Contract with the World

Contract

JANE RULE

With the World

HARCOURT BRACE JOVANOVICH

NEW YORK AND LONDON

FOR SHELAGH DAY

The song on pages 10 and 11 is "Pack Up Your Sorrows" by
Pauline Marden and Richard Fariña, © 1964 (Unpub.), 1966,
1977, 1979 Ryerson Music Publishers, Inc., assigned © 1977
to Silkie Music Publishers, A Division of Vanguard Recording
Society, Inc., and is used by permission. The lines quoted
on page 326 are from W. H. Auden's "In Memory of W. B. Yeats,"
Collected Poems, edited by Edward Mendelson, Random House, Inc.,
copyright © 1976 by Edward Mendelson, William Meredith and
Monroe K. Spears, executors of the Estate of W. H. Auden, and
are used by permission.

Library of Congress Cataloging in Publication Data

Rule, Jane.
Contract with the world.

I. Title.
PZ4.R934Co 1980 [PR9199.3.R78] 813'.54 80–7939
ISBN 0–15–122578–8

Printed in the United States of America

First edition

B C D E

CONTENTS

Joseph Walking

*J*OSEPH RABINOWITZ was puzzled about going crazy. Describing his symptoms to a doctor who disapproved of psychiatry, Joseph was advised to walk ten miles a day to prevent manic breakdown. Since he lived less than a mile from the school where he taught industrial arts, commuting on foot did not complete the requirement, so Joseph set out at six in the morning and walked until eight-thirty, when it was time to arrive at school to set up his classes for the day.

His walking was lonely at first, except for the mute acknowledgment of joggers, nearly all male and nearly all at least ten years older than Joseph, who was twenty-five, bellies pregnant with middle age in their Adidas running suits, blue, red, or manly green, shoes to match. That Joseph could attempt to maintain his sanity in his ordinary clothes was a relief to him, and he was careful to make no particular road a habit so that only very near where he lived did he have the embarrassment of sharing the embarrassment with a familiar heart patient or health freak.

Walking did calm him. He arrived at school able to talk only enough to give adequate instructions to his students. For months he was not even tempted into excitement of the sort that used to start him babbling. His reputation as the school loony began to fade. He even acquired a new nickname, the Rabbit, used only behind his back, as "raving Rabinowitz" had been, but affectionately. Joseph knew how to teach, and he cared for his students as he did for all growing things, learning their individual habits and needs.

Once his body became accustomed to the exercise, however, he sometimes forgot he walked out of necessity and was threatencd again with that old joy. The fires, robberies, and accidents which are the urban raw materials for most people's nightmares and TV entertainments did not attract Joseph or disturb in him anything but ordinary fear and sorrow. But a child running, a light-struck cloud, a small pink shell, bloom on a dying dogwood could shock him with a wonder he needed to express or explain. He had to struggle away from speech, swallowing words as he might his gorge, and run, run until he had no breath left. One morning, walking the seawall around Stanley Park, he saw nothing more extraordinary than a gull landing on the near orange tower of Lion's Gate Bridge, and the sickness of words was upon him.

Joseph tried to think of these attacks as something like hayfever. His friend Ann Geary could have violent spasms of sneezing, set off by things as seemingly harmless as a mouthful of stringed beans or the proximity of blooming ragweed. Joseph had even tried her antihistamines for a while. If it weren't for the embarrassment it caused other people, Joseph might even have enjoyed himself. But just as one couldn't teach through a prolonged fit of sneezing,

Joseph couldn't teach through attacks of words which could flow out of him suddenly at the sight of a boy locking type into the chase, hand and key together so articulate Joseph could not keep silent.

If only he had been good with words, as he was with his hands, perhaps what seemed an illness would have been a gift. What came out of him could not be called poetry, unless found poetry, everything from biblical quotations to lines of popular songs, juxtaposed in a way that seemed to soil as it clarified.

John Geary, Ann's young and dying husband, told Joseph, "You've got to learn to shut up."

John kept his head shaved because his hair had begun to come out in handfuls, and he wore a bulk of clothes to conceal a skeleton daily being robbed of flesh. He did not want his two small daughters to encounter sharp edges as they climbed about him in these last months of his life, and he asked Joseph for dinner often to distract Ann from his own lack of appetite.

He looked like a convict and was, under a death sentence he no more understood than a character in Kafka. At his angriest, he would say, "Hell, I may have more time than you do." At his gentlest, the game he liked to play was "If we had all the time in the world, Joseph, what would we do with it?"

Joseph's honest answer would have been "Keep from going crazy from day to day just as we do now," but instead of answering, he encouraged John in grandiose schemes, one night space travel, another, conversion of the world to solar power, harvesting of the seas.

"Do you think the *world's* dying, Joseph?"

Questions like that John never asked in front of Ann or the children.

"When the pain is very bad," Ann confided, "he sings to be sure he won't moan."

Joseph walked to keep from singing, sometimes now not only in the early morning but in the late afternoon as well and often on into the evening if he was not spending it with Ann and John, hundreds, gradually thousands of miles through the city of Vancouver, out into the university grant lands, down along the beach, among the dog walkers, scavengers, and natural solitaries.

On a negatively safe morning, a mist, heavy with the smoke of fall slash burning, hung low over the water, obscuring the north shore mountains. As Joseph made his way along the beach, his eyes smarting, he was composing a joyless sermon to practical men who insisted that slash burning was simply good housekeeping, a safety precaution, no hazard to health. It was a hazard to pleasure, and didn't people have a right to protect the quality of their visual life? Joseph's preoccupation with sharing a headache with all greater Vancouver kept him from seeing the camera until he had nearly tripped over the tripod.

"Watch it!"

Joseph looked toward the shout and saw a man of about his age, dressed in a London Fog raincoat, standing beside a car entirely wrapped in plastic.

"Is it for an ad?" Joseph asked.

"Heavens, no!" the man replied. "It's Art."

Joseph laughed, disconcerted and delighted at the lightly self-mocking tone in which the explanation was offered. "Is it yours?" he asked, gesturing toward the car.

"The camera is, and it's far too expensive for you to fall over or dance with or whatever you were intending to do," the man answered, walking toward his possession protectively.

He was tall, slightly built, uncommonly handsome, and the flirtation in his scolding made it evident to Joseph that he was homosexual. As he did with men of any other race, Joseph prepared to be particularly courteous and friendly, behavior others might have challenged as inverse prejudice, but was simply kindness overcoming timidity.

"Can you get a picture on a day like this?"

"I *chose* a day like this. It's for *Arts Canada*. There has to be something subtle about it."

Joseph regarded the plastic-wrapped car again in silence. "The only problem is . . . I need a swimmer."

"A swimmer?"

"Just off in the background, in his trunks, at the edge of the sea."

"On a day like this?"

"Yes . . . I wonder, would you mind . . . that is, if you've got on decent shorts?"

It seemed far too outrageous a request to be anything but innocent.

Two months later there indeed was Joseph Rabinowitz, shivering in his shorts at the edge of the smoke-misted sea, just a few yards away from a car wrapped snugly in plastic, on the cover of *Arts Canada.*

He and Allen Dent were both looking at it and laughing at the memory and achievement of their first meeting, while Pierre served them tea in mock-indignant silence.

Joseph had been too shy in those early days of his friendship with them to tease Pierre out of sulking, and later, when he was accustomed to the moods of the household, he realized that Pierre enjoyed jealousy as some women seem to, particularly those who are minimally attractive and insecure with husbands they admire and can't believe their good fortune to be married to. Pierre, seven years younger than Allen, found by him in a gay bar in Montreal when Pierre was sixteen, exaggerated their inequality in any way open to him. Allen was "the man," Pierre the boy wife, adoring, dependent.

When he was convinced that Joseph was a friend rather than a rival, he confessed, "I hate Allen to tell people he picked me up in a bar. It's so unromantic. Why couldn't he have found me, as he found you, on a beach and picked me up and taken me home like a beautiful, fragile shell?"

It was a ridiculous and accurate image of himself, and he dressed to accent that fragility, a body as slender and small as a ten-year-old's, eyes large and dark as the eyes in the Foster Parents' Plan ads.

"The only way to legalize a taste for young boys is to keep an undernourished orphan," Allen said, not only about Pierre but in front of him.

But none of Allen's insults, delivered in the same light tone he used to mock himself or his work, seemed to trouble Pierre. What did hurt or offend him never made any sense to Joseph and seemed of no interest to Allen, who would ignore him until he decided to get over his pique without help.

A peculiarity of the relationship was that the longer Joseph knew them, the less he saw of the negative flirtation between them. It was as if they displayed all the faults they could be accused of as a testing defense, unnecessary with good friends. Instead, Joseph saw how protective Allen was of Pierre, never encouraging the great range of his timidities but reassuring him, helping him to small new self-confidences in everything from keeping a checking account to reading books.

"I'd send him back to school," Allen confided, "but he simply couldn't take it. He's such a natural victim."

Allen never talked with that kind of candid concern about his work. His increasing success as a free-lance photographer, a constant source of pride for Pierre, made Allen the more self-mocking. He called himself vanity's pimp, a political window dresser, a voyeur, a camera for hire.

"He pretends to be hard and cynical," Pierre explained to Joseph, "but he is really very sensitive and suicidal. He cares about his work. He is a real artist, a genius."

"I have one ambition," Allen said on more than one occasion, "to grow up to be a dirty old man and the greatest pornographer of the century."

Aside from his natural flirtatiousness, directed at anyone, male or female, who had not grossly offended him, Allen was, in fact, nearly a prudish man. He never told dirty jokes and was not an admirer of parts of the human bodies. His taste was for an innocence that could accommodate him, like Joseph's.

"I do *like* you, Joseph," he would say. "You never stay long enough to be a bore, and you're the only person I know who believes what I say."

At such statements Pierre ran thin fingers through his long dark hair, listening for criticism of himself in the praise of someone else. He liked Joseph because he could be forgiven the pleasure he gave Allen, because he stopped around even more often when Allen was away on his frequent picture-taking assignments and let Pierre brag/complain about Allen's success and Pierre's loneliness and neglect.

"Once, when he'd been away for a month, sailing on some rich man's yacht, I was sure he wasn't coming back. I was desperate, I was so lonely and frightened. I started wandering around the city—not at night, just in the daytime. I don't really know Vancouver. He doesn't understand why I wasn't frightened in Montreal, but I know Montreal. I'd never get arrested in Montreal. I got busted in the men's room at The Bay. It was awful. It cost him a terrible amount of money, and he wasn't even angry with me. He never even let me explain, and he bought me this beautiful ring."

It was a diamond of the sort advertised in the Hudson's Bay department store ads under the caption "Diamonds are forever."

Joseph didn't mention Allen and Pierre to Ann and John, who would probably find them bizarre and unsympathetic, a symptom of Joseph's own instability. He was, therefore, embarrassed to see that issue of *Arts Canada* on their coffee table. John was past saying anything about it, but Ann nodded to it and gave him a polite, puzzled look.

"The photographer's a friend of mine. I was doing him a favor," Joseph explained on a single note of laughter.

"How interesting," Ann said, and she meant for him, not for herself.

"Where did you find it?"

"At the library."

"Joseph," John called through the conversation, "help me downstairs."

John had an old printing press in his basement. There, before John knew he was dying, Joseph had spent hours with him, at first teaching him how to use it, then listening to him dream aloud about this archaic and at the same time revolutionary machine, by means of which he would somehow—he had not ever decided how—change the world. Over the press he had tacked the statement "He who first shortened the labor of Copyists by the device of Movable Types was disbanding hired Armies, and cashiering most Kings and Senates, and creating a whole new Democratic World: he had invented the Art of Printing."

"Set up anything," John said, "and let's run it awhile. I just like the sound of it."

Joseph took the stick and set quickly:

> What I aspired to be,
> And was not, comforts me.

"Nice," John said. "Who is it?"

"Browning," Joseph said.

Joseph lifted the chase into place, thinking how many months it had been since John was able to do it himself. Three-dimensional now only because of the number of Ann's sweaters he wore, he could hardly sit up. Joseph adjusted the pins, pulled the wheel, and threw the switch, setting the old machine into the rhythmic motion they both loved. Then he took a stack of bookmarks to feed into it. Above the sound, he could hear John singing:

> No use crying
> Talking to a stranger
> Naming the sorrow you've seen
> Too many bad times, too many sad times
> Nobody knows what you mean.

Joseph joined him on the chorus:

But if somehow you could
Pack up your sorrows
And give them all to me
You would lose them,
I know how to use them
Give them all to me.

And listened again:

No use rambling
Walking in the shadows
Tracking a wandering star
No one beside you, no one to hide you
And nobody knows what you are.

"But if somehow," they sang again together, "you could pack up your sorrows . . ." until John sang the last sad verse alone:

No use roaming
Going by the roadside
Seeking a satisfied mind
Too many highways, too many byways
And nobody's walking behind.

Joseph kept on working, hardly able to see, more ridiculously exposed than he had been at the edge of that autumn sea, with a friend who would be dead before there was time to laugh about it.

It was the picture on the cover of *Arts Canada* which was also responsible for putting Joseph back in touch with Mike Trasco, a man he had known in his student days when they were in some of the same courses in education at the University of British Columbia. Joseph answered the phone to "No shit, is that you on the cover of that magazine?"

When Joseph admitted that it was, Mike wanted to argue about it.

"I didn't take the picture," Joseph protested. "I just happened to be walking by."

"In your shorts?"

Joseph laughed.

"Soft sculpture is a pile of crap."

"Actually, it's a car," Joseph said.

"Listen, if you're so big with *Arts Canada*, I want you to come over and see some of the stuff I'm doing."

"I haven't got anything to do with *Arts Canada*."

"But I'm *working*. I'm doing the real thing."

Unable to be rude, Joseph agreed to meet him at an unconventionally early hour at his studio—a shed in the back alley behind Trasco's house.

Joseph walked toward his appointment before the late fall sun was up, the time of morning when only the more modest of workers waited at bus stops, carrying shopping bags and lunch kits rather than briefcases, looking cold in thin coats, coughing. He walked several blocks along the bus route, then chose a residential street where he could watch the first waking lights of family houses, listen to the thud of the morning paper against front doors and the bicycle whir of a paper boy approaching behind him. Dawn on a flat block in the district of Kitsilano was no more than a gray gradually brightening to day, windows fading into small stucco houses, like creatures up on their haunches, approached by six or eight concrete steps, painted red or green, kept forlorn company by winter-saddened hydrangeas or rhododendrons. Even the mountain ash trees had been stripped of their berries by the last migrating birds. The only leaves still falling were from alders, flat gray-green and sodden in the gutters.

Joseph was now coming into an area of new apartment blocks and old houses, each uncomfortable in the other's presence. Mike Trasco's was the last house left on his block, squashed between two long three-story buildings like the token filling in a bready sandwich. There was no room between his fence and his house for a walkway to the backyard, and Joseph decided against presenting himself at the front door, recalling that Mike was married, with children. He walked, instead, around the corner and approached the house from the alley, narrow and cluttered with garbage cans.

He found Mike at the door of his shed, the welcome smell of coffee coming from a pot on the wood stove.

"You *are* really beginning to lose your hair," Mike greeted him with loud cheerfulness.

Joseph looked up at the vigor of Mike's growing abundance, fiercely pruned and finely shining black, the same light of health in his black eyes. He had not seemed young even in his student days, his virility so accustomed that there was nothing of the boy left in him. He was the sort of man who would be in his prime for years before he suddenly, unaccountably, shrank into age. And what he observed of Joseph was true. At twenty-seven he had begun to move from boyhood into middle age, having inherited the nearly colorless fairness of his English mother, nothing but a tendency to stoop from his Jewish father. Mike Trasco lived in a season Joseph would never experience.

The mug of coffee Mike thrust at him warmed his hands and made him feel oddly, domestically welcomed in the clutter of the shed, where the only places to sit were on stacks of lumber or metal.

"There's nothing *here*," Mike explained. "I haven't got the room," and he glared as he looked around at the limits of his space. "But I've got some drawings and some models, to give you an idea anyway. I'm trying to get it together to rent real space, but the *price* on it these days! Guys talk in square feet like they thought they meant quarter acres."

He had got out a large notebook and was flipping through it energetically.

"Are you teaching these days?" Joseph asked.

"No, I'm not cut out for it, you know. I haven't got the patience. Your own kids, you can belt them one when they need it. The punks I had to deal with . . . no way. Here we are. Now just take a look at this to get an idea."

Joseph moved close to Mike in order to see what he was looking at. It was characteristic of Mike not to be able to give space even in such a circumstance. What Joseph saw, peering around Mike's large shoulder, was what looked like a plan for something part bench, part fence, part boat.

"Wood?" he asked.

"Yeah, clean lines but my own." Mike frowned. "Now that's something to *look* at, to recognize. That outsized garbage bag on the *Arts Canada* cover, it's a woman's work. I could tell in a minute, didn't even have to look. They're all doing monumental domestic crap. Soft sculpture! It's a joke! Now look, look at this one."

Again Mike blocked Joseph's view, but what part of the drawing he could see looked like a pile of discarded desk chairs.

"Do you find them or build them?" Joseph asked.

"Built them. *Things* don't need to be rescued. Found art is bullshit. *Form* has to be rescued from usefulness."

"You must have to be quite a carpenter."

Mike turned at Joseph and glared.

Joseph's one note of laughter ended high and hopeful.

"A carpenter builds *things*. A sculptor builds objects of art."

"I only meant . . . the same tools."

There was a timid rattle of the door latch.

"What is it?" Mike shouted.

The door opened, and a boy of about four came in. "Time to eat."

"Oh." Mike looked undecidedly at his sketchbook, then closed it and shoved it away. "Come eat."

"Thanks, I've had breakfast," Joseph explained. "I need to be getting along to school."

"At seven o'clock?"

"It's over an hour's walk."

"Take a bus, for Christ's sake," Mike said, a compelling hand on Joseph's shoulder. "And at least have another cup of coffee."

Joseph did not want to meet Mike's wife because he did not want to see Mike being a husband and father, but, short of explaining the necessity of his walking, which he would not do, he had no ready excuse.

Not until he actually met Alma did Joseph realize he had in his imagination married Mike to quite another kind of woman. Alma was tall, ample-bodied, with a Nordic fairness as shining as Mike's Polish darkness. What surprised Joseph was not her good looks but her intimidating confidence and its effect on Mike.

Mike Trasco, who had seemed to Joseph grandly, confidently male, became in the presence of his wife blunderingly assertive, behavior she tolerated alternately with amused condescension and superior scorn. She didn't shout at him, "Polack! Barbarian!" She hardly spoke to him at all. But her northern eyes, as cold and clear as a well-below-freezing sky, and the serene planes of her face locked him out of her approval with finality. After fifteen minutes in her company, Mike's eyes took on a look of stunned rage. Joseph, who had not before felt in enough sympathy with him to seek him out, became, because of that look, Mike's friend.

Joseph did not dislike Alma, and it would have been impossible at that first meeting to disapprove of her. She did not charm, but her presence had to be admired, calm at the center of all that masculine noise, from squawling one-year-old in his high chair to bellowing husband at the foot of the table.

"Why in hell call me in if the meal's not on the table?"

Shortly she placed a plate before him, mounded with slices of rare roast beef, two stuffed baked potatoes, green beans, and sliced tomatoes. She and the two children were having an ordinary breakfast of fruit juice and boiled eggs. Joseph had accepted a glass of orange juice rather than coffee, which he nearly spilled at the moment Mike's hand slammed down on the tray of the baby's high chair and he shouted, "Eat! Don't dream. You can sleep after breakfast." The four-year-old did not look up from his egg. Alma watched her husband as if she might be attending an ethnic movie.

He seemed to Joseph a fraud of a father, of a husband, perhaps of an artist, too, with all his belligerent talk of aesthetics. But before Joseph left that breakfast hour, he had offered to lend Mike some of his own tools and to see what influence Allen Dent might have with *Arts Canada.*

Joseph took a bus partway back to school, sharing it with a number of students, until he saw, in a garden he looked out at while the bus was loading new passengers, the first Christmas rose. Joseph had to get off the bus and walk, even though he would be late for work.

He did not discover for some weeks that Mike's extraordinary breakfast was really his dinner. He worked at a downtown nightclub as doorman and bouncer six nights a week, came home at three or four in the morning, and worked at sketches and models for sculpture until Alma got up and cooked him a meal sometime between six and seven in the morning. He slept through the late morning and afternoon.

What puzzled Joseph for a time was the apparent material comfort in the house when Mike was obviously pressed for funds. Mike, who could rail at nearly anything his wife or children did, never commented on the good china and glassware that were used every day on a handsome dining-room table, the good-looking clothes his children wore, the expensive toys that blocked the front walk, the English baby carriage. The things that surrounded Mike, aside from the shell of the house, were as unlikely as his wife.

Finally Mike confessed, "I pay the rent. I put the food on the table. If Alma's parents want to clutter up the place with their sort of junk, it's all right with me."

For Joseph it was disappointing to have so simple an explanation not only for the mystery of the things in the house but for Alma's sense of superiority. He was immediately less impressed by her and more critical, silently taking sides with Mike even at his belligerent worst.

"It's easier to dislike the rich than to make money," Allen Dent observed, having chosen for Alma the moment he met the Trascos.

"It's easier to dislike the straights than to be one," Pierre countered; for him no man as beautiful to look at as Mike could be basically bad. "You're jealous."

"I'm incapable of jealousy, and in this case you're fawning over the classic castrating male. He'd kill you."

"I don't doubt that," Pierre said sadly.

"I can't abide people who are serious about their work," Allen said, "particularly if they're bad at it."

"Is he bad at it?" Joseph asked.

"Well . . . no," Allen admitted, "but he might as well be since he can't be great."

"Why?"

"Because that's all he wants," Allen said. "Why do you think he married a woman like Alma?"

"Are you going to help him?" Joseph asked. "Can you?"

"It would be unkind," Allen said.

"Love is," Pierre said.

Allen ignored the remark. Joseph wasn't sure how much of a teasing cliché it was, how much a real message.

"Well, I'll see," Allen said, "but as I told him, he's got to build something first, not just a model."

As he walked with Mike down among the warehouses on the Vancouver waterfront, looking for space, Joseph's concern for his friend shifted from pity to pleasure. In this neighborhood, Mike's muscular swagger and big voice were natural to him and right for his friends there. He returned quick jabs to the shoulder with men half his size and laughed at every greeting. Here was the only place Joseph saw Mike diffident before men twice his age, who embraced him and said things like: "Look at the head of hair on him! Look at those shoulders!"

These were the streets on which Mike had grown up, and though the houses had long since been torn down and the women had disappeared, many of the men stayed on to work as loaders and drivers.

"Maybe I shouldn't come back here," Mike said, "not to work, I mean."

But it was here he could make deals of the sort he understood, reductions in rent for a few heisted bottles, traded goods and favors among people he knew just how far he could trust. If he felt too at home to work as hard as he might have under the eyes of his skeptical wife, distractions made him cheerful. The jokes he could not put up with from anyone else didn't threaten his status here. So he finally settled on space in a warehouse right by the water.

There Mike began to build from the first sketch he had shown Joseph, proceeding as any boatbuilder might at first, so that he had to tolerate only jokes about the seaworthiness of his efforts. With his childhood friends Mike didn't argue that what he made must be redeemed from worth, but they saw it happen before their eyes, a prow turning into a fence, turning into a bench.

"Now don't bullshit me, Mike. What is it?"

Mike laughed loudly and happily.

But to Joseph, who preferred to drop in on Mike at the warehouse now, he would talk earnestly, ideas patched together from old notes taken in an art history course ten years ago. However he put it, with whatever historical authority and elegant terminology, all Joseph could gather from it was that art for Mike must have one quality, one virtue: it must be useless.

Joseph was not argumentative. He was often drawn to people for the contradictions they offered to his own life or way of thinking. Because Joseph cared about a thing first for its function, then for its beauty, he found Mike's disdain for either as attractive as his hair.

"If you don't know how to envy, how can you think?" Allen asked one day.

Joseph, walking, wondered if he ever did think, properly in the sense Allen meant. Joseph's habit of mind was to wonder or daydream. Any systematic process was toward a solution to a particular problem, and he did that as a way to avoid thinking . . . or feeling. Envy? The only person Joseph had ever envied was himself when language charged through him and words flashed out of him and fell like burning flowers.

Allen envied nearly everyone for what he scorned in them and in himself, sexual appetite and worldly ambition.

"If I were not essentially frivolous, I would have been a monk," Allen was fond of saying, at which Pierre would giggle.

"Are you religious?" Joseph asked.

"Not at all," Allen answered, clownishly wistful.

Pierre, alone with Joseph, said, "Allen is my religion. Sex for me is prayer."

Joseph wondered if some women talked together as Pierre tried to talk with Joseph. He suspected not. It was not the feminine in Pierre that baffled Joseph; it was his passionate inferiority. No woman Joseph had ever known enjoyed being inferior. But children sometimes did, children of a good father, as John Geary had been.

"If I have walked seven thousand three hundred miles in the last two years and am twenty-seven years old, how many miles will I have walked by the time I'm thirty-five?" Joseph asked aloud as he walked, trying to avoid bitter questions about death. "Good fathers die is not the answer."

Joseph mourned John Geary in his children's faces and proposed to their mother nearly at once. Ann asked him not to buy her a ring of any sort. She became his wife with the wedding ring she had already worn for ten years, and Joseph told neither Allen and Pierre nor Mike about the ring or the wedding. None of them knew where or how he lived, and gradually he forgot to wonder whether or not that was strange since they all seemed to accept the terms of the friendship without question. He went on dropping in with the same irregular frequency, rarely staying longer than an hour, feeling as wholly there with his untold life as with his interior bones and organs.

Joseph imagined that if a novel were ever written about

the household he found himself living in, he would be represented as an empty space, reserved as if for an antique chair off being mended. Energy centered on Ann, for whom life had to go on quite ordinarily. Joseph had married her for that reason. She had married him, he could only guess, because he had asked her and because it was ordinary for her to have a husband to help pay the bills and raise the children. Joseph was very grateful for the children, who took up so much space for Ann that his absences were no great deprivation for her. The only place he'd been able to fill was a place he had already had, in the basement working at the old printing press. Called to dinner, he still felt more a kindly welcomed guest than a husband. It was not Ann's doing. Joseph had never managed to live where he lived, though he did not ever eat, make love, or sleep anywhere else.

"We don't have to have a child," he said to Ann. "There are two already."

She was not listening to his words but to his desire to give her pleasure, pure pleasure.

"You're an artist in bed," she said to him.

He was flattered, but he was aware that he should rather have been a husband for her, a father for her children.

Occasionally he asked Ann to walk with him, but together they never went anywhere, only along the boulevards and into the grant land bush, the children trailing or kiting ahead out of sight. She took his hand sometimes, and, though he knew they looked like a settled married couple out with their children, he felt more like a high school boy, too shy in courtship to have it ever come to anything. Some months ago her mother had come to visit and had taken photographs. Joseph was surprised to find his own image among them, there on the summer lawn. Ann kept one of the pictures of the four of them tucked into her dressing-table mirror. There was no picture of John, even in the children's rooms. But Joseph knew he still returned to her and to the children in their dreams. Joseph could not rid himself of the expectation of his resurrection and return. But it was not John's place Joseph could not fill. It was his own there by her side, though he loved her. He walked and walked away to Allen and Pierre, to Mike, or to Mike and Alma, a household so substantial, so real in its tensions and noise, everyone from squawling baby to bellowing husband *present* compared to himself and the woman and children he went home to, but never mentioned.

Not even to Carlotta, whom he had met under circumstances which might have compelled him to explain if it weren't always so easy for him to signal detachment. Alma had introduced them with the candid suggestion that they might appreciate each other. Alma and Carlotta were old friends, important to each other, and therefore Carlotta was a problem for Mike, which he tried to solve by alternately baiting and propositioning her.

"Narcissist, onanist," he taunted at the series of self-portraits she had painted.

"They sell," she answered wryly.

"Whore!"

She smiled, and so did Mike.

Joseph was meant to distract them from each other, and he was able to, sometimes by asking Mike to show him a new wrench or saw in his shed, so that Alma and Carlotta could enjoy their long psychiatric conversations in peace, sometimes offering to walk Carlotta home, for she lived only a few blocks away in a single large room at the top of an old house, whose north windows overlooked the city, sea, and mountains.

After several months, Carlotta's place was another of his stops, domestically the most peaceful, for she lived resolutely alone and let him intrude only because she knew he would not stay long. Her basic reluctance to have visitors made Joseph thoughtful to bring a small present or observation to please her, and that was easy because she was both poor and quick-witted.

"We are all twenty-nine years old," Joseph said one day, standing at Carlotta's door, holding out a yellow plastic bucket in which two crabs clicked and bubbled.

"Where did those come from?" Carlotta asked, making no gesture to accept them.

"From Mike. He sets a trap down next to his warehouse."

"I don't accept presents from Mike."

"But now they are from me."

"Why don't you take them to Alma?"

"Not enough for the family. Anyway, she doesn't like them. She's a cook who can't kill."

"It's only practice for the main event," Carlotta said, taking the bucket from him. "Come in."

The dark, narrow staircase smelled of paint even more than Carlotta's room because the windows were nearly always open. Joseph approached the painting on the easel as if it were a person to be greeted and stood some time before it while Carlotta drew water and put the pot on the stove.

"Whose skeleton is this?" he asked.

"Mine."

"Have you really broken that many bones?"

"In my dreams."

"Everyone is also crazy," Joseph said, adding a single note of laughter.

Carlotta turned toward him, her beaked face fierce. "I have finally told Alma there is no such thing as therapeutic art. It's not a category; it's a denigration."

"What did she say?"

"She said, 'Did you remember to eat breakfast this morning?' "

"Had you?"

"I couldn't remember," Carlotta answered irritably. "I think the only thing that really keeps me from killing myself is that I'm too absentminded to manage it."

"There's starvation," Joseph said. "Shall I put the crabs in?"

"No, it's a pleasure."

Joseph watched her reach into the bucket, her long, unnaturally thin arm as rigidly strong as something made of metal, the armored, flailing crab more like an appropriate appendage than an adversary. She plunged it into the boiling water as if it were some revolting part of herself. The second crab, warned, clamped a claw on the rim of the pot and threw itself onto its back on an unheated burner.

"Shit!"

"I'll do it," Joseph said.

He was cautious, could even have been accused of reverence, as he lifted the second crab into the pot, discovering that one of its claws had broken off in its attempt to escape. He dropped it separately into the water.

"It could have grown another," he observed, "given the chance."

"I'm surprised they're both male," Carlotta said, and continued over Joseph's laugh, "I'd think Mike would be pitching all the males back and keeping the females for eating."

"He's not a killer," Joseph said.

"Just dangerously deluded. He doesn't know the difference between stone or wood or metal and human flesh, and that's not healthy for a sculptor."

"Oh, come, he never took a knife to Alma, did he?"

"His prick . . . the same difference."

"A woman can be . . . hard as stone."

"Harder," Carlotta said. "We have to be; otherwise, all of you try to carve us into your own needs."

"Do I?" he wondered, then turned away from her studying look and asked, "Have you got any butter?"

"I think so. Look in the cupboard."

There was no refrigerator. Carlotta kept the place so cold that it wasn't necessary except in high summer, a time she was often fasting. Joseph found an unopened quarter of a pound of butter and a loaf of bread in a health food store wrapper. There were also two tomatoes and an unopened can of condensed milk and several packages of Japanese dried soups.

He carefully ladled some of the crab water into a mug to make soup, then sloshed the rest into the sink to clear it of a streak of black paint floating in a pool of turpentine so that the crabs could be safely cleaned there. He did not ask permission to do that job. Carlotta took the mug of soup and watched him through the steam of it, held always close to her mouth.

"Red's the color of death in Japan," she said.

Joseph gently inserted a thumb at the base of the red back shell and eased it off the body and legs, then let the force of the cold water clean the crab. He did not break it apart so much as disassemble it, leg by leg, like a mechanical toy whose parts could be put away to build something else another day. Only the body had to be snapped in half, and Joseph did that last and quickly.

"Are we all really twenty-nine?" Carlotta asked.

"Yes," Joseph said, beginning on the second crab, "about to embark on the terrible decade. You, Mike, Alma, Allen, and I, all of us." His excluding of Ann was factual; she was already thirty-one.

"I've never liked people my own age," Carlotta said. "That's what made school so awful, sitting in a room with thirty-five other people whose teeth all fell out at the same time."

"It doesn't teach compassion," Joseph said.

"Aren't you going to eat some of this?"

"No," he said, "no, I'm not."

Joseph had walked only five miles that day, slogging, slipping work in the melting of the first snow. Vancouver was a city that pretended real winter never came there, and very few of its residents were willing to take garden spades to their share of the sidewalk. Postmen and milkmen and Joseph galoshed along in one another's tracks, making the footprints that would freeze and break incautious bones a few days later, for old people came out like snowdrops on a mild January day.

For Joseph the cold was like a sedative, as if the flow of words were a shallow stream easily frozen, and he could look in winter at sights that would drown him in words in another season: a raccoon high in the bare branches of a maple on the corner of Second Avenue and Sasamat, a lone child skidding down the hill on the lid of a garbage can, as if his mind could skate on the hard surface of hibernating hysteria. Everyone with allergies loves winter.

"Why don't you ever stay long enough to thaw out?" Pierre asked him, pouring out a cup of tea.

"I'd talk too much," Joseph confessed.

"You? You never do anything but listen. Allen says there's something wrong with you: kindness."

But it took Joseph no effort to deflect Pierre's interest from himself to Allen, away at the moment photographing champion Canadian skiers.

"When it has anything to do with athletics, I'm terrified. All these gay people coming out, writing books about it—even football players! Allen says muscles revolt him and only people like me are in danger of gang rape."

"But aren't you glad . . . or at least reassured that people can begin to be more open?"

"As Allen says, it's like going around with your fly undone."

Joseph would no more argue with Pierre about homosexuality than he would with Mike about art or Carlotta about suicide. All his friends seemed to wear attitudes like name tags, means of identity rather than principle. It was the same with the political parties they supported or actually belonged to. Mike belonged to the New Democratic party because of his working-class background rather than his socialist convictions. Carlotta was really to the left of the New Democratic party but tolerated it on the ground that a country like Canada could never manage a revolution. Alma was a Liberal to maintain social superiority and annoy Mike. All the nicest people were Liberals. Allen voted Conservative out of affected cynicism to serve his own vices. Pierre? He believed in the federal government of whatever party, in Canadian unity because, he explained, "I have embraced my enemy and become his adoring slave." With such a view Pierre would no longer be safe on the separatist streets of Montreal, but he hadn't been in Quebec for five years. Joseph himself was the worst sort of liberal, a naïve humanist who hoped for rather than believed in anything. Ann was his companion in that. They all had outgrown what they knew without knowing anything else.

To be an insignificant man in an insignificant place who could carry such ordinary responsibilities as a job and a mortgage was for Joseph a protective coloring that kept him out of the eye of the eagle, for he had no desire to be claimed for a heroic or melodramatic death in service of his country or his own imagination. But insignificance did not keep him from being a man hunted by songbirds and flowers.

"How do you laugh like that?" Roxanne demanded the moment Allen introduced her to Joseph.

"Like what?" Joseph asked.

"Just the one note, somewhere between a cough and a coo."

Joseph shrugged and turned away to let Pierre help him unwind out of his layer of woolen protection.

"He's really a bird," Pierre explained, instead, "a gull Allen found on the beach. See . . . ?" He demonstrated, pulling off Joseph's cap. "Even his hair is like feathers."

Joseph could imagine it was so, the fair, thinning tufts damp against his scalp, but in no way as remarkable as the head of hair on this young woman, who, as fine and frail-bodied as Pierre, suddenly bloomed like a sunflower into a stiff mass of tight yellow curls.

"I found her in a record shop on Granville . . . working there," Allen explained later. "I've thought for a long time that Pierre needed a playmate."

So Allen had brought her home as if she were some kind of nearly life-sized doll, to please his boy wife. She did. Her size delighted Pierre, and the flatness of her chest, which she displayed in transparent shirts or skintight tank tops with as much vanity as Pierre. Her hair enchanted him, so soft to touch and yet so resistant to any taming. She had small blue eyes, a wide mouth, and a set of large good teeth which belonged in a far larger face. She carried herself with a stiff grace which, along with her diminutive size and extraordinary hair, made her seem the more unreal, as if at least some parts of her animation were mechanical.

Joseph was at first shy of her, and it disappointed him to find her so often there when he dropped by, opening the door to him like a jack-in-the-box. If only Pierre was at home, the two of them would be involved in a project or game of some sort, often requiring the swapping of clothes. Roxanne was teaching Pierre to sew. He was teaching her to cook. Pierre tried to involve Joseph, but he could find no place in their play. Though he was glad for Pierre to find him now so seldom alone or lonely, Joseph was apt to check for signs of Allen's presence before he rang the bell.

Allen treated Roxanne with the indulgent affection men of his temperament often reserve for intelligent dogs. Though she didn't find anything to worship in Allen in exchange, she was perfectly comfortable with him. After a few initial assaultive questions which Joseph didn't answer, she kept a watchful distance from him until one day in early spring they accidentally met walking away from downtown Vancouver across the Granville Street Bridge.

"Walk with me, but don't talk," Roxanne said, her fending-off hand then becoming a link between them.

The noise of the traffic was so great that a conversation would have been impossible anyway. If it weren't for the marvelous views over the newly developed False Creek area or across the Burrard Bridge to the mountains, Joseph would have avoided the six lanes of urging traffic. Leaping off a bridge of this sort must be made easier by all the racket and exhaust stench you'd leave behind. Walking with Roxanne, if he was to set his pace by hers, was like marching in a military band. Did she hear Sousa in her head to block out all the engine urgency, punctuated by horn and brake? She couldn't be smiling unless her private sound track were tuned in somewhere else. Though Joseph couldn't get the noise out of his own head, her absorbed company did distract him. Joseph would have taken the Fourth Avenue exit, but she walked on, determined to go with the main flow of traffic south on Granville Street. They went on until she was stopped by a red light at Broadway.

"I should start west from here," Joseph said.

"All right," she agreed, and turned up Broadway with him.

Joseph wanted to turn off Broadway to one of the quieter streets, but he felt shy of changing their direction twice. Finally he asked, "Where are you going?"

"Oh, nowhere. I'm just following the traffic."

"Following the traffic?"

"Yeah. To listen to it, you know. I just like to listen to it."

"We'd never make good walking companions. I hate it."

"Only because you try not to listen to it. *Shhh* . . . listen."

Dutifully he marched with her for another several blocks, then shook his head and said, "I'm sorry. That's all I can take."

She left him easily, but he stood for a moment watching the stiff energy of her walk before he escaped.

The next time Joseph met Roxanne he was more puzzled than put off. Did she, perhaps, walk because she had to? Joseph had never considered there might be others like himself, but why would she choose the traffic to pattern her miles?

"Do you walk every day?" he asked.

"Sure. I don't have a car."

Joseph didn't feel confident enough to tell her that wasn't what he meant. He did want to find out about her but without being pressed to his own confession.

Ann was the only one who knew that he walked and why.

Perhaps her unspoken skepticism made Joseph the more reluctant to test the credibility of his exercise with anyone else who might put it in the category of a fad diet. It did, after all, work. He babbled rarely and had not gone crazy.

"Do you know what I used to think?" Carlotta asked him one day, standing at her windows while a spring gale blew in. "I used to think mental hospitals were filled with melodramatic neurotics like me, but they're not. They're filled with mild, kind souls like you, most of whom are, of course, women."

"I have read," Joseph said, "that mental hospitals are really simply jails for women who tend to be violent toward themselves rather than other people when they get desperate. I don't know why you think that excludes you."

"Because I'm not a potential suicide really. I'm a murderer."

"Well, I'm not essentially mild or kind either, and when I go crazy, it won't be like a candle in the window being blown out."

She laughed. "I'd like to see that."

"I'm not sure you would."

Because it was spring, squalls bringing the pink snow of ornamental cherry blossom, a new blade of grass cracking the sidewalk, a robin challenging its own image in the basement window, Joseph found himself reluctantly choosing the traffic, the center of the city nearly closed from the sky, the weight of steel and concrete great enough to defy the strongest weed.

At the warehouse Mike had finished his first piece and was now slowly working on what looked increasingly like the wreckage of a schoolroom.

"Didn't you like school much?" Joseph asked, watching Mike deliberately break in two places a chairlike form he had just made.

"I loved it," Mike said. "I was eleven the last time I had a teacher bigger than I was, and at ten I could outspell the principal. I'd have been a poet if I didn't know . . ." He paused and looked out across his work. "Listen, Joseph, I'm going to tell you something important: there is no real power on earth but art, real art, great art, and the greatest is sculpture because it can be big and permanent and *there*. You can't shut the covers of a book on this; you can't take the needle off the record. You have to look at it. You have to face it. It occupies *space*."

Joseph could imagine children climbing about in this deliberate wreckage as if it were a jungle gym. The boat/bench/fence also invited occupancy or siege.

"When the hell is Allen coming down to see this?"

"He said it would be better for you to have at least two of them finished."

"But he is coming."

"Oh, yes," Joseph said. "He'll come."

"Alma likes him. She says faggots are restful." Mike shook his head and snorted. "I told her to get her rest while he was around . . . it was okay with me."

These days even mentioning Alma could bring the look of a wounded animal into Mike's eyes. And that bewildered fury always touched Joseph with tenderness and unease. Alma was not a territory to conquer but more like sculpture as Mike talked about it, monumental, occupying her own space, hard as stone.

"Harder," he remembered Carlotta saying. "We have to be . . ."

Why didn't she or Alma respond to Mike's vulnerability, his large and fragile pride? He could be silly, boring, a bully, but those were his responses to being mocked or ignored or shut out. He had not married Alma's money; he had married her arrogance, thinking he could give it his name and make it his own, but instead, he had taken his worst enemy into his house and heart, and she festered there.

Alma was the first to celebrate her thirtieth birthday. She managed to make the four extra months of her life yet another source of superiority over Mike instead of the conventional shame it might have been.

"I hated being young. Every year older I get will be better. I'll be very good at being eighty."

"Eighty," Pierre echoed faintly, balancing between awe and disgust.

"All of *us* will be dead," Allen said, gesturing to Mike, Joseph, and himself.

"When's your birthday, Allen?" Joseph asked.

"I've had my last."

"Suicide this year?" Carlotta asked.

"No, no. I'm going to be a Dorian Gray. Perhaps you'd like to do the portrait?"

"It's an idea. Does narcissism begin to fade at thirty, Alma?"

"It shouldn't in you," Alma replied, smiling.

Her condescension to other women seemed neither to intimidate nor to offend them. Roxanne, who was meeting Alma for the first time, stood before her offering herself like a flower, and, when Alma picked her for her momentary amusement, calling her Dandelion, Roxanne was delighted.

Mike, in his attempt to be host, seemed more like a waiter in his own house. The moment he stopped trying to dominate, he didn't know how to do anything but serve. Joseph offered to help him with the drinks, wanting him to have an ally.

"If it wasn't her birthday, I'd tell her to get her ass out here in the kitchen," Mike grumbled as he struggled unnecessarily with the ice tray. "If that fucking faggot hadn't brought a bottle of rye, we wouldn't need this fucking ice."

Mike had provided a couple of gallons of British Columbia wine, two large hunks of cheese, a round of Polish sausage, and some dark bread. The food looked crude and out of place on the handsome dining-room table. Mike glared at it as they went back into the living room. "I'm losing a night's pay for this."

The real celebration, Alma made it clear, was with her parents, her sisters, and her children the next evening when

Mike would be safely back at work, taking out his resentment on drunks of both sexes. A new BMW, a gift from her father, was already parked out front behind Mike's beat-up Datsun truck.

"She doesn't need a fucking car. She has the truck all day. She can't run around at night, for Christ's sake, not with the kids. Well, a credit card goes with it, so it's no skin off me."

Pierre would have helped distract Mike if he'd dared, but he had taken Allen's initial warning seriously and admired Mike from a safe distance with his large, orphan eyes. Everyone else in the room had chosen Alma and on her birthday made no attempt to hide it, except perhaps for Carlotta, who had put up with Mike for so long she had developed a nearly affectionate tolerance.

"What did you give Alma, Mike?" she asked.

"She's yet to get it," Mike answered. "The best screw of her life."

"Chained or free?"

"On her birthday she has a choice."

Pierre at the edge of this exchange shuddered, and Joseph laughed the note that always turned Roxanne toward him with the same question, unspoken now, that he had not answered.

Joseph only knew it was one of the ways, like walking, to keep from bursting into words, and he was feeling closer to crazy that night than he had in months.

"You're such a perfect Aries," Allen was saying to Alma.

Her large, graceful hand pulled her fair, bright hair away from her face, the gesture of a woman acquiescing to flattery. She didn't do it often. Her audience was not Allen but Roxanne, and Allen knew it.

Joseph had had his glass of wine, all he ever risked drinking, and he needed badly to get away.

"It's all this hair," he said aloud, "blowing in the wind."

Pierre turned his solemn child's eyes to Joseph, smiled, and offered him a joint.

"No, no, thank you," Joseph said. He had never smoked anything, and he could not stay long in a room where marijuana was being shared because it gave him a headache of a curiously specific sort, like a cork plugged too tight in a verbal center.

Carlotta was the only one of them who shared his suspicion of alcohol and drugs.

"The world already hurts my eyes," she said, and: "Drinking water can make me dizzy and want to vomit. Why spend money?"

Mike, on the other hand, reached for a joint gladly, for it could jail his temper and restore him to visionary quiet even in the presence of his wife, who could then sometimes appear to him as his creation.

Joseph watched him inhale and said, " 'A daughter of the gods, divinely tall,/And most divinely fair.' "

"What's that?" Mike asked.

"Tennyson," Joseph said, "my mother loved Tennyson," and laughed.

Roxanne was smiling at him. "You took the words right out of my mouth."

"Out of Tennyson's," Joseph said, but he saw her unnaturally large, fine teeth and knew, if he didn't get out, he would be stealing everyone's words, shouting, singing, " 'Of all the glad New Year, mother, the maddest, merriest day;/For I'm to be Queen o' the May, mother,/I'm to be Queen o' the May.' "

"Old Joseph coming out?" Allen asked, putting a hand on his shoulder. "I can't believe our good fortune."

"What did you put in his wine?" Pierre asked Mike in genuine dismay.

" 'If time be heavy on your hands,/Are there no beggars at your gate,/Nor any poor about your lands?/Oh! teach the orphan-boy to read. . . .' Tennyson, Tennyson, Tennyson!" Joseph shouted.

"Easy," Allen said, his arm now firmly around Joseph's shoulder.

Joseph let himself feel the firmness, vibrating inside it. He had to get out. He turned to Alma, meaning to wish her only happy birthday and good-night, but instead, he found himself saying, " 'He will hold thee, when his passion shall have spent its novel force,/Something better than his dog, a little dearer than his horse.' "

"Tennyson, too," Alma said, unperturbed.

Joseph turned and ran out of the house, down the steps, stumbling over pedal car and tricycle, the April moon as staged as he felt he must seem.

"Nothing is genuine but madness," he said loudly to a parked car, the BMW, and then he ran as blindly as he could, trying not to think of tulips sheltering all around him in the dark. When he finally reached the house he called his own, entirely out of breath and Tennyson, he let himself in by the basement door, knowing Ann would hear him and recognize his need to be alone.

Standing before the long drawers of type, Clarendon, Newsprint Bold, Bembo, he laughed three times to catch his breath. Then he opened the drawer that held ten-point Stymie Bold, took up the stick, and reached for a capital **J**.

"Jesus began his ministry when he was thirty years old," Joseph said as he set the letter.

ɾ   .

"And died at thirty-three."

Ɛɾ

"On the cross."

ƨƐɾ

"For the world."

∪ƨƐɾ   .

"Joseph?"

He did not know how long she'd been calling him. She was standing right in front of him now, a look of no more than ordinary concern on her face.

"I just wanted to get this set . . ." he tried to explain, gesturing with the stick, knowing the type was too small even for someone used to reading backwards for her to see what he had set. Even if she could, Ann would not recognize it for the crude craziness it was. She was, unlike himself, modestly religious.

In her face was a sound he did not have to make. "Jesu, joy of man's desiring . . . desiring . . . desiring."

Joseph did not wonder, until Ann lay sleeping beside him, whether Mike ever made love to Alma like that, briefly for himself, to get it out of the way, then long for her, hardening her nipples in his mouth, listening to her heart, her breathing, the shallow sounds in her throat to adjust the rhythm of his hand, finally going down on her, sucking her to coming, which she did with an arching heave that forced him out and away from her in violent rejection. Then she wanted his weight, held him to her, and he lay newborn and quiet until she slept. Mike, the father of sons, would not suckle at a woman, be hurled into new life by her and then held tenderly like a child. Mike would not be "an artist" in bed but a man turning a woman of stone into flesh to bear him, to bear his children. Alma resented it, and so did Carlotta. "All of you try to carve us into your own needs." For him to have no real need, to make love for pleasure, her pleasure, was that what this woman sleeping quietly, what any woman, wanted? It was not enough surely, though it was all Joseph wanted himself: to be out of the way and quiet.

Joseph walked for ten days without calling on any of his friends, fifteen, sometimes twenty miles, mostly in the labyrinth of city streets where he had only occasional glimpses of the sea or sky, which, separated from each other, did not have the blatant season of Vancouver gardens, a vulgarity of azaleas, armies of irises, rashes of blooming vines. Ann had begun to sneeze, but Joseph suffered no more than a dull headache from the noise and exhaust of the commuter traffic by the time he got to school in the morning, which dulled him to unthreatened quiet.

"Where have you been?" Pierre demanded when Joseph finally felt recovered enough to stop for a cup of tea.

"Have you had the flu?" Joseph asked. He would not have thought it possible for Pierre to lose weight, but he had. If his normally skintight tank top had not now hung from him, Joseph was sure he could have counted Pierre's ribs.

"Not yet," Pierre said gloomily.

"Is Allen away?"

"Isn't he always?"

"Where's Roxanne then?"

"I've seen her once, just once, in ten days. She's in love."

"Well, I suppose that's nice for her . . . isn't it?"

"It's *going* to be horrible."

"Why?"

"She's in love with Alma."

"Are you sure?" Joseph asked.

"You were there. You saw it happen."

"When?"

"At Alma's birthday party. Allen thought that was why you left. Wasn't it?"

"No," Joseph said slowly. "I wasn't feeling very well . . . I was . . ."

"I thought you were drunk. Allen said . . . well, never mind. Sit down. I'll fix you something. It is upsetting, isn't it?"

"Have you talked with Roxanne?"

"Talked? I've listened. I thought I *knew* Roxanne. We were friends. Oh, I knew she was gay, of course, but she wasn't vulgar about it. Now she can't stop talking about Alma's . . . breasts, and she doesn't even call them breasts. It's disgusting."

"Alma does have beautiful breasts," Joseph said in fairness.

"Are *you* going to start, too?"

"But she's not . . . surely she's not interested in Roxanne?"

"Roxanne *is* wonderful," Pierre asserted. "She's hardly like a woman at all, and she's very intelligent . . . in her own way. Allen says she's probably the only real artist among us."

"Artist?"

"Composer," Pierre said, pretension raising the pitch of his voice.

"I don't know Roxanne, of course," Joseph admitted. "Not well."

"She thinks you're very sensitive and crazy."

"She doesn't like the way I laugh."

"She *does*. She says you are one wind chime . . . like the sound of one hand clapping," Pierre shouted, by this time out in the kitchen.

Joseph followed him out and stood watching him make tea.

"Why have you stopped eating?"

"I haven't," Pierre said. "It's just that I throw up every time I think of her."

"Roxanne?"

"No, Alma."

A woman like Alma, who would marry Mike, surely wouldn't be attracted to someone like Roxanne. For the hours Joseph had speculated about why Mike had married Alma, it had not occurred to him to wonder why Alma had married Mike. Joseph had assumed that any woman, asked, would have married Mike because he was, in Joseph's eyes, a man. Actually the women Joseph had seen with Mike— admittedly only Alma and Carlotta often—were unimpressed by his virility. Did only men admire the masculinity of other men? Then why had Alma married him?

"She's a dyke all right," Pierre said as he arranged cups on a tray.

"Roxanne?"

"No, Alma."

"How can you think so?"

"Why else would she marry Mike? She despises him," Pierre said indignantly.

"That doesn't make sense."

"Of course, it does. If Allen wanted a wife as a cover, he wouldn't marry someone like Alma or Roxanne. He'd marry the prettiest, silliest woman he could find . . . and loathe her. As long as Alma's married to Mike, it wouldn't cross anyone's mind . . ."

"It has yours."

"Not until Roxanne . . ."

"But Alma's got two children . . ." Joseph protested.

"Even Sappho had a daughter, and the steam baths are full of fathers of seven . . . well, in Montreal anyway."

"Mike would kill her," Joseph said quietly.

"Roxanne?"

"No, Alma."

But Joseph did not believe what he said. He was not afraid for Alma. He was, as he had been all along, afraid for Mike.

"I wish Allen had finally taken those pictures."

"He said there was no point. *Arts Canada* just isn't interested in unknown carpenters," Pierre said, his inflection an exact imitation of Allen's irony.

"I don't go begging. I'll be discovered!" Mike shouted from a perch fifteen feet from the ground, on his newest piece, a series of welded ladders and poles, above which suspended from the ceiling was a large triangular shape made of tubing, something between window frame and musical instrument.

Joseph waited for him to come down before he said, "But don't most people at least approach galleries?"

"I'm not most people!"

"What about that big sculpture competition in North Vancouver?"

"It's invitational," Mike said.

"Some of them around the country must be open."

"Listen, Joseph, nothing in this country is 'open' to a Polack bouncer with an education degree and minus twenty cents in the bank. And even if it was, when you look at the shit the 'experts' call sculpture . . . If only I had *space*. Christ, you can't see any of these now."

Mike paced, disappeared into and behind his work, emerged again, as if deep in thought. He did not want to talk about or do anything toward becoming, in the world's eyes, a sculptor. Safer to stay here in his kingdom of uselessness, posturing for his childhood friends, lecturing Joseph, but his own thirtieth birthday was approaching, and there was a crisis in his household. If Mike had been an authentic phony, he'd have had self-protection enough, but he had worked hard in the little time he had, scrounging materials, building. The objects that had begun to crowd the space were, at the least, genuine delusions. For all Joseph knew, they were also art.

"Why won't he try to help himself?" Joseph asked Carlotta. "Why won't he at least try to get a dealer?"

"He did try showing his sketches and models several years ago before he started all this work. Now he thinks he's kidding himself and doesn't want to find out."

"Is he?"

"Who isn't? My paintings sell, not well, but they sell. Mike's right to be scornful of that. It doesn't prove anything, not even that people who buy them care about them, much less know whether or not they're good. My theory is they buy them because they don't understand them. If they did, they couldn't live with them. I couldn't. Could you?"

Joseph looked at the painting Carlotta was working on.

"It's an X ray of my hip, but I stole the color from Georgia O'Keeffe."

"I thought you went to the doctor for . . . ordinary reasons."

"I do. When I'm not thinking about killing myself, I'm terrified I'm dying of one disease or another."

"Do you like Mike at all, Carlotta?"

"Sure," she said, but she turned away.

"Can't you help him?"

"He's married to Alma."

"She doesn't do anything to help him."

"He won't *let* her. She'd get her father to *buy* him a gallery. You know why Mike won't make it? He's too moral about his in-laws, and he thinks art is important. There's nothing important about it."

"Why do you paint then?" Joseph asked.

"Because I like being alone, because I like being poor, and because I'd bore myself to death if I didn't do something, and that takes too long."

"Mike's different."

"Mike's a man."

Joseph might have said, "So am I," but he was irrelevant to this conversation.

"Have you seen Alma since the party?"

"A couple of times."

"Had a ride in the new car?"

"Joseph, you can't stand Alma. She's my closest friend. I'm not going to talk about her. You wouldn't understand."

"I'd like to," Joseph protested. "I don't dislike her. It's only that I feel sorry . . . for both of them."

"For Roxanne and Alma?"

Joseph had not intended to trick Carlotta into confirmation, but he had wanted it. "No, I meant Mike and Alma."

"Sometimes I like you a lot. Sometimes you're a little creep. You should get a life of your own."

He laughed.

"I mean it. Learn a little self-pity. That bout of Tennyson the other night wasn't funny."

"My mother liked the Brownings, too, and Shakespeare and the Bible. Sometimes my head is full of it."

Carlotta began washing brushes at the sink, and for the first time, Joseph realized he had outstayed his brief welcome.

"I like it," he said, nodding to the painting. "It's full of light."

"I'm nearly through with my bones. Next I'll probably have to paint with my own blood."

Joseph nodded and turned to go.

"Joseph, what's the matter?"

" 'I want that glib and oily art,/To speak and purpose not,' " he said without any temptation to go further.

"What's that supposed to mean?"

"I have a lot on my mind. When I say anything, it begins to come out. So I have to try to shut up. I'm sorry about the other night."

"Well, the party was awful anyway," Carlotta admitted. "At least it reminded me to celebrate being thirty alone."

"When will that be?"

"Last week."

"Don't get lost in this new year, will you? I feel as if we could all get lost," Joseph said.

Perhaps he really meant they might simply slip away from him, and they had been too long more real to him than his own life . . . or more important. He expected of them—or at least of Mike and Allen and Carlotta—that they would simply go on growing more and more into themselves, recognizable to him and gradually to the world. Instead, they had begun to flicker across his attentive consciousness, now a shirt (Mike), now a cough (Carlotta), now a gesture of glinting diamond (Pierre). He knew them as he knew different species of birds, could name them, but he could not recognize a whole, particular other self, would falter before any of them, knowing them to be essentially strangers. Did they have selves to kid? "Let no one till his death/Be called unhappy. Measure not the work/Until the day's out and the labor done."

I am morally crazy, he thought, trying not to say it aloud, raised on tag lines my mother believed in, encouraged with, judged by: "Ah, but a man's reach should exceed his grasp. . . ." "All flesh is grass, and all the goodliness thereof is as the flower of the field." He saw Carlotta's exposed bones in clarifying light, lying on a lawn like an offering to the orange flame of an azalea. Mike's ladders and poles began to sprout branches and then leaves. Joseph smiled, then laughed. "They shall mount up with wings as eagles; they shall run, and not be weary; and they shall walk, and not faint."

"We have to fly before we can run," he shouted, his arms stretching out to reach the eagle turning above him. "We have to run before we can walk." And he ran along the beach by the spot where he had first met Allen. "Finally we will walk and not faint." And he walked. "Here lies one whose name was writ in water." He knelt at the edge of the water and wrote "JOHN" in the water with his finger. "I have no such immortal fears." He wrote again, "JOSEPH." And laughed and laughed like a buoy sounding its warning in the dangerously shallow sea.

The blanching of spring into summer, the letting out of school gave Joseph again some small distance between himself and his allergy, radical joy, ecstatic mourning, craziness, whatever it was. There was time not only for his walking but for domestic kindnesses he knew he must develop not only for Ann and her children but for himself. The children were not exactly shy of him, tolerated his reading to them, fixing their toys, even occasionally making them a meal, without complaint, but they did not turn to him ever. A skinned knee on an outing was not cried over unless Ann was there. The six-year-old would not confess to Joseph about being unable to dial a number on the phone, chose disobedience over asking for help. The eight-year-old introduced him to a friend as "my mother's husband." The relief he felt increased his guilt now that the time of silent mourning must surely be over for children as young as they had been. For children as young as they still were, they needed a sense of him as more responsible for them, more loving of them than he had been.

"Should I adopt them?" he asked Ann shyly one night.

"If you want to, it would be very nice."

"Not for them to change their names or call me Dad or anything, just as a legal protection."

"They might like to have your name. They might like to think of you as their father."

"Well . . ." Joseph said.

"You could ask them," she suggested.

"Why don't you? That way they wouldn't feel they had to . . ."

"All right. And, Joseph, it's no more a betrayal than my marrying you."

"No, of course not."

He spent most of the next day walking. When he finally got back just before dinner, Ann smiled at him, kissed him, and said, "Now you ask them."

"Do they understand what adoption means?"

"I've explained it to them," she assured him.

So he went into the living room, where the children were watching television. Usually they took no more notice of him behind his newspaper than he did of them, but the moment they saw him they turned off their program.

"Don't let me interrupt," he said quickly.

"Mother said you wanted to talk to us," the eight-year-old said in a voice firm enough to seem reproachful.

"Yes, well, you see, I thought maybe it was time, now that we're all more or less used to each other, for me to adopt you—that is, if it's all right with you?"

"I can already spell Rabinowitz," the six-year-old announced.

"Mother said, since you wanted to marry us, too, we could call you Dad. Can we?"

"Sure you can, if you want to."

The sense of ownership the children immediately asserted was extraordinary to Joseph. He felt more like a new tandem bicycle than a legal protector, a lap full of children who had never before done more than hold his hand crossing the street. A dozen times a day, one or the other of them would instruct him, "Fathers do . . ." or "Fathers don't do . . ." He was initiated into the intimate rituals of bathing, doing up hard buttons, braiding hair, forced for the first time to acknowledge these children as young females for whom legality already meant permissiveness.

"Do you remember when you were Joseph, you didn't kiss us good-night?"

"Daddy, what is my name? Say my name."

"Susan."

"My *whole* name."

"Susan Rabinowitz."

"And mine, too," the younger one demanded.

"Rachel . . . Rachel Rabinowitz."

He had not really thought about Ann calling herself Ann Rabinowitz, but now that he had, as Ann put it, "married them all," he could think of her as his wife with less surprise and disbelief. If the children felt no more his, he felt much more theirs, and that was, after all, the point. After the first month, hearing either of them shout "Daddy" at him on the public street no longer seemed their calling attention to a criminal act.

Joseph would have liked to say to Carlotta or Allen and Pierre or Mike that he had adopted two children. Particularly he would have liked to speak to Mike, wondering how Mike really felt about his own. Joseph had seen him only as a bluff bully, but now he remembered that Mike also absentmindedly touched his children, as if they could offer the comfort of worry beads. Joseph couldn't imagine himself ever unselfconsciously touching Susan or Rachel, perhaps not because they weren't his, but because they were girls.

Mike was in no mood for anyone else's intimate disclosures, working obsessively to avoid discovering any of his own. He would talk about nothing but money or art.

"I should buy into that damned club and make some real money for a change."

Aside from the fact that he could get money for such a

project only from his father-in-law, being part owner of a nightclub would tie him to it and encroach even more on the little time he had.

"This is a hick town, Joseph. The only action in this country is in Toronto, and that's nothing but a suburb of New York. Nothing's going to come into Vancouver except from the outside with a label like Henry Moore or Barbara Hepworth."

Mike never spoke, therefore, of leaving Vancouver. He was a man not only in domestic chains but imprisoned in a vanished neighborhood, where street signs could still remind him of the fights he had won and greetings from boyhood friends could reassure him of the aesthetic distance he had put between himself and them. Afraid of rejection at the local galleries, which he accused alternately of being run by a bunch of goddamned Americans or local art school types doing their own thing only because they'd never been taught any goddamned thing else, Mike apparently didn't even dream of the large world beyond this city as having any real place for him.

Though Joseph had sometimes wished for a talent with words that might absorb the energy of his hysteria and transform it into poetry, he did not envy anyone who was actually trying to be an artist. Mike's angry frustration had a basis in fact. There wasn't room for anyone but the masters who did live in places like New York and London. Everyone had to work for years in the humiliation of being not good enough until a very few came to be great. As Allen had said from the beginning, Mike did not seem a candidate for greatness.

Carlotta didn't seem to care. For her, anyway, there was some measure of success.

"You can say all you like about being a big frog in a little pond. It takes talent," she said.

Allen, who by now was accepting more and more American and European assignments, refused to call himself an artist at all. "It's business, Joseph, not even big business. I can live like a millionaire on the job, but I'll never be one. The only way Pierre will ever be an heiress is on my flight insurance."

. "Have you ever thought of adopting Pierre?" Joseph asked.

Allen snorted in derisive laughter. "You must have been reading Somerset Maugham's biography. There are two great differences between Maugham and me: I've never made the mistake of fathering a child or accumulating enough money to be fought over."

It was a stupid question and as close as Joseph could get to telling any of them that he was a legal father of two girl children because he would then have to explain that he was married and further explain why he hadn't mentioned the fact for the nearly two years since his wedding. He didn't know why he had kept Ann in the same privacy that he did his illness, nor did he understand why only the fact of the children tempted him to confession. After his tactlessness with Allen, he did have the sense to avoid asking Carlotta if she wanted a child.

Alma might have talked about being a parent, but Joseph was avoiding that house as much as he could, and motherhood, anyway, seemed to him so huge, sacred, and mysterious as to have nothing in common with his own tentative feelings. His not wanting to father a child had something to do with Alma, a sense that impregnating a woman so transformed and alienated her that what tenderness she had once given was obliterated. Adopting Ann's two, on the contrary, had brought her nearer to him, a reserve in herself so deep he had not even known it was there removed from him now. She was more affectionate with him in front of the children, readier to ask his advice, and she paused now before any of his small offerings about the people he knew, inviting him to go on rather than closing him off with "How nice" or "How interesting." With her, as with his friends, he would have liked to begin to close the gap, but his long silence now made it somehow impossible.

On Mike's birthday, at a dawn that promised a day hot as zinnias, Joseph walked down to the warehouse, hoping to find Mike there, but the door was locked. Instead of going back to the house, where he might be involved in a tense family meal, he went home for breakfast, again aware of the great difference between his own life and Mike's. Would Mike be as surprised by Ann as Joseph had been by Alma, not just the fact of her but the kind of woman she was? She didn't look the two years older than Joseph but only because Joseph looked older than he was. She was . . . old-fashioned, like someone out of his mother's or even grandmother's generation, a round, good woman, whose beauty had to be unclothed and surprised. This morning she looked worn, the heat steaming her glasses, dark hair damp at her temples. Joseph remembered only faintly that the children looked like their father, who had died out of his own face months before his actual death, which had lodged in the set of Ann's jaw as a fact. She looked what she was, a woman who had borne two children and buried a husband before she was thirty.

"I'll take you swimming this afternoon," Joseph promised the children before he went downstairs to the press.

Joseph picked up the stick, lifted the four-letter blasphemy out of it, and began to set, using his most ornate capitals for the beginning of each line:

Trasco's Decrees

Soft Sculpture Is a Pile of Crap

There Is No Real Power on Earth but Art

Sculpture Is the Greatest

Found Art Is Bullshit

As Joseph was studying the drawer of ornaments to find a border that was suitable, Susan and Rachel appeared at the top of the stairs.

"Can we play down here where it's cool?"

"Sure."

He pulled out the bottom drawer of one of the type chests and let the children play with the large wooden antique letters he and John had found and bought.

"They're all backwards," Susan complained.

"Write your name backwards, and I'll print you a sign."

It was lunchtime before Joseph finished. He sent the children up with fine new signs for their doors and left the ink on the plate and rollers to be cleaned after he had eaten.

Ann, her back to him at the kitchen counter, said, "Would you just see the girls' hands are clean, John?"

Joseph stiffened, then realized that she had not noticed her mistake.

"That daddy's dead," Rachel corrected, standing in the hall.

Ann turned to him then.

"I was thinking of him, too," Joseph said.

"He always loved the sound of the press," she said. "So do I."

Joseph had a premonition that if he lived into old age with Ann, she would grow gradually free to confuse them, the two husbands for whom she wore the same ring.

It was almost eight o'clock, time for Mike to go to work, when Joseph got to his house with the sign he had made, carrying it carefully because the ink wasn't really dry. He felt cheerful at this afterthought of a birthday present, made while Mike slept. The light was on in the alley shed, but the door of that was locked, too. Reluctantly Joseph knocked on the back door. Alma opened it, her face frankly angry.

"Oh, it's you."

"I just wanted to drop off a sort of birthday card for Mike. Has he already gone?"

"No, he's out there," she said, "sulking."

"Well, shall I just leave this . . . ?"

"No. Pound on the door. Get him to stop behaving like a child."

She turned back without taking the sign.

Joseph went back down to the shed, knocked, and called, "Mike?" and then tried the latch, which gave this time.

The door swung open, and there for a second Joseph saw Mike hanging before him like a huge, obscene joke. "Alma!" Joseph shouted before he stepped forward, touched, and realized that it *was* an obscene joke, a life-sized soft sculpture, self-portrait of suicide. The hand was clay, an exact replica, wearing Mike's wedding ring, glued into the cuff of one of Mike's favorite wool shirts. The arm underneath was as soft as any other rag doll. Joseph climbed up onto the box Mike himself must have used to hang his own image. Joseph's urgent need to touch the head was repugnant to him, but he had to see the face. The hair, when he took hold of it to lift the face up off the dummy's chest, felt real. Then Joseph confronted the death's head, Mike's face serene as Joseph had never seen it. He heard hurrying footsteps.

"Wait!" he shouted, and as he jumped down from the box, he saw what he had not noticed before, the straining point of an erection against the trouser fly.

Alma was at the door before he could warn or stop her. Her scream seemed to go on for minutes, an absolute sound that could not be interrupted, like a river that finally reached a fall of sound which might have been giggles, freeing Joseph to take hold of her and shake her.

"It's a joke. It's a dummy."

He led her back into the house, more worried by her sudden docility than he had been by her scream. Both the children were at the top of the stairs, crying. Since Alma made no move toward them, Joseph went up to calm them and get them back to bed.

"Your dad played a joke and scared your mother for a minute, that's all. She's all right."

Joseph had not been in this part of the house before. The boys' rooms looked like something out of a magazine. From rocking horse to train set, they had everything that could be bought. To reassure and distract them, Joseph admired a toy fire truck with a real water tank and hoses. The older child showed him how the hoses could be cranked after the ladders had been unhooked. His hands, so like his father's, reminded Joseph of the clay hands of the dummy, the wedding ring. He wished Alma would come up and help him. He did not like to leave her alone. Ann would never have allowed her own fright or grief or anger to get between her and her children. These two, Joseph realized, were dissembling for him, pretending to be all right. They seemed to him so appallingly small already to know they must cover up fear. But he accepted it and sent them to their beds.

Alma was sitting at the dining-room table, her head in her hands.

"He's insane," she said quietly.

"He's unhappy," Joseph said.

Alma looked up at him, her face more tired and vulnerable than he had ever seen it.

"Yes," she said, "I suppose he is. I've got past caring."

"I'm going to go take it down before it frightens anyone else."

"I'll go up to the children. Joseph? I'm sorry, and thank you."

Once the thing was cut down, its power was gone. Joseph took the screwdriver out of the trousers, thinking how childish both Mike's humor and anger were, sorry for him. He folded the head and hands under the stuffed body. He found "Trasco's Decrees" where he had dropped it and put it on top of what now looked like a pile of clothes. Soft sculpture might be a pile of crap, but Mike had certainly managed to be successful at it. Joseph hoped his birthday greeting would somehow turn this into something to laugh at. What if it wasn't a joke?

Joseph stood staring. Could Mike somewhere else at this moment be hanging dead? At the warehouse? Joseph hurried back into the house. He could hear Alma with the children. He went to the phone and called the club where

Mike worked, to be told he wasn't there. "It's his birthday. He's taken the night off."

"Alma?"

"I'm just coming down."

Joseph did not want to frighten her, but he had to find Mike now as quickly as he could.

"Could I borrow your car?"

"Of course."

"I'd just like to find him."

"You don't think . . . ?"

"I don't know," Joseph said. "I just want to find him."

At the warehouse, Mike was not hanging dead but swinging alive on the triangle he had strung from the ceiling.

"*You* found it? Shit!" Mike said.

It was hard to have a conversation with him while he was up there. Mike made no effort to get down, and there was no room to join him. Joseph leaned up against one of the poles, always surprised now that they weren't trees, and waited. He should probably find a phone and let Alma know that Mike was physically all right. Joseph knew, contrary to what she said, that she wasn't past caring, but maybe an hour or two of anxiety would remind her that she had real feelings. Now that he was with Mike, Joseph felt apologetic about what he had done, but surely he couldn't have left the thing hanging for the children to come upon.

"Why don't I buy you a beer?" he finally suggested. "It's your birthday after all."

Mike didn't answer.

"Well, I've got Alma's car. I guess I'd better return it."

"Anyone who's a friend of hers is no friend of mine," Mike said sulkily.

"Look!" Joseph shouted. "It scared her half to death!"

"Then it was only half successful."

"Why don't you stop playing Tarzan and come down where we can talk?"

"I don't feel much like talking," Mike said, but with acrobatic grace he swung down off the triangle and slid down one of the poles to the floor. Then he stood looking at his work. "Maybe I could sell this to the zoo for the ape cage."

" 'His glassy essence, like an angry ape,/Plays such fantastic tricks before high heaven/As makes the angels weep.' "

"That's my birthday poem, is it? What was the one you had for Alma? I liked it better."

" 'A daughter of the gods. . . .' "

"No, no, the other one."

" 'He will hold thee, when his passion shall have spent its novel force,/Something better than his dog, a little dearer than his horse.' "

"That's the one," Mike said, and snorted with satisfaction. "Hey? Did you find the screwdriver?"

"Yeah." Joseph nodded.

Mike's bark of a laugh surprised Joseph into joining him. At first it was mirth both strained and angry, but then it began to trill and giggle. As one stopped for breath, the other started up again until they were stumbling weak, crying and unable to make any sound but high sighs of intaken breath.

" 'How sad and bad and mad it was—/But then, how it was sweet' " traveled through Joseph's mind without his being able to say it.

When he finally left Mike, Joseph was calm. The heat had drained out of the air, and he drove through the cool night with a sense of relief.

Roxanne opened the Trasco front door to his knock.

"Is he . . . ?"

"He's down at the warehouse working," Joseph said, holding out the keys to Alma's car.

"Won't you . . . ?"

"No," Joseph said. "It's late. I have my own wife and children waiting for me."

He turned and ran down the steps, unable to believe he had said such a thing, and to Roxanne, whom he hardly knew, of whom he instinctively disapproved. She would tell Alma, who might not tell Mike but certainly would tell Carlotta. Roxanne would also tell Pierre, who would tell Allen. What was the horror of it?

"I am the husband of a dead man's wife. I am the father of a dead man's children. It's no more a betrayal than marrying her. She said so. 'Life struck sharp on death,/ Makes awful lightning.' "

No, no, it didn't, quite the opposite. His house, his family were quite ordinary, sunlit, and he must protect what he cherished from the extraordinary as long as he could, even the beauty of it, for it would make no difference to them whether he was sculpted for death by cancer as John had been or driven into the joyful light of madness. They knew, even the little girls, how fragile and precious the ordinary was, unlike these people he visited, who played at life as if they were immortals, killing themselves nothing but an art to be perfected. Still, they were his craziness under control rather than any temptation to it.

The loveliness of Ann's aging and ordinary face, as she told him she was pregnant, finally sent him into the light, and it was Ann who found him, raving at eagle and gull alike, "Greatness is a Way of Life. Art is Immortal. I am the Redeemer King. Death is Bullshit," the day before school was to begin in the fall. Joseph was committed on his own thirtieth birthday. "What I aspired to be,/And was not, comforts me." "Where the bee sucks, there suck I;/In the cowslip's bell I lie." "I am a part of all that I have met."

Mike Hanging

"YOU shouldn't be here," Carlotta said.

"I haven't any other damn place to go," Mike answered.

"Do you know he's in the loony bin?"

"Who?"

"Joseph, and he does have a wife and kids, only they're not his kids; he adopted them. I've just been there, to his house."

"Come in," Carlotta said.

Mike followed her up the stairs. He never got over being amazed at her thinness. She didn't have more width than a two-by-four. It should have made her unattractive. Perhaps it was simply the contrast with Alma, who looked the kind of woman who should have been hot brine and was instead as dry as a rag. "It's the ones who smell of tuna fish . . . they're the ones . . ."—old schoolyard advice. Carlotta smelled of paint and the expensive perfume Alma gave her every year for Christmas, like peppery lilies and Greek wine. Her body didn't excite him so much as make him curious, and the distance she always kept from him made him suspect she was curious about him, too. Then he wondered what Alma might have said, what lies she might have told. "Girls don't talk about sex. They're more interested in your wallet than your cock."

"I've got nothing but tea," Carlotta said.

"Tea's fine."

The space of this room surprised him. He had not been in it often and tended to think of it as the pitiable place it seemed to Alma, who romanticized both Carlotta's poverty and her singularity. Now that he was sleeping in his own studio, cooking makeshift meals on a hot plate, this room seemed remarkably civilized.

"It's not for rent, so don't try it on for size," Carlotta said.

"I know, but it is a good setup . . . for one person. It sure beats an eighth of a warehouse. I've got to go next door to shit."

She turned her back on him for practical reasons, but he felt the rebuke. Why did women have to pretend only babies had bowels? Or was she, who had never really sided with the snobbish prudery in Alma when they were together, feeling she had to take on Alma's role now?

"Carlotta, we're friends, aren't we?"

She shrugged.

"Look, I'm not going to play the injured party. I don't even *want* to talk about her."

"Then let's not. I don't live alone to be a wailing wall . . . for anybody."

"Joseph used to . . ."

"He was my wailing wall."

"Yeah. I guess it was something like that for me, too."

"I told him he'd go crazy."

"Why did you say a thing like that?"

"Oh, I didn't put it into his head," Carlotta said impatiently. "I just wanted him to know I knew."

"Knew what?"

"That he *was* crazy. But I didn't know why. What did she say?"

"His wife? That he's on drug therapy, and, if that doesn't work after a month or so, he'll get shock treatments."

"Christ!"

"Maybe he can have visitors in another couple of weeks."

"What did he do?"

"I don't know exactly . . . went manic. She said he's done it before, but not so bad as this time. I asked her what set it off, and she didn't say anything very clear, just shook her head and said, 'Death . . . life. . . .' Her first husband died of cancer. He was a friend of Joseph's."

"How long have they been married?"

"A couple of years."

"Why didn't he ever say?"

"I don't know," Mike said. "She's . . . Ann's her name . . . really a nice person, very straight, but not . . . oh, she seems sympathetic."

In trying to describe her, Mike realized she was the kind of woman he never really noticed until he had noticed her. So maybe there were a lot of them around whom you didn't see unless for some reason you had to look. When you did, you saw something in them.

"She wears glasses. She's sort of plump. I want to say she's ordinary, but I don't think I know enough ordinary people to be sure."

Carlotta smiled, and that encouraged him.

"I told her I'd like to do anything I could. I didn't want to go on about what good friends we were when I'd never met her before, and I didn't want to ask a lot of questions. I told her he dropped around occasionally. She said he had to walk; it was part of his therapy."

Mike stood up and walked over to the window. What he wanted to ask Carlotta was why Joseph, with a job he apparently liked, with a kind wife and a couple of sweet girl children, went around the bend, while he, Mike, with a bitch of a wife, two kids he couldn't keep in shoes, and the burden of a talent he couldn't seem to carry or put down, was still walking around loose. But that would mean mentioning Alma, and he was here on too frail a permission to risk that.

"The things you don't know about people . . . even people you think you know," he said instead, turning back to her. "For all I know, you've got a husband and five kids."

"I've got nothing but my bones," Carlotta answered, "and I'm busy exposing them."

"Why don't you ever paint anyone else?"

"I have to work from life, and I don't think I could stand anyone else around for as long as that would take. Funny . . . I did think I might try Joseph."

"Not much to look at," Mike said. "You know, he's hard to remember?"

"Maybe that's why I wanted to do it. I might have been able to stand two of him in the room at the same time."

"Why don't you do me?" Mike suggested, and, when she laughed, pressed on. "No, I mean I'd model . . . free."

"My own private life class? Mike, that's a woman's ploy."

"Look at me! What's the matter with me?"

"You're a man."

"What's the matter with that?"

"I could never use Alma's castoffs. They're not my size."

"All right," Mike said with a sense of angry satisfaction, "you mentioned her. I didn't. For your information, I wasn't 'cast off.' I left."

"After hanging yourself in the shed. I know. I heard all about it."

"Not *all* because I haven't told you about it."

"I don't want to hear."

"Why not? Why not?" Mike shouted.

"I don't want your pain or hers either."

"You women are so hard, and you tell us we don't have any feelings. Why, Joseph has more feeling in his little finger than you or Alma . . ."

"Joseph is crazy."

No hard fist in the gut ever hurt the way these female truths did, taking away not your breath but your point, the whole point. Mike took a deep, shuddering breath around the fist of tears in his throat.

"I wish I were."

"It's kind people who go crazy."

"I am not unkind!" Mike shouted, and slapped her.

Carlotta didn't move, not even to touch her cheek. She looked at him with cold calm.

"You hurt me," he said, hating the guilty petulance in his voice. "And I am a little crazy."

"No, you're not. You've just been a bouncer too long. Throw yourself out, will you?"

"Look, I didn't mean to do that. But don't you understand? A man can take just so much taunting."

"You don't have to take any more of mine. Get out."

"Come to dinner with me. Let's go over to the Orestes and have a decent meal."

He didn't expect her to accept. He didn't even want to take her, but he didn't want to leave without saying something conciliatory. When she walked over to the closet and got her coat, he wasn't sure that she didn't intend simply to walk out. He followed her down the stairs, and only when she went to his truck and opened the passenger door did he realize he was actually going to pay the price of a meal. Was she that hungry? Or was it a punishment she was exacting, knowing how little he liked to spend money?

When he got into the driver's seat, he saw that she was crying. Alma never cried. He didn't know what to do.

"I'm sorry. I really am."

She shook her head and then said, "I can't stand to think about Joseph."

"Let's not. Come on. Let's just go and eat. We'll both feel better."

The first several times they went out, Mike was mildly embarrassed by Carlotta, as if someone might hold him accountable for starving her to that thinness, and her table manners, probably from living alone, were irritating. He wanted and needed to talk about Alma, his obsessive bitterness in the way of his work and his sleep; yet, because Carlotta refused her as a subject, Mike was free, only when he was with Carlotta, to think about something else, and she did listen, agreeing with him often enough to surprise him but not to make him suspicious that she flattered him. Unlike Joseph or Alma in the early days when she still listened, Carlotta actually understood what he said. They were, after all, fellow artists, and, though her sort of painting was too subjective, at least she hadn't any silly pretensions about it. Mike decided that she was, in her own peculiar way, elegant, a woman who attracted men rather than boys.

For a few moments each time he left her, he puzzled over his reticence with her. Now that Alma wasn't there to be offended by his sexual remarks, he didn't make them. He even forgot that one reason for seeking Carlotta out had been a fantasy of sexual revenge. Once she refused an invitation to his studio, but he'd offered it very tentatively. He knew she wouldn't smoke dope, and he was not at all sure that he could discover enough appetite for a first attempt without it. Her independence daunted him, yet he liked the brief moments of independence she made him feel himself. Whenever they encountered her friends or she was recognized as Carlotta, the painter, as she occasionally was, she introduced him as "Trasco, the sculptor." She sometimes now called him Trasco, which made him feel momentarily more himself and less the severed head of a family.

He heard himself say, "I've always liked you, Carlotta," and he meant it simply.

Mike's schedule was too antisocial for him to see Carlotta as often as he would have liked. He had only one night off a week. Since he'd always made it a rule not to make friends among the people he worked with, he knew no one who could help him get through the worst hours between two and ten in the morning. Occasionally, when he felt he wouldn't sleep anyway, he'd take Carlotta to lunch.

"I've got so used to crazy hours, I'd almost forgotten they were crazy."

"There's not all that much to recommend the land of the living," Carlotta said. "And you've got a social life."

"Social life? They're a bunch of young punks and nubiles. It's what you might call adult baby-sitting. Its only virtue is that it pays. If I have to knock a guy down to take his keys away and send him home in a cab, he thanks me with a twenty the next time he's in."

Mike had never talked about his job with Alma, and he had never wanted anyone he knew to see him at work, standing there at the door with his hands over his privates, flexing his muscles, smiling, smiling, calling all the male customers by name. If they were relatively well behaved and generous in their spending, it was his job to be obsequious. With the mean ones he was to be ugly, which had the virtue of being the way he really felt. It was a shit of a job, but at least it paid fifteen hundred dollars a month, which was a damned sight better than teaching, particularly since a lot of it was outside taxes. Saying that to Carlotta didn't embarrass him. She'd done her own time as a cocktail waitress, not in the kind of brain-splitting music and bawdy brawling he lived with night after night but in a good hotel bar. Still, she'd known what it was to be meat, and there wasn't all that difference between being tits and ass and being a muscle stud. She'd still be at it if she'd had responsibility for anyone but herself. She wasn't exactly making it, beyond rent and not enough to eat.

Christ, how he wished Alma had, just for a few months, the taste of what his life, or Carlotta's life, was really like.

Alma didn't even know there was any similarity. She thought her father's money stood as much between Mike and the world as it did between her and the world. How could he really have explained it without sounding like some kind of mean bastard, trying to deprive his wife and children of a half-decent life simply because he couldn't or wouldn't make that kind of money? At least, even if he did take a minimum of what he needed for his own work, he tried not to be a pigheaded son-in-law. Alma and the kids could have anything they wanted as long as it didn't involve him. Alma thought that was pigheaded. He should have given his own effigy a snout.

Mike had not known, until after he had hanged himself, that he intended to move out. Preoccupied with the actual making of the object, he spent his anger in the work and did not really think what it would mean, swinging there in the old shed he no longer used, until it did swing there and he walked out. His message had probably been clearer to Alma than to himself, and even now, two months later, he had not defined the ultimatum of his departure and his silence. Aside from sending Alma the money she needed to run the house, he had not contacted her. He did not know what he wanted to say. Oh, he had a hundred accusations to shout, and that noise went on in his head most of the time. But none of them was new, and none was anything either of them intended to do anything about. He had shouted at Alma more often than he wanted to before he left. Sometimes he had contemplated beating her into submission, but he always finally admitted that would mean beating her to death. Though Alma dead would have been a deep relief to his anger, her body, which never had belonged to him, did belong to her sons. Mike had struck her seldom and carefully since her first pregnancy. That was why it was increasingly easy for her to refuse him, knowing she was in no real danger.

All that women's liberation crap about women insisting on the rights over their own bodies! They'd always had the ultimate power not only over their own but over men's bodies, over life itself. What a stupidly negative, stupidly destructive way to prove it they turned to: flushing unfinished life down the toilet and fucking each other, all the while claiming men are too insensitive, too violent to be part of the human race!

Mike had wanted a daughter, a child for all the tenderness he couldn't spend on sons, who would be his only as they grew into men themselves, comforts of his old age when a daughter would be gone from him.

"No more," Alma said. "Absolutely no more."

Mike would not have tried to conceive a child in anger. Rape is pollution. He was, therefore, helpless, at her mercy, and she had none. He couldn't stand it. He left her. Out with Carlotta he was "Trasco, the sculptor," but in his head he was husband and father of the family he'd walked out on. He could not think past that, nor could he think toward it.

Joseph, sitting in the visitors' room, staring out the window with eyes that reflected rather than saw the October brightness of the day, was no help. When Mike was able to get his attention, it was like a lake after a long drought, a dry bowl you could only remember swimming in. Mike wanted to cry, as much for himself as for Joseph.

"Don't say anything to aggravate him," Mike had been advised.

Mike tried to talk about anything that wasn't important. He was in short supply of such subjects. He asked questions, inane questions: "How's the food? Do you have everything you need?"

Joseph's tongue seemed to have swollen to the size of his mouth, words occasionally struggling off it, hard to understand and understood not worth the effort. The face Mike found hard to remember was blurred even as he looked at it. He couldn't tell whether it was a puffy swelling or a deflation of flesh that made Joseph so out of focus.

Only when Mike was about to leave did Joseph give him any sense that the visit had been important. Joseph took his hand and held it for so long Mike felt it was a gift he'd have to leave there.

"Listen, Joseph, I'll come back soon, all right?" Mike nearly shouted. "And after a while you'll get out of here, all right?"

What Mike couldn't say to Joseph, he couldn't discuss with Ann either; a woman already deserted twice by death and madness would not be a good listener, or anyway would reflect his petulance, the pettiness of his griefs, and he needed them to be their rightful size if he was going to deal with them.

How he envied Joseph this woman, these girl children, the quietness of them. What business had he going crazy?

Trying to keep the critical irritation out of his voice, Mike asked Ann, "What do the doctors say? How soon will he start to get better?"

"They start shock treatments next week."

Ann seemed calm, or at least resigned. Having watched one man shed his flesh and lose his hair with promised cures, watching another cry and shake and be unable to remember might not be as frightening. The skepticism Mike felt about the treatment he kept to himself. They must have improved it a lot since they jolted an aunt of his to blank silence years ago when he was just a kid. It wouldn't still be primitive like that, or they wouldn't be using it.

"If he were my husband," Carlotta said, "I'd get him out of there."

"What would she do with him? He's a vegetable."

"He's on drugs, that's all."

"But off them, he's violent."

Carlotta looked at Mike long and soberly. "So can you be. Nobody's locked you up."

"What's that supposed to mean?" Mike demanded. "Listen, my biggest problem is that I'm not crazy. Have I killed Alma? Have I raped you?"

"Is that what you'd like to do?" Carlotta asked, a coolness in her voice that irritated him.

"At least there would be some dignity in it!"

"Not for me," Carlotta said.

"And your dignity is all that matters."

"No. It doesn't have to be either/or surely. You make it sound as if you're simply waiting for me to be willing to participate in my own humiliation. It won't happen."

"I told you I'm *not* crazy."

"Trasco, I've decided to do your portrait. Will you sit for me?"

"What kind of portrait?" Mike asked, and felt himself blush.

"Something you'll like. I want to redeem social realism from usefulness. I want to do it as if it were the cover of *Time* magazine or a Mao poster. It may even say, 'Trasco, the sculptor, page twenty-three,' or something like that."

"Far out," Mike said.

"Wearing what you have on right now."

Mike looked down at his red and black shirt, his jeans, and his boots, already tired of them before they were to be immortalized.

"With one of your pieces behind you. We'll work in your studio."

"The light's not very good, and it's going to get colder than hell."

"I like the cold," Carlotta said.

Joseph was the only friend who had become familiar with Mike's sculpture, and Mike missed him sharply the moment Carlotta walked in and stood, looking. Joseph had never pretended to understand Mike's work, but he was an interested, often comfortable presence, a soft bundle of attention in contrast with this measuring rod of a woman who knew what Mike was trying to do and would judge him.

"You can hardly see them," he began, shouting at her.

"Don't talk at me," she said, and stepped away from him.

He had to talk. He couldn't stand to see her there, measuring the work that was intended to measure her or any other human figure in its presence.

"You look like a woman in a department store buying a piece of furniture!"

She ignored him. He shouldn't have brought her here like this at the beginning of her day, when she was fresh and cool, at the irritable end of his, when he had stood, literally, all he could. They should have been together first, if not smoking dope, at least having a drink or two, giving him time to explain, to prepare her for what he wanted her to see and think. Independent of him as she was, she was his doubt materialized, and he saw what he always fought seeing: the possibility that these huge frail structures were pretentious nonsense, the manifestation of his year of delusion. His eyes blurred in defensive fatigue.

"Say something!"

"I hadn't expected so much elegance," she replied, a tone of genuine surprise in her voice.

Shapes came back into focus. Mike was free both to see and to remember the hard skill of making imagined architecture into fact. The point, the whole point, was, of course, to call up that quality of surprise, which was his own when he was able to see what he had done. Carlotta had given him back his ability to see. He wanted to tell her how each piece had happened, why it happened, the balance and the hope. But he didn't have to begin at once. She'd be here working several days a week. He could tell her slowly, asking, "Do you know what is useful? Of course, you do: all that leaks or catches fire from toilet to furnace. All that's useful is potentially catastrophic. Art, great art, is beyond catastrophe. There is no point in making things that kill themselves. That's too didactic, too obvious. It could be done by hooking up a tap and letting it drip. Art doesn't *function*, malfunction, die."

He would tell her how it was that he knew all this, not from the books, the critics, but from life, his own, his father's, the prison of opposites which couldn't be transcended except through art which must be, yes, elegantly beyond hunger and dying.

"I want to tell you about the rats and the smell of vanilla, this neighborhood when I was a kid, why I work here, make this *here*. I want to tell you . . ."

Carlotta was smiling at him. Desire, and with it dread, overcame him. She didn't wait for him to make the first gesture, and her terrible thinness at that moment became a beautiful fragility inside the protection of his sure strength which he would fill her with, but carefully, gently. The cot he slept on would never have held him and his wife. He did not want to think about Alma, to remember the fullness of her breasts, withheld from him since the birth of his first son, the broad hips and strong thighs, the abundance of blond pubic hair, the whole lie of her magnificent body. Carlotta was a Giacometti woman, cool and hard as metal. He had never been able to imagine her naked. Feeling her hand now under his shirt, fingering through the hair on his chest, teasing his surprised nipples, he realized that she must have imagined him naked. He smiled down into her fine, peppery hair, then held her back from him, unable to release her for fear she'd not stand by herself, so fragile she seemed to him now.

He was shocked by his need to please her because it made him know how long he had been deprived of anything but trying to assert himself, his tongue in his wife's mouth an aggressive warning, his cock a weapon against her. Carlotta's mouth was all sucking promise. Her nipples, large fruit of her small breasts, hardened at his touch. He felt as clumsy as a child, pulling at her clothes, at his own, but her laugh was fond, full of pleasure, and her own fingers, accurate and intimate, made him laugh in return, nearly alarmed by how sure she was of his pleasure, those long, thin fingers down across his buttocks as she freed him for her mouth. He was lying on his back on his cot inside one of his angry sexual fantasies in which he had forced Alma to suck the life out of him, drink his seed until she choked. But now he was afraid that he could choke the woman so hungry at him, yet afraid, too, that lifting her up and rocking himself into her might hurt her more. He was dangerous, helpless, baffled, tears trickling into his sideburns, until she rose up and mounted him and he felt his palms slip on her wet thighs, his thumbs open a cunt full of juices he had only imagined. For a second he thought he might be sick or faint with disgust, need, gratitude. He bucked into her with a violence which might have thrown her off, but she rode him as fiercely until the struggle was all he wanted, the marvelous grunting hard work of screwing a woman who wanted it so that he now held her, a thumb against her sexual pulse until it was his own, and she came only a second before him, and finally lay all those light bones on top of him in the briny swamp of sweat and come, their exhausted breathing as mutual a rhythm as their fucking had been.

The moment of peace was brief, his hands gradually recognizing the nearly skeletal body of a woman foreign to him, one he had not even really wanted, who had shown him briefly and absolutely what Alma had deprived him of. The anger was in his hands, and he trembled against the desire to break those bones that had betrayed him into such knowledge. Intuitive in sex, she misread him now, for she was stroking his hair, her tongue teasing at his ear. Alma could always sense his anger, as if it had a smell, and grew armor he couldn't penetrate short of murder. This fragile-boned whore had no idea that the hand on the back of her neck could snap all that slippery, steaming life out of her in a second, that the arm across her rib cage trembled with crushing strength to resist a desire so much more compelling, because singular, to destroy the evidence of his betrayal. She mistook it for tenderness, and suddenly it was tenderness for a woman who was his friend and desired him and gave him nearly murderously costly pleasure and didn't know.

Penitent, protective of her, he turned her into the shelter of his arm and willed himself to gentleness, kissing her nipples, stroking her belly and thighs, and then he touched her as Alma had taught him to in the early days of their lovemaking when they still hoped to please each other. Carlotta watched his hand, then cupped hers over his and stopped him.

"I don't think I could bear that . . . yet."

"In ten minutes?"

She laughed.

Then she looked at him seriously and asked, "How am I ever going to get any work done?"

But several nights later she began. She had borrowed klieg lights from Allen, strong enough not only to illuminate but to give an illusion of warmth. Mike, posed before the structure of carefully broken forms, was embarrassed and absurdly pleased.

"You should have your head under a black cloth, telling me to look at the birdie."

Carlotta might not have heard him, her attention was so fixed on him. Mike had never been aware of being in the presence of someone else working as he worked. If he had not been the object of her concentration, he might have resented it. Instead, understanding her simply as he had never understood anyone before, he gave his will to her work, obediently still until he reached a state of near trance.

"Are you tired?"

As he heard her, he knew she had asked the question twice.

"No," he said. "I thought it would be hard work."

"After a night on your feet."

"It isn't," he said. "I stop thinking of anything."

Then he was aware that he was, in spite of the lights, stiff and cold.

"I'll make coffee," he offered. "Are you cold?"

"I have to be to work."

When he brought her a mug, he looked at her canvas, which was nothing yet but blocked spaces.

"I work very slowly," she said. "I warned you."

"That's all right."

"Is that piece named?"

"Nicknamed. Joseph calls it 'School Days.' I don't name any of them. Naming is a poet's work."

"I went to see him yesterday."

"Who?"

"Joseph. He doesn't remember anything that's happened for the last six months. He doesn't know you've been to see him, even that his wife has. But he does know he can't remember."

"Isn't that temporary now?" Mike asked.

"So they say."

"But they must know what they're doing," Mike said, wanting to be reassured.

"He'll be easier to deal with, I suppose," Carlotta answered, clearly indicating the obscenity that was for her. "He's interested in amnesia anyway, treats it like a peculiar holiday."

"Is that what we're all having?" Mike asked.

"Are you?" Carlotta asked. "Is that what this is?"

"I'm a married man."

"There are remedies for that."

"Do you mean I ought to leave her?"

"You have left her."

He had and he hadn't. Surely Carlotta understood that.

"I saw Alma yesterday, too."

"What did you tell her?" Mike demanded.

"Not what you wish I would."

"What's that?"

"That you're the greatest fuck in town and she ought to get you back, on your terms, as soon as possible."

"Why not? Why not tell her that?"

"When anything gets told Alma, you'll do the telling, Trasco. You really want her back, don't you?"

"She's my wife!"

Carlotta sighed and turned away.

"Listen," Mike said, taking her arm and turning her back to him.

"To what? Your delusions of ownership?"

"What's wrong with that? What's wrong with wanting to fuck for life's sake? I wanted a daughter. Is that a crime?"

"Alma's not a piece of raw material to be made into sons and daughters. She's a human being."

"What is inhuman about being pregnant?"

"Try it," Carlotta suggested, "and see."

"Have you?"

"No," she said. "I'm like you. I'd rather paint. Unlike you, because I'm a woman, I know the difference."

"What's the point then?" he asked.

"Does there have to be one?"

He covered his face and wept. If her arms hadn't circled his chest, his grief might have broken his ribs. He did not understand what was happening to him, to his life. He could not believe what he, in fact, believed: that Alma wanted no more to do with him. She was so far from his that he was, as Carlotta had put it, Alma's cast-off property, and now Carlotta was trying him on for size.

"Get out of here!" he wanted to shout, but his throat felt swollen shut.

Her fingers were at the back of his neck, kneading the pain at the base of his skull. They moved under his shirt over the straining muscles of his back. Again her arms were around him, holding his shuddering. He was baffled and shamed by his need of that comfort, his passivity, as she finally cradled him like an infant, giving him her breast. He fell asleep, his face buried in her cunt, and had horrified dreams of being born between skeletal thighs, a thing of forlorn and wasted flesh.

When he woke alone, it was a full moment before the trance of sleep was broken and he remembered where and how he was.

It was three months since Mike had seen his children. Though he knew she had not, he felt barred from them as if

Alma had actually refused him access. He even found it difficult to think about them. Tony, so inaccurately named for Mike's dead father, already wore glasses and used a book as Mike had used fists for self-defense. More than once Mike had had to take a book by force and order the kid out into the street to play, yet Mike wasn't afraid, as Alma had accused him of being, of Tony's brains. Once he grew into them and became whatever he chose to become, a lawyer, scholar, whatever, Mike would be as proud of him as Alma was, but Mike had to see that he also became a man who could fill his physical space in the world, something the brawny little Victor was already teaching himself, untroubled by Alma's scolding or spoiling, because he knew the tests he had to pass on the playground whether she understood them or not. Mike had more trouble disciplining Vic because he wouldn't be afraid. One day he'd be as silly as Mike had been with his father, too impatient to wait until the battle would be equal, and after that they'd be friends. Mike was less sure how friendship would occur between him and his older son, whose defense was like his mother's, withdrawal into silent superiority, but the kid could draw. In that he was Mike's. Sometimes, not exactly missing them so much as simply wanting to lay eyes on them, take a physical and emotional inventory, Mike was tempted to drive by and pick them up on their way to school, but it was a plan too clandestine, too much an admission of the loss of status he felt. To see them, he must be able to walk into the house and assert his right to be there.

To do that, Mike would have to know what he wanted to do with the boys. Sometimes he imagined driving them down to his mother in Arizona, but she already had her hands full with his brother's kids, and there was the complication of the border. One morning, visiting with Ann, he had a fantasy of moving the boys in there, giving them sisters to teach them the lessons about female nature mothers instinctively withheld from sons. But that was even more a fantasy than getting them across the border and had more to do with Mike's own wish that he'd had a sister, that he'd one day have a daughter, like Susan or Rachel.

He could, of course, simply throw Alma out and occupy the house himself, but there was no way he could take care of the boys, go on earning them a living, and work. Carlotta had no motherly interest in them.

The real reason his plans came to nothing was that he would not ever take his sons from their mother. However much Mike disagreed with her, it was not because he thought her inadequate as a parent. Her job was to nurture and protect, his to discipline and challenge. For him the conflicts were a natural part of the job of marriage, as sex was their obvious resolution. Alma apparently thought both conflict and sex were a proletarian plot against her class and person.

What had he hoped to achieve, walking out like that? He certainly hadn't expected to have to carry on with the separation for weeks, now months. Once he had made it clear that he couldn't stand what was going on any longer, he had expected Alma to give in, not simply to avoid the humiliation of being deserted, her cover blown for that silly nonsense with Roxanne, but because she was, after all, his wife, and it was her place to come to him and apologize.

Was it because of Carlotta that Alma refused to make any gesture toward him? He'd waited weeks for Carlotta, but Alma had no way of knowing he hadn't walked out of the house and gone straight to her. Certainly he'd made no effort to hide the fact that he was seeing her, even spending money on her. But shouldn't jealousy or fear of really losing him force Alma to do something?

To hang onto the last shreds of the fantasy that Alma was capable of jealousy, fear, love, Mike did not go to her. He could not bear to know what he did know, that she was relieved to be rid of him.

Without Carlotta he would have hanged himself in earnest. Instead, he posed for his portrait, and the slow work of it became a reason to go on waiting, as if Carlotta were gradually making him whole and life-sized again so that he could claim what was his.

Joseph was better. Ann talked about bringing him home for Christmas. He might even be able to go back to work in the new year. This news, which Mike had waited for so hopefully, made him apprehensive not just for Joseph but for himself. He had not only worried about Joseph but envied him there in that protective environment where other people made the decisions, and sometimes the dreaded shock treatment lured Mike as a violent solution for himself if it could blank out, even temporarily, the last six months. But now even Joseph was being asked to come back, to go on. For the first time since Joseph had been hospitalized, Mike's sympathy for him was clarified of odd jealousies not only for Joseph's wife and children but for the illness itself.

Joseph was easier to be with now, though he was certainly not yet his old self. He talked a good deal more, always a slight agitation in his voice, and, though he could still listen, there was a new watchfulness in his attention as if he expected pitfalls dangerous to himself in what other people said. Mike could tell him about fixing the swing for Susan and Rachel, replacing a pane of glass a newsboy had broken. He could praise Ann's efficiency and calm. But when he mentioned Carlotta's portrait of himself, Joseph drew back in his chair and braced himself for an accident in which he would be involved, so the only thing Mike didn't say was that he had left Alma. Joseph could bear it no more than Mike could. Instead, Mike had to brace himself for Joseph's revelations.

"The one important thing I forgot is that Ann is pregnant," Joseph admitted, and then laughed the note Mike hadn't heard in months.

"Well, that's great!" Mike said. "A kid of your own."

"I didn't think it was necessary."

"Maybe I'm a dinosaur," Mike admitted. "Maybe I'm the only one left in the world who thinks kids are necessary—

yes, kids of your own. It's great you've adopted the girls, but it can't be quite the same."

"If it were, it would be okay. I feel responsible, but not exactly. I mean, I'm sorry for them that I went crazy, but then I think they know I'm only adopted, not 'real,' nothing in their blood or anything serious like that. Don't you feel with kids of your own you haven't any right to be who you are?"

"Hell, no!" Mike said. "You give them life. They're the only people in the world you do have the right to be yourself with, and they have to put up with it—until they're grown. Your own are your own."

Mike believed what he said until he heard himself say it, refusing to admit aloud that he hadn't even felt the right to call on his own sons for months.

"Was your father like that?"

"Sure was. Beat the shit out of me when I was fifteen and so cocky I thought I could take over the house."

"My father was a refugee. When I got my first bloody nose, he wept and said I was the blood on his hands, and could I ever forgive him."

"He hit you that hard?"

"No, no, he hadn't hit me. He never laid a hand on me. He just didn't think I should have been born. He was such a sad man I used to pick him flowers. Susan and Rachel brought me flowers the last time they came, five Christmas roses."

"Listen, Joseph, this place has done you a lot of good. I don't want to knock it, but these guys can make you get introspective about farting if they feel like it. There are things that are just *natural*, and having kids is one of them. It's not as if a kid would change your life all that much—or Ann's either with the girls as old as they are, and being girls."

"Ann will change, won't she?"

"Christ! Women are always changing. Nothing you can do about that. *She* wants the kid, doesn't she?"

"Yes, but mostly because it's something to give me."

"Well, it is, man. That's how it's supposed to be!"

Mike left the hospital, confused by impatience and concern, back to the ambivalence he had felt through the months of Joseph's illness. Joseph didn't deserve a woman who wanted his child, but then Mike thought of Joseph at the age of his own Victor, picking flowers for his sad father. It seemed so like the man who had been Mike's friend. Losing that friend to this new, needy candor must turn Mike into a friend of a sort he had not been before, concerned with Joseph's moods and frailties, involved in his once-hidden domestic life. At least being with Ann and the children gave Mike some sense of a normal world around him. Carlotta might have saved his life, but Ann preserved his sanity, what there was of it.

"Sometimes I wonder if for some people being normal drives them crazy," he said to Ann, having accepted a cup of coffee. "Like Joseph and my wife."

"Has your wife had a breakdown?" Ann asked.

"Sort of," Mike said. "But I don't want to burden you with my troubles."

"Why not? I burden you with mine all the time. Surely you think of me as a friend?"

"Oh, I do," Mike said. "I realize you're about the only ordinary person I know—except for myself."

"But you're an artist."

"Well, yes," he admitted.

"And so you have a way to be yourself most people don't. Joseph has the temperament without the gift."

"Did Joseph want to be an artist?" Mike asked, surprised.

"Oh, no. In fact, he says he feels spared."

"He's very lucky to have you, Ann. A lot of people wouldn't have the patience for this sort of thing. Sometimes even I . . . well, I wonder what he's got to go crazy about."

Ann's eyes were kind, but something in their expression checked Mike. He did not want to seem to her disloyal.

"It's one of the ironies, I guess."

"And your wife? I don't even know her name."

"Alma." He sighed. "I've left her."

"Should you have done that . . . if she isn't well?"

"Part of the sickness is that she doesn't want me around. Actually, she can't stand the sight of me."

"How hard," Ann said, laying a hand on his arm. "How terribly hard."

"Yeah, it is, and I've got the two sons, and I haven't seen them in months."

"But surely, Mike, you mustn't let her stop you seeing the children. They must need you."

"She's a lot better with them if I'm not around," Mike said, discovering an excuse he suspected of being true.

"Is she getting any help?"

"Not professional help. She's got a friend she's close to."

"It seems to me the only comfort in trouble is when you can do something to help."

Among women as tender as this one, as passionate as Carlotta, he had chosen Alma, who had no sympathy in her. Once it had seemed to him a supreme confidence which came out of the security of her childhood. He had admired what was, in fact, coldness and indifference. She had learned to count the cost and found everything human far too expensive, except for her children, and she put a limit there, too.

"I don't know, Ann. We marry too young or too quickly before we know enough. My father tried to tell me. He said, 'You think life's too short, and what you're going to find out is it's too long.' He was already sick then. I thought it was his sickness speaking."

"Maybe it was," Ann said. "People can grow past trouble."

"Where do you get the faith?"

"With John at the last . . . oh, people say it's the drugs

that produce a state of euphoria, but even if it was a sort of hallucination, he did see . . . something. He said, 'I see,' and then he said, 'It's all all right.' I believe life has a shape we can't see except maybe for a moment at the end."

"A shape?"

"Yes," Ann said, obviously not willing to go beyond that.

Mike looked down at her and realized that she was one of those pious little girls in the eighth grade who wore crosses on gold chains, who flunked math and history and never were first in anything but neat penmanship. Even then he'd been chasing the ones who could spell almost as well as he could, who could run almost as fast, who flaunted their tits as much as he did his biceps. He had no intention of building a wren's nest. He'd mated with a mockingbird. He could hear Alma even now, saying with exaggerated piety, "I believe life has a shape."

Well, Christ, it had to, didn't it? And what some people called hallucinations other people called visions. He certainly knew that sense of supreme balance he felt smoking pot was real. Or he could make it real, build it into his work. Maybe for some people, simple, sincere people like Ann, just hearing about it from someone else was enough. "It's all all right."

"Thank you for telling me that," he said. It was the sort of thing Alma sometimes said to Tony to encourage him to confide in her, and it had irked Mike to see his son so manipulated. But he wasn't trying to manipulate Ann. He did want to thank her.

"Would you like to be with us for Christmas, Mike? If Joseph's home, I know he'd like that."

"Why, thanks," Mike said. "I hadn't really thought that far."

"It's only two weeks away."

Certainly he wouldn't go home for Christmas to play disenfranchised Santa Claus to Alma's father. They had tried not to dislike each other and were modestly successful except on holidays, when each inadvertently showed up the other, Mike a stingy, inadequate provider, his father-in-law a buyer of affection who felt no more certain of his daughter's admiration than Mike did. The very first Christmas, before there were children, Mike was simply amazed at the accumulation of things not only for Alma and her sisters but for himself. Christmas in his own home had been primarily a daylong drunk and a feast at which lesser men than his father often passed out. No one ever gave anyone else more than one gift, and in bad years it might be a dollar from his father, socks she had knitted from his mother. Was it that when you couldn't give much, you learned to dislike giving? Mike's brother was as tight with money as he was. They hadn't given anything to each other for years. Alma had taken over sending presents to Mike's mother and his niece and nephew. Since she did not ask him for extra money, she probably spent her own. He never asked her what money she had. It was none of his business. Over the years he had fought with her about every taste and value money could buy, but money itself was never mentioned. Mike wore the expensive clothes his in-laws gave him when he was less and less frequently invited to their house to dinner, and he had a closetful of golf clubs, tennis rackets, skis, and equipment for other middle-class games he had never learned to play. When one of Alma's sisters asked him his favorite sport, he had answered, "Fighting." She gave him boxing gloves for his birthday. The only present Mike had ever objected to was a life insurance policy.

"Jesus, Alma, he might as well have a contract out on me. Is he a secret member of the Mafia, or what?"

Alma told him it was just like having a suit of clothes or a martini pitcher, and anyway, it wasn't for him; it was for the children.

Gradually Mike understood that Alma's parents had not objected to him as a son-in-law because they felt perfectly confident that, propped up by their money, he could at least look and, therefore, finally become the part. When he did not, they tried to overlook what offended them most, the house he rented and his job, by calling him not an artist but artistic, which made it sound something like asthmatic.

God knows, it could seem as much an illness to him, quarantined down there in his warehouse like an untouchable, a leper, unless Carlotta was with him in a cold trance of work, which, because it was hers, only she could break with the aggressive sexual appetite that studying him seemed to give her. Once he had insisted on having her when she first arrived, not so much because he wanted her urgently but because he didn't like the idea of being the object of her appetite. She was only superficially reluctant, but afterwards she couldn't work, and she didn't return to the portrait for more than a week. Alone in its unfinished company, Mike realized he wouldn't work again until Carlotta had completed him and relinquished his space. If then.

Mike had not gone out of his way to avoid meeting his wife. It was simply that unless he sought her out, they had always lived in different territories of the city. She left their house in Kitsilano for visiting her parents in West Point Grey or a sister in West Vancouver. Though shops in their neighborhood were rich with a variety of foods for Greek, Italian, and Oriental tastes, she preferred the Safeway near her parents' house, the shop that carried only French and English cheeses. Mike lived in his old neighborhood and went east to Commercial to shop. He crossed False Creek only to visit Carlotta or Ann.

It was outside Carlotta's he finally did see Alma a couple of days before Christmas. She was getting into her car and didn't see him parked across the street in his truck. He was shocked to realize what a large woman she was, almost gross.

"Cow!" he whispered harshly. "Bloody great cow!"

Moments later, in Carlotta's company, he was sullen with his own betrayed taste, her unnatural thinness as repugnant to him as his bovine wife.

"Why sulk?" Carlotta asked. "Surely you don't expect me not to see her?"

"I don't give a fuck who you see."

"Truth to tell she's not my favorite caller these days. She was bringing me a Christmas present, that's all."

Mike saw the familiar shape of the box Carlotta's perfume came in. He picked it up and looked at the card, which had always read "From Alma and Mike." This one read "From Alma and Roxanne." He smashed the box down and felt the glass break. The concentrated scent exploded into the room like gas.

He turned and ran down the stairs, slammed into his truck, and drove the brief blocks to his house. Alma had not come back. He sat, staring at the house, wondering if the children were with their grandparents. He knew they were not. They were in his house with Roxanne, who slept in his bed, sucked his wife's cunt, and appeared in his place on Christmas cards. And he had let this go on for four months!

"Come to pay a Christmas call?"

He turned to find Alma standing in the street right by his door.

"Where are the kids?" he demanded.

"With Mother and Dad."

"Why?"

"Because I had a hunch you'd turn up before Christmas, and, if there was going to be a scene, I'd just as soon they missed it."

"Scene? You know you're bloody lucky to be alive?"

"Yes, I am."

"If it weren't for the kids . . ."

"What have you done to your hand?"

He looked down and saw that he was bleeding. "I was practicing."

"Mike, if you want to talk, that's fine. It's long past time we did. But if you've come back on some macho trip just to knock me around, forget it."

"Trasco, the wife beater," he said scornfully. "That's what I should have been."

"It would have ended sooner," she said, almost as if she

were agreeing with him. "Do you want to come in? You ought to fix that hand."

He was suddenly aware that he smelled strongly of Carlotta's perfume, and Alma would certainly notice it if she hadn't already.

"I've just smashed our yearly Christmas present to Carlotta," he tried to announce rather than confess. His hand and her concern about it made him feel more like a misbehaving child than a properly outraged husband.

"Whatever for?"

"Because you put her damned name on it, that's why!" he shouted, near ridiculous tears.

She didn't laugh. The distress in her face frightened him.

"Come in," she said. "Please. She's not here."

Alma took him directly to the bathroom, where she washed the dozen cuts, examining them for bits of glass.

"The perfume's antiseptic, but just in case . . ."

She reached for the iodine. Before she took out the stopper, she smoothed a long strand of her blond hair behind her ear, a gesture so familiar to him he was jealous of it in any other woman. In her face intent on her job he saw unconscious tenderness, and he wanted to tilt that face to his to receive what his hand received, but the weather in her eyes changed whenever she looked up at him.

"You're never careful enough of your hands," she said as she finished.

She did not understand in him what she didn't understand in Victor, the natural conflict of uses, the making and breaking a man must do with his hands. She would have him carry them in his pockets, tools as precious as his cock, to be as protected. He half expected her to kiss the hand she had just tended, but instead she turned abruptly away to escape the close quarters they had been in.

"Coffee?"

She was naturally wifely, like Ann. With Carlotta it was Mike who made the coffee. He sat down at the dining-room table to be served, the habit of a table too deep in him for

Alma to break. She had finally acquired it herself, and it had pleased him, even though this table was a bright emblem of the middle class, who could afford the waste space of a dining room, that it had become a center of the house instead, a place to work or rest as well as eat. As she put the cup before him, along with a plate of Christmas cookies the boys had probably helped her bake, Mike felt at home.

"You've lost weight," she observed.

"I'm not much of a cook."

They both fell silent. Having lost his first angry initiative, Mike didn't know how or where to begin. He had never rehearsed this scene in his head because the script he wrote and rewrote was Alma's coming to him and asking him to come home. That was always followed by a long list of his grievances, after each of which she apologized and promised reform. Alma wasn't a woman who apologized. In real life their reconciliations were his doing, rarely with words, usually with a gesture, fixing a porch step or taking the kids for a ride, and it could never be done as a bid for sex. Neither did Alma bargain.

"This has gone on long enough," he finally said.

"Well, it's given us both time, and I certainly needed it. Thanks, by the way, for sending the money."

He shrugged. Being thanked for what was his to do was a habit he'd never broken her of, but he hadn't given in to it himself. To thank for duty was to suggest a choice where there was none.

"You've always been more honest than I am about big things. We were horribly unhappy, and you did something about it."

"Don't flatter me. It was a bad joke. This whole four months has been a bad joke. It's over. We don't have to talk about it."

"I have to, Mike, because it isn't over. Or it's over for me with you. Please—try not to get angry. It's not your fault. I just am really no good at being your wife, and, once I gave up trying, I should have quit."

"Quit? You don't quit! This isn't a game we're playing."

"Oh, Mike, you're so . . . old-fashioned. Who do you know who's managed to stay married as long as we have?"

"I am your husband, not a skirt you wear one day to your ankles, the next day to your crotch, and send to the Salvation Army next week. You are *married* to me."

"But I'm getting a divorce . . ."

"As a Christmas present from Daddy?"

"I don't want it to be ugly. We're not ugly people. You've been as unhappy as I have."

"Don't tell me what I've been."

"But haven't you?"

"That's beside the point. All this is beside the point. We don't have to talk about it. I'm home," he said, and to prove his point he started to take off his jacket.

"All right," she said, and she stood up. "We don't have to talk. We never have been able to. Why should we at this point? The house is all yours."

She got as far as the front door before he caught up with her. If the face she turned to him had been scornful, he might have been able to hit her, but he saw in it such terrible distress he could not even put out a restraining hand.

"Then talk," he said desperately. "Talk."

"You can't listen. It's nothing you want to hear."

"Look. I shouldn't have done it. It was stupid. I'm sorry."

For a moment he thought he was actually going to see his wife cry. Then she turned away, walked down the steps and over to her car, leaving him alone with an apology he'd had no intention of making.

Ten years. Mike remembered listening to a man talk who had served only seven and simply did not know what to do with himself. After several months he'd stolen a car and smashed it into a tree. Neither the nostalgia for prison nor the gesture was comprehensible to Mike then. Now he felt as if he had done the same thing; only it hadn't worked. He'd managed to get back into the jail, but with no one to judge or keep him, that accomplished nothing. Had he been horribly unhappy? He couldn't remember. He was in touch only with the pointless misery of the last free months, which he had tolerated passively, simply waiting for the time to come to an end, for Alma to end it. Now she had. He was free, and he could feel nothing but blankness.

He wandered around the house to discover how few traces of his own occupancy were left except behind closed closet and cupboard doors. He had been much more effectively put away than Joseph, whose domestic litter was evident everywhere in his house so that, on his return, he'd be immediately at home. Even in the bathroom Mike had to rummage in the storage cupboard beneath the sink to find a box with his razor, toothbrush, shaving lotion, comb.

Among the womanly and childish clutter, he could not distinguish any particular signs of Roxanne. The small pair of trousers in their bedroom could as easily have belonged to Tony. It didn't matter.

Tony's room had changed more than any other in the house. On the shelves where his collection of miniature cars had been, there were books, dozens of them, and there was a music stand, though no sign of an instrument. Whatever it was, he probably had it with him. Mike wondered if his son's face would be as hard to recognize as his room after only four months.

He found in Victor's room what he had missed in Tony's. Victor had obviously inherited the childhood Tony was leaving behind, but all in heaps and overflowing boxes. No amount of nagging from Alma, threatening from Mike would ever make Victor orderly as Tony naturally was.

Mike did not feel real. He was as much a ghost as if he'd actually killed himself on that ridiculous thirtieth birthday. In four months children so young would already be accustomed to his absence. Had he really missed them? He missed the idea of them. What he was really losing was the right to their friendship in the future, the bond that only contending for the same domestic space could make. He saw himself a stranger, a derelict, in a concert hall, football stadium, church, old as his father had been suddenly old, but without the right to the attention and care of the strong young men his sons would be.

Mike could not stay in this house, tomb of a failed kingdom he had never ruled as a man should. Why? Was Carlotta right? Was he, like her, only really able to be alone? What was his art worth to him if it lost him the world? What had it ever been worth anyway? If he had given it up, if he had taken a real job, by now at thirty he'd have something to show for his life: a real house on a real street with a real wife and children in it, rather than these people who had been on nothing but a long-term loan from a patient father-in-law, who had finally decided time had run out and written him off as a bad debt. Alma was his daughter; the boys were his grandsons. Nothing here had ever belonged to Mike.

In the basement he found the monogrammed luggage given to him for trips he had refused to take. Into it he piled some of his clothes, including the newest two of his suits. He also took the set of golf clubs and tennis racket, not knowing why, with some vague sense that not to would be petty.

Finally, he went out into the shed to see if there were any tools or materials he should load into the truck. There he found a pile of his old clothes, on top of which was an elaborately ornamented sign.

Trasco's Decrees

Soft Sculpture Is a Pile of Crap . . .

Mike stopped reading. That pile of clothes was his effigy. He lifted it up and found the hidden head and hands. The screwdriver had been removed. So had the wedding ring. He looked back at the sign, obviously left those months ago by Joseph. It lacked the statement Mike had neglected to share with his friend: "Don't make anything that can kill itself." He carried the dummy out to the trash can and dumped it in. He hesitated with the sign. He knew it was meant as a friendly joke, but the pretentious vulgarity of those statements embarrassed him. He felt a thousand years older than the brash, hopeful fake he had been, so kindly listened to by a little fellow Mike hadn't forgiven for going crazy, deserting Mike in his own craziness which he had claimed to be sanity itself. Joseph at least could come home. Self-pity, as sudden and debilitating as a nosebleed, tasted in Mike's mouth and stained his vision. Why hadn't he really killed himself when he had had at least enough self-respect to be able to do such a thing? Now he could break nothing but a stupid bottle of perfume. He crumpled Joseph's sign, slammed down the lid of the trash can, and turned away. He had to get out of there.

After Mike unloaded the truck at the warehouse, he dressed in one of his rarely worn suits and went down to the club where he worked.

"Jesus, man," his boss exclaimed. "Who died?"

"I've got to quit," Mike said, "right now, without notice."

He was willing to forfeit his last two weeks of pay, but his boss was a man of generous gestures and insisted he take an extra two weeks' money instead.

"And anytime, you know, you want to come back, you need anything, you know where I am."

For a moment Mike doubted what he was doing. Here, where he claimed he had made no friends, where he was nothing but a pair of fists, he was being treated with generosity and kindness. But the irony was too apparent. At thirty to be successful at nothing but being a bouncer at a third-rate nightclub was colder comfort than he could stand.

From the club he walked along Georgia until he came to The Bay. It had been years since he'd been in a department store. First he went to the perfume counter. He did not know the name of Carlotta's perfume, but he recognized the bottle.

"Sixty-three fifty," the clerk informed him.

He did not believe it as he counted out the money. Every

year Alma calmly shelled out this kind of money for the smell of a friend. The cuts on his hand must be worn like expensive jewelry.

He wanted to buy presents for his children. He never had. You don't feel empty-handed going home to children you live with. It was different to contemplate calling on them at their grandparents'. He found his way to the board where all the departments were listed, stood being bumped and crowded by people trying to get on the escalator. It was like being at work on a Saturday night with the sound turned off. In all the TV ads of happy shoppers, the man buying a suit or a car, the woman in her new bra with her different brand of instant coffee, there were never other people. The gray, anxious hordes were invisible. Nobody could really like spending money like this. Faintly now he could hear music, "Joy to the world, the Lord has come." Was there any place he could stand to be? He got through the crowd like the bouncer he was.

Carlotta opened the door to him reluctantly. He offered her the bottle of perfume, still in its bag with the sales slip.

"You still smell of it," she said. "I've been airing this place out for hours. I don't know that I can ever wear it again."

"You damn well better," Mike said. "It costs four dollars and two cents a drop."

"I'm touched."

"I'm no good at presents. You know that."

"Well, at least now it really is from you."

"I saw Alma."

"I know."

"I mean after I left here."

"I know."

"For someone who's not your favorite caller, she stops around on the hour."

"Can you imagine I enjoy it?"

"No," Mike admitted.

"She said you looked terrible, and she was afraid you might do something desparate."

"She flatters herself."

"That's what I told her."

"How much longer do you need to finish the portrait?"

Carlotta looked at him intently. "An hour, a year."

"Seriously."

"I don't want to burden you with more bad news. It's finished at your convenience."

"I'm no good at riddles either."

"People as good-looking as you never are."

"It's looked finished to me for a couple of weeks. You overwork it you could ruin it."

"Then it's finished."

"I want to take off is all. I need to get of here for a while."

"Go," she said.

"I don't mean this minute. I want to see the kids. I promised Ann I'd have Christmas dinner there and welcome Joseph home."

"*I* mean this minute."

"What's the matter?"

"Nothing. I'm finished."

"With me?"

"Put it that way."

"Why?"

"Because *you* are and because, like any woman, I want the little vanity of choosing the moment."

Mike had no more considered ending his relationship with Carlotta than he had considered divorce except in moments of angry fantasy.

"Look, Carlotta, I couldn't have made it through these last months without you. You know that. You've been . . . great. It's just that I've got to get away from all this, figure out what to do with my life."

"Go. Figure. What do you need, a scene?"

"No," he said. "What do you want me to do with the portrait?"

"Shove it up your ass! Fuck it! Burn it!" she shouted, hurling herself at him.

If he hadn't been professional in subduing hysterical women, she would have done him real damage. He had only one bleeding scratch on his cheek close to his eye before he had her pinned and helpless. It had always been the unexpected violence of her appetite that excited his own, the dissolving heat of so thin a covering of flesh. He could feel her tense, waiting for a chance to break free.

"I'm going to shove it up your ass," he said.

He was not afraid of her as he had been of Alma. He was not really angry with her. He needed to take her against her will in order to reach the deep compliance there was in her. Before he succeeded, she had torn the pocket off his jacket and bitten him through the cloth of his shirt, and he had, he was sure, broken the little finger of her left hand. Her cunt was hot, frothy, and he rode her until both their backs might break, and she came to him clinging, weeping, a moment before he gave in himself.

He picked her up and carried her to her bed. They both looked like victims of an explosion. He covered her with a blanket and then sat for a moment on the floor by her. He was faint, lost consciousness for a second, came to.

"Why did you need that?" he asked.

She turned her head to look at him, her face thin, very pale, austere.

"I didn't. You did."

He nodded. Then he must have fainted or slept. When he came to again, she was gone. He looked around for a note. There was none. She had changed out of her torn clothes, taken a shower, even had half a cup of tea. He drank what was left, washed his abused face, straightened himself as he could, and wore the damage as he always had from the time he was a small boy, learning how to take his physical space in the world, as if it didn't matter.

Carlotta had been to the studio before him. Not only the portrait but all the small domestic signs of her were gone. Mike was glad because what had suited his vanity, Carlotta's intense concentration on him, had threatened his pride, the role reversal between artist and model. The portrait itself had become too familiar from his searching it for clues and reassurances. It had finally been able to tell him not much more than that he looked like a man whose picture should be on the cover of *Time*, and that was a wearying irony.

Detached from the clock with no job to go to and no further appointments with Carlotta, Mike could not remember what meal to eat, when to sleep. He thought again of presents for his children and had to concentrate to remember whether shops were closed at four in the morning or four in the afternoon. Suddenly he was afraid he'd missed Christmas altogether and had to ask someone on the street. He still had eleven hours of Christmas Eve.

He went into an art supply shop to buy himself new sketching pads, and there he decided to buy for his sons what he had always guarded fiercely for himself: the drafting tools and papers they had never been allowed to touch. In the pleasure of starting again, he chose generously, buying two of everything so that there would be no cause for envy or argument, each one to be equipped for the solitary activity that had given Mike so many hours of concentrated peace. He could stay alive in their hands and dreaming shapes. The clerk gave him two large boxes he'd later tie elaborately with string, a macramé Santa Claus for Victor, a cross for Tony. On the way out of the shop, Mike paused to look at a large, handsomely bound notebook with its blank pages of fine paper. Always a grumbler about cost, Mike had never given in to his own coveting of such objects. He worked with good materials, but elegance was in the extravagance of his imagination, in the poise of line, not in such things as this. On an impulse he bought it, not for himself but for his wife, though he had no idea what use she could put it to.

After he had phoned and asked her when he might drop by to see the boys, he felt as uncertain as a man courting. Would she, would they all see these gifts as just another indication of his self-absorption instead of the hopeful offering of what mattered to him most to share with them?

Several weeks ago Ann had said she'd put off buying the girls shoes because Joseph liked to take them shopping for those and always turned it into a special occasion. She obviously thought it both funny and endearing since, aside from his teeth, Joseph most begrudged spending money on his own shoes. Mike had always thought of fatherly chores as starting his sons out in skills and pleasures, not in things, but part of his pride had been a defense against his father-in-law's obsessive generosity. Might Mike have discovered the innocent pleasure in things if he'd chosen Tony's first pencil box, Victor's first lunch pail, the very things he had scorned because he'd envied them himself when he started school without the stub of a pencil or anything to eat?

The boys were out playing on their grandparents' expansive front lawn when Mike arrived. Victor was the first to spot his truck, shouted out, "Hey, Dad!" and came at a run. Standing on the parking strip, watching the chunky power of his younger boy's body, Mike wanted to reach out his arms not to some vision of a lost future but to this child, whom he'd tended and taught, rebuked and encouraged, loving him simply as he could never love Tony because Tony had always stayed aloof, as he did now, watching his younger brother greet his father. Mike didn't catch Victor up in his arms, hug him, weep into his tender child's neck, tell him how bitterly Mike had missed him. Victor was a son, not a daughter. And Victor, so like his father in his own requirements, jammed to a stop only a couple of feet from Mike, nearly falling down, and said in a soft, breathless voice with a shy, tough toss of his head, "Hi."

Mike put a hand on his shoulder and a playful fist into his jaw. Victor returned the greeting with a fist into Mike's thigh hard enough to make him wonder if he'd have to limp into the house.

"What are you doing? Practicing for a knockout?"

Victor buried his face against the flesh he had struck, his

arms around Mike's leg, as if he might anchor Mike there forever, half wrestler's hold, half hug. Mike tousled his hair, already darkening as Tony's was not, and looked across the lawn at his fair-haired boy, who had not moved.

"Hey, Tony," Mike called. "Get a leg on. I need help with parcels."

It worked. The boy was released into his own running. He was much more graceful than Victor and was already a good skater, one of the many such accomplishments Mike didn't have.

"How've you been?" Mike asked.

"Okay, I guess," Tony answered. "You been in a fight?"

Mike touched the scratch on his face and saw the cuts on his hand. "Would you believe I had an argument with a perfume bottle?"

Tony had his mother's reluctant smile, which made it a pleasure to win it from him.

"Can we open them right away, while you're here?" Victor asked the moment he saw the presents. "Hey, that's *funny!*" he said, pointing to the knotted Santa.

"How did you do that?" Tony asked, looking at his knotted cross.

Mike wished he'd thought to include balls of string.

"I'll show you," he said.

"Are you coming in?" Tony asked, a note of uncertainty in his voice.

"I'm not going to stand out here and freeze."

"Aunt Margaret's in there," Tony said, "and Uncle Peter."

"They just came," Victor added.

Mike felt the anger in him begin to rise. Did Alma think she needed protection? If so, she should have found someone other than that prick of a brother-in-law who couldn't have protected his prize camellia from his wife's Pekinese.

They were all there, his in-laws, and the term seemed to Mike aggressively legal as he shook hands first with Alma's father, then with Peter. The women had not come to the door. Alma and Margaret sat on the couch in front of the brightly burning fire. Alma's mother stood fiddling with the Christmas tree, which was as formal and expensive as everything else in this house. Alma did rise to greet him, a coffee table between them. He was glad he had a box to offer her and saw that she was surprised by it.

"Can we open ours now while Dad's here?"

"I don't see why not," Alma said.

"What'll you have, Mike?"

"Whatever's going," Mike said.

Alma's mother was offering him a plate of fruitcake, stuffed dates, and some of the same cookies Alma had served him . . .was it only yesterday?

"Eggnog?"

Normally Mike would have remarked that eggnog tasted to him like milk pissed in by a diabetic. This afternoon he said, "Fine."

Victor was struggling to pull off the macramé Santa Claus to get at his present. Tony held his up to his father.

"Can I get it open without undoing the cross?"

Mike took a knife out of his pocket and cut the string to keep the cross intact. He did the same for Victor, wishing he had also bought them knives, wanting them to have everything he did that gave him pleasure.

"You always do such clever things with your hands, Mike," Margaret commented pleasantly. She was the sister who had given him boxing gloves.

He picked up the extra string and quickly tied her two intricate knots.

"Where did you learn how?"

"On the docks when I was a kid . . . from the sailors."

"A compass, hey, *funny!*" Victor exclaimed.

Tony did not say anything as he looked at graph paper, sketching pad, a numbered range of pencils, pen and ink, ruler, but the pleasure in his touching with hands so like his father's was obvious.

"Everything's just the same," Victor discovered, looking into his brother's box. "I've got everything he's got."

The adults laughed, knowing that fact would give status to a bottle of vitamin pills.

"Can I draw something right now?" Victor asked.

"Sure," Mike said. "Why don't we just go in to the dining-room table?"

"I'm sorry," Alma's mother said. "It's set for dinner . . ."

"Use the table in my den," Alma's father suggested.

Mike wondered if he had all the money in the world whether he'd ever be comfortable in the wasted showplaces of a house like this. Alma's father probably sat at that desk once a month to do domestic paperwork. His office was downtown. The only real use for the den was the shelter it offered sons-in-law to watch football games and grandchildren at moments like this. The boys sat down at the library table. Tony decided to block out a town on graph paper. Victor began to draw a plane to bomb it.

Alma came to the door and stood watching. Mike walked over to join her.

"They're wonderful presents."

"Alma, I'm leaving town for a while, maybe a month or two. I've taken what I need out of the house. You can do whatever you want about it."

"What about your job?"

"I quit, but don't worry about that. I've got money set aside. I'll send you the usual."

"You don't really have to do that, Mike."

"Those are my kids."

"Sure, but if you're not working . . . Without us, I thought you might be able to get on with your own work, really concentrate, without the burden . . ."

"A family isn't a burden."

"Mike, you should know I'm going ahead with the divorce, and I don't want alimony or anything."

"Are you going to go out and work?"

"I thought maybe, part time."

"I don't want that. I want you at home with the boys. I'll send the money."

Alma began to protest again and then shrugged. She rarely argued to get her way.

"When are you leaving?"

"In a day or two."

"Take care of yourself, won't you?"

"I've got no choice," Mike answered.

The scene was too strange, the boys peacefully working at the library table, Mike having a civil conversation with Alma about the uncivil and unholy thing she had decided to do. Mike could hear the nervous joviality of the conversation in the living room with its silent gaps while they listened for an angry raising of voices or a slap and a scream. Mike had a momentary image of himself, the superstud, beating the shit out of Alma's father and Peter while the women stood by in terror and admiration, but he had already won the princess's hand and lived happily ever after. His father was right. Life was much too long, and Mike was deathly tired of it.

"Thank your father for this sweet piss," he said, handing Alma his empty glass.

Without saying good-bye to his sons or the rest of the assembled guard, he left the house. He stood for a moment on the front steps to acknowledge the admirable and serene view of Howe Sound, the water sapphire blue today, the great mountains white with unviolated snow. From here the city might not have existed, people piled on top of each other thirty stories high in the lonely close quarters of their lives, the long drunk of Christmas just beginning, the taste already cloying.

That duty done, Mike regretted having agreed to be with Ann and Joseph the next day. He wanted to get into the truck and begin driving—south out of this cold country. But he also needed to eat and to sleep. He wondered about treating himself to a meal in a restaurant, but his extravagance had spent itself. Instead, he stopped at a supermarket to buy hamburger, a can of corn, a bag of apples.

In the lineup Mike caught sight of Pierre, three cash registers away, wearing a kerchief over his long dark curls, carrying a woman's handbag. He seemed to be alone. Mike despised Allen, who chose not to be a man, not to be an artist, degraded himself with that embarrassing and pathetic mistake of a boy, with work about which he was entirely cynical, fawning over Alma, condescending to Mike. Pierre was simply pitiful, trying to pass as a little French housewife; he needed a shave. At that moment Pierre caught sight of Mike and gave him a radiant smile. Mike nodded.

Pierre was checked out first and came to stand with Mike while the clerk rang up his few purchases.

"Is that your dinner?" Pierre asked, peering over his own large bag of groceries.

"Just a snack," Mike answered defensively, not able to abide sympathy from Pierre.

"You're not eating properly," Pierre said, a surprising sternness in his voice. "Carlotta's no sort of cook. You can tell that by looking at her."

"My friends aren't feeding me," Mike said haughtily.

"I can see that," Pierre agreed. "I wish . . . well, the trouble is at Christmas we go gay with a vengeance, and, though you'd be very welcome, of course, I don't think . . ."

"Thanks," Mike said. "I'm having Christmas with Ann and Joseph."

"I did know that. Joseph told me last week. I'm so glad he's getting out of there. Every time I went out to see him I was sick to my stomach for hours afterwards. I told Allen, when I go crazy, he can just put me in a cage in the backyard . . ."

Mike accepted change with one hand, picked up his groceries with the other, refusing to meet the amused eyes of the clerk. "Merry Christmas," he said curtly to either of them, and walked away from their rejoinders.

It was after nine o'clock, the stores all shut, when Mike thought he should also have bought gifts at least for Rachel and Susan. Could he make them something? He looked around his crowded studio space. There wasn't time to make anything elaborate like a doll's house. Chairs? He didn't have the right sorts of scraps, and they'd anyway outgrow them too quickly. He was staring at the piece Joseph called "School Days," the one he had the most trouble keeping Victor from climbing on the several times he had the boys with him here. "It's not a fucking jungle gym. It's a piece of sculpture, a work of art, you little barbarian!" Tony had never had to be told, though he could put on his mother's expression of skepticism at such statements, which angered Mike far more than Victor's innocent energy. Climbing in it did no harm. It was sturdily enough built for a dozen kids to play on. Mike himself climbed about on them all, "like an angry ape," Joseph said.

Well, why not? It came apart in pieces he could easily load into the truck by himself. It wouldn't take half an hour to put the structure together again in Joseph's backyard. That problem solved, Mike finally slept and dreamed of apes and children playing in the wreckage of his art.

Joseph, in trousers now too large for him, an old man's cardigan, and carpet slippers, looked more diminished than he had even in the hospital. Beside him Ann, now clearly pregnant, looked a member of another species. Not for the first time Mike wondered why a woman so calm and fruitful had twice been bound to men so obviously mortal. Though he knew it could not have been conscious choice, she seemed to him the female counterpart of those men who chose dangerous occupations, the constant threat of death giving them a rare radiance.

"Can we let him do this?" Ann was asking Joseph as they stood by the truck, watching him unload the pieces of sculpture.

"What is it?" both the children were asking.

"A special sort of jungle gym for the backyard. Your dad calls it 'School Days.' "

Together they chose a place next to the sandbox Joseph had built them. The day was too cold for standing about. Mike insisted Joseph and Ann go back indoors, but the girls, in bright new ski jackets, stayed with him.

"Are you a daddy, Mike?" Rachel asked.

"Of course, he is," Susan said.

"How do you know?" Rachel asked.

"Because he acts like a daddy."

"Not like ours."

"Ours is sick."

"Our other daddy got sick and died," Rachel informed Mike matter-of-factly. "But Daddy won't. Mother says he'll get well after a while."

"Of course, he will," Mike said.

"Where are your children?" Rachel asked.

"With their mother."

"How old are they?"

"Six and nearly nine."

"We're older," Susan said. "I'm nearly ten."

"I'm eight."

"Don't stand on that until I've got it fixed," Mike said, tempted to suggest that both of them go in to help their mother.

Before when he had been there, they had been very quiet. Now they seemed much more like his own nuisancy kids. You did something for children, and they thought it gave them new rights with you instead of obligations. When did that change? With women it didn't. Maybe that was why you could go ahead and spoil daughters since it was their nature to live their lives getting what they didn't earn as the right of their sex.

"Are you cross?" Rachel asked.

"No," Mike said, lifting her up and putting her down on the bare branch of an apple tree, "just busy. I'll be finished in a minute if you'll stay there."

"Look how high I am!"

"You, too?" Mike asked Susan.

She was more like Tony, he realized. Did first children have to be more watchful and testing?

"Okay," she said, and held out her arms to be lifted.

She hadn't the weight of his six-year-old. Once established in the tree, she began to giggle, a pitch low for a girl child and surprisingly sensual. When she stopped, Rachel started up an imitation. For a few minutes they played catch with their laughter, then struck up a silly duet until they seemed nearly demented.

"I'm going to wet my pants," Rachel said.

That set off an hysteria that shook the tree. Mike tightened the last bolt and climbed up on the structure of carefully broken forms to test its stability. The sight of him standing higher than they were sent them into new convulsions, and his threatened irritation, as he looked down at those tiny-boned, curly-headed children, weak with silliness, hugging the trunk of the apple tree, vanished. Christmas morning, with their frail and subdued father, must have been tense with doubt as well as excitement, all being spent now in this paroxysm of laughter. His boys would have been having an only half-playful fistfight. Maybe at this moment they were, except without him there to permit it, understanding the necessity of spending pent-up anxious excitement, their mother would stop them. Little girls giggled.

"Come on," he said, jumping down. "Now you can try it."

He lifted one, then the other down from the tree. They staggered about a moment, unsure of their balance, then made a game of the staggering, until Susan with a quick grace swung herself up onto the first stage of the structure, and Rachel followed.

"Hey, this is fun!"

"Come up here. Come to this part!"

"Mike, look at me, look at me."

What he saw was not the success of his present to two small girls, though they did not interfere with his pleasure. It had been years since he'd actually been able to see what he had made in a space of its own without other structures competing for attention, in bright daylight. It *was* elegant.

He turned to pick up his tools and saw Joseph at the

window. Mike waved and decided to join him to see what it looked like from there.

Joseph moved aside to let Mike have the view.

"Well, what do you think of that? A Trasco in your own backyard!"

Ann came to look. "Why, Mike, it's so clever!"

Joseph nodded and then asked, "Did you ever find the sign I made you?"

"Oh, yeah, I did," Mike said, "yeah," trying not to remember either what it said or what he had done with it.

"I just remembered that," Joseph said.

Through dinner, which Ann served, Joseph spoke rarely, and always when he did, it was to ask a question of Mike and to add that now-familiar refrain "I just remembered that." His hands shook when he tried to pass the cranberry or the gravy. The little girls sat gravely wearing the paper hats that came out of their Christmas crackers, saying no more than "please" or "thank you." Mike worked hard to fulfill the double obligation of eating enough to honor the feast and talking enough to make the occasion the double celebration it was intended to be. He was enormously relieved when he felt he had stayed as long as he was expected to. He carried off with him matching woolen cap and muffler of the same ridiculous sort Joseph wore, touched that Ann had knitted them for him but not able to wear them out of the house.

On the way back to the warehouse, he turned on the radio and heard, "But if somehow you could/Pack up your sorrows and/Give them all to me/You would lose them, I know how to use them/Give them all to me." The weight of Joseph's illness as heavy in him as the dinner he had just eaten, Mike had a momentary glimmer of what might have driven Joseph as far as he'd gone. Other people's griefs could send you mad. Mike no more wanted to shoulder Joseph's calamities than he did his own. It would take a thousand-mile shrug to get them off his back.

Mike had no clear destination. If there had been a town

called Away, he would have headed for that. With the camper top secured on his Datsun, a mattress, sleeping bag, and camp stove stowed in the back, along, at the last minute, with golf clubs and tennis racket, which made him feel he could take a holiday even from the self he had been, he could be independent. If he discovered that the excuse he'd always given Alma for refusing to spend money on a vacation, which was simply that he couldn't stand idle time, turned out to be true, he could always go visit his mother and brother, but he wanted to feel under no obligation to anyone. He hadn't dealt this hand, but he could choose to play it.

Mike realized almost at once that he did not want to drive a thousand miles with only the radio for distraction. The songs only salted his thoughts with a bitterness he had to escape. He needed a companion. He thought of and rejected Carlotta because she hadn't the money to take real time off. He thought of borrowing one of his children and knew Alma would never hear of it. He had no taste for the melodrama of kidnapping. The simple and obvious solution was to pick up a hitchhiker. Mike minimized the danger of being mugged by stowing a heavy wrench on the shelf behind the seat under a blanket out of sight but in easy reach. The mistake a lot of men made with Mike was assuming his size would make him slow.

Driving out of Vancouver early on Boxing Day, Mike was surprised to find no hitchhikers on the road, but at the border, where an American immigration officer asked a lot of unnecessary questions not only about where he was going, for how long, and why but about his job, his bank account, his marital status, he was relieved to suffer being obsequious alone. He knew very well how to do it since his job for the last eight years had allowed him only two choices, knocking a man down the stairs or kissing his ass.

He fanned his credit cards without saying he didn't have American Express because he didn't like the fucking name. He said he was a designer of jungle gyms on a visit to his mother in Arizona. He gave Alma's parents' address as his own. Then he waited with a show of patience, under which should have been written "simulated," while he was checked in the big black book of particular undesirables. Probably a guy like Allen Dent, a real rip-off artist who could cross the border on his own wings, was asked to show nothing but his expensively straightened teeth.

Mike found his first hitchhiker in Blaine just across the border, a kid who was going to Seattle to marry a girl who was apparently the only virgin he had ever met. There was no point in giving him advice. The ones who so willingly let you into their pants before the blessed occasion could just as easily lock the chastity belt and throw the key away the day after the deed was done. Still, if this kid had a taste for deflowering virgins, he'd be safer and happier molesting girls on the playground at a junior high than marrying one. Such thoughts so depressed Mike that he asked the kid about his job, but he didn't have one. His girl clerked in a department store and thought maybe she could get him in there in the stockroom. Then he was back to talking about getting married.

"Married guys are always telling you not to do it, not to tie yourself down. They forget what getting it anytime you like it is worth, you know? You married?"

Mike nodded.

"Everybody is after all," the kid concluded.

Mike heard Alma say, "How many people do you know who've stayed married as long as we have?" When you're twenty, everybody else in the world is married. When you're thirty, everybody else is divorced.

He let the kid off, glad to be rid of him, and drove some miles alone with the worse company of Alma. He tried to think, instead, of Carlotta, but nothing of her friendliness or eager appetite came back to him. The only image he could call up was her lying on her bed, pale as a corpse, just before he passed out. It hadn't even occurred to him to phone to see how she was. He didn't want to know.

Unable to stand his own company, he stopped for a young couple, dressed in jeans, ponchos, boots, and beads. He should have known by their costume that they would be his age, veteran dropouts, on their way to yet another commune, where they'd find again nobody ever got round to planting anything but grass or making anything but each other's women. They hadn't been in the truck ten minutes before the conversation made it clear that for a steak dinner for both of them—at least they weren't vegetarians—she'd fuck. Mike offered each of them an apple and dropped them in Portland. As she got out of the car, she handed Mike a couple of joints. He was sorry then that he'd let them go. What would have been the matter with buying them a meal, smoking some dope with them, then, if he felt like it, having a friendly screw? She wasn't bad-looking.

Mike hadn't done anything like that since he was in high school, when he had to do it, when fucking a girl with a bunch of your friends was as much an initiation rite as being able to knock any one of them down. A couple of the girls they knew were always willing for a buck a piece, but the greater conquest was cruising around until you found a girl or two you didn't know. None of his father's dire warnings about venereal disease and prison terms discouraged Mike. Such dangers were part of the point. Fear was never an excuse. The only way anyone got out of that Saturday night car was to have some place he was getting it free all for himself. Those Saturday nights, once the novelty wore off, simply bored and depressed Mike.

Sex with Alma would have bored him if he'd had it often enough. How many times could you get up enthusiasm for screwing a dead whale? The cruelty of that image amused him. Yet he had not, until Carlotta, ever cheated on Alma, and he'd had plenty of opportunity. Was it just another sign of his parsimony that he wouldn't pay double for anything? It was more than that. Even bad sex with Alma had the wonder of possibility in it, the discovering of a child in her woman's flesh, as you might discover shape in wood or stone. When she had stopped wanting children, Alma had ceased to be his wife. He had stayed with her as long as he had because she was the mother of his children. Carlotta? She hardly seemed to Mike a woman at all. She was his good friend, whom he had finally beaten at her own game, and he regretted it in the same way he had regretted defeating a male friend, though he understood the necessity. It wouldn't have to happen again.

It was getting dark. There was no point in trying to make it to Grants Pass that night. He'd go off the freeway at Roseburg and find some place quiet after he'd had something to eat. He stepped inside a café and was confronted with the loud music he had had to tolerate at work, a cluster of nervously joking and punching teenaged boys by the jukebox, booths of girls who looked no more than fifteen or sixteen with babies in laps, in high chairs, making bloody swamps of french fries and catsup while their mothers gossiped.

"She told me that he swore he wouldn't hit her again, and she said it was her fault most of the time anyway because she nagged him. They've gone to Reno for a second honeymoon. Her mom kept the baby."

"Wouldn't mind Charlie slugging me if I could get a trip to Reno out of it."

"Only trip I'd get to Reno is alone."

A two-year-old in a high chair overturned a glass of milk; a baby began to howl. Mike had forgotten how much even his own children had irritated him at that age. He knew he couldn't eat a meal here without fighting the impulse to silence every child in the place. He walked out, found a grocery store, bought himself more ground meat, half a dozen eggs, and a can of tomato juice.

After he'd eaten his frugal supper, sitting in his camper door, he took out one of the joints he had been given, smoked, and watched the winter stars. The signs he had been watching all day long to read the names of realities that lay out of sight near the surreal highway began to be shapes in his mind to be reclaimed, to hang high in space, making no claim to reality at all. The huge transport trucks which had passed him in both directions all day long began to come apart as easily as pieces of Leggo, not in fantasies of frightening wreckage, but in redeemable shapes. Mike remembered his brother working over an old car, determined to make it run, while Mike, five years younger, understanding nothing about engines, played among the parts as if they were building blocks.

"That's not the way it goes," his brother had shouted at him. "Don't mess with that."

Jud had thought Mike was retarded because he never built anything the way it said to, tried to make something that looked like a boat out of an airplane kit, engineered a stool that would stand only on its seat.

"I want to make it look like it wants to get up, like a bug on its back."

Mike hadn't the language then to talk about movement that didn't exist, illusion, art.

"Art is putting the wrong things together. Picasso knew that."

After a while he'd go see Jud, explain to him the difference between usefulness and meaning.

The next morning there was snow on the ground at Grants Pass, but the sun was shining, and the roads were clear. Mike wished someone else had been driving as he came down the long, winding road into California and approached Shasta. Several times he pulled off and stopped in order simply to look at the views. It was impossible to believe that just a few hours to the south oranges and grapefruit ripened in hot sun. The golf clubs and tennis racket seemed more absurd than ever. There was a grand peaceful familiarity about this landscape, all substance and clarity. Carlotta said she had to work in the cold. Certainly there was nothing in the miniature brilliance of spring for Mike. Flowers got in the way of his stride like dog shit when he wanted to be looking up, as he did now, at the classic shape of a mountain. He would have liked to stay here awhile, but he still had too much need to be gone since there was nothing else to do. Driving became an occupation.

Once he was in the flat, mild Central Valley, he mourned the mountains, nothing here but acres of dusty olive groves. Mike suffered a boredom intense enough to cancel his anger. Late in the afternoon he gave up the struggle against sleep, pulling into a rest area, and did not even bother to get into the back of the truck but lay cramped on the seat. When he woke, it was after dark, and he was back inside a private time which made him feel less and less in touch with time in the human world. But he soon discovered it didn't matter in California. Nothing ever seemed to close down. It was as easy to get a six-pack of beer at four in the morning as it was at four in the afternoon. There were all-night gas stations, drugstores, movies, and there seemed to be a great many more people, not just runaways and derelicts, who inhabited what were unused portions of night and morning in Vancouver. Mike did not feel the outlaw or outcast he often did in his own city. Neither, however, did he feel at home, wandering in Sacramento, San Francisco, Los Angeles, as far south as San Diego.

Mike did not know how to find and make new friends. Oh, he could strike up an easy enough conversation with working stiffs in any city, but he felt lonelier with them than he did by himself. In selling galleries and museums, he always felt awkward and was therefore abrupt with anyone who tried to approach him. Once, years ago, in the Vancouver Art Gallery, one of the staff had mistaken him for the plumber they were waiting for. He had never set foot in the building again, mocked the shows he only read about as the kind of tenth-rate garbage always foisted off on hick towns like Vancouver. When he was in Los Angeles, he put on his suit and went to galleries which handled the really big names, passing himself off as a prospective buyer. The combination of his father-in-law's taste in clothes and his own knowledge was persuasive, and for several hours Mike tried to enjoy the flattering attention not of simple clerks but of gallery owners called to attend him once he had started asking intelligent questions. But it was such an empty trick—masquerading in the trappings of power didn't give him any—and such a cowardly substitute for what he should have risked that he ended his tour full of self-loathing.

What else could he really do? He had no adequate photographs of his work, and he hadn't any Canadian shows to his credit. His work had not been on public display since the student group exhibit when he was graduated. Anyway, these people weren't in it to discover anybody. They were in it for the big money of the big names. He did ask for the names of galleries where lesser-known and local artists showed their work, but he did not visit them at all, even as a rich buyer. He hadn't come down here to be humiliated as a Canadian nobody. He wasn't out to prove anything at all.

Yet the simplest circumstances seemed to turn into tests. He got into more punch-outs than he had at work, and he discovered it was one thing to deal with out-of-shape drunks, another to deal with the young punks from muscle beach. Mike had lost twenty-five pounds in the last six months, and he was eating and sleeping more like a stray dog than a man.

"Why don't you learn to play golf?" asked one peaceable kid who refused to take Mike's aggressiveness seriously "It's more fun and better for you at your age."

If Mike's clubs had been handy, he'd have beaten the kid to death for his good advice.

Well, what the hell was he doing? He was letting the ten percent of his earnings he had religiously saved ever since he was a kid with a paper route leak away like pus out of the last of Job's boils as if that were the painful cure for his pain. Stupid. He was being entirely stupid.

It was nearly the first of February. He wrote a check for Alma and sent her a note to say he would be in Arizona for a while at his brother's. Then he picked out postcards to send to his sons, a picture of dolphins for Vic, named illustrations of desert cacti for Tony. At the same time he scribbled wish-you-were-here messages to Ann and Joseph, to Carlotta.

Mike hadn't seen Jud for five years, not since their father's funeral. They hadn't talked much then, but Jud had told him he was getting rid of his wife, who'd turned out to be nothing but a tramp, and he was taking their mother south with him to look after the kids. It would give her a home and something to do. Mike had been too grateful to be relieved of the financial and emotional responsibility of his mother to think much about what getting rid of a wife had been for Jud. Mike had met his sister-in-law at the wedding when he went down to Phoenix to be best man, and Jud had brought her home to Vancouver a couple of times, but after there were two children, the grandparents had gone south to visit. Mike remembered her as a pretty woman who hadn't much to say for herself. Alma hadn't taken to her, so they'd seen no more of her than duty seemed to require. Jud had his own friends in Vancouver. They were the sort of brothers who never did much together.

Now Mike wondered how inadequate a brother he might have been to Jud at that time. If he'd undergone even a small measure of the pain Mike was experiencing, he must have needed someone to talk to. Maybe he'd been able to talk to their mother. Mike doubted it, remembering his mother in black, mourning with the stoic formality of a peasant a man whose moods she had accepted like the weather, whose pronouncements she had neither believed nor corrected, a man who had loved her clumsily, provided for her at best uncertainly, his only legacy to her two sons he had taught responsibility and frugality by bad example. The only comfort she could have been to Jud was in not questioning his decision to get rid of his wife, in taking over his household and children and making his life more familiar to and comfortable for him than it had been since he left home. When she said good-bye to Mike, she made her simple explanation: "Jud's the one who needs me."

Jud had sent her back to Vancouver several times on short holidays. Though she and Alma always seemed to get along all right, his mother's presence increased tension between him and Alma, who seemed to be unnecessarily always trying to impress her mother-in-law. "You don't have to feed my mother all this fancy garbage. She's just a peasant, you know, like me." Alma even wanted to give a luncheon, inviting friends of his mother's. "Christ, Alma, she didn't have any friends. She wasn't a member of the Junior League." Alma didn't argue with him. Her mother gave a luncheon, and Mike didn't ask who had been invited. Once Alma accused him of being ashamed of his mother, as if he couldn't see for himself what a handsome and intelligent woman she was, perfectly "presentable." Ashamed of her? He would have married such a woman if there had been anyone remotely like her anywhere in his experience.

His mother had, in fact, liked Alma, but Mike knew his mother would no more find fault with him than she did with Jud. Her loyalties were simple and absolute. Yet he had not been able to go to her, as Jud had, with so practical a request. Even if Jud hadn't been five years ahead of him in this, as in everything else, Mike hadn't established himself confidently enough to provide such a solution. And he doubted that he could live with it, if it had been an option.

He was driving east to Las Vegas, on his way to Phoenix, feeling in a hurry and in doubt by turns. The speeches he had composed for his brother seemed less and less likely every mile he drove. And his mother's uncritical approval tasted like nothing more than borsch and pirogi. Since Alma had mastered both, he might find himself more horribly homesick for her than ever. But where else could he go?

He looked toward the next road sign, growing larger and larger as he approached. Death Valley. It felt more like laughing at a bad joke than making a decision as he took the exit several miles farther down the road.

What Mike expected to find were the skulls of old cars and cattle in an enormous dried-up mud hole, the only glamour in such facts that the valley was below sea level and had taken a number of lives, some recently, of people who had tried to cross it unprepared in the height of summer when temperatures rose to the 120s. Death Valley and the Arabian desert were confused in Mike's imagination; Peter O'Toole could have appeared in either, swapping robes for chaps and boots.

Crossing over the mountains to get there, Mike was chilly enough to turn on the heater, but as he dropped down into the valley in the early afternoon, it might have been a summer day in the north, the fresh clarity of air Mike had nearly forgotten in the smog-ridden city. He had thought of barren land always in negative terms, a lack of vegetation, an absence of green. He did not know, until he saw it, that color bloomed in rock, great strokes of ocher, ridges of red, cliffsides of aquamarine. Unlike the northern mountains, clothed in trees, this naked rock exposed the violence of its coming, layers of geological time heaved up to benign light.

Signs, which nearly everywhere in the south had interested Mike more than any view from the freeway, hardly caught his notice here, although they could have fed his schoolboy fantasies, warning of flash floods, of roads patrolled only once a day by helicopter, of the necessity of carrying water, staying with your car if it broke down, under it if the sun was hot. He was watching the mountains, a man driving at the bottom of a vanished sea through sand dunes onto salt flats where crystals had grown up off the surface like the arms of a thousand drowning men, occasionally an oasis of trees, kept alive by hot springs, where there were cabins to rent. Mike stopped at one of these for a local map and information.

Like so many other places along this coast where the Indians had chosen to live, white men had passed through, unable to tolerate what couldn't be cultivated, irrigated, built on. Here the earth's surface was so fragile that half an inch of rain could wash out a road.

At the lowest point in the valley, Mike got out of his truck and looked up to a sign high above him on the cliff face, Sea Level. Here Indians had lived in a tide governed by seasons rather than the moon, on the valley floor in winter, rising to the mountains for the summer, following whatever paths the winter rains or wind had made, leaving no more signs of their presence than a few arrowheads and bones, fossilizing with the bones and shells of other living things, preserved in these monumental pallets of rock.

A death wish as innocent as breath left Mike empty of everything that had tormented him, reconciled with stone, which did not need to be redeemed of anything.

He traveled up out of the valley, free of guilt or desire, free of memory until he was shocked back into himself by the enormous, almost unbelievable vulgarity of Las Vegas and recognized in it his own answer to the desert: the vulgarity or elegance didn't matter so much as filling the space.

By the time Mike reached Phoenix he was running a fever, and it was some days before he was more than momentarily aware of his mother's face or his brother's fading in and out of his dreams, in which he was nearly always dead but not in the serene place of death, images taken from there and transposed so that he was a grotesquely growing tree of salt crystals at his own dining-room table, a flash flood invading his own house, a natural catastrophe rather than a man, whom his wife and children fled from down a road marked by enormous warnings he could not read.

When the fever finally broke and he woke, he was on a couch in a small living room, crowded with old furniture he dimly recognized. There, for instance, was his father's armchair, maroon vinyl cracking, beside it the high square table with the ashtray that had held his father's cigars. It was an L-shaped room, and in the L was the large old kitchen table, over which was a plastic chandelier with bulbs shaped like flames. Though Mike had always fiercely defended the furnishings of his childhood against Alma's, waking to them here was like trying to recognize his father's face in the last stages of illness. He wondered why Jud had let his mother haul this pathetic junk from British Columbia to Arizona. Was he sentimental about it as Mike had thought he was himself? Then he was aware of the sound of quiet breathing just behind him. He turned his head and saw his mother asleep in a chair. His movement woke her.

She rose slowly, looked at him, put a hand on his forehead, smiled, and said, very quietly, "I'll get you some tea."

They had a quiet hour together in what Mike realized had been dawn light, before Jud woke, and then the children, who were no longer children, young David with a voice as deep as his father's, several inches taller, a shadow of young beard, Judy with breasts and eye makeup. The room was terribly crowded with them all in it until they settled to the table under that awful chandelier for the breakfast his mother was cooking for them.

Mike had assumed his brother was modestly successful. He owned a mobile home dealership and had business all around the state. Was he overcapitalized that he kept this large-bodied family in this cracker box of a house? They all could not have sat together in the living room while Mike lay on the couch. He moved to sit up and was too weak to manage it. He was glad no one had noticed, all of them eating in silent concentration. Was that habit, or was it a silence for his benefit? Mike felt like a corpse in the parlor.

When the other three had gone to work and to school, Mike protested to his mother that they should have sent him to the hospital.

"Not here in this country," she said. "It costs the earth. You pay even for the bedpan and the aspirin."

"Is this where you usually sleep?"

"No, no. I have a bed in Judy's room."

"It seems awfully crowded."

"Jud says how could he sell them if he was too good to live in one."

"This is what he sells?"

His mother nodded. "All over the state. Every one has two bathrooms."

When Mike was strong enough to move around a little, his mother put a deck chair out in the driveway for him. There was no yard except for a patch of stones barricaded by ornamental cacti. It was not so much a neighborhood as a kind of permanent camp, as if pioneers crossing this desert had been suddenly petrified. The houses, like wagons, were more places of storage than spaces to live in. The screened porch which ran the length of Jud's house was the only pleasant place to sit.

The only person who did sit for periods of time was his mother, always with knitting or mending in her lap. The others gathered only when they were waiting for a meal, and then they watched television. In the evening the kids took off to the library, the bowling alley, the movies, and Jud, if he'd come home, went back to his office. He traveled so much he was always behind with his paperwork.

Jud apologized to Mike about being there so seldom. Though he had a secretary, a part-time accountant, as well as two salesmen, he wanted to delegate as little authority as he could in order to keep in touch with every aspect of his business. Jud suggested that, once Mike was feeling up to it, Jud would not only show him the layout but take him on one of his trips, if only just out into the suburbs of Phoenix.

It was not his certainly returning strength so much as his restlessness which made Mike accept any excuse to get away from the cramped space of not only the house but the camp, which covered remarkably few acres for the number of dwellings. There was really no place to walk; roads were designed as a series of small half-moons with an occasional straight spur that dead-ended in desert. Though the houses were different colors and the small patches of ground expressive of different tastes, air force insignia in colored stones here, stone mushrooms and tin roadrunners there, they all were essentially the same.

He would go back to try to talk with his mother.

"People like it the same," she explained to him. "There's room for competition, but not much."

It wasn't her own idea. She was speaking for Jud. Mike didn't remember her speaking for his father in that way, but his father had had defenses rather than real ideas or explanations. Mike would have liked to lodge some of his own notions in her mind, but when he tried to talk with her about art, she didn't even try to hide the fact that it was beyond not only her understanding but her interest. For any other subject—marriage, money, child rearing—Mike had excuses rather than conversation. He was superior to his father only in that he knew it, but Mike had been jarred into that insight as his father never had. Mike could not talk to his mother. He was reduced to watching the quiz shows she liked when he needed to be companionable. She was visibly pleased with him when he began oiling door hinges and trying to figure out how to stop the kitchen floor from squeaking right by the sink.

"You've learned to fix things."

"I probably should have been a plumber or a carpenter."

She nodded to the logic of that.

Mike had been there two weeks when he asked Jud to show him his office, which was, Mike discovered, just down the road at the edge of the camp. Jud corrected him twice, calling it a development. The office, too, was one of the same structures, the larger bedroom Jud's office, the smaller one full of office machines. The secretary, a woman in her fifties with blue hair and a great deal of Indian jewelry, had a desk in the dining L where she could greet customers and salesmen, for whom there were comfortable couches and chairs. All the furniture was blandly modern and expensive. The kitchen was well enough stocked to make it clear that Jud, even when he was in the neighborhood, lived here rather than with his mother and children.

For a couple of days he let Mike hang around to listen and ask questions, to get some idea of the scope of the business.

"You're not just a supplier then. You're getting into development."

"You bet," Jud said. "This is the retirement center of the country, aside from Florida, and we're getting ready for the baby boom of the forties. It's the last big wave of population that's coming through, and the service people are already arriving. It's going to last just long enough to see me through."

"What then?"

"Who knows? Who cares?"

Mike drove with Jud to development after development, almost all of them planned around a central clubhouse with swimming pool and tennis courts, often a golf course, a great green serpentine to distract and rest the eyes from the miles of open, flat desert. Nearly none of these places accepted children, and visiting grandchildren under eighteen had to stay pretty well out of sight. As far as Mike could judge, about three-quarters of the population were impressive health freaks, out on the golf links and tennis courts early in the morning, at the pool after a dietetic lunch, in bed mildly sedated by bourbon at nine o'clock. The other twenty-five percent were helped in and out of the hot therapy pool and played cribbage in the shade. Their stroke-distorted speech, arthritic backs, heart coughs did not seem to depress so much as inspire the others to make full use of their own healthy bodies. Nowhere did Mike see anyone reading, not even a newspaper.

"They don't want to know," Jud said. "This is the one I'll move into as soon as Judy's eighteen. I've already got two houses here, renting at seven hundred dollars a month for the season. All the land west to the mountains is going to be developed as soon as some details are sorted out with the Indians and the government."

"Maybe I should come down and open a crematorium."

"Seriously, in about a year I'm going to have to expand. I want to do one of these places myself, and I need a partner."

"Oh, hell, Jud, I don't have any money, maybe five thousand, and I don't know a damned thing about the business."

"I don't need money so much as someone I can trust. You could learn the business in a month. And with your talent you could mount an advertising campaign to leave these other jokers way behind. Mike, I want a chunk of this, and if you'd come in with me, we could have a fair-sized chunk. The money makes itself."

"What do you do with it once you have it?"

"Anything you want," Jud said. "Just anything you want."

"What do you want?"

"Nothing but the kinds of worries I've got now."

"I'm an artist, Jud, not a businessman."

Jud squinted at his brother. "What's to stop you being both? You have to earn a living now."

"Yeah, but I don't have to think about it."

"Don't you think it's time you did?"

"I've got a lot of other things on my mind."

"Like what? Killing yourself?"

Mike looked at his brother, startled, and then laughed. "I've got no immediate plans."

"Good," Jud said. "Come on. I want to show you the piece of nothing we could make into a gold mine. I'll show you some convincing figures when we get back to the office, but imagination is all you need. Imagine, say, one of your sculptures and some sort of fountain at the entrance, which would right away make the place distinctive."

His brother wanted to save his life. Mike, who felt he should have been insulted, was absurdly touched.

The next morning, alone at the old kitchen table while his mother did the breakfast dishes, Mike opened the divorce papers being served to him. At first, the only thing he was able to read was his name, after which was typed: "of no fixed address."

Alma Writing

*M*Y thirty-first birthday. Did I ever once, in the ten years I lived with Mike, tell him I wanted to write? I've never told anyone. Yet he gave me this absurdly pretentious blank book, which has been sitting on my night table now for three months, growing more pretentious and blanker each day. If it had been a house plant, it would have been dead of neglect in a couple of weeks. The only way to kill this book is to fill it with failed hope. Do I always begin things already knowing they won't work? Like school? Like Mike? Like Roxanne? Like this? If I were going to write something *real*, I'd have to make it up. Scribbling in this reminds me of Vic filling pages with what writing looked like to him because Tony was really learning how. So I read *Sita* and think, enviously, "Anyone can do that," and set out to show myself up because, even if I did know enough about language, my life, unlike Kate Millett's, is only life-sized.

If my chief excuse for living were writing it down, would I live very differently? I'd have to. The moment I got out of bed this morning, I'd have to start packing my bags because I wouldn't be having dinner with my parents and sisters and sons—what a crowd that sounds and is—I'd be going off to Roxanne instead to celebrate my real birth. But even if I did that, I'm far too amazed by loving her to be able to write it down. And anyway, when I get up, I'm going to put on the yellow pantsuit Mother gave me yesterday, my yearly birthday suit, which remakes me into a daughter, and live through the day here in my parents' house, where no one will suggest—perhaps because they don't even think it—that I am an embarrassment or a burden, failed wife, apprehensive mother, with no idea what to do with myself or my children because the one thing I want to do is impossible even if I had the money to do it. And I can't leave this house until I'm sure I won't do it.

When I asked Carlotta all those months ago, right after Mike left, if she'd ever made love with a woman, she said, "Other than myself? No." I let that shut me up. It needn't have. Even when Carlotta didn't want to listen to me, she would, then anyway. I suppose I've been half in love with *her* all these years, and I felt—feel—as guilty about Carlotta as I do about Mike. In a way, Roxanne didn't have anything to do with Mike, or Mike and me, except as a way of showing us how bad it really was.

Is that true? I am so guilty in every direction that I can't understand anything.

I suggested to Dad that maybe I ought to see a psychiatrist. He didn't say no; he wouldn't. He simply said, "Why don't you give yourself some time to think things over for yourself? Then, if you still feel it might help, of course." I've spent most of my time trying not to think things over. I haven't the faintest idea what I'd ask a psychiatrist if I saw one. . . .

Why did I marry? Why did I marry Mike? Aside from the fact that he asked me. Probably aside from the fact that he still, even strained and thin, is the handsomest man I have ever seen, and initially that made me feel that I must be attractive myself, not just a great oversized cow of a girl. Surely not aside from the fact that I thought he was an artist, which made me imagine sensitive depths beyond the repetitive pigheaded nonsense which I thought was simply the surface of his mind. Yes, aside from that, too. Those are my excuses.

Because when I was an eighteen-year-old virgin who had never been on a real date except when it was arranged by my parents, my friend Bett, who had already been "ecstatically" married for two years, taught me the facts of life. She told me I was too tall and too womanly (read: one of monstrous tits) to attract boys and too dumb to attract men. She said "shy." I had to get in touch with my own body, and she could show me how if I could just pretend, while she was doing it, that she was a man. It took her three weeks to get my clothes off, another week to get her hand between my legs, and I never did imagine it was anything but her hand. I was so wet I thought I was hemorrhaging, and I was terrified by what I felt, as if I were being raped not by her hand, but by my own body, which had set fire to itself in some Dickensian spontaneous combustion.

"Am I bleeding to death?"

"That's sex, sweetie."

When I refused to play her part, which she wanted me to do just in order to see that I understood how it worked, she lost interest in the enterprise. Since I couldn't even think about her without beginning to shake, we found it easy enough to avoid each other. Someone told me the other day that she's just married for the third time.

I'm not so worried about what a psychiatrist might make of that as I am of the fact that it didn't occur to me until a year ago today that Bett had been attracted to me or I to her. I let myself believe for all those years that I allowed that long, ridiculous seduction in the interest of nothing but self-knowledge. In a sense, because I certainly wasn't in love with Bett, I was right, except, of course, that I didn't want to know. I was so afraid of being betrayed by my own body that feeling nothing but mild discomfort with Mike was a relief. When I realized that at his inaccurate touch I wouldn't begin to melt down my own thighs and burn to my tits, I stopped fighting him off and let him do pretty much what he liked or needed to do as long as it didn't involve me in any active or important way.

One of Mike's arguments for getting married was that women like sex better after marriage, as if the ring had an ancient erotic power. I was nearly sure by then that it didn't. He'd been fucking me on a mattress in the back of his truck twice a week for six months before he tested his theory on a wife in a proper bed in a bridal suite at the Bayshore Inn. I used Vaseline then. I wanted to please him. It wasn't until after Tony was born . . .What is this myth about forgetting birth? If that kind of terrible commotion could go on, juices spurting out everywhere for an audience of people, of strangers, and afterwards I felt a smug exhibitionist, my breasts full of milk, why on earth was I frightened or ashamed of the wet animality of my own pleasure? I used to want Mike to fuck me just after I'd nursed Tony or even, if he could have been gentle about it, while I was. He was embarrassed even to see me nursing, and when a spot of milk seeped out onto my blouse, I had to change at once. I felt almost innocent in my indignation, married to this prudish ape of a man, a sexual illiterate in an age of information overkill. I even pretended to myself that he was perfectly satisfied. He got it up; he got it in; he got it off. And he was on his way to getting the army of children his vanity required, who, in fact, irritated him to violence for the first three years of their lives and were too expensive for him to support after that.

Why did I marry? Why did I marry Mike? To put off for good knowing that I did not attract men because they didn't attract me. I don't need a psychiatrist to tell me that the only kind of man who insists on marrying a lesbian is a man like Mike, for whom even fucking a brick wall is a test of his virility. Oh, there's the other extreme, a man who wants to pass no tests at all. A man like that could not have protected me from myself for so many hard, safe years.

I was safe. Mike did protect me, and he would have gone on even without the children he still wanted, and I would have gone on, yes, even after Roxanne (she might even have made it easier), if I hadn't finally really seen his pain, not hanging there in the shed but on Joseph's face, in Joseph's simple, humiliating words, "He's unhappy."

I don't know how Joseph's wife feels about his going crazy. Maybe she isn't responsible and so doesn't feel betrayed. But if Mike had actually had to kill himself to get away from me, he would have killed me, too. I would have died of exposure. I still have nightmares about the truck smashed up in a pile of cars or going over a cliff, and almost always Mike in miniature is hanging there on the rearview mirror, where he had a nude doll when I first met him.

I couldn't possibly want to get even. In public measure I'm probably way ahead, as long as Mike doesn't contest the divorce. Dad didn't want me to accept the last check, but I told him that would rile Mike, and I don't want Mike angry, even as far away as Arizona. He could so easily, if he wanted to, take the children away from me, have me declared unfit as a mother.

I don't see Roxanne more than once a week. She knows, because of the divorce, I have to be very careful, and even once that's over, we can't possibly live together, not while I have the boys. But at least we'll be able to have an occasional weekend together. I can always leave the kids here. Roxanne doesn't ask for anything. I'm the one who gets hysterical about not being able to see her. I'm the one who suggests crazy escapes, even without the boys. She shakes that great flower of hair against my belly and says no into my navel.

I love her thinness. I love the tiny cups of her breasts, the way she shows them off in tank tops and see-through shirts. I love her low-slung trousers, so beautifully indecent when she leans over; her cleavage, she says, inviting my finger down to tease the pucker of her ass hole. I touch her wherever and whenever I like. She's as greedy as a cat.

And now I'm trying to be Violette Leduc, writing with one hand, masturbating with the other, and I don't think it's disgusting, but it is stupidly, stupidly lonely to lie here in bed on my birthday, my cunt weeping with greed, while Mother indulges me by cooking breakfast for the children. This should have happened to me when I was fifteen. Is conscience always perverse? I had enough sexual shame for a nun at fifteen, but I had no trouble lying in bed any morning while the bacon cooked. Now, with no sexual shame at all, the smell of this morning's bacon makes both hands equally guilty.

Get up, woman. You're thirty-one years old today, even if you are lying in bed in a room that still suffers traces of your childhood. In twenty minutes Vic and Tony will have to be driven across town to school, and Mother may or may not refrain from saying, "If they transferred schools, they could walk." I can't really tell her the truth: that I don't transfer them because once a week, on Roxanne's day off, I can go to her from dropping the boys without having to explain anything to anyone.

I wrote that three weeks ago. Obviously this isn't going to be a diary. There's really no point in filling it with silly excuses and half-baked explanations and guilty confessions, though that's certainly the garbage in my head. I do feel retarded, here in this little girl's room, in a house where I increasingly feel more like a big sister than a mother to my children, whose manners are improving so drastically that something's going to have to give somewhere. Tony will start shoplifting. Victor will be sent home for obscene behavior on the playground. It's hard to believe I'd ever miss the foulmouthed bellowing I put up with for years, but one good "Fuck off!" or "Stick it up your ass!" would some-times be a real relief. Has Mike ruined me for genteel life?

I tried to talk with Dad the other day. He's been saying, "Wait until you have your divorce. Plenty of time then to sort out what you want to do." They not only don't mind having us here: they're getting used to it, and I shouldn't let that happen. But if I suggest moving out, what I'm suggest-ing is Dad's paying the rent on another place, and he wouldn't hear of my going back to Kitsilano. I could get a part-time job, but short of making enough money to be really independent, what is the point?

I've had another check from Mike. I'm putting them in a savings account for the boys, building them a fantasy inde-pendence so that they won't need to come running home at thirty.

It's what Mike has done, too. What a couple of great babies we are! And always were, playing house in that ri-diculous place, Mike carrying out some movie version of the working-class husband, I the superior wife, or he was the abused and I the secret genius. We were *unreal*. We still are, he pouting over his mother's pirogi, I putting off getting dressed for chamber music, from which Mother is staying home to baby-sit so that I can have a night out with Dad.

Most men Dad's age have other women. When Dad gets restless, he squires one daughter or another around town. How can I help feeling guilty—appalled—that all I really want to do, if I can't be with Roxanne, is lock myself into this room like a mooning teenager pretending to be Can-ada's Rita Mae Brown or whoever? I hide the books I bor-row from Roxanne, not because Mother would rummage through my room; she never has, and there would have been nothing to find when I was growing up. I hide the books as I hide so much of myself to be the wholesome daughter of a wholesome father who is waiting patiently for me downstairs.

One of the rare, interesting fights Mike and I had—I didn't usually fight with him since silence daunted him far more—was about language. I told him I was sick not of his feelings so much as the way he belched them out in such vulgar clichés. Did everything from a miscooked egg to an offensive political statement have to be shoved up somebody's ass? What was appropriate about it as a storage for everything he disliked? From what I'd read, it was for men the only secret pocket of the body for storing valuables, contraband.

"It's the working-class equivalent for putting sand in somebody's piggy bank," he said, surprising himself out of sarcasm by how interesting the idea was to him. "What I call tight-assed, you call cheap. Everything you don't like is cheap or vulgar. The money metaphor can get fairly boring, too. You're not going to teach me to price-tag people. I'm not interested."

I went on flinching at "cunt" and "prick" and "ass hole" mostly because I didn't want the children using that kind of language at school or in front of their grandparents. But Mike didn't either. He cuffed them away from his vocabulary as regularly as he did from his tools, and it worked. The only time Victor ever called me a cunt, I was relieved that he had a word to tell me I had humiliated him.

I went on calling people and things cheap and vulgar but with a new self-consciousness about my tastes . . . and my flinchings.

Mike's proudest possession is his body. He's most comfortable in nothing but a pair of cutoffs, most himself. A suit is a uniform that, like all uniforms, diminishes individuality. "You look like a million dollars, Mike," my father said as we arrived for dinner. Mike didn't flinch. I did.

Looking like a million dollars was all I'd ever tried to do. Something that expensive would have to be all right. The only time I'd ever had any confidence in the body underneath was when I was pregnant and when I was nursing a baby. I was then sacred but repulsive to Mike, who, for all his graphic language about everything else, was reduced to talking about buns in ovens. Well, he did finally get over that when I was carrying Victor.

The problem is that I have no language at all for my body or Roxanne's body that isn't either derisive or embarrassing. I don't like to write about fingering her ass hole, which immediately becomes personified for me as a belligerently stupid male, a surreal genie, metaphorical fart emanating from that . . . anus? I think of licorice, which I don't like. We make love without nouns as much as possible, speak directions instead. "There." "Here?" "Yes, there." Adequate for the lovely circumstance of two very present and visible bodies which are wonderfully familiar in fact as well as practice, but a love letter filled with nothing but adverbs is ridiculous. Gertrude Stein tried to invent a new language for lovemaking, but it was more a code to be cracked than a communication. Imagine the limitation of that when scholars are still debating whether "cow" means turd or orgasm.

I heard a psychologist the other day say that when you teach children names for all the parts of the body, "ear, eye, elbow, leg, thumb," and then say, "This is your wee-wee or pee-pee," they know something's funny. We, my sisters and I, called our own our cracks when we were little. Now we don't talk about our bodies except in gynecological terms. We're graphic about Pap smears, D and Cs, loops, pills, stitches, and itches, but we might have been artificially inseminated for all our talk about fucking. This is an accurate word for what Mike did to me, if you add "over." And maybe that is what goes on in Margaret's bed and in Joan's. We don't talk about it.

I didn't miss a language with Mike, only felt assaulted by his. Roxanne doesn't need a language. She makes sounds that begin somewhere deep in her chest, like the startling wind of underground caves, that are measured by her percussive heart, rise out of the tunnel of her throat, in glottal clickings and whole tones, a narrative song repetitive as any legend so that I now know by heart not only what my fingers and tongue experience but what she experiences as the landscape of my adventure. I listen sometimes at her mouth, sometimes at her chest, sometimes ear pressed to her belly as to a shell to hear her gathering tides. She is like a shell, so fragile and intricately interior, sounding and tasting of the sea. I understand why the clitoris is called a pearl, hidden in oystery frills. I am inside her one of the instruments of her song; also, she is the instrument I play, music a faint imitation or memory of the staccato tonguing, accurate fingering, long bowing that makes her body into song. I think, if there were ever a female Beethoven, the climax of such music couldn't be politely endured.

Roxanne said this morning, "I will call something one day 'Alma's Coming.' "

"Do I make a sound?"

She laughed.

Roxanne doesn't call herself a composer, though that surely is what she is.

"I document sound," she says, if pressed to say so.

She is not a talker about her work, as Mike is, needing to make a theoretical point for every nail he hammers, until words are nervous propaganda for something he needs to believe in and doesn't quite. When Roxanne is caught up in work, she is usually listening and invites me to listen, as if we were audience together to something as accessible to me as to her.

I didn't want her to be an artist of any sort, sick of them, all those pretensions and terrors of ego. Mike's sort of art is like Mike's sort of sex, an attack against foreign material. Carlotta's is too often an invasion of herself, masochistic.

Roxanne isn't either pretentious or afraid. Her seriousness is more like a child's, like Tony's, when he is caught up in watching something. Like that incredible picture of Picasso and his son at a bullfight, the child behind his father, with a finger in his father's mouth.

Now when I'm invited to Allen and Pierre's, Allen comes to pick me up. He knows I have my own car, but Allen has certain masculine formalities which are important to him. They are his passport to the foreign worlds he visits even in his own city; therefore, he carries them everywhere. I didn't think anything about accepting their first invitation after I moved in here. I had not been invited before, but Mike and I never were because of his job. Anyway, he wouldn't have gone. I couldn't ever quite believe in Mike's hostility toward Allen as disapproval. I think Mike was envious. Being free to accept was delightful, and, of course, Roxanne was there.

The next morning at breakfast Dad said, "Very nice fellow, that Allen. But I wonder—I hope you won't think I'm being old-fashioned or overcautious—if it's wise to see him while the divorce is still pending."

"It's perfectly safe, Dad," I assured him. "Allen's gay . . . homosexual."

It gave me the thrill of fear without the fear itself to use those words in front of my parents.

"Are you sure? What a shame."

"But he's such a nice-looking boy," Mother protested.

She would probably protest the same thing about me, though I think she's mildly alarmed by the size of all her daughters; our big bones come from Dad's side of the family.

"He's perfectly happy," I said, something I don't believe about any of my friends. Being just over thirty and happy is a contradiction in terms. "He lives with a French Canadian boy who makes him a better wife than most women would choose to be, given how often he's away."

My parents are too polite to attach moral issues to real people—that is, people they have met in their own front hall. And I am too old to be told that such a subject is inappropriate at the breakfast table in front of Tony and Victor.

"Pierre even looks like a girl," Tony explained to his grandparents.

"Well, with all the long hair around these days, just about everybody does," Mother said cheerfully.

"Dad won't let us," Victor said.

Victor with hair to his waist would be more of a Samson than ever. Tony is a different matter. If he doesn't want to deal with ambiguity, he'll have to wait to grow his hair until he can also grow a beard.

Do I not care, as Mother later in private suggested to me, whether the boys grow up straight? The little sermon I preached to her was pure self-defense, and I was even nervous that she'd wonder why I'd gone into the matter so thoroughly as to know the date the American Psychiatric Association voted homosexuality out of the sick and into the personality trait category. But she was too caught up with the argument.

"Then it's a *bad* personality trait," she said.

"I think being able to love anybody is a step in the right direction."

Well, I do, but if Tony grew up to be a gay militant, I'd feel like the original castrating mother, and Mike would kill him. Still, I know it isn't something mothers do to sons, fathers to daughters.

I love Roxanne like a blade of grass breaking concrete to get to the light. And if Tony had to love like that, couldn't I have the courage to be glad? I haven't even the courage to face all I'm breaking. I pretend it's not going on, as if all these months were a long holiday from a self I'll go back to in a house I take care of with Mike banging in and out. Yet every time I'm with Roxanne, I know I'm already leading the life I say is impossible. The more I protest to myself that I can't live with her, the more determined I am to risk everything, even my sons, and that terrifies me.

Allen and Pierre aren't the ideal couple I make them out to be, and if they had a couple of Allen's daughters from a previous marriage, well, I can't imagine. But Roxanne isn't the child Pierre insists on being. She can enter his fantasy: they play dress-up together for hours the way my sisters and I did. It would bore Allen if he had to pay too much attention to it. His game, another of his masculine affectations, is chess, and I play well enough to distract him. Am I his real counterpart, carrying my feminine affectations around to cover an essentially masculine nature? I don't feel at all masculine, least of all making love with Roxanne, who is so enthusiastic about my breasts I have a dream of having a daughter for her so that Roxanne could taste my milk. And she is not playing at being a boy when she dresses in Pierre's clothes, which are often more feminine than her own. She is entertaining him as I entertain Allen.

Why is it so important to me to insist that we both are feminine women? I find the frank ambiguity of Pierre's sex intriguing, the subtle femininity in Allen actually mildly attractive. If it ever occurred to him to take me to bed, I'd go. Yet any trace of masculinity in either Roxanne or me is something to cover up, deny. Is that why, aside from being terrified of exposure, I don't want to go to a women's bar? I don't want to see women in motorcycle drag and think we have anything in common.

Roxanne hasn't been to the clubs since she's known me. She says the only reason she'd go now would be to enjoy making love in public, a desire I couldn't understand at all until the first night we had dinner with Allen and Pierre, and Roxanne stretched out on the couch and put her head in my lap. I have been embarrassed by obvious sexual gestures between men and women, yes, calling them cheap and vulgar, but to see Pierre kiss Allen is an affirmation of my desire for Roxanne. Pierre occasionally kisses Roxanne.

"Do you find him attractive?" I asked her.

She shrugged and said, "He's sometimes very lonely."

"In leap year," Pierre said, "we should all four marry each other."

At that moment it seemed to Roxanne and me an hilarious and wonderful idea, one of the thousand never-never lands we dreamed of living in together. Allen stays aloof from such games, indulgently parental.

I think Allen is the loneliest person I've ever known, far lonelier than Carlotta, for instance. There is a great deal in Allen Pierre doesn't touch. It's not just the difference in their ages. Allen stays aloof from everyone. It's as if he's protecting not himself but other people from something in himself.

Carlotta is even harder to face than this notebook, which at least doesn't talk back with experiences of its own. I have tried to drop in on her several times in the last couple of months, but she's never at home. Then this morning, driving back from taking the boys to school, I saw her on the beach, sitting on a log. I pulled over into the parking lot and just sat in the car for a while, watching her sketch, the only one on the beach on this cold April morning. Finally I got out of the car and walked over to her.

She didn't look up from her work, so I stood looking down at what she was doing: a very accurate sketch of the debris at her feet. Carlotta is the only person I know who can make a pencil drawing sulk.

"I'm tired of not knowing why I don't see you," I said finally.

She kept on working.

"According to everyone in town, I'm the one who should be mad at you."

She still didn't look up.

"Carlotta, you're my oldest friend, really my only friend. I don't want to talk about anything you don't want to talk about, honestly, but I need to know you're around."

"I'm not around," she said, "not for anybody."

"Why?"

"Because I've had enough, more than enough, and I've got work to do."

"Look, the only reason I haven't asked about you and Mike is that I didn't know at the time whether to be outraged or grateful. I couldn't quite believe, after all these years of putting up with him as my husband, you actually wanted him, though you were certainly always nicer to him than most people, and that's one of the reasons we could stay friends. Anyway, it seems to me crazy, now that he's gone, not to see you."

"I don't much like you in generous moods."

"How do you want me to feel?"

"Melodramatic and silly, the way I do."

I sat down next to her on the log. I wanted to put an arm around her, but I was physically shy of her, as I have been with everyone lately.

"I've never felt so silly in all my life," I told her.

"But you're happy about it. You're glad to be rid of him."

"Terribly."

"Of course, he didn't leave you. He left me."

She was crying. I forget how easily Carlotta cries. It's not something anyone in my family does, at least not in front of anyone else. How do you go about comforting your best friend about being left by your husband? I suddenly felt impatient with her.

"Why on earth did you get involved with him? You know what a bastard he is."

"Why did you?"

"The more I think about it, the less I know, but I was twenty-one, not thirty-one."

"And now that you think you've got what you want, will you know any better what to do with it than Mike?"

"I don't know," I said.

"You're as cruel as children, both of you."

I was very cold and very tired. I had been with Roxanne until three o'clock this morning, crazy with need of her, and even now I felt more like an amputated part of her than a person to deal with Carlotta. I had probably stopped here on the beach more for the reason of avoiding questions my mother was waiting to ask me than to make any real connection with Carlotta.

"Where is he?" she asked suddenly.

"In Arizona with his mother and brother."

"Is he going to stay down there?"

"I don't know."

I thought she might try to hit me. There was really no point in fighting over a man I don't want who is a thousand miles away, and I feel so little charity for him I really do find it hard to believe anyone else would want him in the painful way Carlotta apparently does. I left her there on the beach and came home to Mother.

Why do I feel guilty about Carlotta? It took time for me to believe what everyone in town was telling me, that Mike and Carlotta were having an affair. I knew exactly what Mike was doing, getting vengeance and teaching me a lesson. He couldn't have known that, if I felt any jealousy, it was of him, not of Carlotta. I lied to her this morning. To be torn between gratitude and outrage was the sarcastic surface of what was really happening. Her being with Mike gave me an excuse to ignore her, to punish her a little. All along the person I was deserting was not Mike but Carlotta, and the card on the bottle of perfume was intended to hurt her, not Mike. It didn't occur to me until this morning that she might really have taken Mike not to spite me over Roxanne or teach me a lesson but because she actually wanted him.

Mike has always accused me of romanticizing Carlotta. I did see her as a free spirit, made of sterner stuff than the rest of us. While she was attached to no one else, I admired her detachment from me. I even identified myself with it, thinking my secret self, my real self, was detached, too, and, if I hadn't been trapped in the prison of a family, I might be a disciplined and determined writer, paring Joycean fingernails over my characters. In that fantasy Carlotta was always with me, and we stalked about town, being famous and aloof.

I feel guilt about Carlotta because, from the moment I met Roxanne, I felt cheated by Carlotta of all that friendship might have been. Of course, it couldn't ever have been anything other than what it was. It was only in the first few moments of touching and holding Roxanne's thinness that I might really have been making love with Carlotta. Then I wanted to break what I hadn't been able to touch.

"You're as cruel as children, both of you."

But she didn't want me. She wanted Mike.

Am I cruel? I confess, where Roxanne is concerned, I don't care. I've got to be with her.

When Mother asked why I was out so late last night—wasn't I just going to a movie with a friend—I said, "We were invited to a feast, and we went."

I was tempted to tell her how many hours it lasted, what each course consisted of, how little appetite I have now for anything else. For the first time in my life I'm losing weight without dieting, and Mother sees it as a sign of my unhappiness.

Victor hardly ever mentions Mike these days, but sometimes he comes apart at the seams under the burden of Dad and Mother's unspoken expectations, and I have to yell at him, sometimes even swat or cuff him, as his father would, to give him a line to get back into. Mother and Dad don't approve of that. Neither do I, but a seven-year-old can't cope with a vacuum as he's been asked to, as if it had always been there.

Tony, whom I would have expected to miss Mike as I do, with daily relief, begins to draw pictures of him which are all very large and full of black hair. And he asks questions about his father. "Does Dad know I'm learning to play the violin?" "Does Dad know I have to wear glasses?"

I'd suggest he put such information into the postcards he writes every week, but every fact Tony raises is something he doesn't want his father to know, vulnerabilities he's building up against which he may have to defend himself.

"Is Dad ever coming back?"

I say, yes, of course, after a while, to visit. His own sending of postcards to the boys and the religiously prompt monthly checks make me know what I would know anyway: Mike has no intention of forgetting he is a father.

Is Mike biding his time, just as I am, until the divorce is a fact, his parental rights spelled out by law? Does he know what he's going to do any more than I do? Sometimes the idea that he might try to take the boys is a nightmare, sometimes a daydream, but I could no more be made to give them up than decide to volunteer them.

I wish this were a clearly bad place for all of us to be. Living with Mike, I sometimes felt guilty about how much I simply liked my family, as if it were deeply disloyal to him. But the real point is the money, isn't it? And it always has been. But I wouldn't have married Mike in the first place if there hadn't been money. I couldn't have walked into that trap without one guaranteed open door, which I've now walked through. If I have to be dependent, it's certainly safer and more comfortable to be dependent on my parents than on an ex-husband of Mike's temper.

If I hadn't dropped out of school when I married Mike, if I'd finished my degree, I could go out and teach. But I didn't do that. It would take at least a year back at UBC to finish off, and I couldn't face that.

Is there anything I can face? Certainly not one more question.

I have invited Roxanne to dinner. I have kept her so much to myself that my parents didn't know her name until last week, when I said I'd like her to come. Mother immediately suggested I invite Carlotta as well or any other friend, but I said, no, just Roxanne. I told them she was a friend of Allen's. "Such an unfortunate man!" is now Mother's habitual punctuation whenever his name is mentioned. I told them she worked in a record store with a hi-fi store in the basement. Father knows the fellow who owns the shop, a Jewish fellow, quite a nice sort. I told them she was interested in electronic music. Mother, who thinks Stravinsky should have been deported to another planet and the twenty-first century, frowned. Dad asked what instrument she played. Woman and tape recorder. I offered only the second and explained the little I could.

Roxanne's compositions are called things like "Swimmer," "Bird," "Boat," "Fish," "Bridge," and they are made up of the sounds she collects and then manipulates with her various machines. She says they should be played together in different combinations. I have heard no more than two at a time because of the limited equipment in her room, which is also not large enough for the sound. Fortunately she lives over a grocery store so that she—and we—can make as much noise as she likes at night, but she wishes I could hear them as they should be heard.

"A bit like that fellow John Cage?" Dad asked.

A man with Dad's memory can read *Time* and never be at a social loss. It's a kindness in him which he uses to make other people feel at home, and tonight he'll remember every conversational clue I've given him.

Tony suggested himself that he could play for Roxanne. Victor, not to be outdone, offered to stand on his head, but he's not allowed to do any of his tumbling tricks inside this house since they can be more tumble and less trick than makes Mother comfortable. One of the reasons I've asked Roxanne is that the boys haven't really seen her in months, and they like her. She plays with them as seriously as she plays with Pierre. Mother is kindly disposed to anyone who indulges her grandsons.

I can't hope that either Mother or Dad will accept Roxanne. They won't even know they are supposed to. She'll become for Mother "one of your creative friends," a category of decreased expectations. I think Mother is frightened of Carlotta. When I used to spend so much time with her, Mother checked me over for symptoms of temperament until she was satisfied that I was immune. Carlotta is a mass of middle-class conventions compared to Roxanne. It doesn't even occur to Roxanne that she has nothing to wear for dinner with my parents.

I should be nervous. I should be wondering why on earth I asked her, but I do know why. Living here is like being under deep anesthetic, Roxanne a wild, repeating hallucination of another world. I don't want to drag her into this drugged sleep. I want her to wake me here, make me look at her here, and begin to have some sense of what I can do. I am playing Snow White without a wicked stepmother, Rapunsel with no one to lock me in, except, if you wait for a princess instead of a prince, any parents in the story may turn into poisonous toads. But I am not even afraid of her transparent shirt at the dinner table. I wonder why.

Extraordinary! We could have been back in grade school, Mother asking me to take Roxanne to my room to leave her coat and even play awhile before dinner, which we did until the boys banged on my door like obnoxious little brothers, and Roxanne tumbled into the living room like one of them. I think Dad was on the brink of offering her a Shirley Temple when I told him she likes scotch on the rocks.

She had a tank top on under her see-through shirt and was wearing the single pearl and gold chain I gave her for Christmas, a pin made of real butterfly wings in her hair, which she took off and clipped on Victor's glass of milk.

She was like a magical toy, fascinating to everyone. When she left soon after the boys went to bed, she said, "Maybe next time they'll let me spend the night."

Would we get involved in a pillow fight?

"Such amazing hair," Mother said. "I suppose it must be natural."

"How old is she?"

"My age."

"It must be her size. She isn't really like a child," Dad said.

"She's awfully good with the boys," Mother said. "I was afraid Vic would get overexcited, but he really did awfully well, even when Tony was playing. They grow up every day at this age, don't they?"

It was, in fact, Mother who suggested Roxanne spend the night. It was last Saturday, and she suggested it not even as a convenience but as a treat, offering two shifts of Sunday breakfast so that we could sleep over like teenagers and get up to pancakes and bacon after the boys had gone off to the beach with Dad. Instead of wailing into this notebook with guilty fingers that this should have happened to me at fifteen, I lay touching and being touched in this bed in the first innocent pleasure of my life. We took a shower together before we dressed.

Mother said, as we ate second helpings, "Ah, it's nice to have girls in the house again. It's been a long time since I've heard that kind of laughter."

Did I ever play in the shower with Margaret or Joan? So long ago I hardly remember and certainly never the games Roxanne and I had been playing!

Later Mother said, "Roxanne's a funny little thing. She's good for you. You should have her over more often."

I guess, without thinking about it, I expected Mike to come home for the divorce, as if it were an occasion for both of us, or, if it were mine, he should attend as he would my funeral. I dreaded seeing him and at the same time longed to, not simply as a way of ending my relationship with him but as the signal that I, and everyone around me, could stop saying, "After the divorce . . ."

Even this morning, on the way to court, I expected him. And now I feel no more divorced than I would have felt married if he hadn't turned up at the church. My lawyer assures me that I am. "A free woman," he called me. I feel the way I did when I was a kid and stole something. Getting it out of the store was no relief, and as long as I had it, I felt in danger. I remember throwing a pencil box into the sea. It was weeks before I'd go to the beach again because I was sure I'd find it washed up with the tide. I buried a typewriter ribbon—I took it long before I had a typewriter—and waited for a dog to dig it up. By the time I was nine I had learned to steal only what I could eat.

A free woman? I'll never get away with this. I can't eat my wedding ring. If I knew how, I would cry.

God, this is awful! I had a near fight with Dad tonight at dinner. He wants me to take the boys off on a trip somewhere as soon as school is out.

"A change will do you good."

I don't want a change. It terrifies me. Everything terrifies me. I haven't seen Roxanne in a week. I haven't even phoned her. Why hasn't she phoned me? Suddenly everything's up to me. Suddenly everyone expects me to know what to do. I don't want to do anything. I don't even want to take the boys to school in the morning. Mother's done it three times this week. When I try to tell her how awful I feel, all she can say is, "It's only natural, dear." As if divorce had as many recognizable physical symptoms as pregnancy. I want to scream at her kind, stupid face, "What do you know about it? What do you know about anything?" She manages to love her children by not knowing the first thing about them. Motherhood is blindness and platitudes.

Fatherhood is a mortgage on your children you can never pay off. Witness this damned check from Mike today in the mail. He must know by now—he's been informed—that he's not required by law to send anything now that the divorce is final. *Final.*

It doesn't change anything. I wish there were somebody I could talk to who has been through this. I remember trying to persuade Mike that getting a divorce was the most ordinary thing in the world, something simply everyone did these days, and we were somehow retarded not to have thought of it years ago. Everyone did think of it years ago, getting out while Mike and I were struggling to get deeper in. Where is out? Where did they all go, those broken-in-half couples? Out of the country, like Mike, back to Mother and Daddy, like me? I don't know. They simply disappeared.

I want to disappear. Maybe I have and just don't realize it. I'm in the nowhere I've been in ever since Mike left. I want him back to get this over with. To get what over with?

I want to be punished for what I've done, but not like this, not the daily dread of all those years washing up on the shore, undisposed of after all, the garbage still life of all I've done, and the much more I haven't.

If I'm a free woman, why doesn't someone untie all this guilt, all this fear and say to me, "Yes, it really is true. You really are free." What I'm waiting for is to *be* as humiliated as I *feel*, and I know I couldn't bear that. There is no point in it.

Is freedom nothing but responsibility to punish myself, shout "cunt!" and "dyke!" in the mirror? Face myself with my own sins until I'm as sick of and bored with them as I was when they were Mike's to catalogue, until I can feel as superior and defiant as I did then?

I have never paid for anything in my life. And if I'm paying now, I don't even know how to recognize the price.

I have seen Roxanne. She's as unwilling to be angry with me as everyone else. When I tried to tell her how guilty I felt, how fearful, as if I had no right to anything, hadn't earned anything, was in terrible debt to everyone, she said, "That's no way to get out of being loved." That isn't at all what I meant; at least, I don't think it is, though I could hear then what it must sound like to her.

All these months Roxanne has been different from everyone else, a time bomb in my life, dangerous enough to make the risk a kind of price in itself. But now, unless I were graphically perverse and exhibitionist, my parents would accept my living with Roxanne as a reasonable solution. I have to begin to count costs I couldn't pay or she couldn't pay.

"You don't want to have to lie. You're not a hypocrite like me," I said.

"I don't lie. There's no point in making love in front of people who don't like it. It's something to share, not to expose."

She doesn't understand that if we actually lived together, I'd have her in a bra in a week, in slacks that belted over her rib cage. Or if she does understand, she thinks she wouldn't care if it pleased me, just as Mike tried not to care when I dressed him up in suits.

I won't even meet her friends now. When there was no possibility of it, I liked her to tell me about them, about their wild parties and partner swapping. As erotic fantasy it was just fine, but in fact, I'd be as turned off as I was with Mike. I can't even watch the sex in movies. I hate it.

She doesn't believe me: my nakedness, unabashed, my breasts offered up to her, my legs spread wide, so open, so hungry, I could swallow a roomful of her friends.

"You want to earn this," she asks, "and you also want to be punished for it? Is it so good and so bad?"

"Why don't you feel guilty?"

"Nobody ever taught me how."

She is trying to unteach me, and she does at moments when coming to her is the grand performance of my life, as amazing as giving birth but without its pain. I can feel then that I not only wouldn't mind a world of bystanders but would think it is the one act the world should witness, its pure pleasure, its pure joy. But that is euphoria.

Away from her, the safer I actually am, the realer the possibility of taking her not only as lover but as mate, the more guilty I feel, the more certain I am that the only way I could live with her would be to ruin her. Roxanne is wrong. Guilt is exactly the way to get out of being loved.

Taking the boys to the dentist this afternoon, I met Joseph and Carlotta, who had met each other on their way to the liquor store. I had to prompt Tony and Victor into speaking to Joseph. Only now I realize they didn't recognize him. If he had not been with Carlotta, I'm not sure I would have either. I suppose he has to wear out some of his old clothes, but, if I were his wife, I'd draw the line at those particular trousers. He's withered, and his color is awful. I don't remember that he actually stammered before, though he's always looked like the sort of man who would.

He has a daughter two days old and was buying champagne to celebrate.

"I hope that's what you wanted," I said.

"I didn't want anything," he said, and laughed that peculiar laugh.

Is that why I've been afraid to go out? Carlotta and Joseph are the two people in the world who genuinely disapprove of me as much as I do of myself. And they're the only two, aside from Allen and Pierre—who really don't count—to know what I'm doing. They didn't make me at all nervous. My best friend and Mike's best friend both turn out on Mike's side because they share with him their heterosexual pruderies. They were nervous, behaving as if they'd been caught in an obvious conspiracy, a couple of refugees from the year we were thirty. I'm the only one of us who could stand to lose fifteen pounds. I know I've never looked better in my life, and they would have had to say so to each other when I left. They would have had to say, "Well, divorce seems to agree with her." There's nothing like a little real disapproval to give perspective.

Joseph never has liked me. Mike and I pretty well forced people to choose sides. The parties we gave got more and more like intramural sports. I always thought Carlotta was so deeply on my side she could afford to play referee. But she always liked Joseph. I didn't. I couldn't stand the way Mike felt obliged to behave when Joseph was around, Marlon Brando playing the life of Henry Moore. Joseph didn't forgive me for refusing to get into the act.

Why is it that men—even men who pick up their own socks and know how to fry an egg—never manage to believe in themselves without a deeply sympathetic audience? Carlotta has never asked anyone to believe in her as an artist. Roxanne so simply believes in herself she wouldn't know what to talk about. If I'm as much a needy fake as Mike, at least I keep it to myself. I couldn't fawn over him. And that damned dummy was so mean and melodramatic and like Mike I couldn't believe it. It was Joseph who made me afraid. I've wondered how much that night contributed to his crack-up.

I'm sure Mike doesn't have Joseph on his conscience, or

Carlotta either, and why they're loyal to him when he screwed them both so soundly is one of the mysteries.

I miss her. I always did feel a little on her sufferance, but the sense that any minute she might be bored was a challenge. I was almost required to say any outrageous thing that came into my head. A present could never be something small and thoughtful. It had to be extravagant. I didn't have overt sexual fantasies about Carlotta, but I used to like to think of us as a pair, a contrasting pair of women, extremes, of the sort that attracted Picasso. If there had been a hope in hell of Mike's being a Canadian Picasso (which I admit is a contradiction in terms), would I have fawned over him and encouraged him to act out my appetite for other women? Another of my invented flashbacks to before Roxanne which would exclude Roxanne, give me back my innocent misery.

I meet her at Allen and Pierre's tonight for dinner. We haven't been there together for a long time. Allen's been in Europe. If Pierre is alone, only Roxanne is invited. As a couple we'd simply increase his loneliness.

I asked Allen last night why Pierre never went with him. For a moment he kept his eyes on the chessboard, reluctant to take his mind off the game. Then he seemed to realize it wasn't an idle question.

"He's phobic about traveling. Aside from that, most of the places I go I couldn't take him. Since Trudeau got married, single men, unless they are distressed fathers of three legitimate sons, just aren't in. I have a string of good-looking women over two continents."

"Do you feel guilty about that?"

"Heavens, no. As a matter of fact, I was about to ask you to the Gallery Ball, now that you're a respectably divorced woman."

"I'd be delighted."

"Good," he said, and turned back to our game.

"Don't you ever feel guilty about any of it?"

"About Pierre, of course, but sex, if it isn't a tiny bit wicked, is ever so dull, don't you think? Mike must have been an awful weight of responsibility in bed."

"I was."

"Well, my point is made either way."

"Roxanne doesn't feel guilty."

"Of course not. It takes a certain amount of breeding to be morally trivial, as you and I are."

"Morally trivial?" I know Allen jokes and never jokes.

"You've already begun to fret about ruining Roxanne, I expect, teaching her your own nasty middle-class inhibitions, isolating her from her old free life. It's one of my favorite topics for brooding about Pierre, and I have the advantage of being years older, of having found him when he was still a criminal offense. You couldn't even be jailed. The fact is, of course, Pierre seduced me, and he would have been beaten to death years ago if he hadn't found someone to take him in. But the facts haven't much to do with it."

"Roxanne doesn't need my protection—if I *could* protect her."

"No, but she does need your love. There's that, you see. If I go to friends' second and third weddings with you and we're occasionally seen at an opening, that should take care of our need to pass and give Tony and Victor the option of thinking of you as heterosexual if either of them needs it. That way each of us earns the right to an immodest and indecent bed. Do you know, I'm nearly the only man I know who goes home for sex? I attribute it to my impeccable heterosexual behavior in public. I deserve my vice."

Pierre appeared at that moment from the kitchen. "We've decided to make fudge."

Allen sighed and shook his head. "They conspire to turn us into a pair of fat old cows."

It's true that Roxanne mourns every pound I have so gratefully lost, and Pierre needs to imagine that Allen fasts in his absences. I am not sure he doesn't, for all his tales of expense-account dinners with the handsomest flesh of both sexes in all the cities of Europe. I wonder if the only kind of success I can accept in a man is the kind he believes in as little as I do. I admire Allen.

"You have no alimony," he said then.

It was my turn to be more interested in the neglected game than in the turn of conversation, but I answered, "No, I didn't want any, but Mike keeps sending money anyway. He must have got a job down there."

"That shouldn't irritate you."

"He's trying to buy my good behavior."

"Is he? Then he should have contested the divorce."

"Yes, he should have."

"You wanted him to?"

"Oh, Allen, I don't know. I feel so irrational about it. I don't feel free."

"Of course not. When are you going to start looking for a job?"

"I don't know. Would that solve anything?"

"Part of your charm, Alma, is that you are hardly aware of how totally spoiled you are."

"Oh, I know. I do know."

"Allen has a friend who runs the most successful gallery in Vancouver, one nobody ever hears of because it doesn't handle anyone local, only the international giants. There are no opening nights. The place isn't even open to the public during the day. Investors make appointments and fly in from Montreal and Toronto, even from Los Angeles and Houston and Atlanta. His last local employee couldn't resist a second business with the customers, and he felt it lowered the tone of the establishment. He's perfectly willing to supply call girls or boys, but he wants people working in the gallery to be singularly professional.

"I didn't ask him the salary, but it wouldn't be peanuts. You don't type, I suppose, or add, or do anything useful like that?"

"I type," I said. I must have been the only one in the

class for whom it was nothing more than part of a fantasy for future greatness.

"Would you like an introduction?"

"I don't see how I could work full time . . . with the boys."

"It isn't that sort of job."

I wanted to say, "Don't push me," but I've been waiting for months to be pushed in some direction. I think I imagined ultimatums rather than possibilities.

I am thirty-one years old, and I have never had a job. I have never even considered it seriously. I majored in education instead of English not to be practical but because it was easier. Mickey Mouse courses were ideal preparation for the hours I play stupid card games, Monopoly, and put together jigsaw puzzles with the boys. Roxanne says working is as interesting as gin rummy.

If I'd decided to be something outlandish—a brain surgeon, a commercial pilot, a Greek scholar—to work would be the natural outcome. To take a job simply for the sake of a job seems slightly sordid for a woman, particularly for anyone with children. Oh, I know I sound more like Mother than I should, who thinks Roxanne is such a brave little thing to sell records to people.

"Do you work a cash register?" Mother asked her, as if that were one of the central mysteries.

Well, it's a mystery to me, too, and I have Mother's unhealthy awe of the million very ordinary things I don't know how to do, like use a laundromat or put gas in my own car.

I don't suppose the gallery has anything as obvious as a cash register.

Being propositioned by rich men doesn't frighten me. I doubt that it would happen. Might there be a rich woman or two? Allen was careful to point out that the last thing his friend wants is sex-crazed employees of whatever tastes.

Do I think the only respectable reason for doing anything is love? I certainly wouldn't have married for money. In the first couple of years I was very proud that people would know I'd married for love.

If love was really vanity and a need for safety, what is it with Roxanne beyond lust and escapism? If I lived with her, we might lock ourselves into roles as stupid as mine and Mike's, or, what is more likely, we'd fight constantly about the roles we weren't playing. Who cooks? Who pays the utility bill? Who changes the beds?

Mother and I never fight about chores. She never expects me to do anything, and aside from cooking, there's very little to do. Roxanne and I wouldn't have a cleaning woman, not just because we couldn't afford it. We couldn't have someone like that poking around in our lives.

When I'm with Roxanne, I really enjoy doing ordinary things for her. In her room it's like playing house. She hasn't more than a couple of glasses and plates to wash, and her clothes fit into two drawers. The only complexities are her machines, and she keeps them impeccably.

But would I enjoy coming home from work and having to cook the meal, spend the evening doing the laundry, being with the boys, while she was off fiddling with her recorders, night after night? When would I ever read a book or write—or cut my toenails for that matter? I put up with Mike's sculpting and crazy hours for two reasons: it gave me plenty of time to myself, and I didn't want to be with him. I don't even like Roxanne to go to the bathroom without me. Anytime there's a chance to be with her, I don't want to do anything else. The idea of sitting in the same room with her and reading a book is unimaginable.

Why won't I imagine? It has nothing to do with Roxanne. I don't want to be looked at and called "an unfortunate woman," having to work, living with another woman. Being lesbian is a great place to visit, but I wouldn't want to live there. I don't feel humiliated at home because it's temporary.

Any day now I can suggest to Dad that summer will be too much for Mother, the kids underfoot all the time.

School is out next week, and once they've been running around loose for a while, Dad won't be hard to convince. I couldn't stay here and work and let Mother cope all day with the children. Once I move out, there's no way I can have a job in summertime.

If I rented a room to Roxanne, a room to herself, I wouldn't be asking Dad for a house of my own simply for that. I could start using Mike's money. He told me it was to keep me home with the boys. If Dad bought me a house —he certainly has offered more than once—and there was no rent to pay, Mike's money and Roxanne's rent together would be enough—well, not for clothes, but Mother and Dad have always been generous about that.

I simply assume Roxanne wants to live with me. We talk about living together all the time, but it's always in some other place, near other mountains, by other seas, in a house of our own, which never gets furnished beyond a huge bed and sunning mats and certainly doesn't have Tony and Victor running in and out with stomachaches, broken arms, and the obsessive need to tell the plot of every TV program, including the commercials. There is no huge laundry basket for the piles of their dirty clothes. In those dreams, the nearest they've got to us is about a mile down some tropical shore as naked as we are, as absorbed in seashells as we are in our oceanic sex. I have never said to Roxanne, quite simply, "Would you live with me and help me raise the boys?" She can't suggest it herself, but also she may have as many doubts as I do.

I have just read this through. It's hours and hours of nagging myself with guilts and doubts and indecisions. The only changes that seem to have taken place are that from resenting Mike's money I've begun to be grateful for and count on it; from being afraid I'd do that drastically immoral thing of living with Roxanne, no matter what anyone thought, I'm afraid I can't live with Roxanne because of what I think.

This isn't writing. This is to writing what masturbation is to making love, an analogy that wouldn't have demeaned it for me while I still lived with Mike since my own fingers were so much more skillful than his. The lonely pleasing of oneself is certainly better than the mutual displeasure of bad sex.

But I wasn't trying to deal with sex. If this is to have any purpose, it should at least make me more aware of myself, of how I really feel and what I really want. When I admit the worst, I often don't really believe it. When I try to sound as if I'm coming to terms with my life, writing becomes a substitute for doing anything about it. Even when I'm most discouraged, there's satisfaction in the pages I have filled.

If I were at all serious about this, I should at least try to write a story, even if it were about myself. It would be nothing to send to *Chatelaine* or *Saturday Night*, that's for sure. And the sort of little magazine that might publish it would send me nothing but a subscription I wouldn't want delivered to this house. Roxanne already takes them all, *Branching Out, A Room of One's Own, Body Politic, The Advocate, Christopher Street, Conditions, Sinister Wisdom.* I read them the way I used to read *Vogue* and *Redbook,* trying to imagine myself glamorous or matronly, even occasionally the writer of one of the stories. Now I try to identify with Adrienne Rich, whose husband really did kill himself, leaving her with sons to raise. But the differences are enormous. She was an accomplished poet—even W. H. Auden said so—when she was years younger than I am. And now she's years older and talks about herself at my age as if it were another life. She lives in New York and knows all the important women in the movement, for whom sex is political.

All of them, from Violette Leduc to Kate Millett, are artists and radicals first. There must be a lot more women like me than like them for whom loving another woman is nothing but that, with no redeeming politics or transforming art.

I think Roxanne does feel like one of them. She doesn't talk a lot about it, but occasionally she says something that makes me feel the world she actually lives in is the moon's distance from mine. She calls people she's never met—like Pauline Oliveros—sister. I didn't even know she was a famous composer. My only sisters are my sisters, who are not my sisters at all in that sense. We don't know each other either.

No one would be interested in reading the self-doubt and moral dilemma of a woman living safely at home with her two children, protected by indulgent parents who even let her have slumber parties with her little friend and never come in without knocking and never look around when they do, so that this notebook is as safe from them as it would be locked in the vault of my heart. The only one I hide it from is Tony because he seems to look at me more and more often with my own eyes. A ten-year-old.

We read about people who have already been heard of in places that already exist.

I have a title for a novel—I suppose it could be a short story—"The Annals of War." It's out of a Hardy poem which isn't about war at all but about a "maid and her wyte" plowing a field. But that is an eternal story. My wyte was a bouncer, and there wasn't any field to plow. We lived in a world of concrete and other people's flower beds. What's ordinary isn't eternal, not here and now for me.

Two women in a ring of flesh, as if they were continually giving birth to each other, may go back as far as Sappho, but as a symbol they have more in common with war than with peace, fission rather than fusion, destructive of all holy clichés: motherhood, the family, maple syrup, our bacon wrapper flag!

Listen (as Mike would say), I want to record here how often I'm happy, simply happy. When Mike decided to go somewhere with us, I always dreaded it because having an audience increased his sense of responsibility. He shouted and cuffed so much I thought the boys would have permanently damaged eardrums. Now I really like the long summer days when we can go off together, just the three of us, today all day on the Gulf Island ferry. I didn't take a picnic lunch, let them eat those bilious burgers and fries. Ferries are a marvelous way to travel with kids. There's enough room for them to explore, two stories of decks and lounges and cafeterias. They play tag, hide-and-seek, race each other, occasionally rest and actually look at the landscape of islands, and they are as intent as the captain every time the ship docks at one.

Victor is enchanted by sea gulls, which seem to him beautiful flying into the light, hilarious hitching a ride on the deck rail. Tony dreams off into the shoreline, asking of every white beach, "Do you think that's Indian, Mom? Do you think there might be petroglyphs?"

I think how I'd like to take them around the world like this, though I don't suppose a freighter crew and passengers would be as tolerant of their antics. For today going around this world was just fine. We counted twenty-eight sailboats, five tugs, twelve commercial fishing boats, eight other ferries, one carrying freight cars to Vancouver Island, and even saw a cruise ship coming back from Alaska. We followed it through Active Pass with a great sounding of ships' horns. We spotted eagles, named trees: hemlock, Douglas fir, cedar, alder. Tony is very good at that. Victor likes shouting out "arbutus" over and over again until he is silly with repetition, and his spinny giggles seem to me as fine a hymn as any to those distinctively beautiful trees, red branches distributing weight in curious and graceful gestures to balance the tree on precarious rock. They all are in high white bloom this time of year, which will turn into Christmas clusters of red berries.

On days like this I feel both more with the children and more detached from them, a special kind of companionship which is part of the long rehearsal for letting them go. I am proud of Tony's absentminded tending of toddlers, stopping to set upright one diapered fellow, just capsized by Victor's passing speed. I suppose, like his father, Victor has such a smile he can afford to make waves. I've stopped wondering why I can love him so simply, *like* him, when he reminds me a dozen times a day of Mike. I'm just glad I do.

I suppose by the end of August I'll be counting the days until school begins, thinking up places for them to go without me, but right now I feel rich with a summer to share with my children. My apprehensions and theirs, since Mike left, have made us nervously dependent on each other sometimes. Vic hurls himself into my lap as if the force of sitting on me would keep me where he needs me. Tony tells long stories he doesn't want to come to an end so that he won't have to get out of the car to go to school, so that I won't turn out his light at night. Days like this give us back to each other. By the end of summer we should be healthily bored, longing to miss each other.

Dad has bought me a house. He's such an instinctively tactful man I've rarely seen him so nervous about being misunderstood in his intentions. The house is an investment, nothing I need to live in if I don't like it. It was a foreclosure sale, and he already held the second mortgage. I'm always welcome to stay here. This will always be my home, and the boys'. On the other hand, parents shouldn't be possessive. Children—grown children—need a life of their own.

I finally had to stop him, telling him I couldn't ask to move out and put the additional financial burden on him; it would seem too ungrateful when I'd been made to feel so welcome here. But if he was offering me a house, he was wonderfully generous, and I delighted.

"Well, your sisters both have houses. It seems only fair . . ."

It's not the house I would have chosen. For one thing, it has no room to rent. There are only three bedrooms. And, of course, the boys will have to change schools in the fall. Tony is enthusiastic about that, Victor apprehensive with having to establish his territory all over again. The biggest drawback is that it's lovely. It's not really a question of not deserving it. Of course I don't. I am still looking for some sort of punishment I could tolerate, and this house eliminates one more possibility. I don't even have to share a bathroom with the boys. I have my own off the master bedroom, which has a view I like better than Mother and Dad's, which disappears at night, except for the lights of an occasional ship, because they look out on the unpopulated mountains of Howe Sound. This house overlooks not only the sea and the mountains but the great spread of the city, which from this distance and angle looks real, even beautiful, not only all day but all night. It's not a big house. The furniture I already have will look, for the first time, very much at home.

There's a garden. I've never learned to garden, except for snipping off dead heads, watering, raking a few leaves, but it's something I've always imagined I'd do, like having children.

We move next week.

"Why don't we take the boys back with us, and then you and Roxanne can work as late as you like?"

I am getting used to Mother's conspiring with me for my most nefarious pleasures, and I didn't even feel guilty when Tony went silent with disappointment at not spending the first night in the new house and Vic said, "Oh, shit!" Because it came out only in a whisper, we all ignored it.

Roxanne and I had to go on working for a while simply to have advanced the order enough to have earned the pleasure of being alone in this lovely space. And I did want the kitchen settled to get up to in the morning. I could fix the boys' rooms after Roxanne went to work and before I picked them up.

When we finally got into the bed I had occasionally so fearfully and guiltily taken her to last summer, I felt like a woman warrior who had finally reconquered her own kingdom, a bed big enough for acrobatic celebration in a house that could be filled with the noise of victory.

Later, standing naked at the window, looking down over a city I felt I owned, I wanted to propose to Roxanne, who stood beside me, her high small breasts like those of an Egyptian goddess, who is incongruously crowned by a bright aura of hair.

"Live with me," I said. "Really live with me."

For answer, she led me back to bed and made love so gently, so tenderly, with such reluctance to reach any climax that I could feel her wishing there were a way to go on and on at a pitch of sweetness that never had to end, but it grew higher and hotter until it ended for me in a crying joy, for her in a harsh noise in her throat.

We said nothing about it at a hurried breakfast this morning. She refused to let me drive her to work. Has she really made up her mind that it won't work? Or do we have to go through a new period of separation we choose before we can choose to be together? I don't know.

The boys are finally asleep in their own beds after a rackety day of overexcitement and testings, I too tired, too much in a daze of exhausted satisfaction, to be much help to either of them. I did tell Vic I'd warm the seat of his pants if he dared throw one thing out his window, which was his angry solution for being told to unpack and tidy instead of settling to play with every old toy he'd discovered. He knew I hadn't either the energy or the investment, but he took my effort of attention in reluctant obedience. Tony simply asked, in a voice of almost adult weariness, how long moving took.

There's something absolutely satisfactory in the people you love who get put to bed, kissed, and left to sleep alone. For tonight this enormous bed feels magnificently christened and not one bit too big for me alone. I stretch in every direction, yawn, sigh, feel beautiful and beautifully alone.

I've used every domestic excuse I could to avoid writing in this notebook, and with the move there have been enough of them to keep me silent for six weeks, long enough to make me wonder if scribbling here was one of the symptoms of my regressing into childhood. Last week I decided, if I were going to write, I should sit up properly at my desk and write something real. First I tried writing a story about Roxanne and me, but since part of taking myself seriously is trying to write something for sale, I changed Roxanne's sex. She became Robert, still selling records and spending all his spare time documenting sound. To keep him from seeming effeminate, I had to make him restless with his job, as Roxanne rarely seems to be, and I had to make him take his real work not more seriously than Roxanne does but more . . . pretentiously, I suppose. He did think of himself as a composer. I didn't have to write many pages before I saw that Robert was sounding more and more like Mike, and there would be absolutely no point in a woman's choosing between a bouncer and a record clerk, between a closet sculptor and an unrecognized electronic music composer who, never having met John Cage, still called him "brother." I tried to make Robert much better in bed, but a man to be as good as a woman in bed would have to be not only well instructed but impotent. The husband, page by page, became a paragon of manhood compared to Robert, and, though I suppose there are some women, not knowing any better, who would leave a Mike for a Robert, no one remotely like me would.

So I tried turning myself into a man and Mike into a woman, and that was, surprisingly, a great deal easier. I called myself Alan and was a moderately successful businessman of some sort. Alan came out sounding more flippant than my father, less cynical than Allen, with a male kindness I like in them both. Mike, as a woman, was amazingly attractive, perhaps because tending a house and children is so much more human a job than beating people up night after night. As a woman she could sculpt without driving ambition, seem a little silly to herself sometimes but not to other people. I got so interested in what our marriage would have been like that I forgot Roxanne entirely. As a businessman with a wife who wanted evenings for her own work, I didn't have time for Roxanne, to say nothing of avocations like writing. I was looking after the kids.

I did not stumble on a way to write fiction, and here I am back in bed with my notebook. I think I feel about bed the way Mike does about the dining-room table; it shouldn't be shut up for the day, reserved for nothing but sleeping and making love at strictly appointed times. Mike never liked the children in bed with us. The first time Victor climbed into bed with Roxanne and me and planted himself firmly between us, nearly comfortably jealous, Freud shuddered in my bones, but Roxanne laughed. Now, if she spends the night on the weekend, both kids bring everything from the Monopoly board to the soccer ball into bed with us in the morning. Colette wrote in bed.

I didn't try to write when I was married to Mike. I must have had at least as much time to myself as I do now. I didn't use it. I went to bed soon after the children did because I had to be up so early to feed Mike. Then half the time I'd have to barricade the kids into their rooms to go back to bed with Mike, get up twenty minutes later, occasionally stimulated enough to be frustrated, usually dry and sore and angry. All day long he was a sleeping presence, and, if the children's noise woke him early, there would be hours of his irritation to get through before he went off to work.

I sleep much less now. I don't seem to need it. I spend at least as much time in bed.

I wonder if most women who love each other don't live together. The only ones we really know about are probably just the tip of the iceberg. Roxanne and I may be part of a vast majority of underwater women, making love in the back seat of a car on the way home from PTA meetings, in the morning after babies have been nursed and put down to nap. Why is illicit sex always a man on his lunch hour or on a business trip? Or a woman with the Fuller brush man.

There are jokes about steam baths and public toilets as well, but there's never an arched eyebrow about bridge games or meetings of Brownie leaders. Even with the women's movement characterized as a bunch of bra-burning dykes, people still don't believe women have sex with women except when they can't get men or are man haters.

I wasn't honest about turning myself into a man. I simply made up the sort of man I like and depend on. Mike made a perfectly good woman because he stayed heterosexual. As a man I would have been a guilt-ridden fairy, and I would have met Robert in a public toilet at the Bay and never even known his name.

In general I feel horribly sorry for men. In particular I either resent or admire them. I don't even feel sorry for Joseph, though I think I probably should. I would feel terribly sorry for him if he were a woman. I understand what drives women crazy. Men aren't supposed to go.

In this notebook, I touch my imagination as I do Roxanne's body. Here? Here? Is this the beginning of something? Or this? Changing the sexes of everyone I know could be a device for seeing something more clearly, but I'm using it as a cover-up, not simply to hide my being lesbian but to keep my general attitudes and my specific feelings and behavior as far from meeting as possible since they can't meet; they don't even speak the same language.

That last entry seemed to me so silly at the time I haven't written here for a month, but I have written. Now that Tony and Victor are back at school and can walk to school, I get them breakfast and come back to bed and work until lunchtime five days a week. I haven't finished a story yet, but I'm beginning to see why even the beginnings that feel alive start to dissolve five or six pages in. I'm tightening characters into what they ought to feel for some point I'm trying to make, when most people live as far out of the tent of their ideas as I do. I asked Roxanne the other night if ideas got in her way. She said, yes, when she didn't listen well enough or couldn't hear. An idea should come like a bloom on a plant, a song out of a bird.

I've been toying with the idea of taking a writing class at UBC. Then I remembered a cooking class I took when I was ten. I couldn't eat most of the group-concocted messes, but I was enchanted with something called candlestick salad —half a banana standing in a ring of pineapple, a curved slice of apple for a handle, a maraschino cherry on top for a flame, and mayonnaise dribbling down for melting wax. I'd only sliced the apple at school, but I decided to make the whole thing, five times over, for the family. The bananas I bought were too big for the holes in the pineapple. I had to squeeze and shove, and even then the much-handled bananas tilted uncertainly and looked gray from all my effort. Everyone did eat them, and I was fortunate to have a reticent and kindly father and no brothers to make obvious remarks. Mike would have been graphic! My mother said, "If you want to learn to cook, go into this kitchen and cook."

So that's what I'm doing now, hoping to get beyond the stage of candlestick salad sooner alone.

If Carlotta hadn't written a note on her show invitation, I wouldn't have gone. I've broken so many patterns, faiths, expectations in the last year, some even in the hope of consequences, that not turning up at her opening would have been an easy enough first, perhaps easier than going.

It is peculiar to go anywhere with Roxanne. No matter how much people gossip about our sex life, they don't treat us as a couple. A man and a woman don't have to live together to be paired. At their slightest indication, they are treated like Siamese twins. Roxanne and I are two single women at the same party, ten years older than most other single women there. Roxanne doesn't look it. I do. We don't look as if we came from the same generation, or perhaps planet. The surprise of this public separateness is always double-edged: I feel relieved not to be so exposed and at the same time very unprotected. Though Mike at these occasions could be so obnoxious I wanted to disown him, he was nevertheless my husband, the tallest and handsomest man in the room. He was better than a mirror for my vanity. Roxanne doesn't disappear in a crowd; her hair is too extraordinary. The way she turns to anyone who speaks to her, like a flower to the sun, alarms rather than makes me jealous, but she isn't really easily taken in. I know that. Still, she's vulnerable, and I have no convention for protecting her either.

Carlotta, skeletal and composed, is very elegant in a long dress the color of fine ash. She more or less ignores her friends on these occasions, expecting them to do what she is doing: soft-selling to potential buyers. I link arms with a doctor friend of my father's and say, "It must be your training to save lives. Have you noticed that, if it weren't for the medical profession, a lot of Vancouver artists would starve?"

"There are some real collectors," he agrees. "I can't claim to be one, but I always have been interested in Carlotta."

We look together at her X-rayed bones, arranged in tidal washes. He chooses her pelvic bone, stranded alone on an otherwise-barren beach.

"I should have given that to you," Carlotta says, the first time she's spoken to me since I arrived, and I have no idea what she means, peace offering or taunt.

"Too late. I've sold it," I tell her.

We both turn away to other buyers. I don't care about being reconciled with Carlotta. I want to be interesting enough to her so that there will always be at least brief moments between us, which never have worked and never will. I don't mind that now, and, when I did, I didn't know. Long friendships may be seasoned by unrequited love and betrayal. She hasn't given up my perfume.

Allen and Pierre are here, as separate from each other as Roxanne and I are. Pierre has found Roxanne. They stand together in their transparent shirts, Pierre flashing his diamonds-are-forever ring like a newly engaged teenager, Roxanne's pearl perfectly visible between her small, arrogant breasts. There are so many outlandish costumes here that they don't seem out of place. Nor do Allen and I, who are not simply disguised as buyers, since I will help him choose the debris I watched Carlotta sketch with such moody accuracy on the beach that cold day last spring. As we stand discussing it, I am aware that my father's doctor friend has noticed us and is probably deciding I am now half of a less striking but more appropriate couple. Allen does enjoy being one of the most elusive and eligible bachelors in Vancouver, whose name has been linked with a dozen different women, none of whom, he assures me, has had any more illusions or desires than I do. "All lesbian?" I ask, incredulous.

"My dear, I'm not a gossip."

Now he admires my brown sapphires.

"They belonged to my grandmother."

"A woman should wear nothing but real jewelry, preferably at least fifty years old."

Allen's attention is caught by a sound which has been repeating at long but fairly regular intervals, familiar as a friend's voice, but I can't place it until Allen excuses himself and goes over to Joseph. The sound is Joseph's laugh, like a warning buoy in that sea of people. He looks less seedy than when I saw him last, but he's still not a good color, and the vacant hopefulness on his face makes me afraid he won't be able to remember Allen's name. Allen is inviting Joseph and his wife back for drinks after the opening, as I have been invited, with Roxanne.

I wish they weren't coming. I wish Carlotta had other friends, a lover to go off with, and Roxanne and I could go home to bed. I don't realize, until after we're there, that I must not trust Roxanne to understand what she understands perfectly well and can deal with.

Carlotta is elated by the success of her show, jokes about

being the richest rag-and-bone woman in the city. She's free of financial worry for six months now and has a couple of good commissions. There is no one who plays big frog in little pond with more attractive irony. Roxanne and Allen are being a good audience, Allen because he plays her quipping game with her, Roxanne, as always, because she listens. I watch Carlotta contemplate Roxanne's breasts, the pearl which Carlotta touches suddenly as if it were something she herself is wearing, a gesture so uncertain and sexual that it makes me catch my breath.

I am standing with Ann Rabinowitz and turn to her to shield her from something that is shocking only to me, who, in imagination, quite cavalierly changes the sexes of all my friends but never their sexual partners. I feel prudish and silly. There is a spot of milk on Ann's blouse. My own breasts tighten in sympathy, in pleasure. I ask her about the baby. Behind her glasses her eyes are very tender. This is the first time I've ever talked with her, and I feel she's being very careful of me, a manner she may have developed for Joseph, a gentle testing of what I can take. I mention Mike casually to indicate that I'm not fragile.

"He was very kind to me, a good friend."

"I'm glad," I say. "Joseph has always been a very good friend to Mike." And I like admitting that without my own selfish reservations. "How's Joseph getting along? He does look better."

"He is. He has trouble with his memory. It makes his teaching very tiring. But he loves the baby. We all do."

"I'd love to see her."

"Then come over some morning. I bathe her around ten o'clock."

And then feed her? I have such a desire to see those milk-filled breasts, to watch their being sucked by a hungry girl baby, that in this moment I wish I'd let Mike talk me into one more baby, not because I'm envious, not because I want another child but because I want to share the experience with Ann, its marvelous sensuality.

"Why are you the only one not in purdah with your breasts?" I asked Roxanne later, in bed.

She laughed at my lust, and so did I, because she sucked me until I was Ann, until I was everywoman, brimming with milk, frothing, spilling over, an orgasmic fountain.

After Mike and I went to a party, our separately stored-up lusts burst out as accusations of narrow jealousy so that, if he finally did fuck me, it was in assertive ownership and revenge. Roxanne gathers up the details of the evening, hers and mine, and takes them home to be opened and shared, like the presents they were meant to be.

"I'd die at an orgy," I said just after dawn.

"Perhaps."

"This is an orgy, at least four of us in this bed all night."

Lovely, as long as it is fantasy. Roxanne knows that. I think it may be something she regrets about me and hopes I'll outgrow. I can regret it a little myself until I am cooking breakfast for two small boys and wonder at such depravity.

Carlotta is doing a portrait of Roxanne. Carlotta phoned and asked my *permission*.

"You must ask Roxanne. It has nothing to do with me."

"Her body is so much like mine, I thought I might break the narcissistic spell—or extend it. I've already done a couple of male portraits that aren't bad, one of Joseph particularly, but I feel much less certain about doing women. If I could do Roxanne, I might try you. If you would."

Carlotta, as a painter, can do that, simply borrow any friend she wants to study without apology or subterfuge. I've done a portrait of Joseph, too, but he's a twenty-five-year-old girl who cracks up after an abortion. About the only thing left of Joseph is the laugh, which Roxanne has also recorded. She used it in a short piece called "Similes," which has single notes of all sorts of instruments as well as car horns, buoys, bells. Carlotta can't paint his laugh. A portrait can suggest a great deal but reveal nothing. What, after all, *is* a cruel mouth? Just that, if I write it down. But in a face actually represented, unless it is a cartoon, all the features are as ambiguous as those of any stranger—unless, of course, you actually know the person. Will I be able to tell, by looking at Roxanne's portrait, how aroused she is by the exercise? Since it will go on for weeks, perhaps months, Roxanne will go through every sort of mood. Carlotta will catch what she wants. So, whether they're her own bones or someone else's face, Carlotta's paintings will go on saying more about Carlotta.

And my writing? Well, here in this notebook, of course. I haven't really tried to present anyone but me and often at my least presentable. Carlotta has yet to paint herself masturbating with one hand, painting with the other. Maybe she doesn't. Obviously her deciding to do portraits is like my attempting stories to get outside myself, but I don't think I have the right to use my friends for that, except in unrecognizable fragments. If I actually tried to do a word portrait of Roxanne, I couldn't simply catch a passing expression on her face; I'd have to know what it meant. And since words don't trap a subject in space and time, she wouldn't have to be alone or thirty-one years old. I could write something as long as a novel about her, fleshing her out with all her past experience so that she would be a person rather than simply a presence in this notebook, a snatch of dialogue or a yellow tank top in a story.

Major biographical clue: any character in my fiction who wears a tank top is sexually attractive, even though I wouldn't be caught dead in one.

A portrait painter doesn't have to deal with anything but the physical presence. A writer, like a lover, has to deal with the past, with all the acts of the past, and that's impossible. Yet the minute you start paring away at the clutter of events to get at essential experience, you're probably doing the equivalent of removing essential teeth for the line of the jaw. Maybe leaving thirty-one years undisturbed inside the sack of skin and concentrating on the shape and texture of that sack is more possible, as making love is more possible than loving. That is, I *know* Roxanne when we're making love. My tongue by now can call the farthest outpost of her nervous system to attention. I can consume everything alien until her mind is purified of everything but what I am doing and about to do. But do I know her at all when desire hasn't emptied her of a self that remembers, experiences, and grows quite apart from me, and always will?

I don't even know why she isn't living here, but that may be because I don't think about it. I suspect she isn't living here because I haven't made it clear that I want her to. I am not sure I do. So, when I stop to think, I learn something about myself rather than about Roxanne, except that she is tactful.

When we are making love, I am a female multitude with an appetite so various that I can be a hundred women, each a new pleasure to her, but the lovelier the night has been, the more I want time to myself, time when I am not waiting for her to come home, wondering where she is. Then I can think of her as a person instead of the obsession she is to me.

Pierre's history is an important part of his attractiveness to Allen, who is more apt to dwell on him as an abandoned child and street orphan than on his transparent shirts and tank tops. That Roxanne was a foster child is important to Pierre, a way they make common cause. For me she might have been born full grown the night of my thirtieth birthday. What is childlike about her has nothing to do with her childhood; it is an essential attention she's never lost. Carlotta can hardly help catching that in her face, for if she isn't paying attention to Carlotta, she will be to something or someone else.

Roxanne didn't call me; she called Allen.

"She didn't want to bother you. I told her *I* didn't mind bothering you at all."

At first I said I couldn't go and leave the boys alone. What if Victor woke up and needed something?

"There are parts of the world where people Victor's age are supporting their old mothers. Tony'd look after him. Leave a note."

"Can't you just go and bring her here?"

"Yes."

I responded more to the anger in Allen's voice than to any sense of responsibility of my own to go to the police station. I hadn't had time to take in what had happened to her until after I'd hung up the phone and began to wait for him to get here. Once I'd written Tony a note and put on my coat, there was nothing else to do.

I simply couldn't understand how she could have been caught breaking into the store where she works. She has a key. She often goes down there at night to work.

When Allen finally arrived, he explained, "I didn't say she had broken in—I said she was charged with breaking and entering and theft over one hundred dollars."

"Why?"

"Because she was down there running half the tape recorders in the basement."

"But she does that a couple of times a week and has for years. It's the main reason she likes the job."

"And never bothered to ask permission?"

"I don't know. I don't suppose she thought of it as doing anything wrong. I mean, she's sometimes wished she could take me down to hear, but she thought, since I wasn't an employee, it might not be right."

"It isn't even a Maoist plot, but it might as well be as far as the authorities are concerned. I can understand why Roxanne has no sense of private property, but surely by now a little capitalist responsibility could have rubbed off from you. You don't really think all the toys in the world belong to you."

"Why are you so angry?"

"Because you don't take care of her, for God's sake!"

"She's a grown woman, Allen."

"She's no more a grown woman than you are!"

"I am the mother of two real children. I'm not about to

pretend she's another. I don't happen to want her to grow up and leave home."

We couldn't share the anxiety except by fighting with each other. By the time we arrived at the station, I felt Allen was taking me there not so much for Roxanne's sake as for punishment because in some way I hadn't anticipated the danger she was in and prevented this from happening.

Allen's lawyer was already there when we arrived. Allen was so familiar with the procedure I wondered how many times he'd bailed Pierre out of trouble Allen had not been able to prevent in all his wisdom and self-righteousness. I had a sudden image of Roxanne as someone quite alien to me, a hardened juvenile delinquent who might be caught any night she wasn't with me, breaking into buildings, stealing quantities of expensive equipment, or out cruising the streets like a prostitute. The infidelity—mine—shocked me, but I couldn't shake it. In my own safe house and all the way down to the jail I could be sure of what had happened and why. Once in that wretched public place I was exposed, reduced, with nothing to do but shake, while the men played their power games against each other, Roxanne the prize.

When she was finally produced, she looked like one of those mechanical dolls whose spring has been wound too tight and broken, rigid and still. I wanted to run to her, embrace her or shake her or whatever it took to bring her back to life again, but I was as rigid with terror as she was. Allen took her arm, and then he took mine and steered us both out of the building to the car. Roxanne answered his battery of questions very softly with no more than a word or two each time.

"And who was it who found you? A night watchman?"

"The owner."

"The owner?" I asked, indignant. "But he's a friend of my father's!"

"Why didn't you think of that two hours ago?" Allen demanded.

"Don't get your father into this," Roxanne pleaded.

"Roxanne," Allen said, "I hate to face you with the facts of life this late at night, but we're talking about the difference between a jail sentence of a couple of years and dropped charges. Would your father be willing to talk with him, Alma?"

"I'm sure he would."

Dad was able to make the store owner listen to reason. All the charges were dropped the next day, but Roxanne is out of a job, and Mother is a little more formal and dubious about her than she was, giving me one of my attacks of respectability, and I question Roxanne not like a lover but like a lawyer for the prosecution.

Roxanne assures me that she has served time in jail only on morals offenses, never for offenses against property. She served her first term when she was fifteen in a juvenile correction center in some place like Kamloops or Nelson. After that she was put in a foster home where people are paid eight hundred dollars a month to deal with incorrigibles. Roxanne was in and out of jail until she was twenty-one and became a consenting adult. After that, she was careful not to associate with anyone under age, not only to keep herself out of trouble but not to risk jail for someone who had never been.

"They're not good places," she says.

I am appalled. I behave as if I'd just discovered that the maid had syphilis. I don't want someone with a criminal record around the children. I make excuses not to ask her to the house. Since she never questions or protests, it isn't difficult, now that she's not working, to see her in her room during the day. Simply because I'm scandalized by her, I am more obsessed by her than ever. I grill her with sexual questions. I want to hear exactly how women intimidate, rape, keep in bondage other women. I know I'm making her miserable. I can't seem to help it. I want her to act out all her own sexual humiliations on me. I beg to be abused. For I've had a revelation: the punishment is the same as the crime, and I am in a frenzy for it. She won't.

"It's my past, Alma. I can't give it to you any more than you can give me yours."

Often now, when I arrive, she has the same rigid, blank look she had that night at the jail, and again I feel she is a doll wound too tight, broken, and I am an alarmed and petulant child who wants to shake, push, wind tighter the toy I've already broken.

Then she's not at home, two days, three days, a week. I track her down, sometimes at Carlotta's, sometimes at Pierre's. I feel their reluctance to let me in.

"I thought you said you were looking for a job today."

She shrugs. Pierre sulks, wanting Roxanne to himself because Allen is again out of town. Carlotta won't let me look at the portrait. She won't let me stay around while she works. Daily the wall around Roxanne is getting higher. She might as well have been sent to prison. I know I am building it, and I can't stop. She has become the prison of my need, and she won't let me in, angel at the gate with flaming sword instead of welcoming jailor. No, just something I've broken and can't mend and want to smash and want to mourn and want back. Roxanne! Roxanne!

I haven't seen Roxanne for a month. I haven't seen any of them, except for Ann Rabinowitz, who doesn't seem to me one of them. I went first because Joseph was spending all of the Christmas holiday in the hospital, and Mike is no longer around to be the friend he was to Ann last time. I watched her bathe and then nurse the baby. We talked about the care of cracked nipples. Then I asked them all over for dinner, though we agreed the children were just the age to detest each other. But the baby is a real novelty to the boys, and since the girls are so good with her and also just that much older than Vic and Tony, the boys are impressed with them, too.

I feel useful and wholesome around Ann, companionably matronly, and I like her. We've been slow to exchange real confidences, she probably because she hasn't wanted to burden me with hers, I because I didn't believe she could understand mine. Then this afternoon she gave me a surprising opening.

"Mike told me you'd had some sort of breakdown."

"He did? What else did he say?"

"Not much. He thought it had alienated you from him. And he said you had one friend who had stayed close to you."

"Did he tell you I was a lesbian?"

"No," Ann said.

"Well, that's the breakdown, and that's the close friend. I was in love with another woman."

"And you aren't now?"

"Yes . . . no. I'm not seeing her right at the moment. I've been so obnoxious I may not be able to see her again."

"Why?"

"I think it must be more important for me to be guilty than anything else in the world, as if my life depended on it. Have you ever felt that way at all?"

Ann nodded.

"Do you feel guilty when Joseph's sick?"

Two tears, like premature bifocals, caught on the lower rims of her glasses.

"No, I feel angry."

"At him?"

"Not exactly. At the pattern of suffering, I guess. I try to believe it has some point."

"Is that why you had the baby?"

"Yes—and why I named her Joy."

"Mike wanted a daughter."

"Joseph didn't. He may have been right. Sometimes I think it's a kind of joy that shakes him apart. He tries to live his life in camouflage, which doesn't really help because, if it doesn't see him, he still sees it."

"What?"

"Wonder. He seems to be able to deal with it only when he's irrational."

"Do you ever feel crazy?"

She shook her head, and then she smiled. "I've felt wonderful."

"And you can cope with that," I said, laughing.

"Oh, yes."

"Well, apparently I can't. I wreck it."

"Maybe we all do," Ann said. "Maybe that's the pattern."

I share Ann's anger at that possibility. Perhaps it's time I felt guilty about those things I can do something about. Correction may be just a polite word for punishment, but it might also help.

Carlotta wouldn't come to dinner last night; neither would Pierre. Allen came by himself. It has always puzzled me that of all the people I know, Allen is the one I find easiest to talk to. He puts so many people off with his flippant cynicism, though it's usually directed at himself.

"This was supposed to be peace and reconciliation night," I said to him, "but I'm glad you've come alone."

"I never turn down dinner with a handsome woman," he said, "particularly if she has delicious sons."

"Actually Vic and Tony are at their grandparents' tonight."

He sighed.

Once we'd settled with drinks and Allen had paid the appropriate number of compliments to the flowers, the fire, my hair (which I've had cut), I said, "I want to talk about love—honestly."

"You're too ambitious. Only writers talk like that."

"I am trying to write."

"Oh, my God, Alma, not you! How long has this been going on? Why didn't you tell me at once? Maybe I can still help."

He did such a parody of the male friend advising abortion that I had to laugh, and his mock horror—real enough underneath his style—made it easier for me to have finally confessed to someone other than Roxanne.

"I need to do it."

"But I offered to get you a decent, quite interesting job. You go right on confusing freedom and bondage. Freedom is *money*, Alma, not art."

"Well, you manage both."

"I do not. I have never pretended to be an artist."

"You are one just the same."

"I'd rather talk about love, if those are my only two choices."

"Good. So would I. How is Roxanne?"

"Working at a drugstore, one of the few that don't stock tape recorders."

"Where is she doing her real work?"

"She isn't. She says she doesn't feel like it."

"I've been working harder than I ever have in the last month."

"Self-justification."

"What?"

"That's all art is, you know, for most anyway."

"We were going to talk about love."

"So we were."

"Would she see me again?"

"Of course. She's the same fool she was a month ago, only slightly less miserable."

"I don't know what I was doing."

"Shall I tell you? You were having a long, self-indulgent tantrum about your sullied love. I took you down to that jail to give you a taste of the reality Roxanne lives with. I thought it was time. I was wrong."

"How often have you had to bail Pierre out?"

"Once . . . after he'd been picked up in the men's room at The Bay. I took him back to the diamond department and bought him that ridiculous ring. You don't seem to believe in Roxanne's innocence."

"I should have bought her a . . . tape recorder?"

"As a start. You shouldn't punish other people for what only you feel guilty about. Roxanne doesn't feel guilty about loving you any more than Pierre feels guilty about loving me, and if someone as self-loathing as I am can cope with it, certainly you can learn to."

"How?"

"Where are you most likely to find your self-respect? Mine's in making an adequate amount of money—more than adequate, enough to buy off my guilt in ways that please Pierre."

"In writing, I suppose."

"Well, then, all right. It isn't that either of them needs buying off, but at least you could live with Roxanne. That would spare her something."

"You think I ought to earn money and support her."

"Of course I do. I've been telling you that for months."

"Why me? Why not Roxanne?"

"With a jail record and a grade eight education? Are you kidding?"

"I haven't ever even supported myself."

"Think of it as noblesse oblige. That should suit you better than women's liberation."

"I don't feel all that superior."

"Being a snob has nothing to do with feeling superior."

"What has it to do with?"

"Being afraid. You shouldn't be afraid of Roxanne. She's very gifted and very gentle."

"Are she and Pierre having an affair?"

"What has that got to do with anything?" Allen demanded.

"I don't know," I said, and got up to put dinner on the table.

It had never had anything to do with anything before, but, once Allen started talking about money, I began to think of Roxanne as an object which should come with an exclusive lifetime guarantee, very like Mike's image of me. It was the one mistake I had not already made.

"If only you were a man," Allen said as he sat down to eat, "you'd understand what I'm trying to say."

Allen does not know how often I play that game. If I

were a man, I would probably be in love with Ann or Allen. For the first time my lot as myself seems less complicated and more possible. All I really need is nerve.

All my reconciliation scenes were extravagantly penitent and entirely sexual. The reconciliation itself took place over the phone yesterday morning. When Roxanne arrived for dinner, the boys greeted her as if she'd been away on a long trip. She brought them a game involving Ping-Pong balls and cones, which they played all evening. I didn't rush them off to their rooms. Even after they went to bed, Roxanne and I sat in the living room, having a drink.

"I guess I should make the boys' lunches before we go to bed."

"I'll need one, too. I'll make the soup."

The sacramental moments in real life come over lunch boxes on kitchen counters. The ordinary for the reconciled is holy. This house is going to have two cooks and no master.

Roxanne Recording

$\mathcal{R}$OXANNE was making a sound map of the house. What other people might have fixed, a dripping tap or squeaking hinge, she listened to. What other people blanked out—the refrigerator or furnace going on, a plane passing overhead—she heard. She was interested in the difference in tone between eggshells and chicken bones in the garbage disposal. She compared the refilling times of the two toilets. She recorded the boys' feet up and down the stairs, in and out of the house, and she asked them to spend one rainy afternoon doing nothing but sitting down over and over again on different pieces of living-room furniture.

"Victor farted—on purpose," Tony said, outraged.

"It's okay; it's okay," Roxanne assured him. "Everything is okay."

One morning she was out on the front lawn, setting up the sprinkler, and heard Tony upstairs practicing his violin. She got bowing exercises through the slow rhythm of water, falling back and forth like a metronome. The next morning she recorded only the sprinkler, then only Tony's bowing. She wanted her machines to be one-voiced instruments as much as possible, not the garbage cans of sound like radios, everything jammed together at one source.

Roxanne rarely listened to recorded music. Alma's stereo gave some space for the music to happen in but still not enough. It was like putting a whole orchestra into an elevator. She would not listen to symphonies at all unless she could go to the concert and see the numbers of instruments. Listening to a record gave you no idea how many violins were trying to vanish into the same note, an odd exercise to do over and over again for centuries, the obliteration of distinctive sound for volume. But, given a choice, she'd any day rather stand on a street corner and listen to a band march by, each instrument giving her a solo a couple of steps long inside the traveling collective of sound.

Musical instruments were not of major interest to her, and she doubted that they would have been even if she'd had a childhood like Tony's, practicing an hour before breakfast every morning. She would have been out with Victor listening to the neighborhood dogs bark, throwing stones into the fishpond, talking back to the crows. And like Victor, she'd rather shout than sing. The only kind of singing she could listen to was the sort people did alone, where they might imitate for a while the unnatural pretentiousness of the professional singer but soon turn it into the sound joke it was. Most singing was like the resonance of a cleft palate or the voice of someone born profoundly deaf. Learning to sing was like learning to limp. Roxanne had refused in school to carry a tune, except in her head, where she couldn't help it. If she'd been allowed to whistle, she might have cooperated, but only on her own, not with a bunch of others.

One of Roxanne's chief difficulties in learning to under-stand and be understood was that she had so little sense of what was commonly irritating and commonly pleasurable to listen to. Mastering table manners, polite conversation, other people's orgasms, she could quickly get the balance of the natural, technical, and conventional, but it was years before she could believe that there was a common response to sound from which she was excluded. Fingernails across blackboards, cracking of finger joints, tapping of pencils—at first she made specific lists, only gradually began to gen-eralize to any extended tapping or drumming, any machine except for those specifically designed for making a sound and having no other purpose. She finally was able to con-clude that people were irritated or embarrassed or bored or frightened by any sound that was not specifically made to please, while for her that very motive in sound made it less interesting, less true. She was drawn to what she sometimes called weed sound because it was what other people would root out if they could. She named some of her pieces after weeds: dandelion, crabgrass, broom.

"The names of a lot of the sounds I love are ugly. I'm glad I'm not trying to write," she said to Alma.

"Like what?"

"Oh, like the sound of your body shifting in the tub. A sort of grunting sound."

"Have you recorded that?"

"Yes."

Roxanne was working very hard and had been for the month since she'd moved in with Alma. It was intensely interesting for her, and it also kept her from thinking over-much about Alma and herself until it would be useful to do so. Roxanne had never lived with anyone since she'd had a choice because everywhere not her own had been some sort of prison. But she'd always had a dream of living that was shared, erotic and companionable, which would simply go on and on, maybe with one other person, maybe with sev-eral.

Alma was not like anyone Roxanne had known before. When Roxanne first met her, she had been astounded by her physical beauty, the generous clarity of her face, her magnificent size, the prize specimen of a breeder god who had made sure she was fed to a fullness of breast and thigh, teeth perfectly white, skin without flaw. Roxanne's hunger was cannibal, to be satisfied whatever the price. She had known women who used husbands and children against her greed as a lover and had expected it of Alma, but Alma almost at once gave what Roxanne was intent on stealing. She had never known anyone as generous with her body and as selfish with everything else—with things, with space, with imagination, with heart. It was not conscious. For Roxanne it was oddly admirable because so uncalculating. Allen, who worked hard to maintain cynical superiority and was fond of making common cause with Alma, was guiltily generous in ways Roxanne understood. Alma's guilt was never connected with her selfishness. She wanted to be punished—even brutally punished—for the generosity of her body. That was what Roxanne couldn't stand, Alma's wanting pain as if it were something she had earned, something Roxanne owed her as an emotional debt. It was heartbreaking. It was ridiculous. Roxanne didn't understand it. She wouldn't do it.

Now Alma seemed almost to have forgotten all that. Their lovemaking, necessarily quieter, except when the boys were off for the night with their grandparents, was positively domesticated in other ways. Though Alma was shy of the lovely size of her breasts, particularly her nipples, she was learning to use a bra like a purse, something for storing valuables when she went out, and she never resisted the pleasure Roxanne took in them, whether they were working together in the kitchen or making the bed. Roxanne indulged Alma by covering her own more often in public, though it was almost like being blind or deaf to shield what she felt through her tits. Alma did not know there was anything to receive except sexual pleasure.

She was not insensitive or unintelligent. Her selfishness made her a better mother than she would have been without it, functioning for the boys in the ways she felt them an extension of herself, in material and creature comforts, healthily against them as she made it clear this was her house, her life out of which they were expected to grow.

She did regret Roxanne had no room of her own, but it did not occur to Alma to offer to have one built in the basement, where Roxanne had stored most of her belongings since there was no obvious room for anything but clothes in their bedroom. It was not their bedroom; it was Alma's, as it was Alma's house, Alma's children, Alma's life, into which Roxanne would fit if she could.

It wasn't that Alma couldn't imagine so much as that she didn't. Or did only when she was writing, when she often seemed to imagine so much that it ceased to be documentation at all.

It was comfortable, even rather grand, not only for Alma but for Roxanne. There were no calculated thoughtfulnesses that had to be noted and returned. There were very few distracting responsibilities to be assumed since it would never occur to Alma to say, in an aggrieved tone, "These are your children as much as mine," or, "This is your house as much as mine." She was surprised and pleased by Roxanne's ordinary attentions to the children, her willingness to vacuum. She was relieved that Roxanne routinely contributed to the housekeeping money. In emotional ways, Roxanne felt freer of Alma than when they had not lived together. But she had no idea either how long she would be welcome or how long she'd be able to stay. She didn't brood about it or puzzle anxiously. She noticed and worked.

Roxanne still posed for Carlotta once a week. The portrait, much referred to, had only just begun. Before, Carlotta had been sketching. She had begun working with Roxanne dressed, but after a month she said impatiently that this was work for a fashion designer or commercial artist selling shirts. Roxanne traded her clothes for closed windows. It was still very cold. She drank cups of tea and had a hot shower before she left.

Sometimes Carlotta showed her the day's sketches. In no matter what pose, the body had a still attentiveness Roxanne recognized as her own, but the skeletal length of bones was exaggerated. Carlotta was taller than Roxanne. Roxanne was wearing Carlotta's skeleton under her own inquiring flesh.

"I don't want to do that," Carlotta said. "But I'm afraid to make your bones less important than mine."

"They are less important," Roxanne said, putting her length of arm next to Carlotta's, their hands side by side. Compared to the articulate instrument that was Carlotta's hand, Roxanne's looked like a small, timid animal.

"Your flesh is human. I'm not sure mine is," Carlotta said, musing rather than judgmental.

Roxanne touched Carlotta's arm with her fingers. It was hard and cool. She wanted to see Carlotta naked, curious to know the shape of her breasts, the line of hip and thigh. Roxanne assumed Carlotta had not made love with Alma because Alma had not initiated it. Alma had not out of nearly willful ignorance but also because this minimal flesh was worn like armor and kept chilled. Carlotta turned away and reopened the windows. Dutifully Roxanne put on her pea coat and left.

She went on touching Carlotta casually when she felt like it. The temperature of Carlotta's resistance was constant, though her interest increased. Some of the poses she asked for were frankly erotic.

"For Alma's birthday," Carlotta said wryly.

The weekly present Carlotta was sending Alma was Roxanne's intense sexual energy, and Roxanne suspected that was all Alma would get.

When she herself was exasperated with Alma and refusing to see her, Roxanne asked, "Why are *you* so angry with Alma?"

"She's convenient to be angry with. She's near enough to

know that I am, and she cares . . . not enough, of course."

"And Mike isn't?"

"Isn't he ever going to come back?"

"I don't know. He's asked for the boys for the summer. If Alma agrees to that, he may come to get them."

"And her, too?"

"I don't think so," Roxanne said.

"He would if he could, even now."

"Do you really want him?"

Carlotta stopped her more and more agitated sketching and looked at Roxanne as if she had just arrived in the room to interrupt Carlotta's work. Roxanne was disconcerted by the shift, nearly embarrassed.

"I've always been jealous of her. Why shouldn't I have at least what she doesn't want? But he's nothing but crumbs from her table; that's all that's left of him."

Carlotta was crying, sounds more frustrated than grieving. Roxanne would have gone to her then if she hadn't felt she would be only more crumbs until Carlotta raged, "Why don't any of you ever want me?"

Naked, their bodies were remarkably similar except in skin tone and hair color, but Carlotta was not interested in posing for Roxanne. Her appetite was impatient, melodramatic, sex a contending struggle, full of squeals and hisses, until for Roxanne it was rather grandly funny. She felt like the driver of one of those bumper cars at the Pacific National Exhibition, crashing into Carlotta over and over again until she was trapped, stalled, and whimpering at the gentleness Roxanne forced on her.

"I won't come. I won't come," she chanted, and Roxanne listened to the changing rhythms of it, letting it guide the pressure and rhythm of her tongue until she felt Carlotta coming and held her, gripped like a bowling ball that couldn't roll away.

There were three or four occasions like the first one before Carlotta made love to Roxanne in return, with a rollercoaster wildness and uncertainty, rushing over and over again toward climaxes that dropped away in violent changes of direction, until Roxanne was nearly sick with hilarity, and Carlotta moaned and swayed like a trestle about to collapse.

"This is terrible, hard work," Carlotta said, "and I'm no good at it."

Roxanne laughed and hugged her. "We're not in jail. You don't have to."

"Anyway, it gets in the way of work. We don't have time for it."

Carlotta was more cheerful, even humored, than she had been before as if some point had been proved and could now be let go. The drawings began to look more like Roxanne in bone as well as stance. Before Roxanne moved in with Alma, she had put her clothes back on for the portrait Carlotta could now paint.

Roxanne told Alma nothing about Carlotta. She did not trust Alma's use of such information, which might, in her hands, turn into some new form of self-punishment.

The only person she did talk to was Pierre, who had an elaborate understanding of the personal, being interested in nearly nothing else. She and Pierre shared attitudes which were foreign to the others.

"Allen says the gods are not supposed to be moral, just larger than life. That's why I'm always attracted to big men. It doesn't matter about people's flaws, which, after all, are in proportion to their size."

Pierre didn't forgive Allen his absences, his cruelties, his pride. Pierre accepted them, often loudly complaining but neither expecting nor desiring reform. Allen wouldn't be Allen without them any more than Alma would be Alma without her monumental selfishness and misplaced guilt.

"There's no point in telling either of them the truth," Pierre explained. "I would screw you if I absolutely had to."

"Of course," Roxanne agreed, as little able to imagine it as he was.

"It's not necessary. He likes to imagine that he seduces

me away from heterosexuality every time he comes home. If it made me more attractive to him, I'd not only pretend to keep a harem, I'd have one."

It was a fiction modestly costly for Roxanne since Alma got no pleasure from pretending to rescue Roxanne from Pierre and would have been reassured to know it wasn't necessary, but Roxanne had to be loyal to Pierre, who was like a younger sibling, sister and brother in one.

"What Allen doesn't understand is that we need taboos just like anyone else. Simply because I didn't grow up with a sister I couldn't screw doesn't mean I can now or want to, any more than he wants the women he squires around. Does Alma ever pretend she's having an affair with him?"

"No," Roxanne said. "She does think he's attractive."

"I should think so!"

Pierre loved any excuse to talk about how attractive Allen was, from the way his hair grew at the back of his neck to the arch of his beautiful foot.

His worship of Allen's body was very like what Roxanne felt for Alma's, a perpetually renewing wonder that was joyful and holy. She and Pierre had been born again in the same faith. They celebrated and suffered as true believers.

"They don't love us the way we love them, of course. Allen is too much of a man; Alma is too much of a woman."

Roxanne at that kind of invitation took her turn to praise that too much of a woman, Alma. Pierre was more sympathetic to Roxanne's passion unrequited than he was to her present sexual pleasure. Alma could be interesting to him only as the embodiment of an idea of love, not as a female body, about which he had deep aesthetic reservations.

"I'd rather not lie," Roxanne said, "and I'd like to be happy."

Pierre lifted his eyebrows.

"I don't lie to you," Roxanne continued.

"You're not in love with me."

"That's not the reason. She's so safe she doesn't know what's dangerous."

"I know."

"I worship that."

"I know."

"She doesn't go out, you see. When she asks me about my day, I have to lie or skip parts. She doesn't know that every day is a trail of dead cats, arrests, whatever. . . . You know that. That's why you don't go out. I don't surprise you."

"No, but, if Allen was tight with money and made me go out to work, I'd think he didn't really care."

"I don't mind working."

"Well, at least you can stop worrying about dying alone, which is more comfort than Allen gives me."

"She doesn't ever think about dying."

"Neither does he," Pierre said, "except for committing suicide, and he thinks that is a matter of choice."

"If I ever told her we're all dying of cancer, she'd think I was crazy."

"Do you think I can say that to Allen? He couldn't live with it. He just couldn't. He thinks I'm paranoid because I won't let him have his shaving cream in aerosol cans."

"I don't say why about things like that. I just say I don't like it, whatever it is, and she throws it out. I think she thinks I'm whimsical."

"It's a trick to be a bodyguard for someone who doesn't know it."

"Yes, it is."

"But don't get uptight about it," Pierre insisted.

"I'd like to be happy."

"You are, compared to me."

Roxanne was certainly neither bored nor lonely. Her lack of equipment or place to work daunted her only briefly. Since she could collect but couldn't arrange the sounds of the house, she had simply to think about it. In thinking, she discovered the house too small for the mapping she wanted to do. So was the neighborhood. Roxanne wanted to make a sound map of the city. The moment that idea occurred to her, she realized that it was a project she was already in the middle of. If only she could hear what she already had recorded on those thousands of feet of tape stored in Alma's basement, she would know exactly what to do. Instead she had to remember, make notes, describe.

"I need that wall," she said to Alma as they lay in bed early one morning.

"What for?"

"A map of Vancouver."

"What will you do about the closet door?"

"Include it."

"You're going to draw right on the wall?"

Roxanne got out of bed, found a pencil, and then, kneeling on her own pillow, she drew over the headboard a small compass. Then she handed the pencil to Alma.

"You're daring me."

"Yes."

"You don't do that to a house you own. You do it to someplace else."

"It's your house," Roxanne said. "You can do what you want."

"But *you* want to draw on the wall."

"Yes."

Alma didn't agree then. She brought it up again at breakfast after the boys had left for school and was still undecided when Roxanne left for work. If Roxanne hadn't had good training in foster homes, where it was made just as clear that she had no property rights, she might have been more exasperated with Alma than she was. If Roxanne had asked to tattoo obscene poems down the insides of Alma's thighs, she would have stretched out naked and waited. To touch her bedroom wall was another matter.

"How do you feel about the garage door?" Roxanne asked that night at dinner.

The boys were puzzled. Alma explained to them, "Roxanne wants to make a big map of Vancouver, and I don't think it ought to be in my bedroom."

"Do it in my room," Victor suggested. "I like maps."

"She'd never get in over the junk."

"Well, what about the garage door?" Tony asked.

"It seems awfully public," Alma said.

"You let Daddy work in the shed," Victor said.

"Daddy had a studio," Tony said.

"I just need a wall," Roxanne said.

"Well, why not right here?" Alma suggested, making a nervous gesture at the dining-room wall.

That evening Roxanne established the basic grid of streets across the wall she faced domestically twice a day. It would have been better if she could have wakened to it every morning, but, if she got up as soon as she woke, she could work awhile before breakfast. At first she intended only to make notes, a word or two to remind her of the sound she had recorded or wanted to record, but because the wall was first an issue and then a curiosity, Roxanne began to see the map as a thing in itself as well as a score for work to be done. She cut pictures out of magazines, everything from air-conditioning units to national flags. Directions were color-coded, green to indicate what did happen on that particular corner, red to indicate what might happen, gold to suggest what should happen.

"Are you trying to make it look the way it's going to sound?" Tony asked.

"Not exactly," Roxanne said. "I'm just trying to see what it sounds like."

"Oh." He was sitting at the dining-room table, cutting out a picture of the B.C. Hydro building. "Is it going to happen where you show it on the map or somewhere all at once like at the Playhouse?"

"I don't know," Roxanne said.

"It's actually good-looking," Alma said as she set the table for dinner.

They were expecting Allen and Pierre, and for the first time Roxanne was uneasy about the map. Alma's parents had seen it; so had Ann Rabinowitz, and they had all responded with the same bland incomprehension to which Roxanne did not have to reply. Pierre would be playful, as he always was about her projects, and she could handle that, but Allen would see the entirely unrealistic scope of it and know that she was serious. He was quite willing to treat her like a precocious child, though they were the same age, but Roxanne doubted that he'd accept the idea that she was ready to do something with her work. She wasn't sure herself, partly because she had no idea how it could be practically realized. Still, at this point she did not want to be discouraged. She felt the way Alma did about her stories, that she wasn't sure they were good enough to stand rejection. Roxanne asked Alma to seat Allen with his back to that wall.

Allen and Pierre hadn't been there five minutes before Tony said, "Can I show them your wall, Roxanne?"

She hadn't realized until then that Tony was seriously involved. As he explained the images, the color coding, he was much clearer than she could have been, able to give some sense of the map as map, as score, as a number of possibilities, and his audience was far more attentive to him than they would have been to her.

Allen stepped back and looked at Roxanne. "Are you really going to do this?"

She shrugged, aware of how impossible the whole thing really was. If you could get jailed for two years for playing someone else's equipment after store hours, what would you get for playing a whole city?

"I guess it's private property."

"What is?" Allen asked.

"The city . . . the streets and all."

"No, it's not," Tony said, indignant. "It belongs to everyone."

"Do you know any of the people in the music business?" Allen asked.

"No," Roxanne said. "I'm not really interested in music. I'm interested in sound."

"That doesn't matter. What you need is money—obviously, lots of it."

"Not really all that much—if I had the machines—a place to work."

"Alma, why hasn't Roxanne a place to work?"

"She has. She wanted a wall; here's the wall."

Allen and Pierre both laughed, and Roxanne couldn't resist a smile. What was so obvious to everyone else—Alma's reluctance to give an inch—she didn't recognize at all.

Before the evening was over, they had explored the basement, paced out a workshop area, and Allen had extracted a promise from Alma that she would pay for the materials if the work was volunteered.

"You don't know how to do things like that, do you?" Alma asked him.

"No, of course not. I play at being butch, but I don't work at it."

"Joseph will do it," Pierre said.

"Oh, I couldn't have Joseph . . ." Alma began.

"He needs something to do while he can't teach."

"There must be plenty of things for him to do . . ."

Alma didn't want Joseph in the house. Allen was going to insist. As he and Alma grew closer, he bullied her more frequently and successfully. She gave in to give in, not because she agreed with Allen, and that pleased him. Roxanne would almost always rather give up her own way than be accompanied reluctantly. But Alma did need bullying since she did not really know about needs other than her own. She had to be told that you let a crazy friend help you, whether you wanted to or not, simply because he happened to be on the other end of the teeter-totter.

"I don't really know how to handle him," Alma confessed. "He's never really liked me, and he doesn't approve of us. Honestly, sometimes Allen goes too far."

"I'm very pleased about the workroom," Roxanne said.

"Of course, you are. I don't know why we didn't think of it months ago."

"It will give Joseph a chance to like you."

"I doubt that. You know, I don't really think I understand men at all, except for men like Allen. They always seem to be disapproving of something and expecting an apology. Who's Joseph to disapprove of me?"

He came, arriving while everyone was still at breakfast. The matter with Joseph, Roxanne and Pierre had long ago decided, was that he knew and pretended he didn't. He knew everyone was dying of cancer, and he knew there was a point to being careful and loving. He couldn't stand to know. Now mostly he didn't have to pretend because he did forget, really forget, but forgetting wasn't the same as not knowing, like Allen and Alma. Only real ignorance could make you strong. Joseph lacked that.

"I want to tell you something I just remembered, Roxanne," he said, smiling at her. "I just remembered that walk we took across the bridge while you listened to the traffic. Do you still listen to the traffic?"

"Yes."

He laughed his single note of distress.

"I remember because the baby does, too. She stands on the parking strip and claps after a car goes by."

"Funny!" Victor judged.

"Before babies learn to talk," Tony said, "they can hear everything."

"Where did you learn that?" Alma asked.

"I don't know—*Mary Poppins*? Didn't the babies understand the birds?"

"They do say," Alma told him, "that babies make every sound and then only remember and repeat sounds they hear back. That's why, for instance, Pierre forgets his *th*'s. He didn't hear them as a baby when he was learning French."

Roxanne had a curious, faint memory of lying in an enclosed space, seeing nothing but the underedge of a window sill and a ceiling, listening not to a human voice but to a myriad of sounds coming in from outside. The world outside must have been her teacher, and she was still struggling to speak her own mother tongue.

"Nothing is really forgotten," Joseph said. "I've been reassured."

It was not reassuring. Fortunately or not, the bizarre events of any day in the drugstore where she worked distracted Roxanne from worry about anyone not in her presence. Chewing gum, cigarettes, prescriptions for antibiotics, sex magazines, deodorants, eyebrow pencils, vibrators—life is habit-forming, even for the old woman over there by the greeting cards, grunting out pungent turds while she looks for a birthday card for her grandson. Roxanne must clean up after her quickly before someone decides to lock the old lady up. No one gets indignant about dogs, which not only shit but nose each other's private parts just to say hello, but let the manager catch a couple of kids feeling each other up over the magazine rack, and he calls the RCMP.

Roxanne had to work as hard to figure out other people's morality as she did their taste in sound. The first principle was not to assume that what shocked and outraged people was something they didn't do themselves. The manager, for instance, finger-fucked the cashier every time there was a slow couple of minutes. Roxanne didn't object to it. It seemed no more offensive than rubbing a cat's ears or scratching the base of its tail, but you could be arrested for doing it in public, and she'd been jailed for doing it in private before she was twenty-one. Yet it was what everyone wanted, in jail or out of it, a little wild comfort of one sort or another. In a humane society you wouldn't punish people able to find their own; you'd help those who couldn't . . . children, crazy people, old people. But Roxanne knew better. She was very careful to be of no real help to anyone while she was at work.

She had nearly forgotten the dangers at home when she walked in not only to Joseph having a cup of coffee at the dining-room table but to Mike, Victor balancing on the back of his father's chair, Tony standing protectively by Roxanne's wall.

"Where's Alma?"

"In her room," Tony said.

Roxanne acknowledged no one as she went through the room. She found Alma staring out the window at the city.

"When did he arrive?"

"About an hour ago," Alma said, "just after the boys got home."

"It's only the first of June."

"He said he wanted time to look around the old town before he took the boys south."

"Oh."

"Oh, Roxanne, it's terrible, just terrible. When he sat down at the table with Joseph, it was as if the last two years hadn't happened. . . ."

"You don't want to go back to him, do you?"

"Of course, I don't, but don't you see, if you were a man, he wouldn't dare come in like this, expecting me to make him coffee, settling to talk with Joseph as if he were in his own house. And you wouldn't just stand there asking stupid questions . . . just like a woman!"

"I am a woman," Roxanne said wearily.

"Oh, darling, what are we going to do?"

"What do we have to do?"

"Will you stop asking questions, for God's sake, and tell me what to do?"

"I'm trying to say we don't have to do anything except be civil to him when he's here to see the boys. If he hangs around too much, tell him you have work to do."

"He looks so . . . well."

"Good."

"Did you see his car?"

"I came the back way," Roxanne said, looking out the window to which Alma nodded.

There was a sage green Lincoln Continental parked in

front of the house. To Roxanne it was nothing but a cancerous lump in his ego, but it was obvious that Alma was admiring it.

"You ought to go back downstairs," Roxanne said, trying to sound both matter-of-fact and decisive. "I need to change out of my uniform."

"Shall I ask him to dinner?"

I don't know—Play it by ear— Do you want to?— No— Yes— It doesn't matter. Nothing that occurred to Roxanne to say was useful. She shrugged.

"Oh, shit!" Alma said, and slammed the door as she went out.

Roxanne got out of the institution green she wore all day and put on her most transparent shirt, her lowest-slung pair of trousers, and her pearl. She knew, if Mike had come to buy Alma back, she might be tempted not by the money itself but by the respectability of it. Roxanne could compete with respectability only by offending it; she needed to be as visible as possible.

Joseph was leaving as Roxanne arrived back downstairs.

"I'll come by to give you a hand tomorrow," Mike was saying. "We could get it done in a day together."

When Joseph had left, Mike said, "He's not in very good shape, is he? It's nice of him to give you girls a hand. I did as much for him when he was away, but still . . . Well, poor guy. So, how about I take you all out to dinner?"

"Funny!" Victor said.

"You don't change much, *Funny!*"

"You have," Tony said quietly.

"Have I?" Mike asked, smiling.

He was even better-looking, his dark desert tan making his teeth all the whiter, his eyes bright with a warmer fire. He was dressed casually but expensively, his shirt the sort Pierre bought imitations of from Hong Kong, his shoes handmade.

"You never took us out to dinner before."

"Well, I lived with you, son. That was different."

Alma sat in front with Mike, Roxanne with the boys in the back seat of the Lincoln. Mike didn't stop Vic from trying every button within reach, even played a teasing game with him by locking his door and closing his window from the master controls. Tony sat very still and straight.

"You know, I thought I'd hate working for a living— well, seriously. I love it."

"It certainly agrees with you," Alma said.

"Does, doesn't it?" He grinned at her.

Roxanne had been afraid but not jealous of Mike when he was still Alma's husband. At that time she knew he could kill either of them, and that was the only way he could have interfered with their relationship. But it was now not only domesticated but complicated by unsatisfied needs and subtle messages. Mike might enjoy meting out the sexual punishment Roxanne had refused, and Alma could still be roused by guilt to want it.

She was no less magnificent than he. Roxanne had got used to Alma's loss of weight and knew being slender became her. Her face, which could be a bland mask when Roxanne first knew her, most often when Mike was around, rarely took on that defense now. She had learned to say and show more often what she felt. Now it was perfectly easy for Mike to read there that he pleased her. Roxanne's cunt ached, so did the palms of her hands. She leaned on them.

"Seafood all right?" Mike asked. "Damn few fish on the desert."

He indulged the glutton in Victor as they competed to see who could eat the most steamed clams. He encouraged Tony's curiosity about an oyster dish he hadn't tried. He was as attentive over Alma's dinner as if she'd been a nursing mother. Roxanne, who knew shellfish were the sewers of the sea, ordered a dish which had both clams and oysters, a suicidal gesture only Pierre could have appreciated, and it was only a gesture because she could not eat.

"Well, I don't know why I was so thrown this afternoon," Alma said as she began to undress. "I was even wearing a bra because Joseph was around. I think Mike Trasco has turned into a human being."

Roxanne took a fistful of Alma's radiant hair and pulled, hard.

"Hey."

"I'll fist-fuck if I have to," Roxanne said.

"Oh, love, love, don't be silly. These are yours; this is yours. He's always appealed to my vanity, but you're my addiction. You know that. I tried to swear off, remember? I couldn't."

"I'm your friend."

"Of course you are, and my lover and my beloved, and I know you don't like seafood, but oysters for me are like first-course sex with you, and I've been hungry for you all evening . . ."

Her lies were like Roxanne's own, motivated by love, and Roxanne understood them. If she was not, in fact, the cause of Alma's ready wetness, she was its welcome recipient. Alma was not at this moment thinking of Mike sucking her cunt, rimming her anus, preparing her for multiples of coming. Her mouth and hands were busy with the same plans for Roxanne, delicate, shocking, sure.

"Sweet woman."

"Sweet woman."

Out of bed, the ache returned, not just when Mike was around. Roxanne ached all day simply with the possibility of his presence. It was a great relief to her that her workroom was finished in a couple of days, but anytime the boys were home Mike had excuse enough to be there. Alma did nothing to discourage him.

"It's such a relief simply to like the man," she explained. "It makes me feel less crazy to have married him."

Crazy to have divorced him? Roxanne had stopped asking questions. The sexual reassurance she insisted on, Alma gave her without grudge, but lying naked in Roxanne's arms, Alma could still talk about Mike, his new confident kindness.

"He doesn't even object to Tony's violin."

"He calls him owl eyes," Roxanne countered, knowing that here, too, it was her jealousy that spoke; though Tony was far more cautious with his father than Victor, neither boy had eyes for anyone else.

"As a joke. Tony's really looking forward to the summer. It sounds horribly hot to me. Mike says the best time to go is winter. We all might go down for Christmas."

Roxanne assumed that she was not part of that all. She said nothing.

She was not surprised to come home to an empty house and a note on the dining-room table. Mike had taken them out for dinner and to the movies. Alma knew Roxanne would love an evening to herself to move into her workroom. She did go down to the basement, but the place smelled of Mike, and the empty house above her weighed too many aching tons.

She phoned Pierre.

"I'll set another place at the table and give you rats' tails on toast. Allen will come get you."

Allen greeted her with "You must be a mind reader. I'm just home from Ottawa, where I got a lot of good advice. We're going to get you a Canada Council grant."

"What for?"

"To go on with your project, your sound map, whatever you call it."

"I call it 'Mother Tongue,'" Roxanne said.

"Sexist for my taste."

Roxanne managed a half smile.

"I'm warning you," Allen said. "We're going to cheer you up. Before the evening is over, you'll forget Mike Trasco exists. But while you still remember, let me tell you this: she'll never go back to him."

"Why are you so sure?"

"She doesn't need the money; she doesn't want the man. And, though she doesn't think it's quite nice, she happens to be in love with you."

"The workroom is finished. He helped Joseph."

"Good."

There was a strained energy in Allen's voice. Roxanne really wished he hadn't been at home. With Pierre she could have wept and raged and despaired, and his comfort would have been to be as helpless as she was. Allen couldn't stand things gone wrong. He had to fix whatever it was, and the more tired and pressed he was, the more responsibility he seemed to feel. For his sake, she would have to pretend to forget Mike for the evening. Though that would have been a relief, dropping her guard in that way seemed too dangerous. As long as she kept him locked in the vise of her attention, he couldn't take Alma from her.

Once Pierre's delicious dinner, which looked planned for three weeks in advance, had been enjoyed in the sort of leisure only men seemed able to command for a meal, Allen spread the Canada Council forms on the table.

"Tony talked very well the other night, but now you've got to talk. I was going to get Alma to write this up, but we'll have to ourselves."

"I don't know anyone to ask for letters," Roxanne objected, daunted by the whole idea of a grant.

"I've solved that. It's multimedia enough so that I can write one of them, and Carlotta can write one, and I've got some names of people involved in experimental music here in town. The only problem is presenting it clearly. I'll take a picture of the wall, but you've got to go on from there."

"How can I cost it? I haven't the first notion . . ."

"Roxanne," Allen said, taking her shoulders, "stop that! You know the machines you need; you know what they cost. This is a minibudget to get enough done so that you can give people some idea . . ."

"They'll look up and see I have a record . . ."

"And that will be all the more reason for giving you the money. Artists are supposed to be outlaws. It's just clerks in stores who're not."

"But what I'm doing is crazy," Roxanne protested.

"Artists are supposed to be crazy."

"You're a genius, Roxanne," Pierre said. "All Allen wants you to do is admit it."

Confessing on a paper to be sent to an agent of the federal government what she would like to do to Vancouver was like submitting a master plan for robbing every bank in town. If she had to tell the truth, she had in mind a cast of thousands, involving everyone from schoolchildren to professionals. She wanted marching bands of tape recorders; she wanted fifty oboes on fifty different street corners, playing fifty different national anthems in their natural tone of complaint. And that was just the beginning. She wanted this performance to go on for days, for weeks, forever, a display of sound as permanent as sculpture which would transform the city.

"Surely it's against the law?" she asked.

"You simply don't say it's a revolution," Allen said, scribbling notes as she talked.

"But it's disturbing the peace."

"Never mind. Never mind."

They were drinking vodka, and Pierre didn't let the glasses sit empty. Roxanne drank as quickly as Allen without his habit or stamina, and she was also excited. Not only Mike but Alma receded from her mind. Roxanne was cheerfully drunk by the time Allen delivered her home, and it was well after midnight. She did notice, with relief, that Mike's car was nowhere around.

"Where on earth have you been?" Alma demanded.

"With Allen and Pierre."

"I bet!"

"Where else would I be?"

"In bed with Carlotta."

"What?"

"You cheap little cheat! Did you think I wouldn't find out?"

"It happened months ago before I moved in here. It hasn't anything to do with anything."

"How was she?"

Roxanne took a deep breath, knowing it was only the vodka that tempted her to say how hugely funny and really quite bad sex had been with Carlotta, how finally daunted Carlotta had been at the hard work of Roxanne's body. Alma didn't want to know.

"I spent the evening filling out an application for a Canada Council grant. It's Allen's idea. I think it's probably crazy."

"I said, 'How was she?' "

"That's the sort of thing you need to find out for yourself."

"But it's much quicker to benefit from your experience . . . and Mike's. He said she wasn't bad at all, but she didn't like you much."

"This is a silly conversation. Come to bed."

"Don't get near me."

Alma's eyes, in which Roxanne could swim naked, now tried to freeze her out, pale and hard-surfaced as ice.

"What's really the matter?"

"And did Pierre have his bit of a bugger tonight?"

At such an accusation from Allen, Pierre would have waggled his behind. Roxanne knew she should do something sexual, preferably cruel, at least assertive. She couldn't. She felt a pitying sympathy for them both as if she were a third party watching this scene.

"Do you ache all day the way I do?" Roxanne asked. "I didn't know before that jealousy hurts . . . physically."

"What have you got to be jealous about?" Alma asked sarcastically.

"Nothing probably," Roxanne admitted. "But I keep hurting."

"What would you have me do . . . not see him? It's hard enough on the boys as it is without my making it worse. At least they can see there's no animosity between Mike and me."

"So different from you and me."

"Why did you do that to me?"

"I didn't do anything to you. I wasn't even seeing you."

"That's a lie. She didn't finish the portrait until well after you moved in."

"All right, it's a lie, or a sort of a lie. I'd rather not lie."

"I can't stand it."

"Neither of us can," Roxanne said.

She should have been able to reach out to Alma. Instead, Roxanne went woodenly out of the room and upstairs to bed. The vodka was a merciful sedative. She had been deeply asleep when she was roused by Alma's rough love-making, crude name-calling, and tears which came so seldom, always in the dark. If only they could be happy.

It was the night before Tony and Victor were to leave for Arizona. Victor was manic with nervous excitement, Tony quiet with apprehension. Alma was being overly ordinary with them.

"I'm going to miss you guys," Roxanne finally felt obliged to say.

"I bet!" Victor said.

"I'm not kidding. Two months is a long time."

"When your workroom is all set up, can I help with the tape recorders and stuff?" Tony asked.

"Sure."

"Are you going to make a movie?" Victor asked.

"I hadn't planned to."

"To go with the sound track, you know? I'd be in it," Vic offered, and demonstrated some of the monstrous faces and horrifying deaths he was willing to perform.

"Vic, Roxanne is serious," Tony said.

"Roxanne is *funny!*"

"Enough, Victor!" Alma ordered. "You carry on like that, and your father will kill you."

"He didn't hit me once . . . not all the time he's been here. You're the mean one. Anyway, I can hit him back."

"I wouldn't advise it," Alma said.

"You're a girl-fucker!" Victor shouted in high good spirits, and then laughed into the tense silence he had created.

Alma hit him hard in the face. He had a startled, puzzled look as his tongue tasted blood from his nose.

"Don't," Roxanne said, moving between Alma and her younger son.

Later Roxanne wondered whether they would have sorted it out better if she hadn't interfered. As it was, Alma left the room, and Roxanne cleaned up Victor's face. She wanted to talk with him. She wanted to say, "The right word is lesbian, but most people still think that's as bad as girl-fucker. All either of them means is that your mother and I love each other, and that's a good thing." Then she could have told him how to apologize in a way that he could understand. But Victor was not Roxanne's child, and Roxanne's feelings were very different from Alma's. Roxanne was often frightened; she was never ashamed. She didn't say anything, and he sent himself to his room as soon as the nosebleed was under control.

"He didn't mean anything. It's just a dumb thing he heard."

"I know he didn't," Roxanne said.

"Is Mother going to want us back?"

"Tony, the problem is she doesn't want you to go. Neither do I, except it will be fun for you to see Arizona and do things with your dad."

"Why did she hit Vic like that?"

"She was scared."

"Of Vic?"

"Of what the world teaches him."

"I don't learn it."

"I know you don't, and I'm glad."

Alma had no conversation of the sort with either son. The farewell in the morning was stiff with unforgiven misunderstandings, Alma playing the abused and deserted woman, the boys marchers into a forced exile. Only Mike was absolutely cheerful.

As the Lincoln finally pulled away, Alma turned to Roxanne and said, "Don't go to work today. Tell them you're sick or something. I can't stay here alone."

Roxanne agreed readily enough.

"We'll take a picnic and go to the beach," Alma said.

It was a beautiful day. A lot of other people had had the same idea, mostly mothers of preschool children and the unemployed. Alma stripped down to a black bikini, oiled herself, and said, "I bought this for you. Do you like it?" Alma said that of anything new she put on. Roxanne didn't own a bathing suit.

"Yes," Roxanne said.

"No, you'd rather be at Wreck Beach."

"No."

"Have you ever been?"

It was going to be one of those sexual conversations which might set a lovely erotic tone to the whole day but could as easily tip into angry accusations.

"Would you like to go?" Roxanne asked.

"I feel safer among the young mothers," Alma decided. "But we ought to do something a little wild to celebrate our freedom, don't you think?"

Roxanne knew Alma was feeling no more like celebrating than Roxanne did.

"Most of the nudes at Wreck Beach are men."

"So you have been," Alma said.

"Once as Pierre's bodyguard."

"Do people . . . do anything?"

"Mostly look at each other. There are always a few people tangled up in blankets or sleeping bags."

"Would you like to do that?"

"Not at Wreck Beach."

"I want to do something special with you like fuck on the beach or go to a gay bar."

"Why those things?" Roxanne asked.

"I want you to know I don't care."

"Don't care?"

"Next time I'll break his jaw if I have to."

"Oh, Alma, he's just a little boy."

"Growing up to be a man as foulmouthed as his father."

Roxanne savored that moment of Alma's hostility toward Mike, but she had to rescue Victor from it.

"I wanted to talk with him," Roxanne said. "We really should talk to them both. We should do it together."

"Tell them we're girl-fuckers?" Alma asked lightly.

"Tell them we love each other."

"It's none of their damned business," Alma said.

They watched a toddler, running with diapers at half-mast away from a laughing mother toward the water.

"You lose them anyway," Alma said. "That's the whole point."

"Are you afraid Mike won't send them back?" Roxanne asked.

"Yes . . . and no. You aren't being very good at my mood today, darling. I want to forget I *am* a mother. I want to be an irresistibly wicked woman in an amusing and relatively safe way."

The bars were too rough for Alma to enjoy being irresistible. The coffeehouses catered to fifteen-year-olds, so Alma couldn't help be reminded that she was a mother. The only possibility was finding a poetry reading or concert that would attract a lot of women and perhaps develop into a party afterward. Roxanne knew enough women from the women's meetings she had gone to to get a party started, but not on a weeknight in summer.

"You'll have to give me some time. There's no place to go except on weekends."

"I want to *be* a lesbian," Alma said, rolling over on her stomach. "Oil my back."

Roxanne obeyed and let a buggering finger play for a good five minutes in full view of young mothers who simply would not notice anything outlandish or indecent going on on their part of the beach. It frightened her badly, but it also made her drunk with lusting gratitude that this absolutely magnificent woman wanted her not only in secret but out in the bright light of day, to which Alma, out of wonderful ignorance, was immune. She did not know she could be not only exposed but arrested.

Where they couldn't be comfortable was at home. It was contaminated with the boys' absence.

"I don't care where we go, just out," Alma said.

No matter where they went, whether to the movies or swimming, they had to deal with men wanting to pick them up.

"This has never happened to me before in my life," Alma said.

"Kids are great bodyguards," Roxanne said.

"Or husbands."

Roxanne found in the paper an announcement of a talk at UBC in the Student Union Building. "Women's Liberation—Where Now?" She tried not to take the title personally. If she couldn't protect Alma from men on the make, Roxanne could provide more seductive alternatives.

"You mean that's where lesbians go on a Friday night?"

"The more interesting ones."

"Will everyone be a lesbian?"

"No."

"How will I tell?"

"Some of them wear buttons."

"What will I wear?"

Roxanne was nearly always caught off guard by Alma's sudden appearance in any room. She had a style, a presence that attracted attention—her height, her fairness, her simply expensive clothes, the serene planes of her face. Tonight she was in beige raw silk, matching trousers and tailored shirt, thongs on her long, elegant feet. Her ring was a brown sapphire. Roxanne anticipated the stir Alma would cause with pride and apprehension.

There were perhaps seventy women in a room casually arranged for a talk, some straight chairs fanned across the center of the room unoccupied. Everyone sitting down had chosen the couches along two walls of the room. There was no obvious speaker's chair or table. Amiable nods turned into welcoming smiles when it was clear Roxanne was with the woman they had never seen before. Roxanne had to introduce Alma to half a dozen women before they could sit down.

"Who are they all?" Alma asked.

"Judy's a painter; Ann works for CBC; Shelagh's with the human rights office; Dadie's a grad student in sociology."

"How do you know them?"

Roxanne by now was not surprised by Alma's surprise. The fact that Roxanne had been to jail so colored Alma's vision of her past that Roxanne had given up trying to set the record straight. It was a source of mild disappointment to Alma that Roxanne didn't run with a ring of lesbian prostitutes in her spare time.

"The Women's Caucus downtown," Roxanne said.

"There *is* a woman wearing a button. You weren't kidding!"

A woman sitting on the other side of Alma asked, "Who is this very famous feminist speaker from Toronto nobody's ever heard of?"

"She's my sister's sociology prof at York," someone else replied.

"She's *my* sister's ex-lover."

"It should have said so in the *Sun*," the first speaker concluded.

Roxanne smiled. She had forgotten how wryly friendly and kindly rude these women could be. She hadn't made friends with them exactly, but, when she was lonely, she could drift into their headquarters and always find something to do, mailings to get out, posters to make, babies to tend. Maybe there were still dances to go to where, even alone, you could make a good evening, if you were willing to ask for it. Would Alma like to go to a dance?

The speaker arrived. Roxanne was more and more often surprised to find the authorities much younger than she was. This professor might have been twenty-five. She was very good-looking. She was kissing everyone who was interested.

"*She*'s gay?" Alma whispered.

It was not a particularly interesting talk, mostly about women's co-ops, credit unions, banks. Roxanne wished she could interest herself in money, but she was no better at concentrating on it than she was on keeping her mind blank. She listened to the room, the small sounds of restless liveliness women make when they are bored and excited. Alma, beside her, did not move; she was actually listening.

"But that's exactly what's the matter with me," Alma said excitedly the moment the lecture came to an end. "She understands me completely. It's what Allen has been trying to tell me for years: money is freedom. She's right. She's absolutely right. We have to get our hands on money; that's all there is to it. Oh, I want to meet her. Do you think we could just go up and introduce ourselves? I just have to say to her . . ."

"Of course," Roxanne said.

Dadie, the graduate student, caught Roxanne's arm and held her back from following Alma up to the speaker. "There's a party at my place after this if you and your friend . . . ?"

"We'd like that. Thanks."

"I've lost track of you since you left the record store," Ann of CBC said.

"I've got a job out in Point Grey now."

"She new in town?"

"No," Roxanne said. "She grew up here."

"She doesn't look . . . local."

Before the evening was over, Roxanne felt like a sort of press secretary for Alma. People seemed shy to approach her directly and so asked their questions of Roxanne instead. Alma was unaware of anyone but the professor, at whose feet she sat, too busy admiring to care whether she was being admired or not.

"Oh, I wish she taught at UBC," Alma said as they finally drove home. "I don't think I've ever met anyone who understood me like that. I feel as if my life had been changed. Didn't she impress you at all?"

"She's very good-looking," Roxanne said, wanting to give her full marks where she could. "I really don't understand economics, politics . . ."

"Do you want to clerk in a drugstore all your life?"

"Might deliver mail for a change," Roxanne admitted. "One way of paying the rent is much the same as another —oh, not if you're educated, I guess."

"But it doesn't pay anything. You can't do what you want to do without money. And if Allen hadn't thought of it, you never would have applied for a Canada Council."

"I don't really want that grant."

"Oh, if only you'd listened tonight, you're doing just what she said we do, backing away from money because it's power, and we're all terrified of power. Money's turned Mike into a human being; he doesn't have to pretend to have power he doesn't have. With money, Roxanne, you'd be *somebody*."

Roxanne remembered a saying she'd learned from a black friend in jail: "I know I'm somebody because God didn't make no junk." It was not a time to tell Alma about it.

"That doesn't matter to me either."

"What *does* matter to you?" Alma demanded.

"You, the boys, friends, my tape recorder . . ."

"Yes, but beyond that . . . there is something."

Alma wanted to look for it in other lectures, readings, parties. She began to send out manuscripts of her stories and drop hints about her writing until someone suggested that she give a reading. Smoothing a strand of hair behind her ear, she said modestly, "Oh, I haven't published anything." At the end of that evening Alma was explaining to Roxanne that their trouble was defining themselves in male images of success, like being published or performed, when the real value lay in the work itself and sharing it with its real audience.

Alma had time during the day to get on with her writing. Roxanne rarely looked at her wall, out too late at night to get up early in the morning, loath to let Alma venture out too often on her own.

"You're bored with a lot of this, aren't you?" Alma asked suddenly.

Roxanne tried to protest.

"No, but you've heard it all before, the theories about why we're not better than we are. It isn't that you don't understand."

"I've never been very good at the theory," Roxanne said. "I guess what I've always liked about women's liberation is the women."

Alma let out a shout of laughter. Then she looked seriously at Roxanne and said, "You're so honest and so smart and so good, why are you living with me?"

A thing begins for any number of reasons, from the way a nipple tugs at a blouse to on whose lap you happen to be sitting on the way home; a thing goes on for only one reason: love. Roxanne was as sure Alma loved her as she was that she loved Alma. Roxanne would stay through times of jealousy, times of being unable to work, times of long and stupid misunderstandings as long as she loved and was loved, which was the hope of happiness.

"Did you ever go to a consciousness-raising session?" Alma asked.

"Yes."

"What was it like?"

"What I didn't like," Roxanne said, "was people talking about their childhoods: toilet training, sibling rivalry, mother fixations, father fixations. Maybe it's just that I didn't have a family to make me unhappy or a course to teach me everyone is unhappy."

"I had a lovely childhood," Alma said. "You're so silent about yours, I imagine unspeakable things."

"It was very ordinary, except I was raised by a series of people. If I think back, I tend to feel sorry for them. It can't be easy to try to raise kids you don't love. What puzzled me—you always hear people complain that women talk about nothing but their babies—these women never did. They didn't want to talk about anybody but themselves."

"Well, *that's* liberating."

Roxanne sentimentalized motherhood. She realized that she missed Tony and Victor far more than Alma did. Roxanne encouraged herself to go on feeling their absence as a test of how genuinely she loved them and wanted them in her life. But of course, women shouldn't be more interested in their children than they were in themselves. And those meetings, for some of them, were the only time in the week they could let themselves come first.

"Only naturally very self-centered and selfish women make really good mothers," Alma explained. "Kids improve them, but they survive. I, for instance, couldn't have given you up for the boys. If I'd been able to, Tony and Victor would owe me my life. Owing me theirs is enough of a burden."

"What I mainly didn't like about the group was that you weren't in it."

"I keep thinking how brave you must have been to go to all these things alone. I wouldn't dare."

Roxanne didn't say that she went alone precisely to be alone, to have an excuse not to be with the woman she was supposed to be with. When Roxanne finally had the courage to end that relationship, she promised herself that she'd never again get involved with anyone who wasn't bigger, smarter, and saner than she was. She did not tell Alma such things, not so much out of fear of her jealousy as out of embarrassment. Roxanne seemed to herself nearly retarded in learning both how to love and whom to love. Alma would have a good deal less respect for Roxanne's experience if she knew how superficial and negative a lot of it had been.

Alma had three rejection slips in one day.

"You're probably sending them to the wrong magazines," Roxanne suggested.

"A good story is a good story," Alma said glumly.

"But magazines appeal to different sorts of people. I can see that every day."

"Only a hack would think about the audience!"

In the next ten days she had four more.

"Don't most writers have drawers full of them?" Roxanne asked.

"If they send off the stuff they wrote at fourteen. At thirty-three, I'm either a professional or a failure."

Alma had such confidence in her own negative judgments Roxanne couldn't see how to quarrel with them. She certainly was no judge herself. For her what Alma wrote was lies, of the sort Roxanne wished she didn't tell. Alma's characters had only those sorts of bad feelings anyone would be expected to have, and they seemed as good at lying to themselves as they were to each other. But all the stories Roxanne read did that. There was no more point in finding fault with it than with complaining that all violins were playing the same note. Probably what Roxanne mistrusted in Alma's work editors would see as strength, and what Roxanne loved, the quirky speed of it, hurrying when you expected leisure, taking emotional corners on two wheels, counted as a fault.

When the tenth rejection slip arrived, Alma said, "Okay, that's that."

"What's what?"

"I quit," Alma said. "The one thing too long a marriage taught me is not to stick at what I'm bad at."

"But don't you like to write?"

"Not if it turns out to be just scribbling," Alma said. "I've decided you'd better be the genius. I'm going to get a job."

"At last!" Allen said.

Luckily Allen's gallery owner friend, Dale Easter, was

still looking for someone or again looking for someone, and he agreed at once to try Alma out.

"But it's amazing—I get either a salary or a commission, whichever is *greater,* and the paintings he's selling are worth thousands and thousands of dollars. I could make *real* money."

The names Alma reeled off meant nothing to Roxanne, and the calculations of possible income meant not much more. There was one problem.

"I can always ask Mother and Dad to take them when I have to go out of town, but, when it's just an evening . . ."

"I'll be home," Roxanne assured her.

"And if one of them is sick?"

"I can be sick, too," Roxanne assured her.

"What I'm thinking is maybe you shouldn't work," Alma said. "Maybe you should stay home."

"We'll work it out."

"We mustn't get into roles," Alma said. "Do you think money could turn me into a bull dyke?"

"So quit your job the minute the boys get back," Pierre advised.

"No," Roxanne said. "Alma doesn't want to support me."

"Why not?"

"It offends her femininity."

"What about yours?" Pierre demanded.

"Well, I don't really want to be a wife," Roxanne said. "Oh, it's all right for you—it's kinky."

"Why has the holy light gone out of inferiority? The only other person I know who understands it is Joseph, but what can he do with it, being heterosexual, except feel guilty?"

"Is he going back to teaching next month?"

"He says so. He says he's got a new tranquilizer that would have kept Hitler and Jesus at their rightful trades. He says it's peace without its price. I don't think he'll last a month. It's crucifixion year for him . . . for all of you."

"We aren't going to die together," Roxanne said.

"No," Pierre said. "Carlotta thinks she has time still to commit a well-thought-out suicide. She's favoring a menopausal gesture at the moment, but sometimes she realizes her life is a suicidal gesture."

"Is she doing your portrait?"

"Yes."

"I wonder why," Roxanne said.

"Because I'm here," Pierre said with an artful smile.

"I wonder if she'll do Alma."

"She'd kill her first," Pierre said.

"Still?"

"She blames Alma for Mike, says she ruined him as an artist. Now he can't think of anything but money. What's more interesting, I want to know, except sex? Mike could never bore me."

"Alma likes Mike a lot better now," Roxanne said.

"Carlotta's perverse. She's only really interested in impossible, unhappy people. She told me sex with a woman is so normal it's boring. I expect she was referring to you?"

"I expect," Roxanne admitted, and sighed.

"I'm very loyal. I've thought you'd be marvelous in bed—not with me, of course. Alma's color is always so good."

"I am," Roxanne said, "but it doesn't stay interesting unless you're in love or at least obsessed. Carlotta was just curious—and jealous."

"And you?"

"Oh, I'm always curious, and I like Carlotta, and I'm sorry she's so jealous of Alma that she can't love her. It's more convenient for me, but I'm sorry."

"I want to trade shirts," Pierre said suddenly.

"All right."

"You're a little too severe in that, and I'm a bit too limp in this."

They traded shirts and kissed each other on each cheek, a salutation and farewell they used only when they were alone together.

"I'll be glad when the boys get home and you have more

time to yourself. Alma's been very possessive of you this summer."

"I've got used to missing them," Alma said. "I wonder if giving up children is like giving up smoking. Gradually you find other things you persuade yourself you like even better."

Roxanne expected Alma to propose a last week of evenings at meetings, readings, dances, but, though she didn't have regular hours at the gallery, Alma was spending days there to become familiar with both the inventory and the procedures. She was ordinarily tired at night, as Roxanne had been all summer. Roxanne cooked dishes Pierre had taught her, too disguised and delicate for the boys, and they drank wine and sat long at the table.

"You don't ask for enough," Alma said one night. "This is what you've wanted to do all summer."

"When you do. I like to do what you want to do."

"I don't pay attention to whether you're tired or needing to work or to be alone. I do pay attention to you but not to what you need."

"I like it."

"But you must take up your own space. I can't give it to you. I can't even think about it."

"I have what I need," Roxanne said, and it was not exactly a lie since there was the room in the basement which maybe now she really could move into.

"I bought something for you today."

"Show me?"

"There in the box on the chair."

Roxanne expected to find something Alma thought particularly showed off her height, her coloring, her breasts, something Roxanne would admire her in. The shirt and pants she took out of the box were not Alma's size.

"Try them on," Alma said.

"For me?"

"That's what I said."

They were sheer, in greens as near to yellow as maple tassels in the spring, as dark as hemlock.

"You are a flower, an extraordinary flower," Alma said. "That's my first paycheck. How would you like to be a kept woman?"

Oh, Alma, I will go through all the fantasies with you, make all the mistakes, be your flower, your fool, your sister. I am afraid. I am often afraid for you, of you, but, yes, I'll try anything that might possibly make us happy. There is a point.

"Answer me!" Alma commanded.

They made love with an intensity that they hadn't risked all summer, as if they had been too fearful of their freedom to use it, seized it now only because they would very soon have to give it up. Roxanne worked the better on her wall for remembering the night they had begun making love in the dining room, continued in the living room, on the stairs, on the upstairs hall carpet. In their room at night, she felt not confined so much as gathered up there, an armload of flowers in the vase of their love.

In the first month the boys were home, Alma chose to work more often at night than Roxanne imagined was absolutely necessary. Alma's sons got on her nerves.

"Victor, this is not Arizona. This is Vancouver. You wear *shoes* to the dinner table without having to be asked."

"Tony, if you say 'Dad says' one more time, I'll think you had a lobotomy while you were there and haven't a thought left of your own."

"What's a lobotomy?" Victor asked.

"It's an operation that turns a person into a parrot," Alma answered, glaring at her older son.

He glared back. Alma's sarcasm was never as effective with Tony as it was with Victor, who was bright enough to get the message, mostly good-humored enough to put up with it. Tony was more like Alma, able to dish it out without being able to take it.

Roxanne had expected the boys to make comparisons

between their father and herself, but for them she wasn't in it. The rivalry was between the two parents, leaving Roxanne usefully on the sidelines, far less resentful of their new loyalty to their father than she'd expected to be, surprised at the depth of resentment it could stir in Alma.

Because they knew the brand names of mobile homes and swimming pools, Alma complained that Mike had turned them into a couple of rotten little Americans. She didn't like the clothes he'd bought them and was not reassured by Victor's protest: "But that's what everybody wears."

"It was hot," Tony said defensively, but unlike Victor, he didn't wear his Arizona shirts again.

"Do you still want to help me with my workroom?" Roxanne asked him to help him out of one of his sulks.

"Oh, yeah, sure. I guess so."

Once they were working together, Roxanne teaching Tony her system of filing tapes, he dropped his guard and began to talk and ask questions.

"Dad says sooner or later you've got to figure out art is a hobby. When you do that, you can take real work seriously. Is that how you feel? Is this a hobby?"

"I guess so," Roxanne said.

"You don't want to be famous or make a lot of money or anything like that?"

"No."

"Then you're not serious," Tony concluded, but his voice tipped uncertainly.

"I'm serious about sound—but not that other."

"I'm not serious about anything, not about my violin or drawing or anything."

"I keep forgetting how old you are."

"Twelve."

"Ah, look, here's what I wanted to find," Roxanne said, holding up a tape. "It's my terminal tape. I've got the airport, the bus depot, the docks, the train stations. I never did get a graveyard, someone digging, the coffin going into the grave."

"Can you get permission to record something like that?"

"You have to wait for a friend to die."

"Ghoulish!" Tony said with approval. "Is it on the map?"

"No, but I want to put it there."

The map was going through an awkward stage, thick enough with pictures and instructions to look as if it were about to molt.

"I think making it worse will make it better," Roxanne decided.

Victor was only intermittently interested in the map, more because he didn't want to be excluded than because he was drawn to it. It was far more important for him to reestablish himself in the neighborhood, greatly helped by a new ten-speed, given to him not by his grandfather, but by his father. Roxanne was as lenient with him as she could be about times for coming home. He began to take advantage of her willingness to stretch ten minutes to an hour, and finally, she had to tell him, if he couldn't show up on time, he couldn't go out after supper.

"You're not my mother!"

"No, your mother would take the strap to you."

Victor stayed in, playing the TV in the living room at top volume while Roxanne and Tony worked in the basement. The next morning Roxanne found "FUCK" printed in a small, childish hand in a dozen places on the map, most in park and beach areas where there was still room to write. She wished she'd thought of it herself and told Victor so.

Gradually, as they settled into a routine again, Alma was more willing to come home to them, but she was asking something new of the boys; they had to be interesting if they wanted her attention. Otherwise, she either talked with Roxanne or was abstracted. It was more difficult for Victor, who was at a riddle stage and found it hard to remember if he'd asked more than once. But as with so many things Alma did essentially to suit herself, this improved not only the conversation at dinner but the boy's dispositions. And Roxanne liked better winning Alma's attention than being burdened with it as she sometimes had been during the summer.

"Dale Easter is a very interesting man," Alma said. "I'd like to ask him for dinner. We could have Allen and Pierre, but I'd rather we tried just ourselves and sent Vic and Tony to my parents."

Allen had said Dale was very elusive about his personal life and his background. No one seemed to know where he or his money came from, where he lived, with whom.

"Oh, he can be met in the steam bath, but he's not there every night."

At work Alma couldn't get past the impression Dale tried to give everyone—that he didn't really have a personal life, that he didn't really live anywhere. He traveled and worked.

"You listen so well," she said to Roxanne, "he might talk."

In type not unlike Allen, though more expensive, ambitious, and mistrustful, Dale Easter gave a first impression of nearly ineffectual diffidence. It gave him time to listen and to look before the snob or bully in the person Dale was meeting discovered that he responded neither to condescension nor threats. It made him good with buyers and artists alike, each of whom was gradually persuaded that, however Dale Easter operated in general, in this particular transaction he was an ally.

He came to dinner not as boss but as friend, and the first thing he did was admire the paintings in the living room, most of which were early Carlottas. There was one architectural drawing of Mike's and an acrylic seascape by John Korner.

"I wish I could handle some of these locals," Dale said with a wistfulness Roxanne didn't believe. "Korner is an incredible draftsman. He knows how to *draw* . . . but he lives in Vancouver. I told you Allen once asked me if I'd at least look at pictures of local sculpture—look, sure, but what could I do with it?"

More by tone than by any particular comment Dale was able to suggest it was the philistine world of international buyers rather than the local artists who were at fault, yet there was nothing he could do except, just by being in Vancouver himself, put it quietly on the map. Someday people would come to Vancouver not just to buy European and American art.

"Even now, people are buying Group of Seven, and Emily Carr just had to die to be famous. Look at the price of her paintings! Eventually, eventually . . ."

Roxanne then caught only scraps of conversation as she finished getting the dinner. She was glad it was late enough in the year for them to be eating by candlelight. Properly on Alma's right, Dale could sit with his back to Roxanne's wall. But even in candlelight, he noticed it.

"What's this? What's this? Is there an overhead light? Do you mind?"

He stood in front of it for several minutes while the soup got cold.

"Where on earth did this come from?"

"It's something I'm doing," Roxanne said. "It's not really to look at; it's to read, like a score."

"It's a sound map," Dale said. "The only other one I've seen—not nearly as elaborate or interesting as this was in Bonn, Germany, last year at the Beethoven festival. What's this for? When is it going to happen? Where?"

"Oh, it's only something for Vancouver, someday."

"Has Allen seen this wall?"

"Oh, yes," Roxanne said.

"Well, why didn't he tell me about it?"

"It was in Vancouver," Roxanne said.

"Touché."

"Allen's helped Roxanne apply for a Canada Council to put on some part of this anyway."

"If it happens," Dale said, "I want to help, all right?

Anyway, put King Gallery on your map and make it sound however you like."

The Canada Council turned Roxanne's project down on the grounds that she hadn't yet done anything to prove herself capable, no public concert or production of any kind. Roxanne was suddenly indignant, for she had put on magnificent sound happenings, experiences, whatever anyone wanted to call them, a couple of times a week for years in the basement of the record shop. That they had not been public was not her fault. Her one audience had called the police and could hardly be asked to testify to her years of work.

"So put them on again and make them public," Allen said, "and then apply again next year."

"Maybe Dale would let you use the big gallery," Alma suggested.

"I thought he didn't want the public in and out," Roxanne said.

"He seemed interested enough so that we could ask."

"It's impossible," Roxanne said. "I'd need a minimum of ten tape recorders and twenty speakers."

"Surely you can rent that sort of thing," Allen said.

"With what?"

"With Alma's money, and she'll pay for the advertising, too. Charge admission and make something over expenses for next time."

"Who'd come?" Roxanne asked.

"How much money are we talking about?" Alma asked.

"Women aren't supposed to fear failure," Pierre said. "They're supposed to fear success."

"Well?" Alma said, facing Roxanne.

"All right," Roxanne answered without any clear emotional sense of what she was agreeing to.

It would have been easier if Allen hadn't been sent east on a job that would keep him away for well over a month. Once Dale Easter had agreed to let them have the space, he did not go on to offer the kind of advice and support Allen could only occasionally phone in from Ottawa or Halifax or Montreal.

Roxanne had no trouble renting the equipment she needed, but she simply had no idea how to go about getting an audience. When Allen shouted long distance, "Send out invitations," she didn't know who should receive them. Alma didn't think stealing the King Gallery's mailing list would be useful, since only about a dozen of the addresses were inside British Columbia. Her mother's address book, though appropriately local, would not turn up anyone either interested or willing.

Joseph offered to get his students to print not only invitations but posters, and he seemed to know which stores would accept and display advertising.

"Get one up in the store where you used to work," he suggested.

"Are you kidding?" Roxanne asked.

"No," Joseph said, and to prove his point, he delivered a poster there himself and stayed until he saw it displayed.

Joseph also made himself available to help set up the machines. With his help and Tony's, Roxanne could save some time for a kind of rehearsal in the afternoon before the event began. She was not trying to do anything very elaborate or tricky. Once the machines were started, there was nothing else for her to do. But she did want to use the space of the gallery well, speakers placed, volumes adjusted properly. There were no chairs. People would mill around or sit on the floor—if anyone came.

Allen sent a telegram to the gallery, which arrived just before eight o'clock. The only people there were Carlotta, Pierre, Alma and the boys, Joseph and his family. Even Dale Easter hadn't been able to make it. Just as it looked very much like a family affair, half a dozen strangers turned up, young, polite, interested in the speakers and the machines. Then a man in his seventies with a long wool scarf and a loud voice introduced himself to everyone in the room as if they all should know who he was and be very pleased to see him. Finally the music critic from the *Vancouver Sun* appeared.

"This Allen Dent's friend's concert?"

"It isn't exactly a concert," Roxanne said.

"Well . . . whatever. No place to sit?"

"The floor."

Roxanne was cheered by the smallness of the audience because it meant their own contribution to the sound in the room would not be overwhelmingly unpredictable. At the moment that was frankly all that concerned her. She didn't want to be distracted from her own listening since she hadn't been able to hear her own work for so very long. And she wanted Alma to be able to hear. Anticipating that was very like anticipating making love.

At Alma's nervously questioning look, Roxanne nodded and walked over to the tape decks, bunched together on the floor, crouched down, and started up each one until ten tapes were each performing.

For the first few minutes, she stayed crouched there, listening, measuring the distances between messages, their volumes, for it was very important for them not to seem to compete. Then she got up and began to walk around the room, stopping to listen every step or so, like a bird-watcher bemused by a large migration of birds.

She had never had so large a space before, but, though it was exciting to her and she could hear more and more variously than she ever had before, she knew, too, that she did not want sound trapped in a box, even as big a box as this room. If there had been windows to open, she would have opened them, for sound is meant to escape from the prison of its source and die in freedom. That's what she needed, the whole city and time, real time. But even in this confinement of space and time, she heard the positive gatherings of sound so important to her. Sometimes she laughed out loud. Sometimes she clapped. Sometimes she danced a little, her head tilting from one sound source to another.

The others made small clusters in the room, the young

strangers on the floor, Joseph's whole family and the boys backed up against one wall. The old gentleman stood in the middle of the room, braced as if in a high wind. The music critic leaned against the exit door. Only Alma also moved around. Pierre was curled up by himself under the tent of his dark, curly hair. Carlotta watched from an isolated corner. Roxanne was aware of them all for perhaps the first half hour, but then she grew too absorbed in the complexities she was risking to be able to notice anything else. When Alma touched her arm, Roxanne started out of a working trance to discover that they were all alone in the room. All the speakers were silent.

"You've been squatting there for an hour," Alma said. "Everyone's gone home."

There was a write-up in the *Sun*, which quoted extensively a retired musicologist who said Roxanne was a romantic primitive, who was not self-taught so much as self-teaching, as dangerous as it could be refreshing, and the evening had been both. The music critic described Roxanne as someone who seemed to grow out of her own shoes. The headline was: "Yet to Find Her Audience."

Roxanne wasn't sure there was an audience to be found, and she wasn't sure that it mattered. Oh, her friends were all loyal, but aside from Tony, who had glimmerings of what she was about simply because he'd hung around and asked so many questions, Roxanne realized that no one had a clue to how to listen or what to say.

Only Alma was confident enough to say, "I don't pretend to understand it, but I find it fascinating."

Roxanne said, "I don't think there's anything to understand."

"Anyway," Alma said about the write-up, "it's not only happened, it's been noticed."

"And you're out of pocket."

"Not badly," Alma said. "I think I'm discovering what Mike discovered. Your own money is your own money. You can do what you want with it."

"Alma, it was marvelous for me, *really*."

"I know," Alma said. "And I do understand that. It has to happen again."

As far as Dale Easter was concerned, it could happen once a month, and he hoped he'd be in town to attend. Allen wanted a chance to show them how to promote it properly and was delighted that he might have the opportunity.

"He says he'll be home next week," Pierre reported.

"You look seedy," Roxanne said.

"I've found my first lump."

"Where?"

"In my throat," Pierre said.

"You're joking?"

"A little," Pierre said. "You know it will have to be my lungs—I don't want to deny my origins. Everyone in Quebec dies of their lungs. Read Marie-Claire Blais."

"Allen's been away too long."

"Do you think he lies to me?"

"You say everyone in love lies," Roxanne said.

"Maybe he's not in love. We've been together so long he won't let me keep track. He hates to be reminded I'm over twenty-one. What happens when I start to get gray?"

"Dye it," Roxanne said. "Allen will never leave you."

"He leaves me all the time."

Was part of being in love that constant anxiety? Roxanne was learning that Alma's jealous outbursts were simply the language of that dread. If Roxanne hadn't felt it herself so that she heard Alma's fear but listened to her rejection, Roxanne could have, at those moments, comforted and reassured. Instead, she withdrew, which increased Alma's anxiety. But they did come together again in a joy that denied any real doubt. Roxanne imagined similar sexual affirmations between Allen and Pierre. It was time for Allen to come home.

Alma and Roxanne both got home from work so late that they were sharing a glass of sherry while they worked together on a last-minute supper. Victor was watching the cartoons. Tony had set the table and was reading the paper.

"Have you seen it?" he asked Roxanne as she poured the milk.

"No," Roxanne said.

"Is Allen in Toronto?"

"I'm not sure. Why?"

Tony offered her the front page, a thumb indicating the article he had been reading. Roxanne saw the headline, "Pederasts' Party Over," and took the paper from Tony to read about the vice squad breaking into the apartment of a prominent Toronto businessman to find a number of men in the company of boys as young as twelve. An MP and a college professor were named. So was Allen Dent, one of Canada's best-known photographers, who had attempted with his camera to jump out a twelfth-floor window before he was apprehended and taken into custody.

Roxanne read it all twice, then three times. Something like that couldn't happen to Allen—to Pierre, to herself, sure, they were never really safe, but Allen was the man who bailed you out because he knew all the rules, had the money, and never made silly mistakes.

"What is it?" Alma asked coming into the dining room with plates of food.

Roxanne handed her the paper.

"What? That's absurd!" Alma said. "It must be some other Allen Dent. Allen doesn't go to that kind of thing. He told me he didn't."

"What does 'pederast' mean?" Tony asked.

"Homosexual," Alma said.

"Is that against the law?"

"No," Alma said, "not for adults."

"Was he taking pictures?" Tony asked.

"How do I know?" Alma snapped. "Don't ask so many questions."

"Pierre," Roxanne said. "He won't know unless Allen can reach him. Pierre never reads the paper."

"Someone will tell him," Alma said. "Everyone else will know."

The phone rang. No one moved to answer it. Then all three did, but Tony and Roxanne gave way gratefully to Alma.

"Allen!"

Roxanne and Tony waited. Alma said nearly nothing. She listened and agreed.

"He wants us to keep Pierre from finding out until he can get home. He's flying in tomorrow."

Roxanne picked up the phone and dialed Pierre. There was no answer.

"He's never out," Alma said.

"I'll go over," Roxanne said.

"Won't you eat something first?"

"No."

"But if he's not home . . . ?" Tony asked.

No one answered the door, which was locked. Pierre could, of course, have gone out, but, as Roxanne stood on the porch, her apprehension grew. She went around to the back door, which was also locked. There was a good-sized stone at the foot of the back steps. She took it and hurled it at the window in the back door. The door handle, when she reached it, wouldn't open from the inside. Of course, their doors would all be double deadlocks, a way to reassure Pierre when he had to stay so much alone. Feeling increasingly silly but determined, Roxanne found another rock and broke the breakfast-room window, which was low enough for her to climb in. There would be a lot of explaining and glass replacing to do at a time when no one would have much sense of humor, but that couldn't be helped.

Pierre was on the living-room floor, dead, his brains blown out by a gun still in his mouth. Roxanne knelt down and touched the frail arm in the shirt she had so recently swapped with him, wanting to wake him from the horror of it, remove him from his own death. But there was no Pierre, just an animal carcass, struck and broken like any other stray. Roxanne's heart was pounding so loudly that, at first, she didn't realize someone was also pounding on the door. She wanted to hide the body, hide herself.

"Pierre? Pierre?"

It was Joseph out there, come with the same anxiety, the same knowledge. At so crucial a time, he could not forget. She couldn't find a key to open the front door. Finally Joseph also had to climb through the breakfast-room window. His calm didn't seem the heavy tranquilizing it must have been. It made Roxanne aware of how comparatively crazy she felt.

"Have you called the police?" he asked.

"Of course not!"

"They have to be notified."

"It's not an accident. It's not a crime."

"He died of natural causes?" Joseph asked wryly, looking down at the violent mess on the floor.

"Joseph, they'll search this place. What if they find—oh, I don't know—pictures?"

"There's no way to protect him now," Joseph said, "from any of this."

He went to the phone.

"Before you call," Roxanne said, "do you understand? I can't stay. They mustn't find me here."

"You haven't done anything wrong," Joseph said.

"I broke the windows," Roxanne said, and laughed, hearing inside the sound the waver of hysteria. "I have to get out."

She didn't go right home. She wandered, unable to take hold of or put down the complexity of betrayals she did not know how to feel guilty of and yet did. Finding Pierre made his death a fact, as if she had invented it. Leaving Joseph there with the body would drive him crazy all over again. Letting him invite the police into the house . . . that was simply past her comprehension. She could not think about

Allen at all. The dread that grew in her was for and of Alma. Roxanne could not face telling Alma.

"I don't believe it," Alma said. "I just don't believe any of it."

Good, Roxanne wanted to cry out. *Stay ignorant. Somebody's got to, or I can't stand it.* She kept very quiet, terrified of an outbreak of Alma's own guilt.

"Make love to me," Alma said.

She didn't know. She really didn't know. The ignorance of that body was what Roxanne worshiped, all its juices, even its blood, fertile, vulnerable only to greater and greater pleasure, with no foreknowledge of itself as a bloody and meaningless corpse. Roxanne could not forget, but she could reaffirm the precious, the sacred in this beautiful body which gathered her into its own desires until they were hers as well. They would make love, if they had to, all night against the coming morning.

"Is he going to be buried?" Tony asked at the breakfast table. "Can you record him being buried?"

"What are you talking about?" Alma demanded.

"It's on the map," Tony explained, "in gold."

"It shouldn't be in gold," Roxanne said, trying to think of a way to deflect Tony, to distract Alma, because none of them could handle this subject now, or maybe ever. "You and Vic need to get ready for school."

"It's Sunday," Victor said impatiently. "Don't you even know the day of the week?"

"Is killing yourself against the law?"

"Not exactly," Roxanne said.

"Even if you're a child?" Tony persisted.

"He wasn't a child," Alma said, and then, with obvious, deep-breathing self-control, she suggested that both her sons be excused from the table. "We aren't really ready to talk about it, okay?"

After the boys had gone off to their rooms, Roxanne and Alma sat in silence for a good two minutes.

"Did you get his flight number?" Roxanne finally asked. "I guess we ought to meet the plane."

"We're never going to see him again," Alma said quietly.

"What?"

"We're never going to see him again."

"But we can't do that!" Roxanne protested, "he's our friend. He's bailed me out of jail. He's got you a job. And he's in terrible trouble, and who has he got?"

"Roxanne, my sons are twelve and nine years old. Allen is a pervert."

"We all are!" Roxanne cried, tears streaming down her face.

"Not like that!" Alma shouted. "You must promise me. You must promise me . . ."

"I don't see how I can."

"You must," Alma repeated, an urgency in her voice that was not an order so much as a fact of possible life.

Allen Mourning

*A*FTER the initial shock, the sense of somehow mistakenly being caught in the flash of his own camera, Allen had been cool enough, convincing himself as well as his lawyer and then the judge that his presence at the party had been professional, that he had not known ahead of time what kind of a party it would be. He did not say his intention would have been to get evidence to turn over to the police, but he didn't stop his lawyer from indicating that might have been his natural course. The photographs were already in police hands. Allen's sharing in the guilt would do nothing to help his host, who had obviously been set up by one enemy or another. Charges against Allen and several others were dropped.

Allen was angry with the newspapers, but he was too much in the business himself not to know that abusing friendship was a daily minor cost of getting out the news. He did know that dropping of the charges would be duly reported. Not as many people would read that. Some of those who did would assume some sort of payoff. He would get no indignant sympathy in any quarter. He had served too many scandals in a professional capacity to claim the protection of any ordinary citizen. Nobody is ever on the side of the photographer, even at a wedding, and so Allen thought it should be. What was harder to calculate was who would care enough to let it interfere in any way with giving Allen assignments. Certainly the homosexuals in high places in government would avoid him. He'd had his last season in Ottawa for a while.

If editors of magazines ran into outright refusals there, they might be leery of giving Allen the kind of assignment he'd been particularly good at in the past, which was convincing people who were camera-shy and not in need of publicity that it was a privilege to sit for him. He could get into great houses or hospital rooms by indicating that his photographs would serve the real importance of the person or event. He understood people's fear of being trivialized or exploited along with their need to be acknowledged. His job was to allay the fear and nourish the need while getting the best picture he could for his own purposes. His own purposes were always professional. He did not indulge his prejudices. Now his question was how many other people would indulge theirs against him, technically innocent or not.

It had not occurred to Allen that the story would be picked up by the Vancouver papers. No national figures were involved, unless he could make a modest claim for himself, and he didn't ever publicly identify himself with Vancouver. His telephone answering service was in Toronto. He only worried that Pierre might somehow get the story through the gay grapevine before Allen had a chance to explain it properly. He hoped Alma had taken care of that.

On the plane, though he brooded about threats to his income and about the dirty political games being indulged in to put men in jail for such frivolity, as he neared Vancouver, his spirits began to lift. He decided he had managed the whole business remarkably well, given what could have happened, and he'd soon be looking at it as one of the many narrow escapes his life seemed to be made up of. He even toyed with the possibility that he wouldn't have to say anything at all to Pierre. There were the familiar mountains, white with their first winter snows—a marvelous time of year on the coast where you could still sail on a bright November day—out there right under the nose of industry. He probably couldn't persuade Pierre, whose blood had grown thin all these years in a mild climate. It was enough simply to see the sailboats out in the bay. He was home, and he was going to stay at home for a good long while now, the Rocky Mountains between him and the public world, safe even from his own taste for it.

Joseph did not so much meet Allen as join him as he left the airport. Allen's first impression was that it was an odd coincidence, Joseph walking there beside him.

"Is Ann meeting you?" he asked.

"No, she's home with the children."

"Shall we share a cab?" Allen was efficient in stowing his luggage and settling them both. "I'll drop you off then, shall I?"

"I'd just as soon go back to your house," Joseph said.

Used to Joseph's idiosyncrasies, Allen gave his own address and then asked, "So where have you been?"

"Nowhere," Joseph said. "I came to meet you."

Allen stiffened to new attention, but surely there was nothing wrong. Joseph's face was tender; it was always tender. No one would send Joseph as a messenger of bad news.

"That's very nice of you," Allen said. "Even Pierre can't be bothered anymore I'm in and out so often. You're looking well."

"I am well," Joseph said. "Allen, the Toronto business . . . it got into the papers."

"Hell!" Allen said. "Pierre hasn't seen it, has he? He never reads the paper. Anyway, I phoned Alma last night. Joseph, what is it?"

"Pierre's dead. He killed himself."

Allen felt as disoriented as he had when the police arrived at the party. Perhaps he was simply in the wrong cab being mistaken for the wrong person, even in the wrong city, though the bridge over the Fraser was familiar enough, and Joseph was no stranger to him. But Joseph, of course, was crazy.

"I'm sorry," Allen said, wanting to be gentle, for whatever Joseph's grief was, it was real to him.

"I had to notify the police," Joseph said. "Roxanne was afraid, because of the papers, that they'd search the house, but they didn't."

"Well, that's good," Allen said cautiously. "They've dropped the charges in Toronto."

"That's good," Joseph said, a stammer there underneath the will in his voice.

"So," Allen said, taking a deep breath, which he spent on a silly laugh. "Maybe we can get all this straightened out."

"Roxanne had to break a couple of windows to get in because of the double deadlocks."

"That's all right. What're a couple of windows?"

The journey seemed to take hours. Allen staked his patience on arriving, being able to get out of this irrational script and into his own house. Even after they finally arrived, Allen paid the cab driver attentively, remembered his luggage, and he noticed the combination of red berries on the mountain ash and the second bloom of the dogwood, almost as satisfying a signal of the time of year as white sails against white mountains. As he turned the key in the front door, he also controlled a sharp desire to call Pierre's name and end this sinister charade, but he could not yet seem to break that free of it.

Once inside, Allen left Joseph standing in the living room. From room to room Allen went, and there was no one there. He went through the house again, this time as if he had taken out a search warrant, hurling open closet doors, bureau drawers, cupboards, flinging clothes and papers on the floor. Joseph did nothing to restrain him, and he could not restrain himself, though he had very little idea what he was doing. Pierre could not possibly be dead, not with all this evidence: his shirts, his childish underwear, his miniature shoes, his French Canadian novels and cookbooks. It was a silly trick, and Allen would find the clue to it or find Pierre. Finally Allen came out of their bedroom, exasperated.

"All right. I give up. Where is he?"

"At the morgue."

"This is enough of a joke!" Allen shouted. "I've had it! Do you hear me? Where is he? What have you done with him?"

"He couldn't be left in the house," Joseph said. "Allen, sit down. Allen, listen. I have to help you understand. Pierre's dead."

"I don't like that," Allen said.

"I know."

Surely he could call his Vancouver lawyer. They'd bailed Pierre out of silliness before. It didn't matter how much it cost. Allen was staring at a new stain on the living-room rug. He knelt down and touched it with his fingers, then drew back from the dampness.

"I cleaned up as much as I could," Joseph said.

Bloodstains on the carpet? It was like something you'd see in London at a matinee with your aunt. Allen had always told Pierre, if there was one thing he couldn't stand, it was straight camp. Pierre had never betrayed Allen's taste before.

"I'm embarrassed," he said aloud, surprised. Mortally embarrassed.

In the days ahead, Allen came to believe that was Pierre's exact state when he killed himself, his own taste having been so badly betrayed. Guilt made Allen wretched; loneliness was physically painful; the terrible stupidity of it tipped his accustomed cynicism into bitterness.

The only business calls he had were cancellations, some curt, some—usually from magazine editors—nervous with false sympathy. None of it mattered to Allen. He couldn't have worked if he'd wanted to, his hands having developed a palsy which would make holding a camera impossible. But he didn't want to. He had worked for Pierre.

At first he saw no one but Joseph, that because Joseph had come unbidden and stayed. He was a curious comfort. Allen felt less exposed by his own craziness since Joseph had lived through and witnessed all kinds of derangements. But Allen didn't indulge in any false displays of grief either, as he might have with someone like Alma. Joseph had gone through enough pain to be spared anything but what was essential, which was what couldn't be helped.

"I try to blame them instead of myself," Allen tried to explain. "I try to say they killed him, not I."

"He killed himself," Joseph said, as a matter of fact.

At some moments, Pierre seemed to Allen the supreme good example, and Allen wanted to follow him in it, not just to be done with living but to have the last word, a martyr's revenge. Pierre's death had not been publicly linked with the Toronto arrests. Allen's would be, but his pain was too severe for him not to want to see the results of whatever action he took.

"Ann says you must have dinners with us for a while," Joseph said.

Allen didn't want to go, but he had lost his firm hand metaphorically as well as physically, and he had to use anyone else's kindly decision as a way to get from one moment to the next. When that plump, bespectacled little woman gave Allen a sisterly kiss in greeting, he felt himself shaking with a gratitude that also appalled him. He had not known her power to reject until she welcomed him. How could he survive such vulnerability?

Rachel and Susan, who had been such grave, flighty children, had moved into a new season Allen didn't understand. One moment they presented themselves as interesting, intelligent people, but, if you responded in kind, they dissolved into wriggling self-consciousness. If you dealt with them as the silly children they'd become, they resented it fiercely. Allen delighted in the coquettishness of boys that age, who didn't seem to him a mass of emotional contradictions; they were greedy, tender, loyal, self-centered, all of a piece, and they responded predictably, as girls did not. Allen, who had none of Pierre's aesthetic prejudices against women, could only appreciate and understand a female when she had become a mother, that faint fragrance of blood and milk that could linger about a woman years after she had nursed a child, on beyond menopause. Ann, obviously sensing that the girls would be no entertainment, called them away to tend the baby and set the table, leaving Joseph and Allen alone together, as they had been for great stretches of time over the last few days.

"I've just assumed you aren't teaching," Allen said, normal concerns suddenly occurring to him as they hadn't in days.

"I asked for a few days off. By now they don't ask questions."

"I hadn't even thought."

"I'm really well," Joseph said. "I won't even need my regular amount of sick leave this year."

"That's really good."

"I thought it was the tranquilizers, but I've stopped taking them, even in the last few days."

"Is there anything to drink?"

"I'm sorry," Joseph said. "Of course. I forget—I still do forget."

Allen wanted Joseph to be able to talk about himself, his illness, his health, his job, his children, anything. Listening made Allen nervous. He couldn't concentrate on what anyone else said, even Joseph, who was so quiet and brief. All Allen seemed able to do was pick up the broken pieces of these last few days off the floor of his mind and offer them to someone—Joseph—for verification. Joseph had reconfirmed Pierre's suicide a dozen times a day. Allen had progressed to offering it himself as a statement rather than a question. And he had done some of the practical things, disposing of Pierre's body, with Joseph's help. Allen did not identify it. He couldn't have. He simply wrote the check for cremation. He had felt like the commandant of Buchenwald, sending that beloved body to the furnace, but the hysterical grief of that violent act was soon over as grief at gradual decay would not have been. Joseph had also helped him bundle all Pierre's clothes into the car and take them to the Salvation Army bin in the Safeway parking lot. Allen would have felt safer to have them burned, too, fearing their resurrection on another slight-bodied creature, fearing things more nebulous, evidence of a crime. Joseph had let Allen talk when he could, cry, wander off.

"Thank you," Allen said, accepting vodka on ice. "I want to be able to listen to you. I'm sorry."

"Oh, that's all right," Joseph said. "When we both were good listeners, we weren't as good friends."

Sitting at Joseph's table, Allen had a sudden insight into the reason Joseph had kept his domestic life secret for so long, protecting it even more rigidly than Allen had protected his own. It had taken Joseph these years to master the ordinary, be really at home in it. Joy sat next to him in her high chair, kicking a bedroom slipper into the stew which he was trying to dish up. Susan initiated a low-pitched, lusty giggle, but before Rachel could take it up, Ann had signaled them both so that they sat in precarious grown-up postures, waiting for their food. Joseph lived among and for these four females. Allen could have expected antlers to begin sprouting out of those tufts of feathery hair.

Ann was the sort of woman all men idealized if they noticed her, but very few men would have the courage or sense to want to marry her. Men married for lust, for money, for power, for safety and convenience, rarely to be companion to woman as they dream her to be, faithful, fertile, enduring, tender.

The male does not endure—he sells out, goes crazy, kills himself.

"Eat, Allen," Ann said, a hand on his arm.

He picked up his knife and fork dutifully. For her sake, he even made an attempt to notice what he was eating. At this table he could not be pariah, saint, or lunatic if he could help it. He had to be a man, eating his dinner. It had taken Joseph years to master it, but he had. There he sat at the head of his table, feeding his child.

Allen suddenly remembered Joseph standing shivering in his shorts on that first cold day on the beach. His willingness had turned a mildly sadistic joke into an abiding friendship. Why couldn't I have risked being ordinary? Allen wanted to cry out. Why isn't this my table? But he kept silent and went on eating.

Joseph seemed in no hurry to go back to work, but Allen, once he understood, could not accept Joseph's truant company.

"I'm perfectly all right. I have other people I ought to see, some tactful silences to break."

"Oh," Joseph said. "Alma is . . . She told Roxanne she didn't want . . . It's the boys . . . and Mike. Anyway . . ."

Allen grabbed Joseph by the arm. "You can say Pierre is dead with ease. There shouldn't be anything harder."

"Alma doesn't want to see you."

"Roxanne?"

"Alma doesn't want her to see you. She's afraid of Mike, of losing the boys . . ."

"I should have known," Allen said. "What an incredible, healthy bitch she is!"

"I don't like her," Joseph said.

"Well, no, you never have. I do."

"Even now?"

"Particularly now—she's being vintage Alma," Allen

said. "I'm just sorry I'm being excluded from watching the show."

"Roxanne minds."

"Tell her she can't afford to," Allen said in short dismissal. "None of us can."

It was a relief to be alone, to have his obligations of friendship limited to Joseph and his family. Oh, eventually Allen would have to deal with acquaintances, but they all were of the sort to be as glad to delay meetings as he was, if not for the same reasons. Allen did not know whether he had to pull himself apart or pull himself together, and he had to be alone to find out.

Sinking down gradually through layers of shock, guilt, and grief, at bottom what Allen stood on was anger, an emotion far too expensive and dangerous for him ever to have reached it before. But now he was alone. If he made a mistake, he could damage only himself. At first it was like a huge machine, far too heavy and violent for Allen to master as a weapon against anyone but himself. Every muscle in his body ached, and he tried to hold himself in his own arms, whimpering for comfort. Before he could more than catch his breath, it was his anger he was embracing, and the whimper turned to a roar—at Pierre for leaving him, at himself for his cosmic carelessness for his own and Pierre's safety, at the world determined to teach them to kill themselves, the humane and inexpensive alternative to castration or capital punishment.

Sometimes he tried to defuse it, calling himself a closet romantic full of melodramatic unreason, a self-indulgent escape from the cool cynic he had trained himself to be, but, when he tried to retreat to that old security, there was no room in it for Pierre to be dead. Pierre could lie dead in Allen's heart only when it expanded with anger. Gradually, instead of being debilitated by it, Allen was learning new strength to master and use it to some purpose. He was going to have revenge, of what sort he didn't yet know. He only understood that at the deepest level he rejected Pierre's death as punishment. Pierre had to be seen as a martyr in a war that had been going on for centuries because only one side admitted to fighting.

For an hour at a time, Allen could do simple things with his hands like cooking and washing dishes. When the shaking began, he clamped his hands into his armpits and waited, saying, "You're not frightened or ashamed or embarrassed. You're angry."

He had been at home a week when Carlotta telephoned.

"I want to intrude," she said. "I want to do your portrait."

"I want to buy Pierre's," Allen said.

"I've told you, Allen, I'm not selling any of them."

"Not even now?"

"Particularly not now."

"Could I just . . . have it?"

"No," Carlotta said.

She came over, somberly dressed for her own sort of mourning.

"With no funeral," she said, "with no memorial service, we have to do something. At least you should wear a black armband."

"I'm thinking of wearing the gun that killed him strapped to my heart."

"Marvelous!" Carlotta exclaimed. "It's so grossly Freudian."

"But basically practical," Allen said. "I'm thinking of killing some people."

"Who?"

"I'm not sure."

"Well, I'll paint you as a potential murderer."

"What do you want me to wear?"

"The gun, a white shirt." Carlotta studied him. "Do you remember saying I should do a Dorian Gray portrait?"

"No," Allen said.

"So that it could age and you wouldn't."

"And bear my corruption so that I could hide it," Allen

said. "What a cooperative bunch we've mostly been. You know, I'm beginning to be angry with Pierre."

"It isn't corruption," Carlotta said. "It isn't anger either."

"What is it?"

"Age," Carlotta said, "the bones beginning their long quarrel with the flesh."

"How old am I?"

"Thirty-four," Carlotta said. "We all are."

"I don't look it."

"No, you don't," Carlotta said, "but it's there. I can see it."

"I have a good face," Allen said.

"Yes, you do. You're a good man," Carlotta said. "A good man with a gun over his heart."

Allen's tone, like his hands, could stay steady for as long as an hour, in arrogance or self-mocking, but then it broke in nervous laughter or tears. He agreed to pose no longer than forty-five minutes three times a week. It was the beginning of a new structure. On that slight commitment he would build his week.

A month had passed before Allen realized that there would be no work at all from the sources he depended on. He was going to have to look for it, something he hadn't done for several years. He was reluctant, rationalized that another month should pass before he did anything himself. He needed the time to steady himself, and the public air needed that time to clear.

Joseph told him about Roxanne's concert.

"It would do her good to have you there, and there's nothing Alma could do about it."

Far from feeling the loss of Roxanne, Allen had been relieved not to see her. She was so bound with Pierre that her presence could be no comfort to him. He was not as sanguine about Alma as he insisted on seeming to Joseph. Allen did understand her—oh, very well. He did not forgive her her lack of loyalty and ingratitude. His decision to attend was based on his anticipation of her discomfort.

Allen, who usually kept his hair very carefully trimmed and not quite short enough to be accused of being military, hadn't had a haircut since he got home. He wasn't letting himself go. He showered and shaved with the same regularity every morning, once a week did his laundry, changed his bed. He simply couldn't face his barber, in body type and manner so like Pierre, who would have heard and would be tender. Allen could cope with Joseph's sympathy; there was no sexual question in it. And he could deal with Carlotta's, too, partly because she was so ready to withdraw it if he tried her patience at all. Allen could not risk being with anyone for whom concern could be physically expressed, even with the briefest gesture. It would tear his control like a piece of threadbare cloth. So he combed his hair over instead of behind his ears and knew, though it was common enough among men these days, it gave him an air of decadence he had never approved of. His prudishness was nothing but self-protection, about which he no longer had a choice, except with people who did not know who he was. If he had to present himself to Alma as a child molester, he might as well look the part.

She spoke to him. Moral disapproval could never overcome automatic good manners when Alma was caught off guard. She clearly hadn't expected him. What a handsome woman she was! Pregnancy was not the only sort of sexual flowering that became a woman. Alma was radiant.

Roxanne, in contrast, was drawn and withdrawn. Allen could hardly bear better than she their short exchange.

"Thank you for being here," she said.

"I hoped you'd want me to come."

That was all.

"Hiya," said Victor. "Long time no see."

How like his father he was going to be.

Allen caught sight of Tony, squatting over the equipment, a casual guard. He had his mother's fair coloring, but he didn't really look like either of his parents. His face was finer, would be sterner, and, though he was now taking his growth, he was not heavy-boned. He was, as he always had been for Allen, absolutely beautiful.

Dale Easter stepped up, blocking Allen's view.

"I meant to drop you a note."

Allen nodded. He hadn't been out enough yet to learn phrases of comfort for friends embarrassed by their own neglect.

"Also to say Alma's working out very well—first class—just exactly what I needed: brains, taste, inherited jewelry."

"I'm glad you're letting Roxanne use your studio."

"Between us," Dale said quietly, "she just isn't Vancouver. She'll be in Europe next year or the year after. Or she'll go to L.A. I've heard less interesting stuff get top awards at the festivals. She doesn't even know. It's eerie."

"Who's going to discover her?"

"Someone . . . soon," Dale predicted.

He felt about Roxanne much as Allen did himself, and they had the same fostering instinct with her. Tonight Allen wasn't as sure as he had been that Alma was Roxanne's personal salvation. Alma would not betray her as Allen had Pierre. Roxanne, in any case, didn't have Pierre's extreme and dependent sensibility. What Alma would do was possess and limit. But Roxanne's need to work was so fundamental she would manage. By Roxanne's own admission, Alma was marvelous in bed. Perhaps what wore away at Roxanne wasn't Alma at all but the same grief that fed on Allen's bones. She had loved Pierre and been close to him in ways forbidden to Allen's more intense relationship with him. Allen's grief took a sudden generous step forward, knowing that he shared it, something he had not admitted with Joseph or anyone else.

Victor passed him again in an awkward, crouching run, pursuing Joy, who fled away from him with loud, delighted squeals.

"Oh, dear," Ann said, following after, "she'll be part of the show unless I can quiet her down. That Victor!"

Nearly all the strangers were young men as discreetly gay

as Dale or Allen. The militants, about whom so much was written, were a small minority even among college kids. They might read *The Body Politic* or *The Advocate*, but their own outward and visible sign was to be a little too impeccably heterosexual. Since the raid on *The Body Politic*, when the police had seized even the newspaper's subscription list, fewer of the cautious young even subscribed.

Pierre had been nearly the only person Allen knew, aside from the young prostitutes, who had made no attempt to hide his nature or his tastes. It had been one of his deep attractions for Allen, that delicate bravery. Allen found these young men tonight in no way attractive. He resented their presence as trivializing the occasion. They were here the way they'd also be at experimental films or esoteric dance recitals not because they were really interested or knowledgeable but because it was their climate and therefore their source of gossip. He had more respect for drag queens. Flaunting it seemed a more honest defense. Why then didn't he? He hadn't the flair or the guts. He was nervous about a wing of hair over his ear.

Allen was suddenly shaking so badly he had to stand against the wall and let the line run over and over in his head: I am not frightened or embarrassed; I'm angry. It was ritual rather than fact. The police could come anytime. Anyone could be dead. But Pierre was dead, so what did it matter? There was the real anger. Allen braced himself on it and smiled, calm enough to hold a camera or a gun, whatever weapon he chose.

"Deciding who to kill must be a little like deciding who to paint," Carlotta said, "once you make up your mind you're not going to kill—or paint—yourself."

"I don't think I follow you," Allen said without turning his head; he was a disciplined model, used to shutter speeds.

"Well, it's perfectly obvious that anyone is important enough to himself to consider suicide, but that's very subjective—didn't Auden say something about Narcissus being in love with his own image not because it was beautiful but because it was his? Deciding to kill someone else is different —or maybe it isn't. I wouldn't do a portrait of anyone unimportant to me, but you all may be mine to paint simply because you're mine, *there*, like the mountain to climb, and you, for instance, are there because of the traffic pattern of Joseph's nerves. Would it cross your mind to shoot me?"

"Are you serious?" Allen asked.

"Yes. I may in my own way have contributed to Pierre's suicide."

"How?"

"I don't know. Some people believe to make an image is to steal a soul."

"Do you?"

"No, but that doesn't mean it can't be so. The world may basically operate on inadvertent magic."

"I'd be way ahead of you in soul stealing," Allen said.

He thought of the drawers and drawers full of negatives. There were a few buildings, gardens, sailboats, but the vast majority were people interred alphabetically.

"But you don't choose. People are chosen for you . . . to photograph."

"Mostly," Allen agreed.

"I choose—or have the illusion of choosing. Would you, if you killed anyone?"

"Oh, I assume so," Allen said, "unless it was an accident."

"Then how would you choose?"

"If not myself?"

"If not yourself."

"I don't know," Allen admitted. "I can't yet think of anyone who'd be any use to me dead."

"This is just a pose then?"

Allen looked down at the gun in his hand. "It's a metaphor."

"Allen, metaphors don't kill people. That gun killed Pierre."

"Pierre killed himself," Allen said. "I have got that

straight finally. This gun is the last thing he touched, the last power he knew."

And Pierre put it in his mouth, took it like a lover, killed himself, and might as well have castrated Allen with the same bullet, for he would never again as long as he lived aim his desire at other human flesh. It would be easier to kill.

"I don't think about killing myself any longer," Carlotta said. "I wonder if I think only one of us is allowed to in the great scheme of things. That would mean Pierre had stolen *my* soul—or my choice anyway."

"I don't either," Allen said. "I did at first, but only because I really thought I couldn't stand it; I didn't ever *want* to."

"It's changed us all. I think it's cured Joseph."

"How?"

"Maybe the shock, for one thing. He said to me that going crazy wasn't a real alternative, and he was damned well going to learn to live with flowers and be Joy's father. I have a theory about Joseph that his emotional motor was put in upside down, and what ought to drive him crazy keeps him sane; what reassures the rest of us—a tree in bloom, a kid flying a kite—sends him round the bend. Or did."

"He has no impersonal use for his heart. He says he's very glad he's not an artist, but it would have made it easier for him, I think."

"Not in the long run."

"No, maybe not," Allen said.

"Oh, I don't know. You're so much more accessible, sympathetic, *attractive* with the wind out of your sails, but you keep making me want to burst into tears."

"I strike myself the same way . . . for different reasons."

"It isn't your fault, Allen," Carlotta called to him across the great gulf of his guilt. "It really isn't."

"I wonder why, then, I'm being so cruelly punished," he said.

His loneliness for Pierre was at times so intense he either

wandered the house howling or had to leave, drive around the city, call on a friend. He had nearly given up going to the movies because so often someone tried to pick him up.

All his adult life Allen had envied, while he belittled, men who made nearly no distinction among the requirements of their balls, bowels, and bladders. He had friends who'd as soon offer to buy him a quick one in the hotel men's room as in the bar.

"Better for you than a drink. Beats a shoeshine around the block . . ."

It wasn't conscious fastidiousness or moral disapproval that made Allen refuse. It was the foreknowledge of failure. To his great private chagrin, he had a monogamous cock, and he had years ago given up the embarrassment of trying to prove otherwise. Sometimes he claimed clap, sometimes worldly indifference, sometimes moral superiority to keep sexually aloof. He had never had to confess to Pierre because with Pierre he had no difficulty, nor, perhaps because he was away so much, had Allen ever tired of Pierre sexually.

Since women's liberation, too much had been said against unequal relationships, which were, after all, one's first model of love. Allen didn't care how far kid lib finally went in sexual or financial freedom, children would always be dependent on adults. To accept that dependence was to take the responsibility of being superior, living up to its expectations. It wasn't a matter of depriving someone else of independence but of accepting his need to depend, to be protected.

Allen had a theory that, if he could have adopted any attractive boy he saw, he would have had no problem with impotence. Pierre, however, was a possessive only child and wouldn't ever have stood for a rival. That was a generosity Allen could never have taught him.

To wish that Pierre had understood him better was as futile as to wish Pierre was still alive. Allen wished both a hundred times a day, while he also knew there was no way to explain to Pierre what had happened, how it had happened. It was not Allen's apparent infidelity but his vulnerability that had killed Pierre. If Allen could be picked up, put in jail, exposed in the papers, there was no safety left, not even inside a house with double deadlocks, with a checking account that never went under three thousand dollars. Allen could have tried to explain all that away. He, after all, could bail himself out quickly enough, but Pierre couldn't have believed him for long as one job after another fell away and no new ones were offered. In such circumstances you don't stay a man who can bail himself out for long.

Allen liked to believe, because he wanted Pierre to believe, that it was a matter of good taste rather than cowardice that kept Allen from being publicly homosexual. There was something not quite nice, jock vulgar, about the political kisses men gave each other on the covers of radical magazines, and no wonder people were offended. For years Allen had, in fact, been behaving like a common criminal, and he had finally, briefly, been treated like one. He had no more faced the implications than Alma had the night he took her to the jail to bail Roxanne out. It was just beginning to occur to Allen not only that people like Pierre and Roxanne were vulnerable and therefore in need of protection but that he, Allen Dent, could be deprived of his livelihood, locked up.

Was Alma more aware than he of the universal danger? Is that why she had backed away from Roxanne that night and now was avoiding him, genuinely afraid of contagion? Surely she didn't really believe Allen would try to seduce her sons.

Allen had been at home for two months when he was called on by the police for his first questioning. A teenaged boy had been murdered in Stanley Park on a night Allen was having dinner with the Rabinowitzes. It didn't take fifteen minutes, and everyone was rigidly polite. The scattered fragments of what had been more often fear than anger fused in the intensity of the encounter. Allen did not have to tell himself that he was in pure rage when they left.

"Because I went to a dinner party where the young waiters were in jockstraps," he shouted at Carlotta, "I am to be harassed as a child molester, murderer, every time any child reports an incident, every time a body is found in the leaf mold, in the tide? I can't even stand to read those items in the paper!"

"It's because of that homosexual murder in Toronto not that many years ago—a boy—do you remember?"

"Of course, I remember. It would make as much sense to harass me about that as it would to harass you every time a good-looking man is murdered since you have been seen having dinner with one occasionally. Flirtation, even overt sexual behavior, isn't foreplay for murder, even by most of those deranged with guilt—one in half a million maybe."

"I know it doesn't make sense," Carlotta said.

"Do you? How much of a bigot are you, Carlotta?"

"I've tried it myself," she said coolly.

"And found it too normal to be interesting."

Carlotta laughed. "I think that was Pierre's turn of phrase, not mine, though I'd like to claim it. I'm a bitch, Allen, but I'm no bigot. I haven't much sympathy with needs other than my own, and only my own faults interest me."

"What's happening to me really doesn't appall you?"

"No more than what's happening to everyone else. Melodrama isn't necessarily more important. You need to be special. You need to be indignant. Be indignant. Be special."

Allen allowed himself to grind his teeth and then sat in rigid silence while Carlotta worked. After a ten-minute silence he burst into hysterical tears. She took his head in her hands and raked her threatening but very gentle nails through his lengthening hair over and over again. When he was able to catch his breath, she stepped away and left without saying a word. Allen was not sure she would come back, but she did promptly for their next appointment. His relief made him petulant.

"This is going to be a good session," Carlotta said. "I haven't seen you look self-indulgent in months. All your expressions used to be inside that range."

"Has anybody ever simply walked out on a portrait?"

"Mike did," she said, "but not because he was irritated with me, though he should have been. I was preparing to take my lifetime to finish it, and that was something he didn't have in mind at all. He really didn't take to being my muse. It was enough of a disaster to make me wonder if the feminists are right: the muse has to be female. So I tried Roxanne. I don't think she's capable of being a disaster."

"You're not feminine enough to be a lesbian easily," Allen said, taunting and serious.

She regarded him with amusement.

"Well, I'm glad you're entertained," he said.

Finally Allen did trust Carlotta's nearness and self-absorption. Because of them, she was not afraid to try to save his life. She wouldn't spend more on it than she could afford. He didn't have to be afraid for her as he was sometimes for Joseph, though Allen was far more careful of Joseph. Allen did not talk about guns or killing people in front of Joseph, or about the police.

He ate often at Joseph's table, and, aside from quite often bringing a roast, good cheeses, wine, bags of cookies, Allen took a great many pictures of Ann and the children as a way to be grateful. Though he still had a very up and down time with Susan and Rachel, Joy had decided to take physical possession of him, climbing about him as she did her father, who visibly winced, as Allen did, when a small assertive shoe landed like an avenging angel in his totally innocent lap. How old did girl children have to be before they became respecters of male anatomy? Surely the bulk of sex crimes involving children and adults could be laid at the feet of two-year-olds. Joy seemed to Allen already very feminine, with her mother's roundness and small, full mouth. But she had Joseph's eyes and queer, little laugh.

"Ann," Allen asked one evening while he was helping her with the dishes and Joseph was putting Joy to bed, "do you ever see John's face in Rachel or Susan?"

"Oh, yes," she said, her tone easy enough so that he knew it wasn't an inadvertently cruel question, "and not just in their faces—the way their bodies move, their gestures. Just the other day, the way Susan looked up—it could have been her father."

"Is that . . . hard?"

"Oh, no, Allen. It's wonderful. I can remember him young and well."

Allen didn't imagine he could stand seeing anything of Pierre in someone else, even a small child. An eyebrow would seem grand larceny. But Pierre had been young . . . and well.

It was to Ann Allen confessed his growing financial concern.

"Oh, I could last for a year, and after that I could sell the house. I bought it for Pierre."

"You should take pictures of children," Ann said. "You're so very good at it."

Allen laughed. Ann's kindness was often preposterous. Didn't she remember that someone like Alma wouldn't let Allen into the house?

"Let me tell you something about Alma," Ann said, as if she'd read his thoughts. "She thinks she can protect herself. She has to get over that."

"Do you see much of them?"

"Not now. I saw Alma when she was alone, when I was alone. Sometimes she was a little overwhelming, but I do like her. She's honest—maybe partly because she thinks it's her due; she can afford it. Joseph doesn't really like her."

"Do you find Alma and Carlotta both very self-centered . . . for women?"

Ann laughed. "You men always do want us to be better than we are."

"Don't you want men to be better than they are?"

"Rather less good and happier," Ann said.

Happier? They-lived-happily-ever-after was a heterosexual goal which Allen had always read as what a man was expected to do for a woman, as sex was something he did to her. Happiness for Allen himself was very much beside the point, and part of his love for Pierre, his need to protect, was that happiness was so far out of Pierre's range except as it is surprised in transient moments of pleasure which can give an illusion of happiness. Allen had never considered that goodness and happiness were natural enemies; quite to the contrary, perfect goodness and perfect happiness were synonymous. But they were states irrelevant to Allen or Pierre.

Joseph no longer walked with the obsessive regularity he had in the days when he and Allen had first met, but at least once a week he suggested Allen go with him along the winter beach or through the bleak scrub of the university grant lands. On these walks Allen got into the habit of asking questions: "What was it like when you sat for Carlotta?" or "Do you think, as Ann seems to, that goodness and happiness are at odds?" Sometimes it seemed to Allen, in the rhythm of that walking, they were not in dialogue so much as in duet, now one carrying the melody, now the other, a theme introduced by one, developed by the other. He often felt more instrument of an idea than its source. There was a detachment he could not reach with Carlotta because there was never a moment when conversation might not turn into contest. And so he could ask, "Is there always a battle between the sexes even when there's no sex?"

"Ann and I don't fight," Joseph said.

"Did you with Carlotta?"

"No, not really. I often felt Carlotta was very impatient with me, but I didn't take it personally. I decided she had to be irritable the way she had to be cold while she was working."

"I don't know why Mike was her great love," Allen said.

"He's very attractive to women."

"He's very attractive, period. But he's . . . unconvincing. Women don't seem to notice that so much, or they don't mind."

"He's a touching man."

"Surely not to Carlotta!" Allen was sometimes shocked by Joseph's tenderness.

"No. I wonder why what is most appealing about people is so often overlooked or misjudged. Mike's being unconvincing redeemed him for me."

"It embarrasses me," Allen said, and heard the irritation in his voice.

Joseph, however, was not challenging, always only offering what was true for himself. For an hour, sometimes two, Allen could be nearly deprived of his grief even while he turned some of its themes into this long duet.

But much of what Allen had to deal with couldn't be debated while he modeled or sang in the open air. His obsession with Pierre's body, which had been shocked out of him at its cremation, returned first in dreams, sexually explicit without arousing Allen. He would wake in tears, his body aching as if he had flu or had fallen down a flight of stairs. At night, sitting in front of a television program he couldn't watch, he would see instead Pierre in all his sexual guises, and Allen was as sexually unmoved as he was with any stranger. Sometimes it seemed to Allen his body's angry revenge against Pierre's terrible desertion, but in his mind he couldn't be angry with Pierre. He wept for Pierre's fear, horror, sense of betrayal, alone in a house Allen now knew could be as much a jail as it was a safe haven. And wasn't safe. Why did he have to betray Pierre again now in feeling nothing, nothing at all?

He should go away. He should look for work. He should sell the house. He sat. His hair grew.

"I've come to give you a haircut," Roxanne said, standing at the door with a black satchel, halfway between doctor's bag and salesman's sample case.

"Alma doesn't want you here."

"Alma's in Arizona," Roxanne said.

"For Christmas?"

"Yes. She thought a family Christmas would be nice for the boys, and she's tired of the rain."

Allen realized that she was trying not to look around, not to look down at the floor. The last time she had been in this room she had broken in and found Pierre lying dead on the floor. Joseph had let Allen work through his own morbidity, tracing the body's position on the rug, knowing what of the head had been torn away, repeating every nauseating detail until Allen could see it himself though he had not been able to look, in fact, at the dead body at the morgue. Roxanne, like Joseph, had seen. Her exorcising would be of a different order, and Allen could never ask her about it, though he could see it in the vulnerability of her attentiveness.

"I'm not sure Carlotta would approve of a haircut. She's not finished."

"She asked me to," Roxanne said. "Not short—shorter. She says physically we all have one thing in common: we all have amazing hair."

"Joseph?"

"Well, his is peculiar."

"Have you seen him lately?" Allen asked. "He's so much better."

"No, I haven't seen anyone really except Carlotta this morning and now you."

"You look as if you'd taken up Carlotta's fasting," Allen said, trying for a flippancy of tone he'd apparently lost; he simply sounded concerned.

"I eat," Roxanne said. "I don't sleep well. I get tired."

"I should be offering you something," Allen said. "People who live alone develop very bad manners."

She asked for a glass of milk and followed him out into the kitchen.

"Is Alma staying with Mike?" Allen asked.

"As far as I know," Roxanne said. "She wasn't specific, and I didn't ask."

"That surprises me."

"Alma's a surprising woman," Roxanne said without irony.

"To me she's usually overpredictable," Allen said. "I've been hurt by her but not surprised."

Roxanne nodded. "Were you surprised at me?"

"To be honest, I didn't think much about you. I was glad at first not to have to see you. You were too close . . . Just now, when I opened the door and saw you, I was going to say, 'Pierre isn't home.' Still."

"You look sort of awful . . . not the hair. Actually I like that, except it makes you look like some other kind of person."

"What kind?" Allen asked, throwing his head back in a gesture he had learned from his hair.

"More of a brave fool. Carlotta says you're carrying a gun and talking about killing people."

"Did she send you over here to be some sort of Delilah?" Allen asked.

"I don't think so. She says Joseph says you aren't serious because you haven't mentioned it to him; you're putting her on."

"If I kill anyone, I won't kill anyone we know," Allen said. "Not even Alma."

"She's frightened of all the wrong things."

"I understand that," Allen said. "So have I been. I still am. So much for self-knowledge. Roxanne, are you going to leave her?"

"She'll probably leave me," Roxanne said. "She may have already."

"I can't see her being that kind of fool."

"You're not that much alike," Roxanne said. "Let me give you the haircut."

Nor was she, after all, much like Pierre, though they could wear the same shirts. It suddenly occurred to Allen that he should have offered Roxanne some of Pierre's clothes. Well, he might have thought of it if she'd been around. Unisex was a fad, not a fact. No woman, no matter how deprived of flesh, could have the leanness that made Pierre so fragile and elegant. The flattest female chest promised swelling, the flattest belly a potential birth bubble. Roxanne, so thin she was nearly a stick figure, brought to mind images of stiff toys. She was, like other small women Allen had known, heavy on her feet, and he had seen more boys than girls with her head of sandy mist. Still, her body was, by its nature, amorphous. How well Allen had understood Joseph's confession that he was reluctant to father a child, not just because of the child but because of the awful transformation that took place for Ann.

"I haven't told Carlotta that I didn't get my hair cut because I couldn't face my barber. I could have gone to someone else, I suppose."

"You've got to get something to do," Roxanne said, "or find somebody willing to worry about you on a domestic level."

"There's nothing wrong with the way I keep house."

"You're not keeping heart," Roxanne said.

"Isn't that what's the matter with you?" Allen asked gently.

She sat down at the kitchen table, put aside her scissors and comb, and neither looked at him nor spoke for a moment.

"It seems important," she said then with slow difficulty, "to keep heart—and so nearly impossible. It must be that much harder for you with Pierre already dead. If we can't really care, it's just too awful."

"Yes," Allen said, "there's limited energy for what's left to do: figure out whether you're dying of grief or shame or anger."

"I want to be happy," Roxanne said.

"Is that word part of some new feminist plot?"

"I doubt it," Roxanne said.

"Roxanne, anything outside our own hands is out of reach."

"But it's not outside my own reach," Roxanne protested. "I'm happy when I'm working. I'm happy when I'm with the boys and Alma."

"She's left you," Allen said.

Roxanne stood up again and went back to cutting Allen's hair. Allen felt like a drowning man, clutching at Roxanne's buoyant desire, which, since it wasn't strong enough to save him, he dragged down into his own despair. He could not have her bobbing there, a decoy to the great lie.

"Pierre was never happy," he said.

"Of course, he was," Roxanne said impatiently. "Whenever you were home, he was very happy."

Allen moved suddenly out of Roxanne's range and shouted, *"My work made it necessary for me to travel!"*

"Sit down. Stop yelling. I didn't come over here to fight with you. I came over to give you a haircut."

"I wonder if Joseph ever got to feeling the way I do now, sick of the institutional kindness."

She had left the wings of hair over his ears, and by now, used to the greater length of it, he felt protected rather than exposed.

"I ponder growing a beard," he said, inspecting her job and himself in the bathroom mirror.

He hadn't. He had contemplated lying on his bed and letting hair grow as if he were a corpse until years later he'd be discovered entirely blanketed with hair, his own final curtain.

Roxanne came every day through the holiday. Allen had declined Christmas with the Rabinowitzes; so had Roxanne. Carlotta seemed to disappear to undisclosed relatives somewhere in the interior.

Roxanne didn't ask Allen to Alma's house, obviously because that was what it was. Left behind alone, Roxanne became caretaker. Instead, she brought the meal to him, basically duck and wild rice, but it was the trash of Christmas that was her real contribution, broken candy canes, defective paper bells, a Santa on skis who kept falling over, a music box that played the first three notes of "Silent Night" and then groaned like a fly in a trap. She had dozens of things, all collected from the wreckage of Christmas Eve at her drugstore.

"Can you imagine? Nobody else wanted any of it. Nobody seems to have kids any more, or the kids mustn't have anything but the best."

At first Allen only sat to watch what Roxanne took out of bag or box and played at being mock alarmed or offended by whatever she set out on table or sill, hung about the room at random, but then he became intrigued with a plastic drummer who was supposed to drum as he was pulled along and didn't.

"He's not broken. He's just out of line," he said, and in a moment the drummer gave a smart report.

Lots was beyond fixing.

"The Liberty Bell is cracked," Roxanne said. "Why should a Christmas bell with just a bashed-in corner be rejected?"

"What's the matter with this hand puppet?"

"Turn it around; some kid put gum in its hair. I can cut that out."

"Best barber in town," Allen said.

When they left the living room to sit down to dinner, it looked as if half a dozen children had been called away from play.

"What are we going to do with it all?" Allen asked.

"Give it to the children's wing of the hospital or the Salvation Army."

"What kinds of Christmases did you have as a child?" Allen asked.

"Different kinds, lots of different kinds. Maybe that's partly where I got the idea that we ought to be happy because, when people make an effort, that's really all they want."

"Are you absurd enough to tell me you've been trying to make me happy?"

"I guess so," she said. "Anyway, *I* am."

Did he have to be humble if he couldn't be haughty in his grief? Allen had rarely been given anything that really pleased him. Even when he was given what he'd expressly asked for, he found fault with it. The blue of the sweater wasn't the exact blue he had in mind. He wanted the paperback rather than the hardback of Lawren Harris; the hardback was too much a coffee table book. He had never wanted to be given anything for the house; the house was Pierre's, to be given to by Allen. He had been that way since he could remember. He had been afraid not so much of being bought as of being changed by what other people wanted for him.

"Do you have any family left?" Roxanne asked.

"No, no one close. I never knew my father. He left my mother before I was two. Mother died—oh, about a year before Pierre came to live with me."

"What was she like?"

"She had that kind of cold, prim prettiness women develop who've been badly treated by men. She was intelligent; she was ambitious for me."

"How did she raise you?"

"Her parents helped at first. Then she was a librarian. We didn't really like each other. There was a sort of wary gratitude between us, but once I was grown, I think she was afraid I might dive into her blouse again or mount her. And she kept buying me things like rifles and stories about the sea. Once she bought me a dog. I made her take it back the next day. I've never been able to stand extravagance unless there's money to pay for it."

"Where did you live?"

"Surrey—British Columbia's Orange County, without the money. I expect some of our old neighbors are responsible for the trash mail that's come in in the last several months. They've even got morality and the last judgment down to comic-book formula. Have you ever seen any of it?"

"No," Roxanne said.

"At first I threw it away. Then it began to amuse me." Allen got up and went to his desk, opened a drawer, and found three objects that looked like books of raffle tickets. "Take a look."

They were titled things like "This Was Your Life" and "Sodom and Gomorrah." Each page was one strip high and two frames long; all ended in the flames of hell.

"Nobody who sends this stuff ever signs a name. I wonder why righteousness needs to be anonymous."

"Because you have a gun," Roxanne said. "They believe in evil."

"Well, perhaps that's as well," Allen said. "I believe in justice enough not to shoot anyone I lived next door to as a child simply on spec."

"Pierre kept talking about killing himself or your killing yourself, and then he did. Now you're talking about killing other people."

"I don't know how else to say how murderously angry I am," Allen said quietly. "That's all."

"Why don't you come out?" Roxanne said.

"Come out? Where do you think I've been since I was arrested? I haven't been offered a job since. How *out* can you get?"

"But I mean, say something about it. Make a political point."

"For what? Some of your silly little gay rags that are read by twenty-five people who advertise for each other's cocks every month?"

"There's something I want to say—there is no point in my defending gay politics—but there's something both you and Alma are very mixed up about. You can be superior to people like Pierre and me, that's fine, but you can't be superior to yourself. You're as much a cock-sucker as anyone in the want ads. You're as much a fairy and as much a victim. If even Pierre's killing himself isn't enough to jar you loose, maybe nothing is."

"Loose from what?"

"Your worship of the straight world. Your hatred of your own."

"It's not a world. It's a street scene."

"Alma's coming home tomorrow," Roxanne said.

"You get tired of an argument awfully quickly," Allen said. "Well, anyway, I won that one. Alma's coming home."

After Roxanne had gone, Allen paced against the offense she had been to him. Though he had, at one time or another, called himself every ugly sexual name there was, no one else had ever dared to. Allen had not put himself in that kind of sordid situation where he could be degraded. Even his first sexual experience had been with a teacher who was sensitive, guilty, but never vulgar. Yet that little cunt he'd more or less fished out of the gutter, who didn't have the loyalty to call on him unless that bitch Alma was out of town, felt free to call him a cock-sucker, a fairy, a victim!

He slammed his fist into his palm and said aloud, "I am a man!"

Then he found himself laughing, not on the edge of lunacy but in relief. It was exactly what he had to say not only to himself but to the world, in *Weekend, The Canadian, Saturday Night,* and *Maclean's.*

It did not occur to Allen that, once he made up his mind to make a full statement, no one would want it.

"That sort of thing went out in the sixties with Paul Goodman and his crowd, didn't it?" one editor asked.

"A quiet sort of confession, maybe," another began dubiously, "but stuff about not finding work, about suicide —well, excuse me, but that self-pity and melodrama are just what the rest of us are pretty tired of. It may sound unfeeling, but it's like we know old people ache; we don't want to go on hearing about it."

"Allen, look, we haven't dropped you, damn it! You've dropped us. You haven't been here in months, and you know, the grapevine did let us know maybe you needed to take a holiday. Toronto isn't a hick town, what do you think? There's plenty of work. I'd have given you this article on the asbestos strike except I assigned it just this morning."

"Take my advice," said yet another, who had been spared the raid because he had been home with the flu. "Just let it keep blowing over. Take an assignment here and there—turn them down, too, if they're at all, you know—and in six months, a year, you'll be right back where you were. *I* can't begin; you can see that, but once other people do, I promise you . . ."

It was to this man Allen, who had been ironic and polite with all the others, shouted, "Do you know how many queens and cock-suckers like you are in this business and therefore can't help me out?"

"I have a fair idea," came the cool answer.

"Maybe it's time people had a specific idea," Allen said.

"I wouldn't get into that if I were you. Contrary to a lot of arguments you hear, the police are very cooperative about blackmailers."

"I wouldn't *dream* of blackmailing you," Allen said. "I was just thinking about some sort of billboard, maybe called 'The Queens of Industry.' There might be a series of them: 'Fairies in Politics,' 'Cock-suckers in the Civil Service,' 'Queers in Communication and Education.' Just for everyone's information, because there may be some people being screwed who don't know it or don't know why."

Not only office doors but also private doors in Toronto began to close on him. At the sound of Allen's voice, the apartment intercoms went dead, and no buzz followed for building doors to open. By the end of two weeks there wasn't anyone in Toronto media willing to talk with him, and none of the assignments suggested or promised had come through.

An old acquaintance, taken too much to drink to be careful enough about anyone or anything, admonished Allen, "There's screwing and screwing, Allen, old man, and you're into the wrong kind."

At the end of the third week, Allen walked into the office

of *The Body Politic*, and there sat the men who were willing to kiss each other in public to make a political point. They had in common with college professors, which one or two of them seemed to be, a wardrobe not required to grow up and leave home. They had the clean, tumble-dry look of students, eyes young and grave above misleading beards. Allen might have been only a few years older than some of them; he felt like their grandmother, dry cleaned, clean-shaven, eyes rheumy with accustomed grief.

"No, sorry," was the answer there. "We bully the shit out of people to come out, but we don't witch-hunt our own."

Flicked by their quiet tone of superiority, Allen said, "You know, this magazine is nothing but a larger closet—it doesn't even get into the real world."

"All you guys are the same. Anything under half a million circulation isn't real. The fourteen thousand people who take *The Body Politic* read it, cover to cover."

"Of course, they do," Allen said. "You're preaching to the converted."

"Listen, brother," another said, "if this is a closet, it's your closet, don't shit in it. If you want to break out, don't kill your fellow prisoners; shoot the guards."

"What I'm telling you is," Allen shouted in desperation, "the guards are faggots! The cops are faggots; the editors are faggots!"

Somebody took him out for a drink and talked about sociological paranoia, grief-related pathology, the health of collective living and working.

"I don't really think you understand what's happening to me," Allen said finally very quietly.

He had never before really cared what he was asked to do; some assignments had been more interesting than others, some humanly or technically challenging. Since his first year of learning to use a camera, he had not been interested in choosing what he photographed. He simply wanted to be the very best in how it was done. Now Allen had his own subject, and no one, not even these young radicals, dared deal with it. No one would allow his revenge to be news. Very well. He would turn it into art.

Allen had for years been the trusted photographer at gatherings where discretion nearly always was overcome by vanity and sentiment. Even the most vulnerable of men—politicians—have need of recklessness, and Allen's collection of compromised men included Cabinet ministers as well as university presidents, doctors, and other tycoons. It had been a source of great amusement to many of them that the man who had done their most nobly exposed public faces, the portraits that inspired the nation, also had photographed their private pleasures. Allen Dent was, of course, to be absolutely trusted. He was one of them, and he did not have as much to lose only because he did not have as much.

The revolutionaries dreamed impossibilities: if tomorrow every homosexual in the country suddenly turned green (or lavender), social attitudes would have to change. Well, Allen had offered to do nearly that single-handed, and no one would let him, as censored by *The Body Politic* as by *Weekend*.

Allen returned to Vancouver inspired.

"Any work?" Joseph asked him.

"Not a thing," Allen answered so cheerfully Joseph looked alarmed. "I decided something when I was back there. I decided that begging to be put back to work when I don't even need that kind of money is crazy. I'm missing the opportunity of my life. I should be putting together a show of my own, an Allen Dent retrospective. I think even Dale would be interested in it."

"A great idea!" Joseph said.

"I need time, and I've got it. I think it could be sent right across the country, and, once I get that sort of attention, a really good press, I can more or less go back to work at what I want anytime . . ."

Like Roxanne, Allen needed wall space, but a great deal more of it. He stripped the walls of his house of the mirrors and hangings he had bought gradually over the years for

Pierre. Then he had to repaint, and it took three coats of white to cover Pierre's taste for dark gold. Having that long chore to do gave Allen the time he needed to think before he actually settled to going through his files.

He had no intention of using any of the incriminating material he had in the retrospective. Those pictures would be used only as the basis for selecting the portraits he would hang. Among them he could also use his portrait of Auden, reading with the Russians, one of Allen's first assignments to take not only a great but secretly deeply cherished face; of Isherwood, recently enough to be a gay activist; of Ginsberg; of Kate Millett. He could also include portraits of his friends: Alma, Roxanne, Carlotta (Pierre would say she hardly counted), Dale Easter. And Pierre, of course, would be the refrain. There would be portrait after portrait of Pierre. This show would be Pierre's memorial as well as Allen's revenge. And he did not have to *say* anything, even start the rumor. To anyone at all aware, the principle of selection would be obvious, and the show would be the talk of Canada without a newspaper's or magazine's ever mentioning the testimony it was.

"When are you going to finish?" Allen asked Carlotta. "I'm awfully busy with my own work, and I'm tired of this gun."

"Good," she said. "I'm tired of your face. Another week."

He did not tell her he had discovered he'd already shot his enemies. Now all he had to do was hang them.

Enemies?

Yes, every damned one of them, down to Pierre himself. This was a memorial to betrayal.

Carlotta finished her work. Joseph called round less often. Ann occasionally dropped by with a casserole or a cake.

"I know you're working hard. I don't want to interrupt. I just don't want you to forget to eat."

Joy toddled around the living room, where enlargements

of various faces had already been put up. She stopped in front of the marvelous ruin of folding flesh Auden's face had become, pointed, and said, "Lady."

"No . . ." Ann began.

"Don't correct her," Allen said. "It's a marvelously androgynous face."

When Joy pointed to a languorous Pierre and said, "Girl," Ann blushed.

"He would have loved that," Allen said. "It would have pleased him absolutely."

"Will there be any children?" Ann asked.

"No," he said. "None."

Tony Trasco's face, gravely young and inquiring, was immediately dismissed from Allen's mind. There would be no wishful thinking in this show. Behind each portrait there must be one indisputable fact: homosexual experience. Those famous and self-confessed should be placed strategically near those famous and closeted. Where he had a choice, Allen selected the more formal, the more serious, the more respectable, except in the photographs of Pierre, who would flaunt through this crowd, exposing them all.

"Well, since I don't do photography," Dale said, "it wouldn't set a precedent, and I think a retrospective a marvelous idea."

"I'd like to take it right across the country this spring, summer, and fall, travel with it," Allen said.

"I'm afraid I can't help you there. I don't even have a Toronto contact. All my business is in the States and Europe. I'd be glad to see what I can do in L.A. or Houston or New York."

"No," Allen said, "I want this one to stay Canadian."

It did not take him long to locate galleries in all the major cities. A couple of phone calls to Ottawa made it clear that there was Canada Council money available for Allen and for the galleries, if they applied, to help finance the project. There could even be a catalogue.

"Once you're doing the right thing," Allen said to Joseph, "everything just seems to fall into place. Before I leave here, I'll put the house on the market. That will give me money if I need it . . . and freedom. I'm going to have a good look around this country and see whether there's someplace else to go."

Allen began to go out again in the evening, to chamber music, to the theater. He could still attract the smiles of unattached young women, but he also now stirred gossiping ripples across the clusters of respectable men, the chartered accountants, university teachers, doctors, several of whom would hang in the show, all of whom could. Allen wished he had done more working and playing in Vancouver just for the purpose of this show. Still, he had done enough so that no one in the city would be in any doubt. All this crowd would go to the opening—oh, yes, surely. They'd be delighted to pay homage to this elusive darling, who now, because slightly tarnished, was more attractive than ever.

Allen was excited. Sometimes, as he hung a new print, he laughed aloud in satisfaction. The pictures of Pierre, which at first he wasn't sure he could stand, seeing that future/past of Pierre's blown away head in every whole angle, began to feel companionable. In fact, Allen could sometimes even talk with him.

"You'd say this isn't a very nice thing to do," to a face of Pierre with a shadow of beard, the kind of photograph Pierre would have destroyed if he'd had a chance. "I know that. It isn't. If you were alive, I wouldn't do it. I wouldn't have to."

One of his mother's favorite expressions to stop him from a course of action dangerous or distasteful to her had been, "Well, it's your funeral."

It was Pierre's funeral. He had, as another stupid old saying went, asked for it.

It was not until the night before the opening, when he and Dale finished hanging the last photograph, that Allen felt the real impact of what he had done. It was Pierre's resurrection among illustrious, if preponderantly guilty, witnesses, his Pierre: young, ambiguous, enticing, who had shot himself in the enormous silence Allen had re-created here, in sorrow, in revenge.

"This is—ah—very good stuff," Dale said, moving restlessly about the room. "I wonder only about—how shall I put it? Since it is my gallery, I wouldn't want people to think that my vanity had been served . . ."

"Your photograph stays," Allen said.

"And Alma's? I'm not sure . . ."

"And Alma's."

That night Allen couldn't sleep. Before the next night was over, he would know what he had done or was beginning to do. All his life so self-protective, so circumspect, it was an entirely new experience to be apprehensive about *failing* to be exposed. People must see, see and explain to each other, until the news traveled out before the show, preparing audiences all across the country. The catalogue, simply titled "Allen Dent: A Retrospective," gave the name, title, occupation, and place of residence of every person photographed, except for Pierre. "Pierre" was the only identification of his pictures, ten of them.

It was noon when Alma arrived at the door, larger than life, as she had often seemed.

"You've put on weight again," Allen said, smiling at her, not inviting her in.

"You have got to take my picture out of that show," Alma said.

"Whatever for?" Allen asked. "It's a lovely picture."

"Do you really think you're going to get away with it? Do you really think all those important people are going to let you do that to them? Screwing children may be too apolitical an offense to put you behind bars, but this isn't. This is libel. This is slander. I'll sue."

"For what?" Allen asked, all bewildered innocence.

"You bastard!"

It was a heady pleasure, seeing Alma as angry and as helpless as she was.

"Regretting your friends often only makes it worse," he

said, his voice teacherly as it had often been with Alma in the past, to no effect obviously.

"Those pictures of Pierre—they're just ludicrous. You know that. You're making a fool of yourself is what you're doing."

"A small price for the pleasure," Allen assured her.

"What do you think you're trying to prove anyway?" she demanded, genuine bewilderment modestly undermining her anger.

"I'm not trying to prove anything," Allen said. "You work in a gallery. You know art isn't propaganda. Its pretensions are quite different. They're concerned with truth, if I recall the gist of my fine arts elective."

"Don't you *care* who you hurt?"

"No," Allen said, smiling, "not one bit. Surely you, of all people, can understand that."

She looked as if she might strike him, restrained herself because of the deep lesson she had learned from Mike, no doubt, who had never been taught you didn't hit back.

"Allen, I would probably be a very different person if I didn't have children. As a mother, I'm asking you to take my picture out of your show."

"Pierre is my even better excuse for inhumane behavior, and he's dead."

"Exactly! Tony and Victor are very much alive . . ."

"And therefore as unsafe as you and I are."

"You're a sick man," Alma said. "You have to be stopped. You will be stopped."

She hesitated, obviously wondering if there was any angle she'd neglected. Then she turned away.

In the late afternoon Alma's father telephoned.

"Allen, I hear there's a picture of Alma in your retrospective."

"That's right."

"She seems awfully upset about it, and I wonder if there's any way to have it removed from the show. I'd be very glad to buy it for whatever amount seemed reasonable to you . . . for the inconvenience to you as well."

"It's not for sale," Allen said. "It's not a selling show."

"I see. Well, perhaps simply for removing it . . ."

"It can't be done, I'm sorry."

"Oh, surely anything *can* be done. We're reasonable men."

"No, I'm not," Allen said.

"But you've been a friend of Alma's. There's no reason why you'd want to threaten her reputation in any way. She feels she's in rather inappropriate company . . ."

"On the contrary, the whole show is a monument to pretension and hypocrisy. She should feel right at home."

"I hadn't taken you for a man who would make enemies foolishly."

Allen whistled the melody for the line "Freedom's just another word for nothing left to lose," knowing Alma's father would not pick up the clue.

"Well, I'll have to see what else can be done."

Allen was elated. There was nothing anyone could do.

The next phone call came at 6:00 P.M. It was Dale Easter.

"The gallery's just been closed by the fire department," he said. "I never did intend to have real shows here; I didn't even check out the regulations."

"But they can't do that!" Allen protested. "Not just like that with no warning. Who sent them?"

"I suppose, when I applied for the party license, the liquor board notified them . . ."

"Alma's father has done this."

"Allen, I'm sorry, but I'm not going to fight it. I thought at first Alma was being paranoid, but she isn't, is she?"

"About what?"

"About what this show really is. It's hot enough to burn my place down without any fire, never mind the exits."

"Damn it, Dale, it will put you on the Canadian map!"

"All-star to bush league. Who needs it?"

"If I can't get this show to the public . . ."

"You may in another six months get back to what you ought to be doing. Do you think I would have agreed if I'd realized what you're up to? Do you think any of the other galleries would go along? Use your head."

"You won't show it."

"No, Allen, I won't."

"If Alma hadn't said anything, you'd have been none the wiser."

"Until after opening night. A lot of our acquaintances would be very amused at how badly I failed Canadian identity tests. There I was, saying to Alma, 'I not only didn't know he was gay; I didn't know he'd ever been a Cabinet minister; I didn't even know his name!' She's invaluable to me, that woman."

"If I took you and Alma out of it?"

"No way," Dale said. "Just no way."

Allen stood, shaking with frustration. His mind moved from hanging the show in his own house to kidnapping Tony. Nothing that occurred to him would work. The only way he could succeed with this show was to call no public attention to it, and that, in Vancouver, was now impossible. The question was whether or not he could get it out of town and into Edmonton without interference. If he could once get a gallery run of a couple of weeks, he was sure he could keep going. Dale had neither contacts nor interest in stopping him outside town. Alma's father would not have the influence in other cities he did here.

At just past eight Carlotta turned up. "Will you tell me what's going on?"

"Alma didn't like her picture in the show. I wouldn't take it down. So her father had the building closed down."

"Dale's not going to stand for that, is he?"

"Even if Dale offers you his gallery for a show, don't accept," Allen said. "He just doesn't have the feel for things Canadian, you know?"

"But he was so enthusiastic about it. What's really going on? What kind of a game are you and Alma playing?"

"It's called 'Fighting for Your Life,' " Allen said.

"Are you going to give it to the papers?"

"No," Allen said. "I'm not going to do anything. In two weeks I'll get it to Edmonton, and it can start there."

"But this is your town. Before I'd let Alma's father shut me down, he'd hear about it first thing on 'Good Morning Radio,' second thing in the *Province* for breakfast, and throughout the day. How can you let him run you out of town?"

"It doesn't much matter to me here, to tell the truth. This is really a Toronto show taking its time about getting there."

"You know, that's the trouble with you continental types. You don't recognize home ground even when you're ankle deep in it. Vancouver needs this show, Allen. You can't let it be shut down—not even by a bunch of red-necks, for God's sake, but by a crazy personal friend."

"By now Alma means more to me than that. She's closer to being my wicked fairy godmother."

"Well, since I'm all dressed up with no place to go, and it's your fault, perhaps you should take me somewhere for a drink."

"You are looking very elegant," Allen admitted, "but I'd just as soon not meet other people on the prowl because the show didn't open. I don't want to have to explain."

"Well, I do," she said, gathering a great web of black shawl around her.

"I'd rather you didn't," Allen said, hoping the mildness of his request would be more effective than a more dramatic command.

The item in the following evening's *Sun* said simply, "It was doubly disappointing last night when the fire department closed the King Gallery. This was the first time its owner, Dale Easter, had agreed to show not only a Canadian but a local artist's work. Allen Dent, who has an international reputation as a photographer, had mounted a fifteen-year retrospective, which will now not be shown in Vancouver at all but open in Edmonton in two weeks. Dale Easter has no plans for other shows and therefore is not interested in going to the expense of complying with fire regulations. Vancouver art lovers have missed their one opportunity to see the King Gallery as well as the work of one of our most well-known native sons. Allen Dent was born in Surrey . . ."

From there on it read like an obituary, which seemed appropriate enough. There was nothing, Allen was relieved to see, that suggested motives more complex than safety. If rumors had begun to circulate, they were nebulous enough for the media to ignore. By the time the public had actually been exposed to the show, rumors would be too specific for the media to do anything but censor them.

Most of the world was, after all, like Joseph, for less salutary reasons. It didn't occur to Joseph to question the fire department's action, though he lamented it. What Allen needed in the cities ahead of him were several more Almas with no personal investment in closing the show down but with enough perception to recognize what he was doing and enough malice to report what they knew at the right cocktail parties.

Allen had cleaned out the house of everything but furniture the real estate agent said would be helpful to sell it, and he had arranged for that to be stored as soon as the house was sold. He was packing a generous couple of suitcases to take to Edmonton and on across the country when Roxanne arrived.

"I came to say good-bye," she explained, and when Allen expressed neither gratitude nor admiration for her courage in coming to see him, she added, "because I'm leaving Vancouver."

"Going south with the migration this time?"

"No," she said, "I'm going alone."

"Then there is a straw that breaks the camel's back? By now I could as easily believe in the Easter bunny."

"I don't agree with Alma about a lot of things, too many, I guess, but I wish she could have figured out how to burn down as well as shut down that show."

"You?" Allen asked, incredulous.

"Yes, me. It's a terrible thing you're doing."

"Justice can't always be good-looking," Allen said, liking the cynical flippancy of tone that had gradually come back to him.

"If what you're doing is just, then what the police did to you in Toronto was merciful."

"That's certainly Alma's view."

"No, it isn't. She hasn't got a view, really. She's too frightened and guilty and self-righteous to think, and so are you."

"On the contrary," Allen assured her, "I've thought very carefully. It was you who suggested I make a political statement in the first place. This is my political statement."

"What's political about betraying your own people?"

"Some of us require betrayal to see the light . . . like me. I'm doing unto others what's been done to me."

"You really are too much, you people," Roxanne said, shaking her head. "Where do you get the crust to be so sure you can get even and have the right to?"

"I'm nothing more than poor white trash from Surrey, you know," Allen said. "I still don't have to grovel."

"Don't knock your mother. She raised you. If she was still alive, if Pierre was still alive, you wouldn't be doing this."

"Of course not. It took me awhile to see that I was without obligation and could do what I think is right."

"It's not right! It's what you want to do to get even. It won't work."

"How do you know?" Allen demanded. "What could you know? You're not just innocent of the real world; you're stupid about it. You should go out and do some dealing with it before you come here telling me what to do. You, who betray all your friends, neglect your work to be not even Alma's lover so much as her housemaid, baby-sitter, caretaker, who gets paid in bed privileges rather than cash, because Alma's tighter with her purse than her cunt—you come here to teach me what's right?"

"Something horrible seems to be happening to all of us," Roxanne cried. "You used to be a person I trusted."

"I could have said the same about you."

"But you understand what I was trying to do, don't you? You understand I was only trying to love her."

"Of course, I understood. You understand me now. We just don't approve of each other."

"I am your friend, Allen."

"Where are you going . . . anywhere in particular?"

"Dale keeps telling me about L.A. and San Diego, and I know some women who've gone down there."

"What did make you decide?"

Roxanne hesitated, then shrugged. "Since she hasn't told me, I guess technically . . . oh, what difference does it make? She's pregnant."

"Pregnant?"

"That's right."

"That woman does nothing by halves!"

"Or everything," Roxanne said wryly. "Anyway, you probably ought to take her out of the show, for credibility, if nothing else."

"Not on your life!" Allen said. "She stays."

"Why? Why does it matter to you so much?" Roxanne asked.

"It's a beautiful show, Roxanne, with perfect moral balance, perfect ambiguity: funeral and resurrection, betrayal and tribute, vengeance and justice. I'm obliged to nothing else now . . . surely not the likes of Alma. Why should you be pleading for her even now on your way out?"

"I love her," Roxanne said.

"Love excuses far too much."

Allen looked at her thoughtfully—the toy he'd found in a record shop and brought home to Pierre, another joke turned into a friendship by its victim because she was so attentive and detached. The people closest to Allen shared an indifference to being seen as foolish, unlike himself or Alma, so endlessly and vainly self-protective.

"I'll send you a postcard somewhere along the way," Roxanne said.

"I hope you never come back," Allen said.

"I hope your show burns down in Edmonton," she said.

They caught each other in an awkward, hard embrace, each the size but blatantly wrong sex of the other's lover. For a moment after Roxanne left, Allen wondered if they both were being blind, but he quickly decided he, at any rate, was not. Allen might have settled for the negative solution Roxanne would be for him, but Roxanne had a different kind of future. She went south, her attention intact. Allen left for Edmonton, an artist at last, without the grace to be amazed that he could have been driven to it.

.

Carlotta Painting

*K*NOWING Alma was alone and pregnant should have encouraged Carlotta to effect their reconciliation. Her anger with Alma had never been much more than a convenience, Carlotta's defense against Alma's preoccupation with Roxanne. But as long as they were estranged, Carlotta could put off thinking about a portrait of Alma. Eventually it had to be done, but Carlotta postponed it as long as she could by practicing on other people.

"But I'm nobody special," Ann protested. "I'm not really one of you at all."

"What kind of a group do we seem then?" Carlotta asked.

"You're all so very clever, aren't you? I knit." She laughed at the comparison.

"I'll do you knitting. Then it won't seem such a waste of your time."

"Oh, I didn't mean you to think I'm too busy . . ."

"Then say you will."

"Of course, I will," Ann said.

Carlotta decided to work in Ann's kitchen. She liked the irony of light from the kitchen window which looked out onto the sculpture she had used in her portrait of Mike.

"Is it really all right if I knit? May I keep my glasses on?"

Ann was the only one who did not assume she was doing Carlotta a favor. Carlotta was not used to being asked for this kind of reassurance, and she was surprised that her simple attention was enough to keep Ann's color high, her body alert. If Carlotta hadn't baited Joseph occasionally, she might as well have been studying a sack of potatoes. Pierre disappeared into a dream that left his face blankly idiotic. Sometimes Carlotta debated painting each of them as they were reduced by stillness; she had sketches of Joseph as more bundle than person, Pierre as a retarded child, Allen's face cooked with grief. Her only sketches of Mike were done badly from memory, obsessive pages of his genitals with a hand, foot, ear, hairline, sometimes faintly drawn on the same page to suggest an actual sexual view.

Mike, after all, was the first one. Carlotta's motives had been so confused it was a wonder she had accomplished anything at all. She could look at the painting now with some detachment. It was so obviously the image of Mike she had wanted him to have of himself so that he'd finally have the courage to take the great risks his dreams required. Instead, inadvertently, she had exposed his fantasy to him as a fantasy, and he had rejected it. But he would have rejected even more violently any image that had revealed him as the stunned and drifting man he actually was. Carlotta could hardly have discovered the idea of himself that had emerged in Mike when he went to Arizona.

Carlotta wondered what kind of idea of self Ann held,

who so obviously expected to be exempt from Carlotta's professional attention. Ann did not think of herself as clever, did not think of herself as anyone else's subject matter, raw material. Yet Allen had taken dozens of pictures of her, and in them Ann seemed perfectly serene under his attention. She was not exactly self-conscious now, posing with her knitting for Carlotta, but she was aware and wary.

"I didn't get over the shock of you for a long time," Carlotta said. "In a sense, you were more of a shock than Joseph's crack-up. Not just to me, to all of us. He'd been getting odder and odder for some time. I understood him by thinking of him as very lonely, without a life of his own, living at the edge of other people's. And all the time there you were . . . and the children."

"You were a bit of a shock to me, too," Ann said, smiling.

"Me? Or all of us?"

"All of you. Well, not so much Mike, though he seemed an awfully definite person."

"He felt cheated, you know. He assumed, once he'd discovered you, that all of us had secret lives."

"I knew Joseph had friends. I think he thought of me and the children as . . . vulnerable? or maybe simply not fitting in."

"*We* didn't fit in surely."

"I would have thought Joseph would have chosen friends more placid."

"You thought we'd probably driven him crazy."

"Well, yes," Ann admitted, "in a way. You're all so agitated so much of the time, and so was he, but, of course, that really made him feel less peculiar. And he seems to . . . not exactly understand but have no trouble with what you do. To this day I can't imagine why Mike went to the trouble he obviously did to build that thing in the backyard. Those evenings Roxanne put on didn't make any sense to me at all. I don't know what to listen to or how to take it. Joseph said he didn't either really, but it finally reassured him because a lot of energy, agitation, was under control."

Carlotta laughed. "What a marvelous definition of art!"

"Is it?"

"When I'm working hard, anxiety turns into excitement."

"Is that why creative people lead anxious and unhappy lives?"

"Do you think we do?"

"Don't you?"

"Well," Carlotta said, feeling goaded and not liking to be victim of her own technique, "I don't think of anxiety as a sort of style we've all adopted. It's just there pretty constantly to be dealt with."

"But most of us avoid a lot of anxiety."

"How?"

"By not being ambitious, I suppose."

"Joseph's never been ambitious," Carlotta said.

"Spiritually he has. He's called himself the father of God . . ."

"Drugs can do that to anyone," Carlotta said. "I'm not ambitious, and, though I'm over being suicidal and don't even fast anymore, I stay this side of insanity only by painting."

"But you're very ambitious," Ann protested.

"Oh, in a sense. We all have our contracts with the world. I wouldn't object to a show in Toronto or Montreal or even New York. But that sort of prestige isn't necessary. Selling is, so when yet another gallery here folds, and people like Dale Easter are above dealing with local talent, I can worry, but that's different. The anxiety I'm talking about doesn't attach itself to any convenient meaning. It picks up fear like radio messages from a door hinge, a flower in someone's hair . . ."

Carlotta had stopped painting, moved to the kitchen window, and finished her sentence, staring at Mike's "School Days," on which Joy had begun to climb.

Why did Ann's assertion that Carlotta, that they all were

ambitious seem an accusation she had to defend herself against? She turned back to Ann.

"I think maybe we're all anxious because we haven't been ambitious enough."

Were anxiety and ambition linked? Was there anyone in the world who wasn't, at least secretly, anxious for—if not working for—a special destiny of some sort? Carlotta didn't want to pose those questions to Ann, whose small, full lips had gone smug, whose eyes behind her glasses were distressed. She had no ambition because her life was what she had been promised all along. How unfair a judgment that was! Ann had buried one husband and seen another through a bad crack-up. She was one of the world's real heroines. Carlotta had no idea how to represent that because she couldn't feel it, except as a kind of resentment. Her mended little finger and heart were no match.

Carlotta's abiding passion was envy. She had envied everyone everything, yes, even Joseph his madness, Pierre his suicide, Allen his grief. Everything outside her own experience was not her own so that her potential for poverty was limitless. She had tried to believe in that poverty, to live in terms of it, not only materially but in her work, painting only her self. When it became clearer and clearer that it was so slow a suicide as to take the form of a long life, she began to doubt her choice. These portraits were exercises in self-doubt, extreme exposures to envy in order to die of it or become immune.

"My mother's a religious fanatic. She believes in humility and pain," Carlotta explained. "Mike said he was jealous of kids with new clothes, with bikes. I was jealous of anyone with a broken arm. I used to lie awake at night to figure out how I could break mine without more pain than I could stand. I'm a coward about pain. What were you jealous of?"

"Talent," Ann said. "Obviously I still am."

"But you have a talent for living," Carlotta said, amiably combative now.

Ann might really be able to teach her how to confront other women without feeling as though she were dealing with some aspect of herself which might be her enemy: Roxanne's lesbian sensibility, Ann's motherhood, both of which seemed to Carlotta extremes of femininity which challenged her own narrow and self-protective taste for men, whom she also envied but in a more natural and less confusing way.

What little pity she had, Carlotta reserved for men. It was certainly there in the portrait of Joseph, done during the time he still longed for invisibility. She had made him, therefore, transparent. The image did not become insubstantial because she set him down in Queen Elizabeth Park in May. He hadn't actually posed there. At that time he couldn't have been among so many flowers without a straitjacket. His torso burned with tulips. His brain was a blooming tree.

Pity outlined the portrait of Allen, his definition so sharp he looked something structured of the most fragile glass with only the thinnest veil of undisguising flesh, the gun more like a vital organ torn from his chest than a weapon clutched to it, his eyes the empty room he lived in.

Carlotta had struggled so negatively hard to keep Roxanne from being nothing more than a failed self-portrait that finally she had caught no more than Roxanne's attention—victory at a basic level, but that was all. Their peculiar sexual encounters did accomplish the one thing: distance. Though Carlotta had anticipated its opposite, she could use what she had instead. Intimacy with anyone else had put Carlotta almost immediately in touch with the violence and vulnerability she had assumed was at the center, in one form or another, of everyone. But she had known only men. Roxanne was no more vulnerable naked than with her clothes on, maybe because she went around exposed by choice. The only thing she had to impose as a lover was gentleness, which had made Carlotta feel childishly immodest, as if she'd been caught masturbating by an adult too timid to punish her.

It was nearly as hard for Carlotta to admit to herself that she included Roxanne's finger up her anus in her masturbating fantasies as it was to know how much more often she recalled Mike's raping her than any of his gentler lovemaking. Pierre's suicide had shocked her into knowing that her own toying with that violence had to be put down and left behind once and for all. With it went the fasting, which had always produced more negative hallucinations than she should have lived with. But sex unflavored with some sort of humiliation, defeat, would be without climax. It wasn't really the physical violence that had excited her. Carlotta, if she wanted sex, usually had to make the first aggressive suggestion. To know Mike wanted her whether she wanted him or not was her triumph in that affair. She had had the power to make him violent and ultimately vulnerable . . . for a few moments anyway.

It had taken her months to admit that, if he hadn't left, eventually Carlotta would have driven him away. She didn't attract, entrap, whatever the talent was, men domestically not, as she always supposed, because she wasn't as attractive as Alma, but because she didn't want them.

Ann obviously did. There was not much else about her that could attract. Oh, she wasn't bad-looking, and she had a good deal more presence than Joseph. Once you really looked at Ann, you didn't forget her. Men as different as Allen and Mike tended to idealize her, but the woman they courted was Alma.

"Do you think men are more vulnerable than women?" Carlotta asked because talking with Ann was a way of keeping her mind on Ann.

"Oh, I don't know," Ann said.

She had been in the middle of counting stitches, and she held her hands still as if they could remember the number while she was distracted.

"Ah," Carlotta said, "that is what I want. Exactly."

What everyone in the world wants, just that kind of attention.

Roxanne and Ann rather than Joseph and Ann would be companion pieces.

With Pierre dead, with Roxanne and Allen and Mike all gone from town, with Alma banished, Carlotta was more alone than suited her. But she was also too much in the wrong company of Ann and the children to have energy in the evening to go out to find people. She read a little, but she had a limited tolerance for the printed word. She didn't own a television, not because she scorned it but because she was afraid of it, as she was of alcohol and drugs. Escapes from anxiety were not cures; only confronting and controlling it were.

That was why doing Allen's portrait, which should have been the hardest of all, was so simple, so clear from the beginning. He was such a manifestation of her own existential anxiety with its murderous terrors, except that he had a focus: Pierre.

Carlotta brooded about Pierre, his awful loneliness, a child playing dress-up day after day in that empty house. He had called more often than Carlotta remembered to call him, and she did his portrait more as a way to keep him company than as a requirement of her own imagination. He had become really interesting to her only now that he was dead. If you had to worship something, it was obviously better to have the object of worship something less fragile than another human being. Pierre should have stayed Catholic. Or maybe he had. Maybe suicide was his only escape, the only renunciation that worked, Allen only incidental to it.

She had a message from Allen that the show had been well, if silently received, until it got to Winnipeg, where it was not only announced and noticed in the paper but reviewed there and on local radio with as much "pretentious snot as could be found in Susan Sontag." The tone was definitely Allen, and Carlotta tried to feel reassured. She wished she had been able to see the show herself, not just the catalogue. The rumor around town was that there had been too many famous queers in the show. Even though homosexuals were said to be not only willing but anxious to oppress each other, surely Dale Easter hadn't shut it down for that reason. Allen's own explanation of Alma's displeasure sounded like her imperious self but wasn't really plausible either. Uneasy curiosity about that made Carlotta both wish to see Alma and put it off.

Then Mike phoned.

"I have a favor to ask."

"Where are you?"

"In Phoenix."

"Oh."

"Listen, Carlotta, I got married last week. I didn't want to say anything beforehand to Alma. It's not as if I should ask her permission. But probably she ought to know. Could you just sort of let her know?"

"I don't suppose you really are a bastard at all," Carlotta said. "You just sometimes seem like one—a matter of method probably."

"Well, look, I can't send her a formal announcement."

"How about a warm, personal letter?"

"She'd have to answer it."

"How long has it been since you've heard from Alma?"

"Months," Mike said. "Since Christmas."

"All right. I'll tell her."

"You know, just so she knows."

"I hope it's a good idea," Carlotta said.

"Oh, it's great."

"Does she have a name?"

"Bunny."

"Bunny."

"Yeah."

"Well, Trasco, good luck."

Carlotta didn't phone. She went directly to the house. She was not accustomed to Alma out in West Point Grey, tended to think of her still in the neighborhood, but this house, ablaze with azaleas, open to the whole view, did suit her much better. Victor answered the door.

"Is your mother here?"

"Yeah. She's in her room."

Since he didn't offer to go get her, Carlotta asked, "Where is that?"

"Upstairs at the end of the hall."

It was easy to find behind the only closed door, on which she knocked. There was a pause and then a surprised "Yes?"

"May I come in?"

"Lot!"

The door swung open, and Carlotta was caught in an uncalled-for embrace.

"You've put on weight," Alma said as she finally let her go. "You look almost healthy."

"So have you. Are you still pregnant?"

"How did you know? Who told you that?"

"Allen."

"But how did he know?"

"Roxanne told him on her way out of town. He told me on his way out."

"But she didn't know! I hadn't told her!"

"She knew."

"What an unholy mess it all is! I wonder if anyone, leaving home, ever actually says good-bye. Mike said he didn't know he was leaving until he'd been away for weeks, but Roxanne knew. She packed and moved all her things while I was out of the house, and she did say good-bye to Tony and Victor. Why didn't she say?"

"She probably wondered the same thing about you."

"I hadn't decided what to do, that's all. I thought Roxanne would probably love a baby, me having a baby. But when I actually was pregnant, it seemed more complicated than that. If Mike were like most men and didn't really care about children, it would be fine. He's very possessive about his children."

"It's Mike's?"

"Well, of course, it's Mike's. Who else could it be?" Alma asked impatiently. "And I was afraid of making her jealous. Roxanne's terribly jealous."

"But you're still pregnant?"

"Well, she's gone. If she'd asked me to have an abortion, maybe I could have."

"Is it too late?"

"I suppose so. Anyway, I've decided to have it."

"Will you tell Mike?"

"I was just trying to write to him," Alma said, gesturing to a mess of papers on her bed.

"You weren't thinking of going back to him . . ."

"Well . . . oh, Lot, can you understand this: can you understand that knowing I'm lesbian hasn't really turned out to have much to do with the way I want to live? I did try. I even tried to turn myself into a feminist. The first time Mike came back, just going out to dinner with him, just walking along the street . . . to feel so blissfully ordinary. And then at Christmastime to see the boys with him, Tony particularly—I don't know how to keep him from veering off. All the time Roxanne was here, I kept worrying . . ."

"But you haven't been in touch with Mike for months."

"I've felt so guilty, you can't imagine. It isn't as if I didn't care desperately about Roxanne. When I first realized, I really did wonder if she and I could somehow . . . and then she just left. That's been devastating. I couldn't really think for a while. Maybe going back to Mike is a crazy idea, but what else can I do?"

"Something," Carlotta said. "Mike just phoned me to tell me he's married again. He wanted to let you know without exactly confronting you with it."

"What's her name?" Alma asked.

"Bunny."

Alma's incredulity shattered into laughter. Carlotta

joined as well as she could. She knew this was as close to tears as Alma would get. When Alma recovered, she walked over to the window and looked out over the view.

"I'm going to be thirty-five day after tomorrow. It seems old to be an unwed mother."

"Can't you get rid of it?"

"I wouldn't," Alma said. "I'm not a secret Catholic or anything. I've even marched in abortion parades. But I wouldn't have one."

"It would be preferable to throwing yourself off Lion's Gate Bridge or anything like that."

"Not after Pierre, thanks, and there's Victor and Tony."

"How will they feel about your having a baby?"

"I've already told them. Victor called me an old fart, but he'll get used to it. Tony's the problem. We haven't exactly been on speaking terms since Roxanne left. There was getting to be too close a thing between them. I guess he blames me. What am I going to do? I've been asking that question for the last five years, and every time it's about something worse."

"Ann Rabinowitz thinks we all lead very agitated lives."

"She's such a nice person, why can't I be like that? Bunny. Did you really say Bunny?"

Carlotta nodded.

"I feel sorry for her. Isn't that awful? I don't really think I'm quite in focus. I shouldn't feel relieved. Or anyway, I shouldn't say so, particularly in front of you. You've always really disapproved of me, but you never used to mind. Have you come back just to say this for Mike?"

"No. I've been meaning to come. I decided I didn't know why I kept aspiring to teach you a lesson, since no one else was ever going to. Everyone else I was trying to be loyal to has left town. I've run out of perfume."

"But everyone is teaching me a lesson."

"Maybe inadvertently."

"It's all revenge. There's nothing to learn from that, is there?"

"Nobody's being vengeful."

"Allen is," Alma said.

"What's all this about Allen?" Carlotta asked.

"Didn't you ever see the show?"

"How could I? According to Allen, you're the one who had it closed down."

"I had to, for all of us. You were in it, too, you know."

"I did know," Carlotta said. "Frankly I was flattered, and it was a good picture. Did you really object to being in Auden and Isherwood's company?"

"But it was everybody," Alma said, "from his personal friends to a United Church minister, a college president, a member of Cabinet—all gay; that's how he chose."

"I hardly feel I qualify," Carlotta said. "How do you know? He couldn't have told you since you weren't on speaking terms."

"I didn't have to be told. Allen's gossiped to me for years about these people. I could see for myself."

"How very clever," Carlotta said.

"He won't get away with it, not once the show gets to Toronto," Alma said.

"I think he may."

"Anyway, Roxanne did agree with me about that. She did think it was a despicable thing to do."

"Why?"

"He's doing exactly what was done to him, only to dozens of people—and his friends. How many suicides does he want committed? What does he think he's proving?"

"I'm not sure."

"Why is it so hard for you to disapprove of nearly everyone but me?"

Carlotta laughed. "You have all the privileges, why should you have the rights as well? And you do do awful things, *awful* things."

"I didn't ever make love with your husband."

"I didn't have one."

"Or your woman lover."

Alma's voice dropped a tone, and Carlotta realized that her frivolous attempt at intimacy with Roxanne had troubled Alma a good deal more than Carlotta's much more important affair with Mike.

"At the time you seemed to be through with them. . . ."

Alma was sitting cross-legged in the middle of her bed, the now-pointless letter to Mike scattered about her. There was no energy in her for an argument, and perhaps there was no point in trying to distract her with it. It hadn't been Carlotta's intention to paint her friends at the crises in their lives, but over and over again that seemed to be when their need and hers coincided. Or they were always in crisis, as Ann thought.

"Don't leave me alone now, will you?" Alma asked. "You're the only one left."

"No."

Carlotta hadn't before begun a portrait while she was still working on another. Once she had started Alma's, she wondered why she had put it off so long. The tension Carlotta often had to create between herself and her subject was natural between herself and Alma, who never cared whether she pleased Carlotta or not as long as she was interested. For the first time, since doing Mike's portrait, Carlotta's attention was caught rather than forced. Though she privately thought Alma was risking far too much to have another child, she was as a goddess of fertility irresistible, except apparently to Roxanne.

"I used to think that it was you I wanted to go to bed with, you I was leaving," Alma said.

Carlotta snorted.

"I still have rape fantasies about you. I was jealous of Mike, you know, not of you."

"Well, I was jealous of you and always have been."

"It's flattering," Alma said.

"Women are meant to be rivals, not lovers."

"Do you really think so?"

"Yes. That's why all this attention to Persephone and Demeter can't explain anything. The myth for women is Arachne and Athena."

"I'm your Athena?"

"Exactly. Women don't worship their goddesses; they correct them. We have to because all our goddesses, like you, are prosocially aggressive."

"I must have missed that particular lecture."

"You're for the status quo, for marriage, for motherhood, and no matter how often, how clearly, how passionately one of us spins out the errors of that life, you banish us. You turned Roxanne into a spider. You turned me into a spider years ago."

"That's very exciting," Alma said, brushing a long, heavy strand of hair behind her ear. "I could have seemed simply dull instead."

"You're never dull, just stupidly mistaken and immortal."

"You're very hard."

"I wear my skeleton on the outside, which is your doing. Don't complain."

Carlotta liked the irony of their sexual discoveries, useless to each in the way she wanted or needed to live, the natural envy of their bond, the deep familiarity. She even half believed what she said: artist as finder of the flaw, which was always discovered in the distance between an idea of the self and its needs, but she was really more interested in the idea, more concerned with portrayal than betrayal, unlike Allen.

"I did try writing," Alma said. "I worked at it. Then I collected a lot of rejection slips, and I realized I was too old for that kind of failure. I'm too old for any kind of failure really."

"That's why it's called the prime of life."

"What's so lovely about being pregnant is you don't have to ask, 'What's the point?' Finally it isn't yours to make or even necessarily to see. There may be generations of people born just to make *one* possible—a Joan of Arc or an Einstein."

"Genes don't make geniuses," Carlotta said. "Cultural necessity does. If you lived in the States right now—I mean, if you'd been raised there, you wouldn't be having another baby; you'd be getting on with writing and probably publishing it."

"No, I wouldn't . . . I'm not as much of a conformist as you think, and anyway, it's not all that different down there. You never go there. You just read books about it."

"It's cheaper."

Carlotta didn't really mourn the loss of Alma's stories to the world, or even to Canada, so why did she taunt? Because Alma's self-justification was so simpleminded and smug, because Carlotta's own, if she ever voiced it, would sound both pretentious and preposterous. Canada no more needed painters of uncertain direction than writers of dubious insight. Certainly she wasn't painting in response to any cultural necessity. Was her drive then no more than the idiot goading of one great-grandmother or another in her blood who otherwise would wait out eternity without a point?

"Why do you paint?" Alma said.

"To say, 'See, we exist.' It seems a lot of work when any mirror has the same message."

"A mirror doesn't say it matters."

Carlotta looked up sharply to catch the color of Alma's fading blush. Then they both laughed.

"I'd forgotten you do that when you're pregnant."

Working as hard as she was, Carlotta sometimes forgot to eat. Ann could read hunger in her face, would cook her something or make her a sandwich. Alma didn't notice, her own sudden cravings the prerogative of pregnancy from which Carlotta was excluded.

"One of the things I wondered about when I was writing was what could a portrait possibly say? What does a face *say?*" Alma asked.

"Start with the obvious: though any portrait may not, it can say sex, age, ethnic background, nationality, class, occupation, marital status, all the vital statistics. Character is in the bones, the set of the mouth, the eyes. Psychological history is the skin."

"You mean scars and whatnot?"

"Obviously, yes, but if I only meant that, you'd have no psychological history at all."

"But isn't most of it clichés out of old wives' tales: the weak chin/weak character, long nose/long cock sort of thing?"

"I'm not inventing your face. If I exaggerate characteristics, I move toward cartoon. Faces are, after all, a lot easier to read than books."

"I don't agree," Alma said, "except faces of people you know well."

"I only paint people I know well, and the only thing I can't paint is our hot air," Carlotta said.

"But nothing anyone says is irrelevant really."

"Neither is the color of your eyes."

Carlotta stopped on her way out of the house to look at Roxanne's wall. She had thought she wanted Alma in some kind of relationship with the view. She had done sketches of Alma standing by the window, sitting up in bed. But maybe she should be painted into Roxanne's sound map of the city.

"Tony won't let me touch it," Alma complained.

"Quite right," Carlotta agreed. "It's an extraordinary piece of work."

"You mean to look at."

"Yes," Carlotta said. "What baffles me about Roxanne is that she does complex things like this but is so . . . simple? ordinary? . . . as a person. Is she?"

"I don't know," Alma admitted. "Sometimes I think she's just so tactful she should be a secret agent. Why didn't she say she knew I was pregnant?"

Carlotta shrugged, still studying the wall, instructional

and aesthetic, only inadvertently redeemed from usefulness by the impossibility of Roxanne's living here.

"It's the only thing she left behind. It would be easier to live with if Tony didn't make it into a shrine."

"Maybe she intends to come back," Carlotta said. "Would you have her back?"

"Not if I could help it," Alma said. "I treat her so badly, for one thing."

"Yes."

The puzzle was Roxanne didn't seem to notice or, if she did, didn't seem to mind. Carlotta remembered how lightly Roxanne took Carlotta's weary disgust in that kind of sexual requirement. Carlotta didn't even know how impersonal a revulsion it was until Roxanne accepted it without offense. Was she stupid or insensitive, or did she have a deeper instinct for self-preservation which didn't depend on anyone else's concern? Carlotta had been able to lie under the weight of Mike's first revulsion until it passed. But to laugh at it as if it had nothing to do with her and then to excuse him from the chore of her desire she could never have done. She had wanted to be in love with him. Roxanne obviously had no interest in being in love with Carlotta.

"I started out this project," Carlotta said to Ann, who was counting stitches again, "making love with my model. If being a *ménage à trois* had occurred to us all those years ago, Mike and Alma might still be together. It didn't occur to us. It didn't occur to me. Are you absolutely heterosexual?"

"I don't suppose so," Ann said. "They say nearly nobody is."

"Seriously?"

"Well, I can imagine it partly because of the way I feel about the children. If Joseph were a woman, I can imagine still being attracted to him. That's all pretty theoretical, I admit. Only after Alma told me about herself and Roxanne, that's what I imagined."

"I *can't* imagine."

"I don't think it's anybody's place to judge. Oh, I felt terribly sorry for Mike. You do feel sorry for the one left. Love can feel like bleeding to death when there's no container for it. I'm awfully glad he's found another woman. He sounds happy."

Carlotta was angry with Ann for being able to describe inadvertently so accurately the way Carlotta had felt after Mike left. It should have been her unique hemorrhage, not something that could be ascribed to Mike because it was also obviously the wound Ann had suffered at John's death. There should perhaps have been comfort in such evidence that Carlotta was an ordinary member of the human race, but she resented it. Why should Ann so comprehend Mike's suffering when Carlotta had been in the process of describing her own?

Carlotta noticed that Ann did the same shifting of center with the children and with Joseph. She didn't take anyone down so much as over a peg so there was less jostling for attention. When occasionally Carlotta stayed for supper, the aura, as distinctive as burning candles, was limelight defused.

Carlotta's mother had set up such competition for her attention and approval that all her children thought of their siblings as their worst, because most knowledgeable, enemies. Carlotta hadn't spoken to a brother or sister in years. She had gone so far as to drop her last name from everything but documents which absolutely required it.

The Rabinowitz children got such carefully divided attention from both Ann and Joseph that they had little practice at grandstanding. Carlotta was not surprised to hear that neither Rachel nor Susan excelled at anything. Aside from having no need to, they could also sense their parents' fear. It was amazing that Ann risked calling the baby Joy. They were so concerned about the disfavor of the gods they might instead have named her Sorrow or at least Doubtful.

Alma's boys, by contrast, were exceptional in everything

they did, not always to anyone's pleasure. Victor's specialty these days was breaking rules no one had ever thought to make up like: "No chalk-eating contests at lunch hour." The only thing you could be sure about Tony, Alma said, was that, if everyone else got there in a downhill race, Tony would be doing it cross-country. Carlotta understood that. She hadn't known, until she got to know the Rabinowitzes, that there were more than two options: the limelight or the dark.

"How could you avoid knowing?" Ann asked. "Most of us do live in the ordinary light of day."

It must come in through the window, a kind light that would temper even John's death in her attentive face.

Often the worst time for Carlotta came in the early morning, when, half awake, she would dream her breaking bones. Because she was too busy with the portraits to paint what she had dreamed, she tried sometimes to retrace and explain dreams to herself as a way of stopping the noxious metallic fear in her mouth which otherwise could go on all day. Anxiety, like all other negative emotions, can develop strong immunities, and soon the explanation became a dwelling on dreams which served to increase their power. Once, impatient with the burden of what the night had dragged in like a cat hunting down her nervous system and bloodstream, Carlotta said aloud, "That's silly!" She felt marvelous all day. It was so simple she didn't like even telling herself about it. If banishing a neurosis were really that easy, no one had any business having one, a point Ann had been making one way or another for a long time. It was with some ironic but real relief that Carlotta discovered her minimizing scorn could also be incorporated into her anxiety, so that soon she was not only afraid of her phobias but newly ashamed as well.

"I'm getting a headache every time I go to Ann's," Carlotta confessed to Alma. "I sometimes wonder if I simply can't stand kindly normality."

"I never realized you worked so slowly. You must get so bored!"

"No, just anxious."

"It must be like trying to ride a bicycle an inch a minute. I don't see how you don't fall off."

"Are you getting bored?"

"Resigned," Alma said. "I thought at least you'd ask me to bare my breasts."

"I've decided envy in me is a kind of lust, and I must curb it."

"You did decide on the bed."

"Only because you obviously live in it."

"On the contrary. These days I'm rarely in it except for you."

"Dale working you fairly hard?"

"He's gone most of the time. But there's been a real increase in interest. It has to do with inflation. People are investing for capital gain. It often feels to me more as if I were a stockbroker than an art dealer. I don't so often talk about the quality of the painting as I do the potential of a rising market for one particular painter or other. I made five thousand dollars last month."

"What I make in a good year," Carlotta said.

"I need the money. I've had a real row with Mother and Dad about this baby. They want me to go away to have it and put it up for adoption. For the baby's sake, they say, so that it won't grow up with the stigma of being illegitimate. Nothing to do with their own good name at all. At one point Dad—without actually coming out with it—threatened at least a cut in my allowance. I realized I could get along without him. I don't really need Mike or his money either."

"Can you go on working?"

"Dale's perfectly agreeable. Why didn't you ever tell me that living alone is so delightful?"

Carlotta wondered how she could paint the gulf between them. It was not simply that Alma had twenty times the money, lived in a painting world entirely alien to Carlotta, and thought living with two and a half children was living alone; Alma didn't see the differences.

Allen sent a note to say the Toronto opening was next. He was sorry none of his close, personal friends would be at his possible crucifixion. If Carlotta had had money to spare, she would have flown east for it. She couldn't feel the easy condemnation that Alma did, though Carlotta didn't doubt that at least part of his motive was character assassination. She was surprised to find she did not feel threatened. If anything, she felt modestly unworthy to be among those martyred.

The review in the *Globe and Mail* was superb. It compared the photographs of Pierre to the circus boys of Picasso's Blue Period, but it credited Allen with insights beyond those of even that genius. Many people had recognized the androgynous in the very young and in the old before our masks for the world had formed and after they had dropped away; few people had really explored the essential bisexuality in all of us. Allen had been able, so the reviewer claimed, to reveal, even in the most delicate face, a subtle masculine component. In portraits of our leading politicians, he could discover a surprised tenderness, a delicacy of gesture. We are all revealed as creatures not so polarized as the bra burning, etc. etc. etc.

Carlotta went to her mirror to see if she could spy in her self that subtle masculine component which might make her whole and self-sufficient.

"It makes me just sick!" Alma said. "How can he get away with it? Imagine turning that sort of cheap, dirty trick into some kind of testimony about our essential spiritual selves."

"I think it's magnificent," Carlotta said. "It might just release the humanist locked up inside Allen."

"Don't they remember the gross indecencies he was charged with not even a year ago?"

"He's not a mere photographer now. He's an artist. Gross

indecency is supposed to be his raw material which, by the alchemy of aesthetics, is transformed into illuminated beauty. Do you know how?"

"I certainly don't."

"It's because you're so successful at disguising self-loathing as self-righteousness. Allen really stinks of nothing but your guilt."

"I have no sexual interest in children."

"But what you're terrified of is that you'll be accused of corrupting them by living with Roxanne. You want to pretend that's no sexual influence at all. And of course, it is—probably a good one for the world they'll have to live in, though it's hard to know."

"Tony and Victor have absolutely no idea—"

Alma stopped in mid-protest. For once even she could read Carlotta's face.

More sins were probably committed "for the sake of the children" than made any sense unless they really were the incarnation of Old Nick they sometimes seemed to be. Children, all innocent inadvertence, tempted parents not only to Alma's blind hypocrisies but to her greed. All selfishness and unloving piety are sanctified "for the sake of the children." For their sake, too, sex is kept disgusting.

Carlotta had begun to sketch the children, not with any notion of doing their portraits but because their body stances were so much more speaking of their moods and needs than those of most adults. It took a great deal longer to teach children to express emotions only in guarded, preordained ways than it did to housebreak them. Their faces generally didn't interest her much, aside from genetic recognition.

"Oh, they interest me," Joseph said. "I know erosion shouldn't sadden, but it does. Young faces are so intelligent, even the ones that turn out to be not very bright. And they're so beautiful."

"I resent them, I suppose," Carlotta admitted. "They have nothing to do with me."

Lack, resentment, envy—they drove her to work toward

a remarkable generosity because she represented what she envied in others rather than her envy of it. She had worked so long on manifestations of her self that the act of painting became associated for her with what was essentially hers. In work she, therefore, had the illusion of possessing what she admired. Instead of projecting herself onto her subject as she had had to struggle to avoid with Roxanne, she was learning to let the subject overtake her.

It was the brooding power of Alma's self-righteousness rather than its hypocrisy that became more and more obvious on the canvas. The bed began to look like a relief map of a large country, and behind the bed, Carlotta decided to put Roxanne's map.

"That's where she wanted it in the first place," Alma said ruefully. "I can't think why I didn't let her."

Would Roxanne feel an ironic triumph to have her work finally given place in Alma's bedroom? Or would it seem to her blatant plagiarism? If she felt anything at all, she would be too tactful to say. Carlotta realized she was waiting for Roxanne to come back. She had had a couple of cards without return addresses saying no more than any holidayer would.

Carlotta was also waiting for both Allen and Mike to come back. For her, places like Toronto and Los Angeles were not real. They were an illusion, into which actors went when they stepped offstage. Carlotta thought of all her absent friends as wandering in shadowy places, among ropes and unused props. She had never traveled, not only because she didn't have the money but because she could not imagine herself anyplace else. Once the painter Joe Plaskett had asked her to call on him in Paris. He might as well have suggested she could step into one of the paintings of his Paris room and find her face in one of its mirrors. But she had understood him. He was as obsessive about himself, his room, his faces, as she was about her physical and psychic territory.

What made an artist was perhaps the lack of that imagination which was supposed to be at the heart of their craft. Even Carlotta's friends in town, if not objects of her intense concentration, soon became nothing more than scraps of gossip, rags of memory. "I can't imagine!" was for her a cry of pain at the center of her anxiety. Perhaps only those who suffered a poverty of images for their emotions had to paint or write to survive. Mike was then not a failed artist but a man restored to a life he could imagine. Carlotta could not. He was by now far realer to her as an object in her painting than he was as a man she had tried to love.

"We have less imagination than other people," she explained to Ann.

Carlotta would never say such a thing to Alma since Alma was one of those Carlotta was presuming to explain to Ann. Carlotta never made common cause with Alma to her face.

"The most disgusting thing has just happened!" Alma announced before Carlotta was even through the door, and she looked where she stepped in case it was something which left physical evidence. "This *creature* came to the door, size forty-six tits in nothing but a T-shirt, a voice deeper than Daddy's, saying she'd come all the way from Toronto because she'd fallen in love with my picture in Allen's show."

"Wait until people see my portrait of you. There will be double lines around the block," Carlotta promised cheerfully.

"Lot, did you hear what I said?"

"Of course, I heard."

"This is exactly the sort of exposure and humiliation Allen intended."

"You're such a spoiled woman. I'd probably have been flattered."

"How can you joke?"

"Because it seems to me funny. I suppose it gives you

some sense of justification about shutting the show down here in Vancouver."

"Ask if I needed any!"

"What did you say to her?"

"I ordered her off the premises and told her I'd call the police and charge her with trespassing if she came back. You can actually do that. It's the way Daddy got rid of a boy Joan didn't want to see anymore."

"The concept of sisterhood hasn't much touched you," Carlotta observed.

"What would you have done?"

"I don't know. I have never had a chance to practice rebuffing anyone."

"What a liar you are! Just between Mike and me, you've practiced for years."

"Oh, *you*."

"Well, it's true. If I ever did run off with a bull dyke from Toronto, it would be entirely your fault."

"So you pretend to be outraged, and, in fact, you're intrigued."

"Sometimes I think we live in different worlds," Alma said.

Since Carlotta always thought so, it was perverse of her to say, looking out Alma's bedroom window, "But we have almost the same view."

A fact of Vancouver was that the million-dollar views weren't yet reserved for millionaires. Carlotta paid a hundred dollars a month for hers. She would not, however, trust the police to deal with her unwelcome guests.

"What if people are doing this to people all over Canada?" Alma demanded.

"I've thought about that. I imagined a student going into the office of a particular university president and saying, 'Man, you turn me on.' "

"Don't you see at all how dangerous it is?"

"No," Carlotta said. "I think you enjoy the paranoia, and so does Allen. Pierre killed himself because he was a shallow, vain little creature who didn't know what else to do with his loneliness. We don't even know that he was ever told about Allen's arrest. It could as well have been a coincidence."

"I just don't want to be associated with any of it. It's all a sordid mess, and it has nothing to do with me."

Carlotta got a fine highlight on a cheekbone.

As Allen had lost weight before her eyes, Alma, of course, gained, life swelling in her belly and breasts. Every mood flattered her, whether she was being vain and silly or affectionate and witty. Carlotta had only to catch a few of the hundreds of right moments to have what she wanted: woman being woman.

"I am rather fine," Alma said, a hand on Carlotta's shoulder, admiring the painting.

She was the only one of Carlotta's models who simply enjoyed her own image. Mike had been nervous at first and finally bored. Joseph laughed at his in his chronic distress. Roxanne took only polite notice of hers. Pierre had peered and poked very much as he must have at his image in the mirror. Allen depended on his to keep himself believing in his own anger. Ann grew more and more embarrassed by hers as it neared completion.

"You're flattering me," she'd say.

"How? Doesn't it look like you? Aren't those your gray hairs?"

"Yes, but I look—oh, I don't know: healthier than I am."

"Aren't you healthy?" Carlotta asked.

"Well, ordinarily, I guess. Joseph loves it. He keeps saying, 'It's so *like* you,' in a pleased, surprised way; so in some way it must not be like me at all."

"I get an idea, usually a very simple idea to keep the mood under control. This is unagitated woman in the ordinary light of day. But you're alert, you see. I have your attention. That's what Joseph likes about it. That's what everyone will like about it."

"But I'm not a very good listener," Ann confessed. "Half the time I'm planning tomorrow's dinner at the same time."

"Well, that's in your hands. I haven't left it out."

"I do like what you do, Carlotta. I really think I do understand it."

"That's because I am a minor Kitsilano artist who has made certain mistakes on Commercial and in West Point Grey. We share a territory."

"In school we were taught that art should instruct and delight."

Carlotta laughed. In the old days Mike would have taken up such a challenge and lectured Ann to neither enlightenment nor pleasure about art as the redeemer from usefulness. What Carlotta believed she never admitted to anyone: art heals, even its own motives if it has to. "Art as the-Scab-on-the-Wound School," she could say wryly to herself, but she would not be misunderstood to mean art is therapy.

"Art doesn't need an excuse, does it?" Carlotta said, to answer something. "It's only artists that do, and there isn't any excuse for us really."

There was something else in the portrait of Ann Carlotta didn't talk about. Though there was a window, though the light came in cheerfully enough, there was a subtle claustrophobia in the space the figure occupied. When Carlotta was sure it was nothing but the truth, she declared the portrait finished.

Alma would be her last. In this Carlotta was confronting and transforming into myth what she envied most, celebrating all she was not. She would finish it before Alma was again blasted seedpod, sore and milky, confronting unwed motherhood in an intolerant neighborhood without even the blessing of her ridiculously indulgent parents. If Carlotta went on with figurative painting, she would invent the images she had so far only been able to take from life. What a relief it would be to work in solitude again, her muse at last outgrown.

"If it's a girl, I'm going to name it Carlotta," Alma said.

"You know I don't like children," Carlotta said.

"You could be her godmother. It's taking an interest in a child that makes them interesting."

"I don't believe in God."

"A courtesy godmother then."

"Why involve me? It has nothing to do with me."

"I need somebody with me," Alma said.

"Your mother . . . ?"

"I'm not going to ask her."

"But what about the boys?"

"They're old enough to stay alone."

Carlotta's dreams no longer tampered with her own fragility and pain. They were instead confrontations with the life in Alma's womb, often so horrifying and repulsive Carlotta woke physically sick. They stayed so vivid that she was for a time afraid she couldn't finish the portrait before the baby was born. Then to finish it became an obsession to hold Alma inviolate against the hideous jokes played even against the gods. What if it was a mongoloid? Was Alma also afraid, knowing she was old enough to be in danger? Though she was resolutely cheerful, surely some nights her own dreams must be filled with the possibility of retribution.

There was a letter from Roxanne with a return address in San Diego. She was working at the Music Center there, being taught how to talk about what she was doing, being given phrases like "sound decay," "natural drift," "sonic meditation." Soon not only her work but her conversation would be incomprehensible to someone like Ann and an increasing irritation to Carlotta, except, of course, that Roxanne wasn't around to be irritating. Carlotta missed her more than she would have expected to and suspected that Alma missed Roxanne less once the physical addiction was over.

Did Canadians always have to go south of the border or across the ocean to learn how to talk?

"All right, international art is megalomania and packaging," Dale Easter said, "but we can't go back to village cultures."

"What about McLuhan's global village theory?" Alma asked.

" 'Global' is the operative word there," Dale said.

"Or small is beautiful?" Alma tried again.

Carlotta wished she hadn't said she'd stay for dinner. Alma, without having broached the subject to Carlotta, was obviously trying to manipulate Dale into offering Carlotta a show. Though she was fretting about where she was finally going to show these portraits and some of the sketches, she would not have accepted an offer from Dale. He was not interested in things Canadian, and she did not want his patronage. Tony sat stiff with boredom, Victor trotting one leg through the main course and now dessert. She was sorry for them that she was not Roxanne, who always seemed so natural around children, as if they were as easy to talk with as anyone else.

"Art is elitist, Alma. Surely you've got enough experience now to know that. There's no such thing as a best-seller in drugstore terms. The 'small' world of painting has to be international, the world of collectors and curators."

"Carlotta sells quite well right here," Alma said.

"How much a year, Carlotta?" Dale asked, turning to her. "Five . . . six thousand?"

"Now that there's Art Bank," Carlotta said, "and if you count the dentist bills I pay for with paintings."

"You see? We often make that in one sale."

"Even the artists we sell had to begin somewhere," Alma protested.

"Alma," Carlotta finally said, "don't push him. If I weren't here, he'd explain to you that the portrait work I'm doing went out with the invention of the camera except for subjects like the queen."

"I wouldn't," Dale protested. "I admire you for doing what interests you. I really do. It just isn't mainstream, that's all."

"Women-Can't-Piss-on-Fire School," Carlotta said.

Tony suddenly laughed and then blushed.

"I'm not being vulgar," Carlotta hastened to explain to him. "It's Freud, and he was perfectly serious. So, of course, is Dale."

"Art is sexist," Dale said. "I can't really help that. There *is* Emily Carr. More to the point, there's Bridget Riley, alive, relatively young, with every coveted award, prices as high as any man's."

What a lot of conversational weight names had to carry, particularly for someone like Dale, who didn't like to argue to impress. He could spend a whole evening correcting your view of him with his famous names until he was convinced you agreed. He didn't have ideas so much as explanations.

Carlotta thought no less of Dale Easter than she did of a group of women who ran a storefront gallery on Fourth Avenue where only women's work was exhibited, carefully screened against male content and shown only to other women. At least Dale's bigotry wasn't foolish. He made a great deal of money. Still, she didn't agree with him even at the end of the evening, and he knew it.

"If you'd flatter him just a little," Alma said. "He's impressed with how much you make. He says he bets there aren't many in town who can make that much selling just in Vancouver."

"He wouldn't give me a show," Carlotta said. "He doesn't meet fire regulations."

"There wouldn't be any trouble about that."

"When your father sees this portrait, he may close the show on his own initiative."

"More likely he'll buy it."

"I wish I didn't have to sell it, or any of them. But I can't afford not to now that they're all done."

Finally Carlotta found a gallery out in Surrey operating on a government grant to bring culture to the boondocks. It advertised its shows and concerts on huge billboards on either side of the freeway. Technically it could exhibit but couldn't sell; however, it was glad to refer anyone interested in buying directly to the artist.

"What's the gimmick?" Alma asked.

"Taxpayers' money," Carlotta said.

"They don't take any commission at all?"

"And I don't even have to pay for the invitations. They don't serve wine, maybe Kool-aid and Oreos."

"When?"

"The first two weeks of October."

"Oh, good. The baby will be here by then. Nobody should have a September baby. It's like living with a wood stove all summer."

"What do you know about wood stoves?" Carlotta asked.

"I visit the poor."

Carlotta's mother heated her cabin with one, not because she was poor but because she liked hard work and deprivation. She cooked on a hot plate in summer, which was much hotter in Kamloops than on the coast, but not for comfort: to save wood. It was that heat, as well as her mother, which had driven Carlotta to the coast. Even now, in August, the sea breeze cooled both Carlotta's and Alma's rooms.

"I'm nearly finished," Carlotta said. "I'm really finished."

Alma looked with her. "I wish I could tear it up at night so that you'd have to begin again in the morning. I'm going to be horribly lonely now."

"You'll have the baby soon."

"It's not the same. Do you miss sex?"

"Not much," Carlotta said.

"I sometimes wish there were whorehouses for women."

"Well, it's easy enough to come by if you want it—as close as the nearest bar."

"Not if you want a woman."

"There are those kind, too, I'm told."

"Roxanne wouldn't take me. She said no one in them was

over fifteen. We did meet other lesbians, but, you know, they're just people after all, and you can't just go up to a person and say, 'I want to make love' or screw or whatever."

"Why not?"

"Would you?"

"Go up to someone? Sure, if I felt like it."

"Make love with me."

"Alma, you're eight months and twenty days' pregnant."

"I don't mean now. I mean . . . ever."

"No," Carlotta said gently.

"I didn't think so," Alma said. "Well, anyway, I don't have to go on wondering."

"You said being lesbian isn't the way you want to live."

"I know," Alma said. "But the option was going back to Mike—never another man. I just couldn't."

That night Carlotta dropped in at the bar of the Vancouver Hotel, where she'd once worked as a waitress. Her second drink was bought for her. She was home two hours later, her point proved, fifty dollars in her wallet. She sometimes thought it was the only kind of sex she really did understand, and she didn't miss it. She did need the money. How many more years could she reasonably count on her body's paying the rent? The five pounds she'd gained made her look younger, but thirty-five was watershed year. The twenty to twenty-five years between whoring and the old-age pension might teach her new motives for fasting.

Carlotta felt a senior citizen indeed, as well as the wrong sex, as she sat in the maternity waiting room of the Vancouver General Hospital at four o'clock in the morning.

"I should have just called a taxi myself, I know," Alma had said apologetically, "but I have to know there's someone else there. I have to know I'm not by myself."

"Are you scared?"

"Lonely," Alma said.

To remark on a condition natural to Carlotta as if it were

something that needed accommodating, if not correcting was another of the great differences between them. Since Carlotta couldn't be with Alma now, she wondered what earthly good she really was sitting there among half a dozen boys young enough to look blameless. When you didn't have children to measure your own aging, you had to be startled like this into knowing you must be taken for an expectant grandmother because you were old enough to be one.

"I'd rather be her," the tall, thin, nervous youngster sitting next to her said.

"Who?"

"*Her*. Having it. Instead of being guilt-tripped about it the rest of my life."

"If that's all you give her to complain about, she's lucky," a dark square of a boy said from across the room.

"Man, I don't have a job. *She* did, until just a couple of weeks ago—no maternity leave, nothing."

"Get them all pregnant and back in the kitchen, maybe there will be work for us."

Carlotta got up and walked out into the hall. She'd never been any good at other people's nervous systems. To deal with such vulnerable stupidity was beyond her.

"Carlotta?"

She turned to confront a nurse.

"Mrs. Trasco says that you should go home. It was a false start, but we're keeping her here."

"Tell her I'll be at home with the boys."

Carlotta had not meant to offer that, though she knew it was the other place Alma wanted her to be. Was she, in fact, trying to be Alma's mother? Perhaps Carlotta had got to the age where, whether she was good at whatever or not, she did it. How alarming! Not even to get exemption for ineptitude.

It was dawn. The first buses were running empty in her direction. It would be a couple of hours before a transfusion of people would revive Broadway, as pale and still as something dead now in the tender light of a day that would be hot.

"We don't stand the heat," Carlotta said out loud in the back of the bus, an old crone, the wicked fairy godmother dismissed from the birth.

Tony was up, sitting at the dining-room table with his hands folded over the note his mother had left him, facing Roxanne's map as he always did, the only one in the family informed rather than framed by that wall.

"Is she all right?"

"So far," Carlotta said, hearing how little comfort that would be to him. "I'm sorry. I don't have to tell you how bad I am with children since you've had so much firsthand experience."

"I'm not really much of a child," he said.

"It's your own fault," Carlotta said, dreading the possibility that he'd complain about either parent.

"Do you ever hear from Roxanne?" he asked.

"Yes. She's in San Diego at the Music Center there. I think maybe she'll come back for my show."

"I hope my dad's not."

"Why? I've asked him."

"That baby's my dad's, isn't it?"

"Tony, if you want a heart-to-heart about that, you ought to have it with your mother, not with me."

"She won't talk to me."

"I thought it was the other way round. Are you going back to bed, or should we have some breakfast?"

He was oddly companionable in the kitchen, letting her take charge while he anticipated each thing she needed.

"How did you know I'd have tea?" she asked him as he put boiling water in the pot to heat it.

"Mother doesn't know how you stand to drink it first thing in the morning."

He had such a grave face until he smiled. His teeth, which were like his father's, were too bright for his fairness.

"Well, you listen to her anyway," Carlotta said.

"When I used to ask Roxanne questions, she answered me."

"Maybe that was a mistake she made," Carlotta said, using a clamp to turn the bacon.

"It's not a mistake to understand."

"Well, so the baby is your father's. As far as I'm concerned, it's a bit of useless information."

"Then she really did want us to go back to him. She really did want Roxanne to leave, and it's only because he married that other person . . ."

"Bunny."

"Bunny, that we didn't go back."

"I don't think even your mother knows that. You can't outguess someone who is also only guessing."

"But he always wanted more children. I can remember they used to fight about it. So how is he going to feel?"

"You want a fried egg?"

"Sure."

How did she know how Mike would feel? For all she knew, this Bunny might have presented him with triplets by now. There had been no communication between them since that phone call all those months ago.

"Roxanne wouldn't mind a baby, I don't think," Tony said. "She just thought Mother would go back to him."

"If you care about Roxanne, don't wish her back here. She's not one of us."

"She's *real*," Tony asserted.

"Maybe that's what I'm saying."

"Then I'm not either." He lowered his voice in anger, as if he were afraid of it.

"So, when the time comes, you'll go."

Victor was standing in the doorway in his pajamas with an erection he apparently hadn't noticed.

"Cock-a-doodle-doo, stupid," Tony said. "Go get dressed."

"Where's Mom?"

"At the hospital having the baby."

"Oh." He turned and went back upstairs.

Carlotta felt as assaulted by Victor's mindless penis as she did by Tony's questions. She wished she had never come. Now she felt trapped, having given this number to the hospital.

"What time are you off to school?"

"School doesn't start until next week."

Carlotta couldn't be stuck here all day. The only other option seemed to be to go back to the hospital. Tony at least wasn't stupid.

"Is Allen coming?"

"Home?"

"To your show."

"I imagine so," Carlotta said.

"Then I guess I won't be allowed to go. Do you know why Mother won't speak to Allen? Because she thinks I'm a queer."

What did Tony want from her? Was she supposed to deny it?

"You'll probably have to stay home to baby-sit, whether he's there or not."

When she had fed Victor breakfast, Carlotta decided that sleep might be the most practical solution. The boys could answer the phone and call her.

Carlotta lay down on the bed which had held both Mike's urgent fucking and Roxanne's tenderness: the tongue, the probing finger preparing her for Mike's assault. If she and Mike and Alma had ever . . . but Carlotta could not imagine Alma as a lover; she was irretrievably a rival who even now took over her own bed and cooled whatever appetite Carlotta had tried to conjure for her own comfort.

Tony woke her at noon with the information that Alma had gone back into labor.

"Is that all right?" he asked.

"Yes," she assured him without knowing what else to say.

What did she know about birth anyway? Probably with

the sort of sex education they had in the schools these days, Tony and Victor knew more about it than she did.

"I think I ought to call my grandmother," Tony decided.

"She doesn't want her," Carlotta said. "She was emphatic about that."

"Well, Victor and I are still speaking to them, and Gram said, when the time came, we should go over there . . ."

"You'd certainly be fed better. And why not? They're not going to stay mad at a new grandchild. But tell them she doesn't want them . . . yet anyway."

He was a nice kid, really, and he did have a lot on his plate. What was Alma thinking of, burdening him with a version of her own guilt? Well, she burdened everyone, one way or another. Why else was Carlotta going back to the hospital, fear a pain in her chest, unable to believe in anything but the awful?

The baby was born ten minutes after Carlotta arrived at the hospital, a "perfect" child, that peculiar adjective used to describe a creature with all its fingers and toes, unambiguous genitals, and a head the proper size, though with how many of its marbles no one yet knew. A girl. Carlotta.

"It must be so nice to have a baby named for you," the nurse said. "I do like your painting very much. There's one in my dentist's office."

"My last crown," Carlotta explained wryly. "You're sure she's all right? She doesn't have a third tit or cleft palate or anything?" Confessions of only the most ordinary of her nightmares.

"Perfect. She's perfect."

"And her mother?"

"She said she didn't want to do it too easily or we'd think she was a peasant," the nurse said. "She's one of these women made to have babies."

When Carlotta saw her, however, Alma's face was stained with fatigue. It was as if the baby had, in a morning, stolen ten years of Alma's life. But she was euphoric.

"I knew it was a girl. I so wanted a girl."

"The boys have gone to your parents."

"Well, I can't help that," Alma said.

"I can't be your mother. You'll have to make friends with her again . . . or your sisters."

"It was Tony's idea, wasn't it? He could take care of himself. He's perfectly capable."

"You should make friends with him again, too."

"Oh, Lot, I know I should."

In spite of herself, Carlotta was interested in the baby. It was so small a package to contain all that would become a woman, and it was so concentrated on the process of breaking itself in, unmannerly urgent at the breast, like a straining weight lifter accomplishing the movement of its bowels, and it slept as patients do under anesthetic after major surgery. Yes, it was terribly dependent, as everyone always remarked, but Carlotta was more impressed by the imperiousness of its commands which could jar even Victor out of his own hedonism to answer an infant need.

As Carlotta studied and sketched the baby, she became acquainted with the source of her own bodily preoccupations, the intensity with which she had concentrated on her own parts and processes. She had not been a doted-on only or much younger child. She had had to compete from birth as one of a litter for the attention of a parent who anyway saw in an infant's lying in its own excrement the equivalent of some self-imposed adult penance. To survive in the most friendly of climates was an amazement. What the baby was teaching her was a new respect for herself.

Tony was particularly good with the baby, untroubled by changing the dirtiest diaper, which sent Victor retching from the room.

"It shows she works, that's all," Tony tried to explain to his brother.

It was Tony who found the baby a name for herself. "Tot" he called her, and then so did everyone else, though Carlotta avoided any name as much as she could. She felt both identified and usurped.

Finally the real grandparents arrived with a carload of

pink and white peace offerings. Tony let them in. The baby didn't really need a father. None of them had. The grandfather had always been the stallion in the field. That fuss was over.

"Once you give in to it, some semblance of normal life is reassuring," Carlotta confessed to Joseph, who was helping her frame some of the sketches.

"I think it's relatively easy to explain," Joseph said. "That is, the source of terror is the source of comfort. Running from one means being deprived of the other."

"I couldn't go as far as you have, however."

"In either direction," he agreed. "But I didn't know it was normal to be afraid of what makes you happy."

"Is it?"

"Oh, yes," he said, and laughed.

"But you're on the other side of that now."

" 'In the prison of his days Teach the free man how to praise'—I'm reading poetry myself now."

Praise. Carlotta walked about the gallery, looking at the portraits and sketches of her friends, work that had intermittently occupied her for the last five years. She knew—if anyone bothered to be critical—she would be called slick, flattering, and an anachronism. Perhaps one of the reasons she liked Vancouver was that she was rarely called anything at all, being outside the world of academic connections, without a school. She had been able to follow her own needs in developing her skills. She had suffered only the doubts she herself cast about her work. She could see she had achieved what she was after: envy transformed into praise for these people given her and as defining to her as the sky or the sea or the line of mountains. She was considering the transparency of Roxanne's shirt as it compared to the transparency of Joseph's body when she was startled by her own name called in a familiar voice.

She turned to discover Allen walking across the gallery

toward her. They embraced. Then she stood back from him and studied his face.

"Well?" he asked.

"You're barely recognizable," she said.

Oh, any stranger would have known him as the avenger in his portrait, the gun at his heart. He would have to wear a putty nose or grow a beard to avoid that until he aged enough to leave only a few traces of that intensity of feeling. The emptiness, which had been as fluid as tears, had hardened in his eyes. He had come to terms with permanent damage.

"What a place!" he exclaimed. "How did you ever find it? Aren't you terrified you'll be cut up and sold for baked goods at the next church supper? Do you really know where you are?"

"Under the protection of the federal government."

"I doubt it. Remember, I was born here, home of the enemies of Canada Council or any other federal funding body in support of the obscene arts."

"What's obscene?" Carlotta asked.

"This marvel of Alma, for instance."

He stood and looked for a long moment. Carlotta studied with him, trying to find anything in the least objectionable about that majestic pregnancy.

"In this community the schools use the censored text of *Romeo and Juliet* which cuts out the nurse's references to pregnancy. Our English teacher used to point out all the baudiest puns the prudes didn't get," Allen explained, still looking at the painting. "You admire her just the way I do."

He turned to look at the portrait of Roxanne and said simply, "Tits."

"Oh, Allen, come on!" Carlotta protested.

"Art, like the brassiere, must be uplifting."

"People like that aren't going to come to a show like this."

"Don't count on it. There's a lot of civic pride."

He stood before the portrait of Pierre, his body stiffly attentive, a mourning that had become formalized.

"He was both weaker and more eager," Allen finally said quietly. Then he turned to Carlotta and said, "I want you to take my portrait out of the show."

"I wouldn't consider it!"

"For your sake," Allen said urgently. "I still get hate mail from around here. The people I went to school with are aldermen and ministers and schoolteachers and parents now. You can get away with mother-fuckers like Roxanne and loonies like Joseph, even the monster mother, Alma, but you can't get away with me, not here."

"You're a *fine* one to talk about what can't be got away with!"

"For my sake then," Allen said.

"What you really *want* is community outrage," Carlotta said to him, "and you know by now you won't get it, so you want to protect yourself from disappointment."

"We needn't quibble about my motives," Allen said amiably.

"We're not going to quibble about anything."

"I owe you a drink," he said. "I want to take you out for dinner. I need to know the lay of the land before tomorrow night."

"And I need to know what it's like to be an artiste in Toronto."

"No. I dine out on my pain only when someone else is paying the bill. How I've missed you, Carlotta. In fact, I've missed everyone, even Alma. How is our bitch goddess?"

"She's just had her baby—well, nearly four weeks ago, a girl."

"And Tony is more beautiful than ever, and I'm still barred from the house."

"I assume so," Carlotta said.

"There's such security in knowing old friends don't change."

Over dinner, when she asked him hopeful questions

about where he lived, who his friends were, Allen parried in a flippancy perfectly familiar, but there was no longer that central vulnerability, Pierre.

"Were there ever any real consequences of that show?" Carlotta finally asked.

"Real? No. Those people don't take artists seriously. They pay more attention to their gossip columnists than to us."

"In Vancouver, yes, but I thought maybe in Toronto . . ."

"I'm the fellow with the clever gimmick: androgyny in the prime of life. You know, even junior executives are supposed to be in touch with their own feelings these days, to climb over heads without leaving any marks, to fire tactfully. The only people who take me seriously enough to dislike me—aside, of course, from the friends of my childhood—are the radical lesbians, who, like Roxanne, think I shat in my own nest."

"They're not admirers of nuance."

"I don't suppose political people can afford to be, but it's why they are so very tedious. Ordinary people, on the other hand . . . won't you reconsider and take me out?"

"No."

Carlotta had a presentiment that Allen would someday contradict his disappointed cynicism with a rash political act; then she realized the presentiment was instead a recollection. That made her feel old, grandmother to their past selves as well as to the baby.

She was fixing a last pot of tea for them back in her room when the phone rang.

"Lot?"

"Yes, Alma."

"They're *both* here."

"Who?"

"Mike and Roxanne."

"They came together?"

"Of course not, but they're here. Roxanne arrived only about half an hour after he did."

"And you want me to take one or the other of them off your hands."

"Is there any way you could?"

"Allen's here with me at the minute."

"Oh."

"I imagine he could pick up Roxanne. Is Mike alone?"

"Yes, his wife's seven months pregnant and didn't want to travel."

"Do you want us to come get her?"

"Could you make it look . . . accidental?"

"Are you going to let Allen into the house?"

"Well, of course. After all, Mike's here. I have to go now. Could you come soon?"

There was real glee in Allen's energy as they set out for West Point Grey.

"Roxanne doesn't deserve to be rescued, of course, but what a reunion!"

Tony opened the door to them and blushed. Allen didn't give him a chance to refuse them entry, stepping across the threshold, putting an affectionate arm across the boy's shoulders, and turning him into the living room, where Mike sat in the chair that had once been his exclusively, holding the baby in his arms. Roxanne stood, as if about to depart. Alma was between them, blocking their view of each other. Victor leaned on the back of his father's chair.

"This is turning into quite a party!" Alma said, successfully surprised. "Are you just back in town, Allen?"

"That's right."

Mike was getting up out of his chair, deftly wedging the baby against his chest with one arm, offering his free hand to Allen. Carlotta had forgotten the impact of Mike's beauty, or he had grown even more magnificent. His radiance did not draw her; on the contrary, it made the impossible distance between them all the clearer. The only time he could ever have been accessible to her was when he had lost the confidence which now seemed as bright and strong as his teeth. Only after he had released Allen was Allen free to greet Roxanne. He kissed her on both cheeks, bringing the memory of Pierre palpably into the room. Allen and Alma went through no overt ritual, perhaps because each knew this was an emergency rather than a reconciliation.

"I was just on my way . . ." Roxanne said.

"Don't rush off now," Allen said. "In a few minutes I'll give you a ride. I just stopped in to say hi."

"Have a drink," Mike said. "I know there's plenty. I just fixed one for myself."

He was not aware of the feud between Allen and Alma; she would not have told him anything about it. He was aware that he might be taking up more space than anyone else wanted him to, for he suddenly handed the baby to Tony, turned to Alma, and said, "Would you like me to help?"

"Please," she said.

She had hardly left the room when the infant storm began in Tony's arms.

"It's time for her feeding," he explained.

Alma returned at once, sending Tony to help his father. Then, without asking permission of anyone, she opened her blouse and offered a large dark nipple to her infant daughter. Mike and Tony came back with drinks for Allen and Carlotta.

"Drink time for everyone," Mike said, moving to stand beside his ex-wife and the baby.

This tableau in its ordinary balance of family life was what Alma had often thought she wanted back, but at the center of it now, she was unaware of it. Her whole attention was on the child.

Carlotta looked over at Roxanne, who had all but physically vanished. Did she feel banished from that kingdom or freed of an obsession? Allen was not looking at Alma at all. His eyes rested on Tony.

"I'd rather watch the hockey game," Victor announced, breaking the moment into acceptable pieces.

"We get to do that tomorrow night," Tony explained. "I'm sorry I won't be at the opening, Lot, but Tot's too little. We're going to stay home with her."

"You'll have to see it later. There are some sketches of you and Vic."

"Really?" Allen asked. "For sale?"

"I think my grandfather's spoken for them all," Tony said.

He wasn't in the least flirtatious with Allen, but the special gravity of his tone and expression was disturbingly attractive. Even Carlotta could see it, or she was admitting to her conversion: children are people.

"Where are you staying?" Carlotta asked Roxanne.

"I hadn't thought . . ."

"Here," Tony offered quickly. "You can have my room. I'll bunk in with Vic."

"Sure," Vic agreed. "Because Mother sleeps with the baby."

"Thanks anyway," Roxanne said. "Maybe I'll see you awhile after school tomorrow."

"But Dad can't stay," Tony said in a soft, urgent voice. "He's married to somebody else now."

Roxanne made a gentle face at him, as if he'd said something unworthy of his own perception. He colored again, but he didn't retreat from her.

"Come home with me," Carlotta offered. "And let's go now."

"I do believe he's in love with you, Roxanne," Allen said as he drove them back to Kitsilano by way of the beach.

The bay was filled with the dark shapes of freighters, waiting for prairie grain on its way to China. Someone recently had tried to persuade Carlotta to go on one of the China tours because she would understand and be drawn to their poster art, as most of the others going would not. China for Carlotta was a large warehouse next to a railway line where people selected fur hats, blue shirts, and political buttons to distribute to their friends back home. So the freighters were there as props for foreign mythologies.

"It's a different world," Roxanne was saying, not having taken up Allen's taunt about Tony. "Everyone there is doing things, and there's money—not government money, private money, because people really are interested, really believe in the importance of what we're doing. It's crazy."

Allen dropped them off. Carlotta didn't like to think of him spending the night in a lonely hotel room, underlining all that he had lost here. She knew he wouldn't go to the baths or the bars. But there was nothing else to offer him. She felt very meager with Roxanne, too, the bed narrow and lustless. It was a long way for friends to come for so little.

"I shouldn't have asked you," Carlotta said.

"I had to come," Roxanne said urgently. "I have so much to tell . . . "

Some small part of it was a new lover, not so magnificent as Alma had been (and here she paused for a tribute to Alma's breasts and thighs, which Carlotta had never risked painting for Alma's sake), but human in ways Roxanne thought finally necessary. The greater length of telling, some several hours, was exactly what Carlotta had expected and dreaded. Roxanne had discovered the vocabulary for what she did. If there had been a trace of egotism in that new wonder, Carlotta could have told her to shut up and go to sleep. Instead, she drank cup after cup of tea, her nails making bloody half-moons in the palms of her hands to keep herself awake. Finally it was Roxanne who fell asleep in the middle of one of her own jargon-laden sentences. That aura of hair rested on the pillow; that comically generous mouth in too small a face was still. Was there something essentially simpleminded about someone greatly gifted? Carlotta had no doubt at all that Roxanne would go on to hear her work in the fictitious capitals of the world. Yet she lacked—what was it? A kind of complexity or sophistication. There would always be something of the uncritical worshiper in Roxanne, no matter how many goddesses fell.

They all—Joseph, Ann, Allen, Roxanne, Alma, and Mike—arrived early for the opening, more in the mood of performers than guests. The children had been left at home. The length of the drive out of town, the lack of familiarity with the gallery, the fact that it was a school night made Joseph and Ann decide to leave Joy in the care of Rachel and Susan, as Tot was left with her brothers, in the novelty proud rather than resentful of the responsibility, or so Alma reported it.

"I can only stay an hour. It's such a long way. Tony's got a supplementary bottle in case of emergency, but I'm the emergency. I should have had twins!"

She was so proud of mother's milk she might have invented it. Since the thought of it created mild nausea in most of the others, there was a physical space left around her, across which various needs for attention had to travel and did.

"This is more effective," Allen was saying. "Paintings are, on the whole. But there were lots of subjects at my opening in Toronto, and they did give the impression of having been cut adrift from the walls to be free-floating images in the room. You're positively diminished, of course," he said, smiling at Alma.

"And you might have escaped from a ward for the criminally insane," she retorted.

"I'm the only certifiable nut among us," Joseph said.

"It doesn't show," Mike assured him, "in your portrait or in you."

As soon as other people began to arrive, Carlotta felt anxious as if she or her friends were in real danger, as if she had inadvertently exposed not only Allen but all of them, for they seemed terribly vulnerable there in their flesh, where each move, each gesture could betray. The portraits, in contrast, seemed safe from harm. If she had not been distracted by a number of her regular collectors, she would have obeyed an instinct to herd her friends into safety in the office, in the back alley, anywhere except here where their portraits were like "wanted" posters for the criminally free.

It was odd to have her familiar personal paranoia extend as far as her imagination had, to include her friends.

"Nice to have you on my side," Carlotta said to Alma's large and handsome father. "I was afraid you might not like Alma's portrait."

"Marvelous!" he said. "Simply marvelous! One goes on too long thinking of one's children as children."

"I don't want to sell you every sketch of Tony."

"Oh, I'm sorry, but I must have them."

His confidence was such that he spoke as if the decision were up to him rather than to Carlotta.

"But I've spoken for one of them, sir," Allen said, suddenly at Carlotta's elbow.

"You remember Allen Dent?" Carlotta asked.

"Indeed." Alma's father nodded but did not offer his hand.

"The fire regulations in this building seem ideal," Allen said, his tone gallant.

Alma's father agreed and excused himself.

"I always did like playing 'bite the hand that feeds you,' " Carlotta said, light and cool as she always needed to appear to be, fooling other people as a way of fooling herself.

The crowd grew, became a kind of obstacle course to get through. Carlotta felt trapped in it and at the same time the cause of it, caught in her own net along with her friends. Allen had started taking pictures. The exploding flashes illuminated face after face that she didn't know. She heard the word "tits"; she heard the word "radical." She heard, "I want to buy the flower man."

Mike was standing beside her. "I'd forgotten how young we were. I didn't remember it like that at all."

"What did you expect to see?"

"The error of my ways?"

"The error of mine!" Carlotta said, and laughed.

"Are you all right?"

"It's such a crowd. There are so few people I know. Where do you suppose they all come from?"

"Off the big road, I guess, following the billboards. They didn't spare the advertising," Mike said. "I'd like to see you before I go back. Do you have any time tomorrow?"

Before she could answer, there was a sound or a feeling, as if the crowd were one great beast that had torn a muscle or a tendon. Carlotta looked toward a sigh, contraction, whatever it was. Then someone screamed.

"Is someone hurt?"

"Has someone fallen?"

There were shouts, several sharp grunts, and the mass began to bubble in the vicinity of Roxanne's portrait.

"There's the faggot who does it to kids, right there! Allen Dent. Get him!"

Then, only five or six feet away, Carlotta heard and identified the sound of a bucket of liquid being emptied against the wall. She looked and saw red paint like a bloody explosion, drooling down over what had been the portrait of Alma. As the man with the bucket turned around, Carlotta recognized him. He was the trick who had paid her last month's rent.

"Why, you prick!" she shouted.

"That will teach you, you two-bit whore, not to bring your filth into this community!"

Mike's arm had come down around Carlotta's shoulders, and he placed his body between her and the man who spoke.

"Let me go," she commanded in a quiet but clear voice.

She felt his arm fall away as she lunged forward. She could think of only one thing. She wanted his eyes.

"Lotta, don't kill anybody," she heard Mike shout at her.

As she felt scalp and skin under her nails, her thumbs hungering for the eye sockets to blind the bastard, suddenly her arms were clamped to her sides from behind. There were cameras flashing everywhere.

"Let me go!"

It wasn't Mike. She was being held and dragged back out of the crowd by a uniformed policeman.

"They're ruining my paintings!" she was shouting. "Those

bastards have ruined my paintings. Get them, why don't you?"

She saw Allen, blood pouring out of his nose, shoulder to shoulder with Mike, punching it out with half a dozen men.

"Who the hell are these apes?" Mike shouted.

"Old high school buddies," Allen answered. "Meet our local aldermen."

Out on the sidewalk there were more photographers, more policemen, several on their way in, one holding Roxanne, whose shirt had been torn off, whose shoulder was bleeding.

"What in hell is this?" Carlotta demanded. "Why are you arresting *us?*"

For answer, she was escorted to a waiting paddy wagon.

Joseph and Ann arrived on the sidewalk under police escort, Joseph stumbling as if he'd been pushed, Ann arguing.

"We didn't throw the paint, Officer. We're the artist's friends."

Several unknowns made flying exits before Mike emerged, the frustrated bouncer, a policeman on each arm, bellowing like a bull, behind him Allen, who was being dragged rather than helped. Everyone was in the paddy wagon before Alma appeared, bathed in red paint, explaining regally to anyone who would listen that her father was in there somewhere and would have them all dismissed from the force if they didn't release her at once. She was a nursing mother. Then she saw all the others looking out of the door of the paddy wagon.

"All of you?"

"All of us," Mike said, holding out a welcoming hand.

"What about the baby?"

"She'll be all right."

"My God, Roxanne! Are you hurt?"

"Some," Roxanne answered. "So's Allen."

Alma rummaged in her handbag and found cotton to put

under Allen's upper lip, to clean up the cut on Roxanne's shoulder.

"Are we really going to be taken to jail?" Ann asked.

"Looks that way," Joseph said, and for once his note of laughter was signal rather than warning; Allen and Mike began to laugh with him.

"I'm so damned proud of them all," Allen said, under his stuffing of cotton. "The people of Surrey care enough about art to start a riot! Things like that don't happen in Toronto."

"And the police care enough to join them," Mike said. "Makes a man proud to be a Canadian."

"But who's behind it?" Ann demanded. "It was obviously all planned. Even the press was there. The police were using our portraits to identify us all."

"I am," Allen said. "They came to get me."

"*I* went to bed with the prick who was throwing the paint," Carlotta said.

"They've ruined the work. Don't you care?" Roxanne was shouting. "Is it nothing but a big joke to you? They didn't come because of Allen. They didn't come because of Carlotta. Blame the weather. Blame the stars. They came. They always will."

"No," Ann said, "that's unjust."

"It will be all right," Alma said soothingly. "Dad will be there."

The silence that fell was deeply embarrassed. Inside it Carlotta felt responsible for both the terror and the silliness of their circumstance. She had painted them all into this ludicrous corner, images of envy transformed, offensive deities of the big frog in the polluted little pond, where she, where they all had to live. She saw again the face of the man she could have blinded, felt the intimacy of his scalp under her fingers. She had not blinded, she had not killed him, that payer of her rent, committing a rape she would not consent to, ever. Adrenaline drained out of her like a hemorrhage. She began to shake so violently that she might have to hurl herself to the floor to stop it. Arms held her. Ann's? Alma's?

There was Mike's voice: "We'll sue the shit out of them."
Joseph's very near: " 'All things fall and are built again.' "
"Surely you can," Ann was saying. "You can paint us all again."

Quieting, Carlotta pulled back away from that multiple embrace and discordant song, seeing them all, Joseph, Ann, Mike, Alma, Allen, and Roxanne, escaped from their destroyed portraits, survivors who had already grown far beyond her fixed ideas of them. Because they were all here now together, their lives would change again in ways she couldn't predict.

"I can't imagine," Carlotta said. "I can't imagine."